Shifting Skin

Chris Simms

www.chrissimms.info

W F HOWES LTD

This large print edition published in 2009 by
W F Howes Ltd
Unit 4, Rearsby Business Park, Gaddesby Lane,
Rearsby, Leicester LE7 4YH

1 3 5 7 9 10 8 6 4 2

First published in the United Kingdom in 2006
by Orion

A CIP catalogue record for this book is available
from the British Library

ISBN 978 1 40742 803 1

Typeset by Palimpsest Book Production Limited,
Grangemouth, Stirlingshire
Printed and bound in Great Britain
by MPG Books Ltd, Bodmin, Cornwall

FSC
Mixed Sources
Product group from well-managed
forests and other controlled sources

Cert no. SGS-COC-2953
www.fsc.org
© 1996 Forest Stewardship Council

To the boglins, big and small.

I'm a different person, yeah
Turned my world around

'Lola's Theme', Shapeshifters

CHAPTER 1

Jon Spicer looked around what used to be his weight training room and sighed. Bare plaster walls faced him, exposed surfaces still raw from where he'd scrubbed them with sandpaper. The carpet was hidden by dust sheets that stretched from skirting board to skirting board. In the corner the steam machine looked like the victim of a clumsy shave, scraps of dry wallpaper stuck all over it.

He started peeling apart last week's local paper, separating the pages and laying them across the small table in the middle of the room. Immediately, and even as he tried to look away, his eyes were snagged by the front-page headline: BUTCHER OF BELLE VUE STRIKES AGAIN.

Quickly he flipped the page over, but it was too late. The horrific details of his latest case came streaming into the last place on earth he wanted them: the nursery.

The latest victim, Carol Miller, had been a midwife at Stepping Hill hospital. She was good-looking, her strong facial features complemented by a curvy, full figure. The sort of woman his dad would refer to in his strong Lancashire accent as 'proper breeding material'. In his own way, he would have been right. She'd given birth to a thickset baby the year before. Jon had watched as the infant drained an entire bottle of milk without pausing for breath, blissfully unaware of the tears streaming down the face of his grandmother above him. Jon had sat with his tongue frozen in his mouth, thanking God the bereavement counsellor had come with him to inform the woman that her only child was dead. The counsellor had kept up a soothing murmur, the actual words of secondary importance to the comforting tone of her voice.

'What will become of our Davey?' the woman had gasped. 'His father's not around and I'm not well. What will become of him when I'm gone?'

The wrinkles round her eyes deepened and she started sobbing again. Jon could feel her looking at him and he kept his eyes fixed on the counsellor, willing her to break the silence with an answer. Say something, he pleaded in his head, because if you don't I'm going to fucking cry.

Pushing the memory away, he picked up the paint tray and decorating implements. He banged them down on the table, then placed the tin of paint next to the tray. Getting his blunt nails under the lid, he began to pull, increasing the force until the pain in his fingers got too much. 'Bastard,' he cursed, glaring at the tin like it was trying to insult him. He glanced around for a suitable tool, and spotted the scraper lying next to the steam machine. Only able to fit the corner of its blade under the lid's rim, he cautiously increased the downward pressure. The seal broke with a pop and the blade jerked upwards, gouging into his thumb. Pain shot through his hand and he drew the scraper back, ready to slash the side of the tin in retaliation.

Get a grip, he told himself, placing it on the table and examining his thumb. The red line ran across his knuckle, merging with an old scar from where an opposition player had stamped on his hand while wearing illegal rugby studs. Jon sucked the back of his thumb, then blew a thin stream of air on to the wet skin, the coolness detracting from the pain. He peered into the open tin, frowning at the purplish red paint inside. Then he picked up the plastic spoon and scooped a dollop of viscous liquid into the tray.

Immediately an image of the pathologist dropping Carol Miller's liver into a stainless steel tray appeared in his head. As the pathologist had stepped across to the mortuary's scales, Jon couldn't help staring at the corpse on the autopsy table before him.

She had been found early in the morning, naked except for her knickers, stretched out in the middle of a small park in Belle Vue. The skin from her upper thighs, stomach, chest and neck lay in a neat pile beside her, muscles, tendons, ligaments and subcutaneous fat exposed to the world. The Home Office pathologist who attended the crime scene quickly concluded that she had been moved there from another location. Lifting one of Carol's arms, he pointed to the long grass beneath it. 'No blood. If she'd been flayed here, this whole area would be soaked.'

Jon had stepped out of the white tent shrouding the body and looked around. He was standing in the centre circle of a badly neglected football pitch. It had rained during the night, washing valuable forensic evidence off the body and blurring the many footprints in the patches of mud around it. The area was overlooked by residential properties. Dotted in the unkempt turf was lump after lump of dogshit – apart from late at night, the animals' owners must be using the area as a toilet for their pets almost continually. Even now a woman with a brindle Staffy was hovering beyond the perimeter tape, surreptitiously watching. The ghoul. Jon walked round the white tent, putting it between him and the woman's inquisitive glances. He looked at the modern, cheap council stock, ground-floor windows elongated and narrow to deter burglars. They had a defensive appearance, like machine-gun slits in pillboxes.

Beyond them a large church spire thrust upwards, the flat grey sky making the green copper stand out. Jon shook his head: there was little evidence of the forces of good in this grim place. He dropped his eyes back to earth, looking at the scattering of seagulls waiting at the far end of the pitch. Their hunched postures made them appear resentful of his presence on their feeding ground.

Behind him came the low rumble of traffic, a steady stream of it passing along the A57. He moved away from it, stepping between the team preparing to go over the immediate area on their hands and knees, and walked over to the park's perimeter fence. Rubbish was piled against its base, deposited there by the unrelenting wind that blew across the bleak expanse of grass. At the top of the park was a basketball court, the cracked concrete furred with patches of moss. Fragments of glass crunched under his foot as he paced across it. On his left he counted another gate into the park. That was the fifth. By the time he'd circled the perimeter he'd counted seven more. Twelve possible entry points for the killer. The whole place would need sealing off. He halted under a wiry tree, noticed the beginnings of leaf buds on the bare twigs above him. He took a little comfort in the thought that spring would soon be here to transform the desolate place.

Why take the risk of leaving the body here, in a park overlooked by so many houses? Perhaps the victim was being made an example of. Some sort of warning?

Jon had to agree with the pathologist. There was no way this was where the killer had carried out his . . . what? Surgical procedure? He walked back to the tent and stepped inside. 'There was a bit of disagreement about the first victim – whether her killer had any surgical knowledge. Assuming the same person is responsible for this one, what's your opinion?'

The pathologist was about to take a glove off. He stopped, allowing the rubber to snap back over his wrist. 'As I understand it, the first victim only had the skin from her chest and upper arms removed?'

Jon nodded.

'And here we see he's removed the skin from her throat, chest, stomach and upper thighs. In both cases it's not a particularly difficult procedure to perform. Anyone with the most basic know-ledge of surgery, probably even a butcher, could manage it.'

'Really?' Jon was surprised.

The pathologist smiled. 'Ever peeled the skin off a raw chicken breast? Not much more to it than that. You just use the tip of a very fine scalpel to help divide it from the layer beneath – some-thing to think about next time you're making a casserole.'

Jon felt a wave of revulsion at the pathologist's reply. He'd sat in on a lot of post mortems over the years. But he never could get used to the macabre comments that bounced between the mortuary staff with the same ease as the pre-match banter in his rugby club's changing room.

'So he may not have medical training?' he asked, suddenly aware of the muscles moving beneath his flesh.

The pathologist stood up and removed his gloves. 'He's got some skill, but it could have been gained from practising on dead pigs, for all I know.'

'Jon! Have you seen the local paper from last week?' Alice's voice, calling up from the bottom of the stairs.

He blinked once or twice, waiting for the images to fade. Then he looked at the sheets of newspaper covering the table in front of him. 'Yeah, it's up here.'

'You're not using it to cover that table are you?'

'Well, it's last week's, babe. This week's is by the sofa, I think.'

She began puffing up the stairs, slow footsteps eventually reaching the top. 'There was something in the classified section I wanted,' she announced, slightly out of breath.

Jon turned to the doorway. His girlfriend stood there, strands of blond hair haphazard on her shoulders, football-shaped stomach forcing its way between her T-shirt and tracksuit bottoms.

Jon's eyes moved from the strange blue line that had appeared beneath the tightly stretched skin. 'What was it?'

'One of those abdominal crunchers.'

'I thought you were buying Chloe's off her?'

'Someone else beat me to it. She forgot to mention she'd also put an ad up on the noticeboard at her hospital.'

'That was good of her.' Jon lifted the tray off

the table and put it on the floor. He peeled the paint-covered spoon off a sheet of newspaper, leaving a thick daub of red behind. 'Are you sure this shade isn't too bright?' Carol Miller's blood was still in his mind.

'Jon, it's going to be a nursery. We want it bright and cheerful.'

'Yeah, but red? Isn't it meant to close a room in? That's why they paint the ceilings of boozers with it.'

'Ah,' she countered, 'but we're only using it for the skirting boards and doorframe. The rest of the room will be in that bumblebee yellow.'

Jon started shuffling through the pages, scanning the columns of advertisements.

'There you go.' She stepped over and slid a page towards her. 'Health and Beauty section.' She traced a finger down the 'A' column. 'I thought so: ab cruncher, ten pounds. Bargain.' She tore the corner of the page off.

Jon looked at her enormous bump. 'Are you sure that's a good idea at this time?'

Alice giggled. 'It's for afterwards, stupid. God, if I can hardly do my own shoelaces up, how will I use one of these? But once the little one's arrived, I can start working my abdominals and pelvic floor, get my stomach back in shape.'

Jon stepped behind her and spread his fingers across her swollen belly. 'I quite like you with a bit of a pot.'

She laid her hands over his, leaned back against

his chest and turned her head to look up at him. 'Will you still like it when it's just a saggy fold of flesh?'

Jon made an effort to smile. 'Of course. It will be a part of you.'

She squeezed his hands. 'And what about the pelvic floor stuff? Pissing in my knickers every time I run up the stairs?'

She had plunged him into something he had no knowledge of and he tried to drop his hands away. She clutched them tight, laughter rippling through her. 'It's all part of the process. You'd better get used to this sort of stuff. Just be thankful it won't be you in a few week's time, legs up in stirrups, squeezing out a great big bundle of joy.'

Jon grinned. 'You know I'd share the pain with you if I could.'

'Yeah, right.' She released his hands and headed out of the room, trailing the scrap of newspaper behind her.

Jon put the paint tray back on the table, eyes drawn once again to the clot of congealing paint. A conversation with Carol Miller's mum began playing in his head. He'd asked what her daughter's state of mind had been like. How happy she was. The old lady had replied that her daughter had been unhappy with her weight ever since giving birth to Davey. She'd tried all sorts of diets but never succeeded in removing the two stone her pregnancy had left her with. At the time Jon had begun to screen out the answer, letting the

9

mother ramble to a conclusion, his next question already lined up. But now he scrutinised her words more carefully.

The old lady had said Carol had tried Weight Watchers and a soup diet, but recently she'd returned from work having spotted something that had given her fresh hope.

'Ali?' he called. 'Your mate Chloe's ab cruncher. You said she'd sold it on the noticeboard at her hospital.'

'Yeah.' Her voice floated up from the front room.

Jon stared down at the classified section of the newspaper. Buffered up against the last column of the 'Health and Beauty' entries was the start of the 'Personal Services' section: ad after ad of massage parlours, adult saunas and escort services. He looked back at 'Health and Beauty', seeing the unwanted mountain bikes, exercise bikes, mini-steppers, rowing machines, power sliders and flexi steps. He smiled cynically at the two sections' proximity: if attempts at making yourself look good failed, you only had to travel across the page and buy your-self a shag.

In the front room he crouched down to stroke his boxer dog's ears. 'This noticeboard, is it in the hospital reception or something?'

Alice put the torn-off corner of newspaper on the table. 'No, it's in the staff room of A and E, I think. I know all sorts of stuff gets pinned up there. It's how she found her flat. One of the consultants was advertising.'

10

'Do you reckon every hospital department has one?'

'I'd have thought most would. Why, what's on your mind?'

He made his voice sound casual, 'Nothing much. It just started off a train of thought.'

'About this case you're on?' Her voice had dropped a notch. The previous year, Jon's hunt for the Chewing Gum Killer had placed his family in extreme danger. The nature of his work was an area they both still skirted round nervously.

Jon nodded and stood up. 'I just need to pop out. I won't be long.'

Alice's eyes slid to the clock on the video. 'Half past eight at night? Can't it wait until tomorrow?'

But the thought was an itch he couldn't ignore. 'I'll be back in no time.'

She let out a long sigh and Punch glanced up, sensing her frustration as it billowed across the room. 'Well, at least wash the paint off your hands.'

He stood at the kitchen sink, one hand under the stream of water, watching the curls of red snaking down the plug hole. So far his delving into Carol Miller's life had revealed very little. She hadn't been seeing anyone since her husband had disappeared two months after the baby was born. The grandmother had found herself looking after Davey a lot more than she had planned – Carol's income had plummeted and she'd been forced back into midwifery as a locum, filling in last-minute staff shortages at Stepping Hill

11

hospital's maternity ward. Usually that meant weekends and evenings.

Although she still had the terraced house in Bredbury, the rent was getting harder and harder to meet. The grandmother had been expecting Carol to ask about moving back in very soon. Until, that is, she turned up in a Belle Vue park with large portions of her skin cut off.

He dried his hands on the tea towel, pulled a jacket on over his old rugby shirt, then tucked his warrant card into the breast pocket. On his way to the front door he paused at the door into the front room. Punch's big brown eyes watched him dolefully. Alice kept staring at the magazine on her lap.

'Want anything from the shop at the garage?' he asked.

'No thanks.'

'OK, I won't be long.' He bent over the arm of the sofa and dropped an awkward kiss on the top of her head.

He pulled up in the car park of Stepping Hill hospital twenty minutes later, then followed the signs directing him to the maternity suite.

The front doors were locked; a notice instructed him to buzz the intercom if the time was outside normal office hours. A camera stared down at him from its wire cage above the door. Jon got his warrant card out, held it towards the lens and pressed the button.

His arm was beginning to ache by the time a crackly voice said, 'Hello?'

'DI Spicer, Greater Manchester Police.' He pushed the door but it remained locked.

'Yes?' the voice said.

'For fuck's sake,' Jon muttered under his breath before looking up and saying, 'I'm investigating the murder of Carol Miller.'

'Oh.' The lock buzzed open.

The foyer smelled fresh, the painted walls almost pristine. He wondered if the maternity ward they would be going to for their baby's birth at Withington hospital would be so recently decorated.

A sign by the lifts told him that reception was on the third floor. As he waited for the lift to arrive blue light began to flicker across the walls around him. He turned to see an ambulance pulling up in the emergency bay outside. The driver jumped out and jogged round to the rear of the vehicle. Seconds later the back doors were thrown open and a gurney was wheeled out. The mouth of the woman lying on it was drawn tight and Jon could hear her moans, low and guttural, through the glass. Two male paramedics started pushing her towards the doors, the woman's partner flapping along behind, a large bag hanging from his arm.

As they wheeled her into the foyer the lift arrived. 'Hold the doors!' one of the paramedics called. Then he looked down, 'Nearly there. Keep breathing and don't, whatever you do, start to push.'

Jon had stepped into the lift and he kept his

finger on the button with two arrows pointing away from each other.

'Cheers, mate,' one of the paramedics said with a smile. 'This pair of charlies' – he nodded jovially at the couple – 'didn't want to bother anyone by coming in early. Waited until her contractions were nice and close. A bit too close, though!'

Damp hair plastering her forehead, the woman was deaf to his attempt at humour, eyes tightly shut, focus directed entirely inwards. The moaning began again and Jon saw a glance of concern flit between the two paramedics. He wondered if he could jump back out of the lift, but the doors were sliding shut.

Jon looked at her partner, searching for clues as to how he should handle himself when it was his turn. The man began to brush strands of hair from her forehead and Jon thought what a futile gesture of comfort it was. But what else could he do? He was no more part of the process, no more able to share in what she was going through, than the rest of them. Jesus, thought Jon, everything about parenthood scares me shitless.

'God,' she growled. Her tone was masculine, like someone straining to lift a barbell in a gym. She began a shallow and desperate panting and her eyes snapped open, the look in them giving Jon the impression of a wild animal in pain. Her eyes settled on him for a second before shutting again, and somehow he felt guilty for being a man.

At last the lift came to a halt and the doors

14

opened. A midwife was waiting for them and the group sped off to the nearest delivery room. Jon found himself alone in a corridor plastered with thank you cards and badly taken snaps of women lying on beds, tiny babies clutched in their arms. He leaned closer for a better look, alarmed at the lines of exhaustion on so many of the new mums' pale faces. Except for the pride shining out from their sunken eyes, they looked ideally suited to a hospital ward. And the babies. So small, so fragile. Dough-like features as if their faces had not yet formed, and some with plastic nasal tubes taped to their tiny cheeks. Not for the first time he looked at his thick fingers with their network of nicks and cuts from rugby matches and thought he was the last person on earth suited to this sort of thing.

'Can I help you?'

Guiltily he dropped his hands to his sides and looked at the bird-like woman who had appeared silently at his side. 'DI Jon Spicer.' He started rumbling for his ID, uncomfortably aware that he was wearing trainers, paint-flecked tracksuit bottoms and an old rugby shirt beneath his jacket.

'I just spoke to someone on the intercom about—'

'Yes, I heard. I'm Sister Cooper.' In order to meet his eyes she had to bend her head back. 'They certainly breed them big in the police nowadays.' Her eyes snagged on the bump in the bridge of his nose before dropping to the club badge on his chest, where they found an explanation for his injury. 'Rugby player?'

Jon nodded, never sure whether the admission would bring a knowing smile or a wary look.

Sister Cooper smiled. 'So was my husband. He's confined to criticising it from his armchair nowadays.'

'Oh well,' said Jon. 'I suppose you get to spend more time with him at the weekends now.'

'More's the shame,' she rolled her eyes theatrically. 'Always under my feet, he is. Like a lost puppy, now he doesn't play.'

Jon laughed.

'Please.' She waved him on down the corridor and into a staff room. A couple of other midwives were sitting on the padded blue seats that lined two sides of the room. 'Do you need to speak in private?'

The midwives had obviously been tipped off he was coming and were already beginning to stand. 'No, that's fine,' said Jon, gesturing. 'Please don't get up. I just need to check something.' He moved a copy of the local newspaper out of the way and took a seat, aware of the fact that his towering form didn't exactly encourage a relaxed atmosphere. 'I was talking to Carol Miller's mother and she mentioned Carol was trying to lose a bit of weight. She said Carol had come back from work excited about discovering a new way to regain her shape. I'm interested to know if you have a staff noticeboard where people advertise things for sale.'

'It's right behind you.' Sister Cooper pointed above his head.

Jon craned round and saw a noticeboard plastered with pieces of paper. He stood up and started to scan them.

Salsa lessons. Spanish teacher. Thursday evenings.
Panasonic video camera.
Income tax and preparation of accounts.
Garden maintenance and lawn-mowing services.
Britax Excel 3 in 1 travel system.

'Did she mention anything to any of you?' he asked over his shoulder.

One of the midwives said, 'Yes. Is there an ad for a rowing machine up there? One time she was talking about how effective rowing machines are for burning off calories.'

All three of them joined him and they began searching through the notices together. Within two minutes they'd checked the entire board, but without success.

Jon was about to give up when Sister Cooper announced, 'Here you are.' She was lifting up a large sheet with a photo of a Nissan Micra for sale. Beneath it was a plain postcard.

York Sprinter Rower. Computer screen showing strokes, time, distance, calories. Cost £139, will accept £80. Never used. Call ext. 241 and ask for Pete.

Jon removed it, hoping none of the women had seen the extension number. 'I just need to borrow this. Thanks very much for your help. I won't take

17

up any more of your time.' Hoping his exit wasn't too abrupt, he started for the door.

'DI Spicer?' It was Sister Cooper's voice. He turned round. 'How are Davey and the grand-mother? Are they coping?'

'Social services are helping out. Apparently there's a cousin as well . . .' His voice fell away.

Sister Cooper gave a tight smile and Jon retreated from the room, a woman's shrieks following him all the way to the end of the corridor.

Outside he walked round to the hospital's main reception and approached a woman behind the desk. Discreetly he placed his warrant card on the formica surface and asked if there was a list of internal phone numbers he could look at. She opened a drawer and removed a clipboard with several sheets of A4 pinned to the front. He traced a finger down the columns, searching for extension 241. Eventually he found it within the section headed 'Porter's lodge.'

CHAPTER 2

She found herself lying on the kitchen floor, blood clogging the vision in her right eye, cheek pressed against the fake marble tile. There was a piece of pasta beneath the cooker and she wondered whether the small brush in the cupboard under the sink would be able to reach it. He hated mess. Her face was one big blot of pain. Bottles clinked in the front room.

What's happened to our marriage? she thought. It was good once. It was normal. If only we still had Emily, things wouldn't have ended up like this.

Slowly she got to her knees, feeling as if the weight of her skull had trebled. Drips of blood fell onto the floor with a steady ticking sound. Reaching up, she curled her fingers over the edge of the sink and got stiffly to her feet. The J-cloth smelled faintly of sour milk as she dabbed the blood from her eye.

'Taped over Man United. Stupid bitch.'

It wouldn't be long before he came for her again, rage re-stoked by the alcohol. She opened the cupboard door, leaned forward and tried to reach the floor cleaner, spotting her gin hidden behind the bleach just before her vision darkened. She heard a bottle bang down on the coffee table in the front room, followed by a sharp intake of breath.

He was really going for it. She changed her mind about cleaning up, knowing how the whisky set his demons free. Following a routine that was getting more and more frequent, she grabbed her handbag off the top of the fridge and unbolted the back door.

As she walked unsteadily to her car she thought about how their life had gone wrong. He'd always got a bit lively after a drink or two. Things would get knocked over in the front room if his football team let in a stupid goal. She'd seen the occasional flash of aggression in the pub. Not enough to attract other people's attention. Just sneers at young and boisterous groups. People he felt were lacking in respect.

But he hadn't drunk enough for her to perceive it as a problem. That only happened when his career started to stall. As he was passed over for promotion again and again, the resentment began to build, a dark anger at the world. Trying to get him to talk about it only led to accusations of being a nag.

As she reversed out of the drive he appeared on the front doorstep. The surprise on his face turned to a snarl and he staggered across the lawn. 'Where are you going?'

Her hands were shaking as she got into first gear and accelerated away, the whisky bottle bursting against the back windscreen.

As usual she drove aimlessly, the occasional heaving sob doubling her over the steering wheel. The bleeding above her right eye had started again and the tissue box in the glove compartment was empty. Looking around, she realised she was driving through Belle Vue. The bright lights of a bingo hall were on her left and she turned into the car park, pulled up next to an empty coach and walked towards the entrance. A ripple of nudges went through a group of elderly women in the foyer and they stared at her through the plate-glass windows.

'Can I use your toilets, please?' she asked the red-coated man at the door.

He looked her up and down. A woman in her late thirties with messed-up hair and a bloodied face. 'Are you a member?'

'I'm sorry?' she replied, taken aback by his callousness.

'Have you got your membership card with you?'

She shut her eyes. 'I just want to use your toilets.'

'It's members only.'

She opened her eyes, saw his look of undisguised distaste. Shame suddenly filled her and she turned away from him. There was a motel on the other side of the car park, its neon-lit sign advertising rooms for £39.95 a night. She set off across the tarmac, trying to keep some dignity in her step.

A low hedge separated the two properties and she squeezed through a gap into a dark and empty car park. Directly behind the building she was just able to make out the greyhound racing stadium, unlit floodlights looming in the dark. She pushed open the motel's front door, immediately noticing an ashtray on the counter overflowing with butts. To her side was a rack for holding pamphlets. '*Manchester's Attractions*', said the card at the top, but the shelves below were empty.

She pinged the bell, then immediately placed her hand on the metal dome to stop its sharp echo. The office door opened slightly and a thin woman with lank brown hair slid through the gap. Her pale, narrow face emphasised her large brown eyes, which moved around like those of a frightened deer.

The woman who had just walked in off the car park was immediately reminded of a girl from her school. She'd come from a poor home and always wore second-hand uniforms and jumble-sale shoes. Her stick legs were never clad in tights, and during cold weather the skin almost went blue. The girl constantly suffered from a runny nose – colds in winter, hay fever in summer. As a result, a hanky was always pressed to her face and the playground joke was that her thinness resulted from her losing so much fluid through her nose.

She gestured towards the inner doors. 'I just need to clean up. Can I use your toilets? Please?'

The receptionist's eyes went to the doors behind

her as if she was expecting more than just a lone woman. 'Jesus, you need more than a sink.' She stepped back into the office and almost immediately re-emerged with a green first-aid case. 'Here. I don't think this has ever been used before. I'm pretty sure it's full.'

She put it down on the counter and unclipped the lid. Inside were bandages, plasters, safety pins, antiseptic cream and a pair of blunt scissors. 'The toilets are just through those doors. Wash the blood off and we'll get you patched up.'

'Thank you.'

The hinge on the door into the toilets was stiff and the place smelled awful. She stood in front of the mirror and looked fearfully at her face. God. Her right eye was swollen half shut, dried blood caked her cheek and clotted her eyebrow. A fresh drip emerged from the split in her skin and caught in her eyelash.

She looked around for paper towels but the dispenser was empty. So were the toilet-roll holders in the first two cubicles. The last had a small stack of tissues piled on the cistern.

Five minutes later she stepped back into the reception, a tissue pressed to her eyebrow. 'Seems it doesn't want to stop.'

The receptionist frowned in sympathy. 'Was it a john?'

'Sorry?'

'Your face? Was it . . . ?'

Her mobile phone started to ring. Picking it out

23

of her handbag, she saw her husband's name on the screen. She turned it off and dropped it back. 'Jeff. My husband.' The admission brought tears to her eyes.

The receptionist's face softened further. 'Let me see your face, you poor love.'

'Really, you don't need to. I can do it myself.'

The receptionist peered at the cut. 'These butterfly plasters might do it.' She smeared antiseptic cream over the cut, then applied two of the plasters. 'I've got some ice in the back. It will help with the swelling. You look like you could do with a cup of coffee as well. I'm Dawn, by the way.'

'Fiona. Thank you so much for this,' she replied.

The back office looked as dilapidated as the rest of the motel, but the chairs were soft and the coffee hot. She sat down, and her resolve to return to her car instantly crumbled. Reaching for her handbag, she took out a packet of cigarettes and held it out to Dawn.

'Cheers,' she said, sliding one out.

Fiona held a flame to it and then to her own, took a deep drag and sat back in the seat. Bustling around the room, Dawn wrapped some ice cubes in a bandage and passed it across. Fiona regarded her, thinking that her concern seemed to extend beyond mere sympathy. 'This has happened to you as well, hasn't it?'

Those eyes again. They moved with a look of perpetual alarm. 'How could you tell?' she asked.

Fiona was surprised at how quickly her crestfallen

24

look had appeared. She guessed Dawn was used to people seeing through her fragile front to the vulnerable person beneath. 'Your kindness. It's the sort of thing one shows to a fellow . . . you know.'

'Survivor. The word you're looking for is "survivor".' But it didn't ring true, coming from her lips. Dawn sat down. 'I've suffered, yes. But in the past, not now. I'm with a good person now.' The comment was more than emphatic: it was defiant.

'I'm glad for you.'

'And you? How long has he been doing this to you?'

Breaking eye contact, Fiona lowered the ice pack and readjusted the cubes inside. 'On and off over the last few years.'

'On and off? But more and more often?'

Fiona pressed the ice pack against her forehead and shut her eyes. More and more often? In truth, she couldn't tell; her recent past had merged into one long nightmare. 'He's under a lot of pressure at work. He's always so sorry afterwards.'

'You mean, once he's sober?'

Fiona opened her eyes, surprised at the accuracy of the guess.

Dawn leaned forward, anger in her voice. 'They're always sorry the next morning. But that doesn't last for long. In fact, it lasts for less and less time. It's a cycle, don't you see? It's a cycle that just gets faster and faster. You have to get out of it.'

Fiona closed her eyes again, but the tears had escaped down her cheeks. 'You know that's not so easy. We've been married almost twenty years. I haven't anywhere else to go.' She started getting ready to stand. 'In fact, I should get home. He'll be asleep now. It'll be safe.'

'He's not coming back,' Dawn said quietly.

'Sorry?' Fiona replied, half out of her seat.

'The man you married. You're hoping he'll come back one day, aren't you?'

Fiona pictured her husband of all those years ago. Slim, a full head of hair, the quantity surveyor eager to work his way up the construction company. She thought of him now. Overweight, balding, face ravaged by drink, the strength she'd once found so reassuring now used against her.

'He's gone,' Dawn continued, laying a hand on her shoulder. 'Don't go back there tonight. Stay here – there are plenty of empty rooms.'

Fiona gave a hollow laugh. 'I don't have any money.'

'Sod the money.'

'I can't have you risking your job because of me. What if your manager found out?'

Dawn smiled. 'I'm the night manager. As long as you're out before the day manager arrives at seven, there's no problem.'

Fiona looked around the room uncertainly. 'Who actually owns this place?'

'Some business conglomerate down in London. I've never seen them. It was built for the

26

Commonwealth Games last summer and it's been dying on its arse ever since. Please don't go back to him. You'd only be setting the whole process in motion again.'

Fiona sighed. 'Staying the night here won't achieve anything, other than to aggravate him further. I'll have to face him at some point.'

'Why? Have you left any children back there?'

Fiona gave an aggressive shake of her head. She couldn't face that one, not now.

'Then put a stop to it for ever. Leave him.'

Fiona stared at the floor. 'Don't think it hasn't occurred to me. But leave him for where?'

'Get a good night's rest, and tomorrow I'll put you in touch with some people. There are houses you can go to, places where you'll be safe.'

'You mean women's refuges?' Fiona said. 'But they're for . . .'

'Battered women.' Dawn completed the sentence for her. 'Women from all walks of life, of all ages.' Her voice dropped to a whisper. 'Women just like you.'

Dawn got to her feet and removed a bottle of brandy from a cupboard. The sight of it made Fiona's stomach clench with longing. 'You could do with a splash of this,' said Dawn.

Trying not to appear too eager, Fiona extended her cup, watching the rich chestnut liquid as it glugged from the bottle. As she took a thankful sip, more tears spilled silently down her cheeks. 'Is that how you escaped? By going to a women's refuge?'

'More than once,' Dawn replied, taking a generous sip herself. 'I'd begun to believe that I was one of those women who always fall for the bastards of this world.'

'And now?'

'Now I'm happy. You know what I reckon is most important? Companionship. A partner in life who treats you as equal. To be honest, sex isn't really that important.'

Fiona almost shuddered at the thought of what her drunken husband would do to her in the bedroom.

The outer doors of the motel opened, and low voices sounded in the foyer.

'Dawn!' A woman calling. 'You back there?'

'Two seconds,' Dawn whispered, getting up. 'Yeah, hang on.' She hurried into the reception area.

'Got a spare room?' The woman's voice again.

'Yup. For the night or . . . ?'

'An hour.'

Fiona leaned forwards to see out the door. The woman was standing on the other side of the counter, hair tied in a ponytail, long red nails tapping impatiently on the fake wooden surface. Next to her was a man in a suit, looking awkward.

'That's twenty pounds,' Dawn said to him.

'Ah. Right.' He fumbled for his wallet. The money was handed over, but Dawn didn't open the till. Instead the notes went straight into her back pocket. She passed the woman a key. 'Number four's free.'

The couple went out through the doors and Dawn came back into the office. Fiona looked at her inquisitively and she shrugged. 'That conglomerate? I couldn't live on what they pay me. It's the only way to make ends meet.'

Fiona's mind was working, 'Earlier on, when you asked if it was a john, you meant a . . . You thought I was a . . .'

Dawn looked embarrassed. 'I wasn't sure. Your clothes weren't right, but most women who book in here are working girls. I'm sorry. As soon as you started speaking, I could tell you weren't.'

Fiona took a gulp of her drink, suddenly realising why the man in the bingo hall had been so callous earlier. She laughed at how her life had shifted.

'What?' asked Dawn, smiling nervously.

'Nothing,' said Fiona. 'It's just that if anyone had told me this morning that I'd be sipping brandy in a brothel in Belle Vue tonight, I'd have thought them mad.'

Dawn's face relaxed and she held the bottle out again.

Fiona extended her cup but, before tipping the bottle, Dawn said, 'So you'll stay here tonight?'

Fiona felt like she was teetering on the edge of a cliff. 'What are these refuge places like?'

'Heaven compared to what you're suffering at home.'

Fiona took a deep breath. 'OK. I'll give it a go.'

Dawn's face broke into a smile and she topped up Fiona's cup with brandy.

Fiona wrapped a towel round herself and tried to step out of the shower. The brandy was coursing through her veins and she had to grab at the shower curtain. A couple of hoops were ripped off before she regained her balance. Wiping steam from the bathroom mirror, she looked at her face. Aside from the injuries, a good-looking woman with wavy brown collar-length hair looked back.

'You can do it,' she said slowly, words slightly slurred. 'You can leave him.'

The ice had reduced the swelling a bit and she hoped the bruising wouldn't be too obvious. She wished she had her make-up bag with her. Instead, all she had was a miniature toothbrush and tiny tube of toothpaste Dawn had found in a desk drawer.

Not surprisingly, acting as night manager of a run-down brothel wasn't Dawn's life ambition. As they had worked their way through far too much brandy, she had outlined her plan to emigrate with her partner to Holland, as soon as they'd put enough money aside. Renting rooms out by the hour was going a long way towards letting them realise their plan.

Fiona hung the towel on the rail, then, not trusting her balance, sat on the toilet to put her knickers back on. Carefully she walked across to the bed, peeled back the bedclothes and climbed in. The sheets had worn thin from washing, but they were cool and clean. She flicked the light off and let her head fall to the side.

She woke with a start some time later, certain that someone had opened the door. Her head was spinning and she had to feel at her sides to make sure she was still lying in bed. Keeping absolutely still, she heard a set of room keys fall to the carpet. But the sound was from the next room, not hers. Jesus, the walls were thin.

Groggily, she got up on one elbow and pressed a button on her watch. Its face lit up: 3:36 a.m.

A feminine giggle, the door shut and then she heard a man's voice, words indistinct. The bed creaked as someone sat on it. The woman said something, words impossible to make out. Shoes hit the floor and a belt jangled loudly as it was clumsily unbuckled. Fiona's eyes widened. Surely it wasn't a prostitute and her client?

She could hear the murmur of voices, and the bed creaked as they moved about on it. Fiona lay back and started breathing slowly, unable to resist trying to listen. Silence for a few minutes, then the bed began to creak rhythmically. The man started to grunt lightly. Oh God, they were having sex and she could hear everything. Fiona raised her hands to her ears, squirming.

He began grunting more loudly, then said something and the creaking stopped. Her voice now. More creaking and Fiona guessed they were changing positions. The belt buckle jangled once

31

more. Fiona shut her eyes, embarrassed yet fascinated by the noises. Now the creaking started again, accompanied by gasping. Their movements got wilder and she wondered what the man had requested. Jesus, it was starting to sound like a wrestling match. The headboard started banging against the wall and the gasping was replaced by a stifled moan. Fiona opened her eyes. It wasn't the sound of pleasure. The moan changed to a choking noise. Fiona sat up, all attention. In the darkness it felt like the bed was lurching away from under her. The girl was fighting for breath. Was he strangling her? She listened as the movements and noises became weaker. Finally they stopped.

Fiona kept absolutely still, nausea building in her stomach. The belt buckle again, then the bed creaking. A single pair of footsteps crossed the room. The bathroom taps came on for a while. Fiona willed someone to say something. If they started speaking again, she would know the girl was all right. The footsteps came back across the room.

Still no talking. The bed creaked, there was a grunt of effort and then something heavy thudded to the floor. Fiona slipped out of bed, heart racing. The footsteps moved around for a while before they crossed the room, slower, more laborious. Concentrating on keeping her balance, she tiptoed over to her door and peered through the spyhole. Like a nightmare sequence in a horror film, the fish-eye lens gave a distorted view of the corridor. She heard the door to the next room open and her view was suddenly filled by brown material. She glimpsed wavy chestnut hair, then he was gone. Moments later the door at the other end of the corridor from reception banged shut.

She went into the bathroom and splashed cold water on her face. Had she really just heard a prostitute being murdered? Two glasses were by the sink and she filled one, gulped the water down. Her eyes were bloodshot and her head felt full of cotton wool. She drank another glass, then went back to bed. A chill went through her and she drew the covers up. The person had been carrying something over his shoulder, obscuring Fiona's view of his face. But whatever he was carrying, it was heavy.

She should go and tell Dawn. She'd started to fold the covers back when the doors from reception burst open. Drunken laughter. Someone running down the corridor, turning and running back. A key turned and a door slammed shut. Fiona sank back down in the bed. Everything seemed worse at night, she told herself. At home innocent rattles became the sounds of burglars testing the patio doors, the creak of wood the sound of a rapist's foot on the stairs. She decided to wait until morning, see if daylight could put things in perspective. Uneasily, she lay back and closed her eyes.

As soon as her watch reached six thirty, Fiona

33

climbed out of bed, wincing as the action set off a pounding in her head. She drew the curtains. Weak daylight filtered into the room, the streetlights lining the A57 still on. Mist filled the bingo hall's car park. Thank God, her car was still there, the only vehicle left. She examined her face in the bathroom mirror. The cut above her eyebrow still looked nasty: some swelling remained and the beginnings of a bruise was gathering below the skin, screaming that she was married to a wife beater. While she dressed, nose wrinkling at the stale smell trapped in her clothes, she thought over what had happened in the night. She decided to tell Dawn, see what she reckoned.

Out in the corridor Fiona looked uneasily at the next room. The door hadn't shut properly. She pushed with her fingertips and it swung open. The room was identical to the one she'd slept in. She walked nervously past the bathroom doorway into the main part of the room. The top blanket was stretched tautly across the bed, the pillows plumped up.

Nothing looked as if it had been touched. Fiona glanced into the bathroom. The sink was bone dry, every surface wiped clean. The possibility that she had imagined the entire thing occurred and, fearful of seeing an abused woman with the beginnings of madness staring back at her, Fiona avoided her reflection in the mirror.

No. She couldn't deny the glimpsed figure passing across the view from her spyhole. Staring at the bed once again, she thought of the object on his shoulder. It had been wrapped in something brown – the same shade as the blanket covering the bed. Fiona turned and checked the top shelf of the flimsy wardrobe. One spare pillow, but no spare blanket. The discovery gave her suspicions some foundation and she got down on her hands and knees, scanned under the bed. A small white object lay against the skirting board. The tips of her fingers just reached it and she slid it out from the shadows.

Looping curled script gave the business card an exclusive air: *Cheshire Consorts. Evening companions for the discerning gentleman.*

Fiona flicked the card over. Scrawled in biro on the back was the name Alexia, followed by a mobile phone number.

She went to the window, eager for a glimpse of normal life going on outside the horrible scenario unfurling before her. The daylight was getting stronger, more cars flowing past on the A57 towards the city centre. Back out in the corridor, she saw Dawn emerge from the room nearest reception and dump a pile of sheets into a linen cart.

'I was just coming to give you a knock. The day manager's due any minute. I need you out of here.'

Fiona hurried down the corridor, gulping back the emotion that threatened to erupt as tears. 'Dawn, I know this sounds mad but, I think I heard someone being strangled last night.'

'Where? Outside your window?'

'No. In the next room.'

'What do you mean?'

'I could hear everything through the walls.' She breathed deeply, forcing herself to slow down. 'A couple came in just after three thirty this morning. At first the sounds were them, you know, having sex. But then they changed to choking. It was horrible. I'm certain he killed her. Not a word was said after the struggling stopped. I heard him moving around the room, there was a loud bump and then he walked across the view from my spyhole, carrying something wrapped in a blanket over his shoulder.'

'I'd have seen him come through reception,' Dawn stated flatly.

'He went out the other way, through the fire-escape door at the other end of the corridor.'

Dawn's eyes skittered nervously towards the door to room number nine. 'No, I don't think anyone was in that room last night. Listen, Fiona, you've got to leave. I could lose my job here.' She opened the doors to reception and beckoned. 'Come on.'

Fiona hesitated, looking back down the corridor, wondering if the sounds could have come from another room. She pressed her fingers against her temples, trying to suppress the ache pulsating through her skull. 'But Dawn, that door wasn't properly shut. I looked inside and the spare blanket is missing.'

Dawn's voice was agitated. 'Half the spare blankets are missing in this place. Please, you've got to go.' Her hand flapped more desperately.

Fiona walked reluctantly through the double doors and across the reception area to the exit. Dawn produced a sheet of paper. 'Here. This place is run by decent people. I rang last night after you went to bed. They're expecting you to call.'

She looked at the number, knowing she had nowhere else to go. 'Thank you, Dawn. You've been so kind.' As she folded the paper into her pocket she felt the business card in there already. 'Look! There was this as well. Under the bed.'

But Dawn's eyes were on the main road. 'That's him.'

Fiona looked, saw a silver Volvo turning into the car park.

'Take care, Fiona.' The outer doors swung shut.

CHAPTER 3

'Come on, boy.' The man waited as his elderly labrador climbed slowly down the front steps and on to the garden path.

Once on the pavement the man glanced towards the A57 and the park on the other side. Ever since the lady's body had been found there he'd been put off walking his dog around its litter-strewn confines.

Instead he turned in the other direction, walking along Mount Road, the greyhound racing stadium on his right. This early in the morning the neighbourhood was unusually quiet. Mist filled the street and, as he paused to light a cigarette, the only sound was the scrape of the match and the drip of water hitting the damp pavement as it fell from the glistening tree to his side.

The man continued past a shop. Tip-Top Electricals, all appliances bought and sold. Fridges. Freezers. Washing Machines.

After a couple of boarded-up houses he came to the offices that stood on the corner of the grassy area around which he now walked his dog. *Belle Vue Housing Offices* said the graffiti-covered sign, a few crocuses flowering in the bare earth beneath it. The building's windows were clad in metal grilles, and a spiked rail ran below all the gutters.

The sun had seemed about to come out, but now its promising glow faded once again. The morning felt heavy and subdued, as if waiting for something to give it a kick-start. He breathed out smoke and it soon churned to a stop in the motionless air above his head, hanging there like a phantom.

His dog began to pull excitedly at the lead. 'Bit eager today, Prince,' he said, not sharing that enthusiasm. He undid the clip and watched the animal disappear into the thick haze.

He stepped over the tyre tracks joy-riders had gouged in the grass, and walked for a short while. 'Prince!'

No response.

He waited half a minute, then tried again. Tutting, he cut across the verge in the direction the dog had vanished, soon spotting paw-prints in the dew-covered grass. As he moved forwards the mist seemed to recede at the same pace, never allowing him to see more than about fifteen metres ahead. Eventually he discerned a dark form in front of him. 'Prince,' he said impatiently, 'what are you doing?'

Prince's head was down, nuzzling a discarded white sack.

'Come on, will you.'

The dog looked up, a bluish loop in its teeth.

The man squinted, then walked closer. It wasn't a sack. It was a corpse, white skin ending at an expanse of red where the abdomen began. The swathe of raw flesh continued upwards to where the person's face should have been.

The dog began to slink guiltily away, the section of intestine dangling from its jaws.

Jon Spicer walked into the incident room expecting to be one of the first people in. But there was a man sitting at the desk opposite his. Late twenties, dark brown hair that had been freshly cut, crisp pale-blue shirt. So this is my new partner, Jon thought.

The day before, his boss, Detective Chief Inspector McCloughlin, had mentioned with a meaningful wink that he was being paired up with someone. New resources had been released to the murder investigation and Rick Saville, promoted to detective sergeant only a few months before, was one of seven new officers assigned to it. McCloughlin had described him as 'slick'. Scrutinising him from across the room, Jon wasn't sure if the word applied to his ability as an officer or to his appearance.

He thought about the meaning of McCloughlin's wink. Last summer he'd fallen out with the DCI over the Chewing Gum Killer investigation. Jon suspected Rick Saville had been paired with him to report everything they did back to McCloughlin.

Easy, he told himself. Reserve judgement. As he

crossed the room Saville glanced up, spotted him and immediately began to rise.

'In early,' said Jon, taking his suit jacket off and hanging it on the back of his chair. 'Rick Saville, isn't it?'

'Yeah. Good to meet you.' Not overdoing his smile.

Jon shook the sergeant's hand, feeling slightly less pressure returned. Jon kept his grip, waiting for the subtle press of fingers that would indicate membership of the Masons. Nothing happened. Maybe he was a DS this early in his career because he actually merited the rank.

'Where are you joining us from?'

Rick sat down. 'I've just completed a stint at Chester House – a project for reducing bureaucracy.'

'And did it amount to anything, apart from producing more paperwork?'

Rick smiled briefly, though his eyes remained guarded. 'Not really.'

'I take it you're on the accelerated promotion scheme, then?'

He nodded. 'I did my two years' probationary down in Chester, but all the action's up here, so I applied for the fast track with Greater Manchester Police as soon as I could.'

'Graduate?'

'Yes, Exeter University. History and Law. You?'

Jon shook his head. 'Joined as a bobby over twelve years ago.'

41

'You've done bloody well to make DI by now, then.'

'Cheers. How do you find the accelerated promotion scheme?'

Rick kept his hands on the table, interview-style. 'Very challenging, to be honest. It's all the tests – they never seem to end.'

Jon leaned back and looked at the paperwork spread out on Rick's desk. Statements from friends, relatives and associates of the Butcher's second victim.

Rick saw the direction of Jon's gaze. 'A bit of homework. All these tests I do, it's a hard habit to break.'

Jon sat down. 'Any first impressions?' he asked, turning his computer on.

Rick tipped his head to one side. 'Not really. I just wanted to familiarise myself. But this second victim, Carol Miller, she seems to have been called in on a lot of evenings and weekends to cover the maternity ward.'

Jon shrugged. 'That's the nature of locum work, isn't it? You're on call for when the full-time staff cry off. Which is usually evenings and weekends.'

Rick tapped a biro on the pile of documents, neither agreeing nor disagreeing. 'Her last twenty-four hours . . . She left the baby with her mum just after five in the afternoon, but she wasn't on duty in Stepping Hill until seven. You don't leave your baby two hours earlier than you need to, surely? Yet Carol Miller's mum was under the impression her daughter had left to go directly to work. So what was she up to?'

Grudgingly, Jon admitted to himself that he was impressed. Of course, the discrepancy hadn't escaped the investigating team. Many suspected Carol was hiding something. Attention had turned to her phone records. 'That's what a few of us are wondering. Maybe she just needed a break from the little one, but didn't want to admit it.' He opened his briefcase and took out a perspex folder. Inside was the card from the maternity ward's noticeboard.

His first thought was to keep everything back from his new partner, at least until he could be certain if he was McCloughlin's stooge or not. He glanced across the desk. Rick's eyes were roving back and forth across a witness statement. Skim-reading – something Jon couldn't master, hard as he'd tried. Watching the younger officer absorbing information like a sponge, he suddenly felt threatened.

He looked at the card again, knowing that teamwork was far more effective.

'I had a thought yesterday, sparked by something my missus said. Carol Miller was always trying to lose weight, but never very successfully. Then she got excited about something she'd spotted at work. Last night I checked the staff noticeboard on the maternity ward at Stepping Hill hospital. One of the midwives mentioned Carol had been talking about getting a rowing machine. I found this.' He spun the postcard across the desk.

Rick trapped it under one hand and picked it up. 'A rowing machine. Did you try the extension number?'

Jon shook his head, 'I thought it might be more interesting to catch him face to face. His shift starts later this morning.'

By now the room was filling up with members of the investigating team. Behind their desks was McCloughlin's private office, separated from the rest of the room by a flimsy partition wall. The phone on his desk began to ring.

'Where's the boss?' asked Rick, the word sounding odd coming out of his mouth.

Jon shrugged as Rick got up. He skirted eagerly round his desk, stepped into the office and picked up the receiver. Far too keen, Jon thought, knowing he would now have to take a message. Turning his head slightly to the side, he listened to his new partner.

'Hello. DCI McCloughlin's phone . . . No, he's in a meeting I think . . . Well, I don't know. I mean, I don't know where the meeting is. Can I take . . . Right, I see. Hang on.' He now sounded totally flustered. 'Jon? This guy's insisting on talking to the SIO.'

Jon swivelled in his seat. 'Who is it?'

'The radio operator downstairs. Can you . . . ?' He held the phone out as if it was a piece of equipment he no longer knew how to operate.

44

'DI Spicer here.'

'Jon, it's Sergeant Innes,' voice sounding strained. 'Who's the tool that picked up the phone?'

'My new partner.'

He heard an exasperated sigh. 'Where's McCloughlin?'

'I don't know. Have you tried his mobile?'

'It's switched off. A call's come just come in from near a patch of waste ground by the Belle Vue Housing Offices. Are you near a box?'

'Hang on.' He transferred the call to the phone on his desk and turned to his computer screen. 'I am now. Go ahead.'

'Have a look at this FWIN.'

Jon typed the Force-Wide Incident Number in and the operations room report filled the screen. 'Oh, shit, another body.'

'Yes. Minus her outer layer – and I don't mean clothes. I've told the nearest uniformed units to get over there and secure the scene. The major-incident wagon's also on its way.'

Jon scanned through for the exact location of the incident. 'Off Mount Road? I don't believe it.'

Anger surged through him. The bodies were being dumped right on their doorstep, and Jon felt as if the killer was deliberately goading him. He felt his grip tightening on the telephone receiver. 'OK, we'll get over there. Leave a message on McCloughlin's voicemail will you?'

Before he'd hung up, Rick was in his face. 'Mount Road? Where's that?'

'Put it this way. With the traffic at the moment, it would probably be faster to walk there.'

Despite that, they drove, Jon anxiously listening to the police radio for any sign of McCloughlin's whereabouts as they fought through the commuters clogging the A6, siren only slightly speeding their progress.

Finally they turned off the main road on to Kirkmanshulme Lane, only to join the end of a stationary queue of cars. The oncoming lane was just as choked, and Jon realised there was no way of cutting through. 'Bollocks,' he said, his fingers drumming angrily on the steering wheel.

Rick looked out of the side window. 'Belle Vue. Strange name for such a grim-looking area.'

Jon glanced at his passenger, then at the surroundings beyond their windscreen. 'Belle Vue? In its day this was the biggest leisure park in Britain. There was a zoo, complete with mangy lions and miserable bears, a huge roller coaster, boating lakes, dodgems, miniature steam railway. Even a speed-racing track.'

'Where?' asked Rick, twisting in his seat, trying to find evidence of what Jon had just described.

'This whole area. The speedway track was over there, where that car auction site is. One of my earliest memories is of coming out here with my dad, getting sprayed with the red grit that the bikes used to kick up as they roared past. I used to wear a pair of old flying goggles to protect my eyes. They still race, but at the greyhound track nowadays.

Of course, you're not allowed to perch on the barriers at the bends any more.'

'I bet there was hardly any trouble, either.'

Hearing the wistful note in his voice, Jon let out a short cough. 'Don't you believe it. There's no harking back to a lost golden era with Manchester. The housing around this area was shocking – still is, in fact.' He nodded at the road in front. 'There are houses just up the road in Gorton on the market for five grand. Negative equity is alive and well around here. When the leisure park was first built it was surrounded by back-to-back terraces crammed in around the cotton factories and chemical works. Smoking chimneys, open drains, the stench from the knacker's yards.'

'You make it sound like a Lowry painting,' Rick laughed, a note of disbelief in his voice.

Jon's eyes narrowed slightly. 'That's because it was, man. Lowry painted life as he saw it, no gloss. When my family first moved over here from Galway they lived in an area called Little Ireland in Ancoats. You've never heard of it?'

Looking a little bored, Rick shook his head.

'Engels described it in his *Condition of the Working Classes in England*,' Jon replied, resisting the temptation to make a comment about his partner's university education. 'It was the worst slum he'd ever seen. Hundreds of Irish families shared cellars as their homes, slept on straw. You're from Chester. Did you never learn about the region's history at school?'

Rick reddened. 'I went to boarding school down in Surrey.'

Jon clenched his teeth. Should have bloody guessed.

Rick broke the awkward silence. 'So it wasn't all polite promenading, then?'

Jon sighed. 'People needed an escape. Working in a factory all week was tough back then. That's what led to the music halls and drinking dens. I've read about what used to go on and it was pretty much the same as today, including the drunks, the prostitutes, the gangs.'

'Gangs?'

Enjoying the fact he was giving a history lesson to a graduate in the subject, Jon nodded. 'Scuttlers, they were called. Peaked caps, bell-bottom trousers. They'd form a group and steam into people – knock them down and rob them. Manchester's always had gangs. Three lads from one were arrested for breaking into the zoo. They got into the bird enclosure and kicked a load of penguins and pelicans to death.'

'Recently?'

'No, late fifties. My granddad told me about it. They all got packed off to borstal.' He paused, then couldn't resist adding, 'Their grandkids are probably the ones mugging clueless southerners who come to study at Manchester University today.'

Rick started to pick nervously at a thumbnail. The last comment had definitely hit home.

Eventually they started inching past the huge expanse of a multiplex cinema's car park. It was empty except for a group of lads racing radio-controlled cars across the smooth asphalt.

A pang of guilt played in Jon's head. Trying to make up for his cutting remark, he said, 'The lake was right there, massive thing with an island in the middle. The roller coaster was called The Bobs, one of those old, creaking wooden things. The cars rattled round it, looking like they were about to fall off at any moment. There's not much my old man admits to being scared of, but he happily let me know that The Bobs terrified him half to death. I was too small to be allowed on – probably saved me from a lifetime of nightmares.'

'So it was all here when you were growing up?' Rick asked, sounding chastened.

'Yeah, just, though it was well past its heyday by the time I was old enough to visit.'

'What happened to it?'

'It closed down during the seventies, bit by bit. Bigger and better attractions elsewhere: Chester Zoo, Alton Towers, Blackpool. Plus tastes change – there used to be a huge ballroom where they held the national brass band contest. Not much demand for stuff like that any more.'

Rick was staring at the cinema. 'How long's that been here?'

'The Showcase? Early nineties, maybe. After the last parts of the park were demolished this place was waste ground for over a decade. The facelift started with that. Burger King and Pizza Hut sprang up on the back of it, and so did the bingo hall. But I hear they're all struggling again. The Printworks in the city centre is dragging huge numbers of cinema customers away. If the Showcase folds, it'll revert to wasteland again, I suppose.' Jon thought about the processes of decay and regeneration that seemed to wash regularly across the city like a tide lapping at a beach.

At last they turned on to Mount Road and a couple of minutes later they pulled up by the Belle Vue Housing Office. Council workers were crowded in the car park, staring through the metal struts of the fence. The mist had burned away, and across the grass several uniformed officers were attempting to keep a small gathering of locals at bay. Jon and Rick started across the grass, warrant cards ready.

'Has someone been killed?' A council worker in a shiny grey suit called through the fence. The eager note in his voice riled Jon. 'It looks like a corpse.'

Jon paused and stared at the man, took in his pallid skin and fish-like eyes. 'So do you.' He carried on, leaving gasps of shock behind him.

Without turning his head, Rick murmured, 'Please, don't mince your words.'

He smiled to indicate sarcasm but Jon's face remained stormy. 'One thing I hate is members of the public getting a thrill from this sort of thing.'

As they reached the rendezvous point in the

outer ring of tape Jon noticed a young man nearby lining up the crime scene in the viewfinder of his camera phone. 'If I hear that click, I'll impound your phone as evidence.'

The man lowered the phone, an uncertain expression on his face. A uniform stepped over and, as he noted down their names, Jon nodded towards the man with the phone. 'Take his name and address.' Then, louder, 'The perpetrator of a crime often returns to where he committed it.' The man looked as if he wished he'd stayed at home.

Jon and Rick proceeded to the inner cordon. The pathologist and crime-scene manager had yet to arrive, so no one was entering the circle of tape. Beyond it was the body. Like the first two victims, she was naked except for a pair of knickers. Unlike the first two victims, her face had been removed.

Jon felt his throat contract. Shit, we've got an evil bastard on our hands.

Rick looked away first. 'That's grotesque. It's like something from that exhibition.'

Jon turned his head. 'What exhibition?'

Rick looked up at the sky. 'What's his name? Von Hagen, that's it. He removes the skin from corpses, preserves them, then puts them in various poses. The exhibition was down in London not long ago.'

They turned back to the dead woman and regarded her for a little longer before Rick added, 'She seems too young to have lost that many teeth.'

Jon nodded. The smooth and supple skin that remained on the corpse's limbs was that of a young woman, yet half of her teeth were missing. Keeping his eyes on the body, Jon began walking round the perimeter. With each step the sense that he was viewing some sort of display increased. 'You should investigate that.'

Rick looked at him enquiringly.

'That Von Hagen thing. It occurred to me when looking at Carol Miller's body – why risk dumping it in the middle of a public park? He must be trying to make some sort of a point. I thought it was a warning, but maybe it's a display.'

He looked around. Once again houses bordered the grass: a council terrace down one side, more-expensive-looking properties with large rear gardens on the other. Several worried owners stood behind their fences, exchanging comments. Above the roofs he could just make out the tops of the floodlights that ringed the greyhound track. A solitary phone mast towered over the scene, topped by ugly panels of grey metal. 'If only there was a camera on that.'

About five minutes later the Home Office pathologist arrived.

'Fast mover,' observed Jon as the pathologist folded his long limbs into a white suit.

'The call came through when I was on my way to work. It was easier to come straight here.' He slipped on white overshoes and, laying down footplates before him, approached the body.

While Jon waited for him to complete his initial examination, the major-incident wagon pulled up in the Housing Offices car park. Several officers approached the crime scene, carrying poles and a white plastic canopy. As soon as the pathologist had properly surveyed the body Jon said, 'What do you reckon?'

'Well' – the pathologist stood up, one knee popping loudly – 'she's been here most of the night. There was a heavy dew and some mist this morning. I don't know when the dew point occurred – I noticed my car had a light covering when I took the dog out for a walk at about eleven o'clock last night.' He looked at the sun, still low in the sky. 'The side of the body still hidden from the sun is soaking, as is her hair.'

'Any idea on time of death?'

'Rigor mortis is pretty well established. The facial muscles are stiff, though whether the fact that they've lost their layer of skin is relevant I'd have to find out. Despite that, the limbs are also going. Her being out here all night would have delayed its onset, but I'd say she was killed a good twelve hours ago, maybe more.'

'And the lack of blood around the body. She was moved here?'

'Just like last time. One thing I'm not sure about is the damage to her abdomen. The wounds are very rough.'

'Dog bites,' said Jon.

The pathologist looked dismayed and Jon was

pleased to have broken through his professional detachment.

'What's your opinion now on this guy's medical skills?' Jon asked, hands in his pockets.

The doctor looked at him, regret tugging at the corners of his eyes. 'To remove a face in its entirety like this takes a lot of time and skill.' He crouched, extending a finger to the victim's hairline. 'He's created a coronal flap by cutting from one ear, across the top of the forehead to the other ear. Then he's peeled the skin away – not particularly hard where the forehead is concerned, since the peri-cranial flesh is quite loose and you only have the frontalis muscle to worry about.' He pointed to his own forehead and raised his eyebrows. 'That's the one that lets you do that. Next, I imagine he made incisions down the sides of the face and right along the jawline. This is where it would have got complicated. The muscles in your body are attached to your bones by tendons. Your facial muscles differ from all your other muscles in that they attach directly to other muscles or to the skin, which is why the human face is capable of such an amazing array of expressions. The movement of one muscle has an effect on its neighbour – a kind of ripple effect, if you like.

'Whoever did this has divided the skin from the ocular muscles – which surround the eye – almost perfectly.' He pointed to an exposed eyeball. 'Just a tiny nick here, then he's carried on down the face, leaving all the muscles around the nose perfectly intact – I forget their names, *levator* and *Compressor naris* or something. Next, he reached the mouth. He's removed her lips, with the result she now looks like she's grinning for kingdom come. Perhaps that's what he wanted.'

'So he's had formal training of some description?' Jon asked, relieved to look away from the mutilated corpse.

'He's got surgical knowledge, without a doubt. The key to surgery is all about finding a plane – the layer between the dermis, or outer layer of skin, and the sub-dermal tissue. Once you've found your plane, you make your incision along it and the skin lifts away quite easily. But to find your plane and keep it while navigating all the contours of the face and its delicate arrangement of muscles? That's quite a feat.'

Jon nodded his thanks and turned away. When he got his hands on whoever was doing this, the bastard had better admit to everything straight away. Otherwise it would take more than the duty officer to stop him visiting the sick fuck in his cell and beating a confession out of him with his bare hands.

By the time McCloughlin showed up, the body was shrouded by a white tent. The pathologist and photographer were inside and flashes kept going off, making it appear like they were in there enjoying a particularly morbid party.

'DI Spicer,' McCloughlin announced, rubbing his hands together. 'First to the scene again?'

The comment wasn't accompanied by a smile. On the Chewing Gum Killer case, Jon had arrived at a crime scene ahead of McCloughlin and the observations he'd made had eventually led him to the killer. It still bristled with McCloughlin.

'Sir, I picked up the call to your desk phone,' Rick intervened.

McCloughlin didn't seem bothered and Jon glanced at Rick. So, the arrangement you have with McCloughlin extends to taking his phonecalls?

'And Jon took the opportunity of teaching you how to crack a case all by yourself?' McCloughlin walked off without waiting for an answer.

Rick spoke from the corner of his mouth. 'Someone got out of bed the wrong side.'

Jon's hands were clenched tight in his pockets. 'I guess that's our cue to bugger off.'

As they set off back to the car Jon spotted a petite figure with tousled black hair hurrying across the grass towards him. She was struggling slightly with what looked like a large plastic toolbox: Nikki Kingston, the crime-scene manager. He'd used just to fancy her, but with what they'd gone through during the Chewing Gum Killer investigation, the bond between them had deepened to a level he'd never dare let Alice know about. 'Nikki, you've got this one?'

She smiled up at him. 'Jon Spicer. My lucky day.' Her eyes lingered on his for another heartbeat before she turned to Rick.

Jon coughed. 'Nikki Kingston, crime-scene manager. DS Rick Saville, my new partner.'

Rick's businesslike exterior underwent a fractional softening, and Jon noticed a lightness in his touch as he clasped her hand.

Nikki turned back to Jon. Something was sparking in her eyes and jealousy jabbed him in the chest. 'So, am I reporting to you?' she asked.

He shook his head, 'I'm on another part of the investigation. Carol Miller, mainly.'

Her eyes widened. 'You mean this one's connected to the Butcher? I was just told it was a naked body in a field.'

'It is. Except her face is about two feet away from the rest of her.'

'Oh, Jesus,' Nikki winced.

Jon gave her a grim smile. 'See you in the incident room.'

She turned and started towards the crime scene again.

The walk back to their car took Jon and Rick past a makeshift ramp made from an old door and a few breezeblocks. Bicycle tyres had scoured the grass in front of it and left muddy tracks across the door's surface. As they stepped round it Jon spotted something.

'Nikki!' he called.

She turned, saw the urgency of his wave and came back.

'Is that a latex glove?' Jon said, pointing. It lay in the long grass beneath the door, fingers slightly curled as if caught in the act of trying to crawl from their sight.

She squatted down to get a closer look. 'Yes, and that looks like blood covering it.' She examined the ramp. It had been knocked out of alignment with the breezeblocks. Treading carefully, she scrutinised the area around the door. Pointing to a heel mark in the muddy patch by the foot of the ramp, she said, 'Looks like someone could have bumped into it.'

Jon looked back at the tent covering the body. With a finger he drew a line in the air back towards the road. The ramp was right in the way.

'What are you thinking?' asked Rick.

'Our man dumps the body and sets off back to his vehicle. Only it's dark. He walks full into this ramp, stumbles and drops the glove.'

Nikki was nodding with excitement, 'Don't go any nearer. There's another footprint there, too. We need to get this area taped off.' She turned towards the main crime scene.

'Nikki!' He caught her hand. 'When McCloughlin asks, it was Rick who found the glove.'

'No way,' Rick protested. 'It was your find.'

Jon didn't take his eyes off Nikki. 'You heard me?'

'Whatever,' Nikki replied with a frown, twisting her fingers from his grip and running away.

In the car Jon began indicating to do a U-turn, then changed his mind. 'Let's go for a coffee.

If we get back to the incident room now, everyone's going to be pumping us for information, and there's no way I'm taking the wind out of McCloughlin's sails.'

'Why's he got it in for you?' Rick asked.

Jon ran a hand over his knee, wondering how much Rick knew. 'It's old history. I had a stroke of luck.'

'The Chewing Gum Killer?'

Jon looked out the side window and nodded.

'That was the favourite topic of conversation last summer in Chester House.'

'Well, there you go. You know already.'

'Yeah, but it was McCloughlin's case. He was SIO, he gave the interviews on the TV and to the press when it was all over.'

'His case, but my collar. You know how it is,' Jon said guardedly.

'So why did you tell the CSM to say it was me who found the glove?'

'We shouldn't have even been there before him. The last thing I needed was to find what may turn out to be a crucial piece of evidence.'

'So you got her to tell McCloughlin it was my find?'

'Yeah,' Jon answered, hating the fact that Saville now had something on him.

In the coffee shop, Jon tipped a sachet of white sugar into his black coffee. Rick carefully tapped half a sachet of brown sugar into his latte, then reached for the pot of chocolate powder to dust the foam on top. When he spotted Jon watching him, he suddenly changed his mind.

'Anyway, back to the present,' said Rick, sitting down. 'First victim.'

Jon took a seat opposite him. 'Angela Rowlands.'

Rick sat forwards. 'Forty-two years old. Divorced for just under two years. Got the three-bedroom semi in Droylesden as part of the settlement. Worked part-time as a legal secretary in a solicitor's just off Deansgate.'

Jon nodded. 'You've done your homework.'

'That's just surface stuff. I'm hoping you know something more interesting.'

Jon took a sip of coffee and grimaced slightly with pleasure at its sharp taste. 'Her daughter, Lucy, lives down near Castlefield, doing very well in web site design. Lucy told us her mum had been very lonely since the divorce. Hurt too. The husband dumped her for a "younger model", to use Lucy's words. Rowland's stage in life: mid-forties, married for twenty years. She was in a routine. It was safe and comfy, but totally devoid of single men. Lucy had encouraged her to get out and start trying to meet someone, but apparently the idea terrified her.'

'Don't blame her,' Rick leaned back. 'Playing the field after being out of it for that long?' He shook his head.

'Exactly. Apparently, Lucy took her to a singles' night at a bar in town. Lucy did very well, but her mum didn't get a second glance. After that

Lucy suggested she try dating agencies – but only the upmarket ones.'

Rick toyed with his drink. 'Ones that advertise in the broadsheets?'

'Yup. And at several hundred quid just to join, they're not cheap.'

'So we've got her coming into contact with various men, none of whom had a previous social connection with her. Have we got the list of people she had dates with?'

'Only just. They were reluctant at first, because their members' records are strictly confidential. Then someone pointed out to them that having the Butcher of Belle Vue on their books was probably more of a risk to their profits than a few disgruntled members. Rowland received dozens of member profiles, but only had around fifteen actual dates, we think. Each one's being looked into now.'

Jon downed his coffee in one gulp. 'According to Lucy, she hadn't had much luck with any of them. Her confidence was low. Before the divorce she'd only ever dressed up for a few gin and tonics at their local every Friday. Now her wardrobe was hopelessly out of date.' He tapped a forefinger on the table to emphasise his next point. 'Then she mentioned to her daughter over the phone that she'd decided to do something. She sounded nervous and excited. She wouldn't say what, just that it was something she should have done a long time ago.'

'Did Lucy find out what she was up to?'

Jon shook his head. 'Next time she saw her mum, it was in the mortuary. We've gone over her phone records and bank statements, but nothing of much help there.'

Both men were silent as they turned possibilities over. Jon looked up. 'What about the porter selling this rowing machine? That was a surgical glove back there. They must be two a penny in hospitals. How about nipping over to Stepping Hill hospital?'

Rick looked uncomfortable. 'Shouldn't we run it by McCloughlin first?'

'Strictly speaking, yes.'

Rick hesitated before pulling out his mobile. 'I'll give him a quick ring, then. May as well play things by the book.'

Jon gave a noncommittal shrug as Rick made the call.

CHAPTER 4

Rick snapped his phone shut. 'Yeah, he says to get over there, but stressed just for a chat. What did he think we were going to do, batter him?'

Jon knew the comment was directed at him. In McCloughlin's view, Jon's temper was his Achilles' heel, a constant threat to his career.

Half an hour later Jon laid his warrant card on the counter in the main reception at Stepping Hill hospital. A different woman looked up at him.

'Could I use the phone please?' he asked. 'Internal call.'

'Here you are.' She turned it round and put it on the counter.

Jon dialled 241. He was about to give up when the phone was answered. 'Is Pete around?'

'Pete Gray?'

'I don't know his surname.'

'Well, there's only one Pete works in here. He's on his way with some supplies to the surgical wards. Left two minutes ago.'

'Cheers.' Jon handed the phone back and looked at the site map. A very cheerful volunteer with the name 'Sue' on her badge pointed out the way they needed to go. Thanking her, they set off down a long corridor, passing a procession of hospital staff, patients and visitors. Soon they reached a T-junction and followed the overhead sign. At the next crossroads, they could see the surgical ward immediately in front. Jon glanced to his left; a man with a large paunch was swaggering towards them, pushing a trolley piled with boxes. As he got nearer Jon said to Rick, 'Check out the box on top of his pile.'

The label said: *Mediquip Inc. Powder-free surgical gloves. Sterile. 24 boxes of 200.*

'Pete Gray?' Jon asked. Taking in the porter's jet-black laquered quiff, Jon guessed he was in his late forties and clinging to the same haircut of twenty years ago. When baldness hit, it was going to hit hard. The heavy gold neck chain seemed incongruous with the simple white overalls he was wearing.

'Yes?' he said, slowing down.

Jon held his warrant card up. 'DI Spicer and DS Saville, Greater Manchester Police. Once you've dropped that lot off, can we have a quick word?'

The porter seemed to think about this for a second, eyes fixed on Jon's badge. Nervously he raised a hand to his chin. No wedding ring. 'Here? What's it about?'

'Perhaps a café area would be more comfortable,' Jon replied, ignoring the second question.

Pete's eyes flicked from Jon to Rick and back again. 'OK.'

He pushed the trolley through the double doors, Jon and Rick watching him through the windows.

'Him selling a rowing machine? No wonder. He obviously didn't get much use out of it,' Rick said quietly.

Pete re-emerged and, confidently now, led them to a quiet café area round the corner. After they'd all got a drink, Pete walked over to a table with a discarded copy of the *Sun* on it, peeling back the front page to stare at the page three girl beneath. 'I wouldn't kick her out of bed. Tits are fake, though.'

Jon studied his face. With the build-up of flab on his cheeks and below his jaw, there was a faint resemblance to a Las Vegasera Elvis. In his younger days he'd probably been quite the ladies' man. The way he passed judgement on a topless model some thirty years younger than him suggested that he thought he still was.

'How long have you worked here, Pete?' Jon placed a white plastic stirrer in his upturned cup lid.

Pete finished pouring a third sachet of sugar into his coffee. 'About eight years.'

'Ever have to work nights? I could never get used to them when I was in uniform.'

Pete's shoulders relaxed a little. 'I don't mind them, actually.'

Jon stretched his legs out to the side of the table, took a sip of coffee. Allowing a note of boredom into his voice, he said, 'This is just routine stuff because your name was thrown up as part of an ongoing investigation – it shouldn't take long. Were you working yesterday?'

'Yeah, I finish at eight in the evening.'

He wasn't quite sure why, but Jon was getting a feeling about the man. Keeping it casual, he looked away, appearing to be more interested in the Give Blood poster on the wall. He was about to ask his next question when Rick jumped in, 'What did you do for the rest of the night?'

A wary expression slid across Pete's face. 'Watched a couple of videos.'

Jon tried to steer the conversation back to just a chat. 'A couple? You a film buff?'

'Just Elvis ones.'

'I think I've only ever seen *Viva Las Vegas*. What else was he in?'

'Loads.'

The man had clammed up and Jon could tell he was only going to get more tense. Cursing Rick for having jumped in so clumsily, he decided to go for it. 'Did anyone watch them with you?'

'No, I live alone.' Guarded now.

'Pete, are you into exercise?'

'Not really.'

'What about rowing?'

He shook his head.

'You've never tried a rowing machine?'

Pete blinked. 'Oh, yeah. I've tried it a couple of times.'

'At a gym?'

'No, I bought one. The thing's still in my house.'

'Must clutter the place up. Ever considered selling it?'

The stream of questions was irritating Pete and he tried to reverse the flow. 'Why? You want to buy it?'

Jon laid his forearms on the table. 'Did Carol Miller want to buy it?'

He watched as connections came together in the other man's head. 'I've never laid eyes on her.'

'Was she looking to buy your rowing machine? The one you're trying to sell on the noticeboard of the maternity ward?'

Pete ran a hand back and forth across his chin, eyes shifting to the side. 'We spoke. She was interested, but she never followed it up.'

'You spoke? You mean over the telephone?'

'That's right. She rang me – internal call.'

No record of calls made on an internal phone system, Jon thought. He was considering his next question when Pete spoke first. 'I don't like where this is going. I'm not prepared to continue.' He finished his coffee and got up.

Jon shrugged. 'One last thing before you go. I've been meaning to see *Viva Las Vegas* again for a long time. Where do you hire your Elvis videos from?' He could check on Pete Gray's story with the shop.

'I have my own collection.' He walked quickly away.

Jon waited until he'd disappeared round the

corner. 'Well, that got him all shook up.' Rick's face was blank, completely missing the joke.

Jon pulled an evidence bag from his pocket, then, using the end of a pen, picked up the cup Pete had been drinking from and dropped it inside.

'What are you taking that for?' asked Rick.

'It'll have his prints and DNA on it.'

His partner laughed incredulously. 'You're not seriously thinking of trying to use that as evidence in court?'

Jon gritted his teeth and waited for the flash of annoyance to pass. 'No. But it could come in useful if any DNA's recovered from the third victim's body.'

With a little shake of his head, Rick stood up.

As they crossed the canteen Jon stared at the back of Rick's neck, thinking that his new partner had a lot to learn and deciding that he wasn't the one who'd do the teaching.

CHAPTER 5

The woman shook her head. 'Don't worry, love. We've had women turn up here in just their nighties before. Barefoot and everything.'

Fiona saw the woman's eyes shift to the cut above her eyebrow yet again. She turned away to look around the bedroom. It was more like a nun's cell: narrow single bed, tiny table next to it, simple wardrobe in the corner. The only splash of colour was three dahlias in the vase on the bedside table.

'Talking of nighties, we've got spare ones, or pyjamas if you prefer. Clothes and basic toiletries, too. A lot of people donate items.'

Fiona smiled. 'Thank you, Hazel, you're so kind. I don't know what to say.'

'You can say that we can take some photographs of your face.'

Her voice had hardened and Fiona looked at her with surprise.

'Photographic evidence makes it more difficult for him to get away with it.' She was staring intently into Fiona's eyes.

69

'I . . . I don't know. What do you mean, "get away with it"?'

Hazel backed off. 'I'm sorry. I shouldn't let it anger me like this. What I mean is, if there comes a time when you want to press charges or divorce him, it helps to have some kind of record. A written diary is good, but photos are far, far preferable. There's no pressure for you to do anything now, except get better. But it helps if we can get some record while the injuries are still fresh.'

They stepped out of the room, Hazel gesturing to the many doors in the short corridor. 'With the exception of the two family rooms and the old servant's quarters up in the attic, all the bedrooms have been divided. It's a bit like a mini-hotel, complete with my office just inside the front door. Shall we go down?'

'Actually, do you mind if I make a quick call in private?' Fiona said, glancing back into the empty room.

'Certainly,' Hazel replied. 'But I must stress that this address has to remain a secret.'

Fiona nodded and then went into her room and closed the door. She lifted her mobile out of her handbag and switched it on. Before she'd even found the business card from Cheshire Consorts, her phone was beeping with answerphone messages.

She listened to the first, heard Jeff's drunken threats, and deleted it. The next three were him again, angrier and more drunk, remorseful and pleading, then snarling and vicious. She deleted

70

them, too. The last was from that morning, a colleague from the salon ringing to see if she was OK.

Noticing her battery charge was getting low, she reached into her handbag and took the card from Cheshire Consorts out.

What the hell am I doing? she thought. Isn't my life messed up enough without getting involved in this?

She was about to screw the card up when a memory from the day her daughter died bobbed up. She'd been lying there, listening to Emily's light footsteps as she ran out of the house. Just lying there, not doing a thing. At some point every single day of her life since, she'd paused and thought: If only I'd got up . . .

She ran a hand across her forehead, trying to wipe the thought away. Opening her eyes she stared at the card again. Damn it, she'd let down one vulnerable person in her life. She wasn't about to do it again with this Alexia. She took a breath in and called the mobile number written on the back of the card.

When it was eventually answered, all Fiona could hear was what sounded like traffic going past. After a few seconds she tentatively said, 'Hello? Is that Alexia?'

'You what?' A male voice, pitched high with the question.

'I'm trying to get hold of Alexia. Is she there?'

'Who's this?'

'A friend.'

'From where?'

'From . . .' Fiona searched for an answer, but failed to find one. 'Put Alexia on, please.'

Silence. 'Who are you?' Fiona demanded. 'Why have you got Alexia's phone?'

Still no reply.

'It was you in that motel room last night, wasn't it? What have you done to her?'

The phone went dead.

Fiona stabbed at the redial button, but got the 'number unobtainable' signal. She hugged herself, waiting for her heart to slow down.

The office door was open. Hazel waved her in and said, 'OK. If you could sit in the corner.' She opened a drawer and took out a Polaroid camera. 'Now, if you'll lift your hair away from your face. Lovely.' The flash went off. 'I'll just get a close up of that cut on your eyebrow. Has a doctor seen it yet?'

Fiona shook her head. 'I was planning to go to A and E later on.'

'I think you should,' Hazel replied. 'You don't want to end up with a scar.'

She photographed Fiona head on and from the other side. 'Great. How about a cup of tea while I get your file sorted out?'

Two other women were sitting at the kitchen table, one hunched over the late morning edition of the local paper, a cigarette in her hand.

'Sarah, Cathy, this is Fiona. She'll be with us

for a few days.' Hazel retreated from the room and Sarah got up and reached for the kettle. Fiona sensed a well-established routine.

'Brew?' Sarah asked.

'Thanks,' Fiona replied. She fought the urge to brush an imaginary hair from her forehead, knowing the gesture was just an attempt to hide her injury. Nervously she reached for her cigarettes, realising she only had a few left. She held the pack out anyway. 'Cigarette anyone?'

Cathy looked up and Fiona saw livid burns running down the side of her face. A large chunk of her self-consciousness evaporated.

'No, thanks,' Cathy smiled, holding up her own by way of an explanation.

The headline on the paper's front page caught Fiona's eye: HAS THE BUTCHER CLAIMED ANOTHER?

'Milk? Sugar?' Sarah asked, but her voice seemed to be coming from far away.

Fiona's voice came out as a croak, 'Can I?'

'Be my guest.' Cathy slid the paper across and the front page filled Fiona's vision.

A grainy photo, which, judging from the elevation, had been taken from an upstairs window. There was a garden in the foreground. On the grassy area beyond stood a cluster of uniformed policemen and a few onlookers in plain clothes. A tent was being hastily erected.

Fiona's hand went to her mouth as she read the opening paragraph.

A dog walker made a gruesome discovery early this morning on waste ground almost in the shadow of Belle Vue's famous greyhound racing stadium. As yet police have refused to confirm whether the Butcher has claimed another victim but, as our reporter at the scene can confirm, substantial swathes of the victim's skin had been removed.

Fiona looked up and turned desperately from one woman to the other.

Cathy's chair scraped slightly as she shied away, 'Do you know something about this?'

'I heard . . . I heard something last night. I was in a motel. Oh God.'

'What did you hear?' Sarah's hand was frozen on a carton of milk.

'Something horrible.' Fiona stood up and hurried back to the office.

Hazel was writing Fiona's name at the top of some sort of form. She looked up. 'What's wrong?'

'I need to use your phone. Please.'

'Of course. Here.' Quickly she evacuated her seat. 'Are you OK?'

'I just have to . . .' The sentence was left unfinished as she began dialling a number. 'Janine, it's Fiona. Is Alice there?'

'Fiona! We tried your home number and mobile when you didn't come in this morning. Everything OK?'

'I'll tell you later. Just put Alice on, will you?'

'OK. She's just finishing with a customer. Wait a second.'

Fiona kept her head down, discouraging any questions from Hazel who was hovering at the door.

'Hi, Fiona. How are you?'

'Alice, your other half. Jon. He's in the police, right? Quite high up?'

'Yes, he works on major incidents. What's wrong?'

'Listen, I need to speak to him. It's about this Butcher of Belle Vue thing.'

CHAPTER 6

They had just pulled up in the car park of Longsight police station when Jon's mobile began a stifled warble in his pocket.

He glanced at the caller's identity and was surprised to see Alice's name. She always tried to avoid calling him at work. Afraid it was because the baby was coming early, he signalled to Rick that he'd catch him up. 'Ali. Are you OK?'

'Fine. Can you talk?'

Relieved, Jon leaned an elbow on the car roof. 'Yeah. What's up?'

'I work with a woman called Fiona. She does make-up and facials.'

'The one with the violent husband?'

Alice's voice dropped to a whisper. 'Yeah.'

There was a moment's silence as each waited for the other to go on.

Alice spoke first. 'She called me just now. She wants to meet you.'

'About the husband? Ali, I'd love to sort him out, but there are trained officers she can speak to in the Domestic Violence—'

'She thinks she heard someone being killed last night.'

'What?'

'She thinks she heard someone being killed last night.'

'Where?'

'In the room next to hers. She was staying in some run-down motel in Belle Vue.'

Jon cupped a hand over his ear to hear more clearly. 'You said Belle Vue?'

Forty minutes later he found himself sitting with another coffee. He thought back to Rick reaching for the chocolate powder, then changing his mind. Strangely self-conscious behaviour.

As his eyes scanned the people passing the window, he searched his memory for the one time he'd met Fiona. It was a few years ago when the salon staff were out celebrating Melvyn's birthday. Jon was coming off a late shift and had agreed to pick Alice up at the end of the night.

When he'd arrived at the wine-bar he could see the evening had been a good one. Empty bottles littered the table and they were all sitting around with pissed looks on their faces. Jon had taken a seat next to Melvyn and Alice. On spotting him, Melvyn introduced everyone, then instantly reached for a bottle of wine and began filling a glass.

'Just a small one,' Jon had smiled, his outstretched hand palm down.

'Bollocks. Get a taxi,' Melvyn replied, filling it right up.

Jon shook his head, the grin still on his face. 'It'll take hours to catch you lot up and this place shuts in ten minutes.'

Alice had slumped against his shoulder and was fumbling with a packet of cigarettes as she resumed an earnest discussion with Melvyn about who was the sexiest, Ewan McGregor, Johnny Depp or Keanu Reeves.

God, she's going to be hung over in the morning, Jon thought, lighting one for himself and looking around. Fiona was at the other end of the table, clutching a glass of wine, deep in a serious-looking conversation with the woman at her side.

Jon had found himself studying her. She should have been quite a glamorous woman but something was marring the impression. Her face was pleasantly proportioned, no single feature standing out as wrong. Her light brown hair had been professionally cut and styled, probably by Melvyn, Jon had guessed. She was wearing a pale blue cashmere top, the neckline cut just low enough to show off a glittery necklace.

But everything was being undermined by something. Ready to look away the moment her eyes turned towards his, he scrutinised her more closely. Was it her eyebrows? Had she plucked them a little too vigorously? Applied liner at a slightly harsh angle?

Finally it came to him. The negative impression

wasn't as a result of any single feature, it was more the expression on her face. The lines at the corners of her eyes and at the edges of her mouth all emphasised it. They slanted downwards and the skin along her jawline seemed loose and somehow tired.

Her face hinted at the slow and cumulative effects of pain. He'd seen a similar drawn look appear on his granddad's face as the cancer really began to take hold. Jon was just wondering what was eating her when something caused alarm to flicker in her eyes.

He looked to his right and saw a heavy man standing just inside the door. His arms were crossed and a large belly pressed out over his belt. He nodded towards the door and Jon spotted a set of car keys hanging from one hand.

Fiona started scrabbling around for her handbag, hurriedly saying goodbye to the colleague she'd been talking to. Her movement was picked up by Melvyn and he glanced round for an explanation. Seeing the man by the door, he called out sarcastically, 'Jeff! Good to see you. Joining us for a quick one?'

The man stayed exactly where he was and shook his head.

'Yeah, and fuck you, too,' Melvyn muttered.

Fiona was now standing, agitation and embarrassment on her face. 'See you all on Monday,' she said, struggling slightly with her words.

Melvyn got up and hugged her, then watched

with a pained expression as she lurched across the bar and out the door. Jon looked around and saw similar emotions on everyone else's face.

Melvyn sat back down with a sigh. 'Fucking arsehole.'

'That's Fiona's other half?' Jon asked.

His question had gone unanswered as they all broke into conversations about why she stayed with him.

A woman walked through the coffee shop doors. She was wearing a strange mish-mash of clothes, her hair was down over her forehead and she tried to keep her head bowed as she glanced quickly round the room. Their eyes met. Simultaneously recognising her and seeing the damage to her face, Jon held up a hand.

She moved towards him. 'How did you know it was me?'

'We were introduced once. I was picking Alice up from the pub. You were there with the other staff from the salon.' She was looking blankly at him. 'Jesus, you really were pissed.' He touched the scar above his own eyebrow and smiled. 'Besides, Alice said we had something in common.'

Her eyes dropped in embarrassment and Jon cursed his clumsy attempt at breaking the ice.

'What else did she say about me?' she asked.

He chose his words more carefully. 'Not a lot. Just that your husband gives you a hard time.'

She sat down, lit a cigarette and looked him in the eyes. 'My soon to be ex-husband.'

Jon hoped so, but he'd heard that line plenty of times before. Abusive relationships fought hard to keep their participants in place. 'I can put you in touch with specially trained officers. Start the ball rolling to make sure he can't come near you again.'

She shook her head. 'Thanks, but it's OK.'

'Where are you staying?' said Jon, eyes straying hungrily to the smoke curling from the tip of her cigarette.

'Sorry, would you like one?' She held the pack out.

Jon pursed his lips. He'd agreed with Alice to give up last year. Apart from one lapse, he hadn't smoked in almost six months. Most of the time it was becoming less and less of a problem, but certain occasions brought on an urge like the need for a cool drink on a summer's day. A little voice told him it would be OK. She was a fellow smoker. She'd understand. Word would never get back to Alice. He wrestled the temptation down with a shake of his head. 'Trying to give up, thanks. So, where are you staying?'

'I've got a room just round the corner.' She gestured vaguely towards the street.

'In the refuge on Stanhope Street?' Jon kept his voice low.

Fiona's face went from shock to realisation. 'Sorry. They told me to keep the address secret. I should have known the police would know about it.'

'How long are you there for?'

She sighed, and a tremor passed across her lower lip. 'I don't know. I really don't know.'

'Are you OK, Fiona? We don't have to do this if you're not.'

She smiled bleakly. 'Am I OK? I've just walked out on my husband. And then what I heard last night . . .' She ground the cigarette out, drilling the filter hard into the ashtray. 'Be strong, Fiona. Be strong,' she said under her breath. Then she looked up. 'I want to tell you about last night.' Despite her determined tone, a shiver went through her.

'Can I get you a coffee first?'

She smiled. 'Thanks. A latte, please.'

Jon returned a couple of minutes later. He placed a froth-filled cup before her just as she lit another cigarette. 'Take your time,' he said, sitting down.

Fiona told her story, starting from when she'd staggered into the foyer of the Platinum Inn and had sat with Dawn in the back office, sharing a few drinks. She began to falter when she had to describe the sound of the couple undressing.

'OK, Fiona,' Jon helped her along. 'They were on the bed by now.'

She nodded.

'And I'm guessing you could hear them getting down to business? Pardon the pun.'

'Yes. But then I heard them speak again and they moved. Changed – you know – positions I suppose. And that's when the struggling began. And this awful choking sound. She was fighting to breathe.'

Jon knew the autopsies on Angela Rowlands and Carol Miller had shown evidence of strangulation. In the background the milk steamer's splutters ground to a halt.

'Eventually they stopped moving. Then one person got up, went to the bathroom and the taps came on. He wandered about the room for a bit, went back to the bed.' She broke to spoon foam into her mouth, fingers trembling. 'Then there was a thump, like something heavy being dragged off the bed and onto the floor.'

Jon tried to keep his thoughts objective, but he couldn't stop the waves of excitement running through him. He dragged his eyes from the tip of her cigarette again.

'I crept across to my door and looked through the spyhole. One person left that room, moving slowly, something big and heavy wrapped in a blanket over his shoulder.'

'Did you see his face?'

'No, just a flash of reddish-brown hair, but I reckon that was the girl's, poking out from the top of the blanket. He headed away from reception to the door at the other end of the corridor. He must have left through the fire exit.'

'Did any sort of an alarm go off?'

Fiona shook her head. 'You should see the place. It's falling apart. I doubt the alarms even work.'

Jon ran the information through his head. The motel was a few minutes' walk from where the third

83

body had been found. But where had the victim's skin been removed? Did the killer have a van in the car park or had he even left the building at all? Could he have taken her to a storage room or perhaps the basement?

'Fiona, do you know what time of night this was?'

She nodded emphatically. 'Three thirty in the morning they woke me coming into their room. He left at about four I'd imagine.'

Jon's excitement vanished. 'You're absolutely sure on that?'

'Yes, I looked at my watch.'

'And it was three thirty in the morning?'

'Yes. Three thirty-six, to be exact.'

An image of the killer had just started to materialise in his head. Blurred and indistinct maybe, but just enough to create a tingle in his veins. It was a sensation he found completely addictive. Now the hazy silhouette evaporated like a mirage. His lips tensed in regret. 'Fiona, I'm telling you this in confidence. The body found at just after six this morning. It had been there all night, not placed there just before dawn.'

Fiona frowned. 'But I heard . . . What I heard, it wasn't just sex.' Her jaw set tight. 'I really think I heard someone being killed.'

Jon took a deep breath and looked up at the ceiling, wondering how much brandy she'd shared with the receptionist. Halogen bulbs glared down at him.

'And I found this.' Fiona patted her pockets and pulled out a slightly crumpled business card. 'It was under the bed.'

'Under which bed?'

'The one in the next room. Number nine. The door hadn't shut properly. I looked around it this morning.'

'And?'

'And it was spotless. The bed looked like no one had slept in it. The bathroom was immaculate. Everything had been wiped clean – to destroy evidence, I suppose. This was the only thing there. Oh, and the spare blanket was missing, too.'

The card was still in her outstretched hand, shaking slightly.

Jon looked at it. It could have been lying there for days. 'Fiona, you were attacked by your husband last night. You mentioned you had quite a bit of brandy with the night receptionist—'

'Don't say I imagined it!' she hissed.

'I'm not. I'm certain you heard something. But this motel – it's used on an hourly basis by prostitutes and their clients. All sorts are going on. Doors banging, people coming and going right through the night.'

'I heard what I heard.' The card was thrust defiantly towards him.

Reluctantly Jon took it, read the printed writing then flipped it over.

Fiona jabbed a finger at the scrawled biro. 'I tried her number. A man answered. He hung up on me and when I tried again the number had gone dead.'

Jon raised an eyebrow.

'Go on. Try it yourself.'

As he took his mobile out he got a surreptitious look at his watch. This was taking up too much time. He rang the number. It went through to a number unavailable announcement.

'See?' Fiona insisted. Her voice was beginning to grate. 'He's stolen her stuff. The phone's probably been shoved down some drain by now.'

'OK.' Jon got ready to stand up. 'This Platinum Inn. I'll stop by and ask some questions, I'll speak to Cheshire Consorts and I'll check who this mobile number is registered to.'

Fiona relaxed a little. 'Thank you.'

'I've really got to go. I'll call you. Have you got a mobile?'

She gave him her number.

When he walked into the incident room on the top floor of Longsight station, a new buzz was in the air.

Rick was at his desk, a couple of other officers complimenting him on spotting the glove. Jon saw the look of pleasure on his face, the easy way he was taking credit for the find. You'll go far in this job, he thought.

As he got to their desks Rick finally saw him. 'It was blood on that glove.'

Jon sat down. 'That's great news. Anything on who the girl is?'

'No. She's been fingerprinted and a DNA sample's been taken. All missing reports for young female adults are being checked now, and word's gone out to the neighbouring forces to do the same.'

'Door-to-door around Belle Vue?'

'As we speak.'

The other two officers moved off and Rick quietly said, 'McCloughlin announced that I'd found the glove to the whole room. It's been a good way of meeting everyone.'

That surprised Jon, and he thought that maybe there was no link between Rick and McCloughlin. But then he realised Rick could easily have told McCloughlin the true story and the announcement to the incident room could be just McCloughlin keeping up the pretence. 'What about that footprint?'

'The CSM – what was her name?'

'Nikki Kingston,' Jon replied, slightly irritated at the defensive note in his voice.

'Apparently, she shoved a bucket over it and sent for a casting kit.'

Jon grinned in admiration of her efficiency.

'But the best is yet to come,' Rick carried on.

'Go on.'

'The glove. She's testing it for fingerprints, something about amino acid deposits in sweat showing up on latex. If whoever dropped that glove is on NAFIS, we could have his name and address in a few hours.'

Jon looked around. 'No wonder everyone's looking so happy.'

Rick stood up. 'I'm desperate for a leak.'

Jon waited until Rick had gone out, then picked up the phone and dialled Nikki's number. 'Nikki, it's Jon. This glove.'

'Bloody hell, Jon. Anyone else and I'd tell them to call back later. It's right in front of me. We've already lifted a partial from the wrist where he gripped it to pull it on.'

'Enough for a match?'

'No. But there should be others – on the inside at the fingertips, for instance. If he wasn't wearing them long enough to get them all smudged, they could prove useful.'

'Great. Listen, can you tell me who made the glove? Can you see the word "Mediquip" on it?'

'Hang on. There's something on the back.' Her words were drawn out and Jon could tell she was squinting, face inches from the glove. 'Yes. It says "Size 8" and "Mediquip Inc". Good news?'

'Could well be,' Jon replied, trying to suppress the excitement in his voice. He placed the bag with Pete Gray's cup in on the desk. 'Last thing, Nikki,' he said, lowering his voice. 'Can you run a couple of tests on a cup for me? Fingerprints and, hopefully, saliva for DNA.'

'Are you taking the piss?'

'I don't mean straight away,' he protested. 'Just when you get the chance.'

She sighed. 'You owe me. Big time. Where's it come from, anyway?'

'A suspect left it behind at an interview.'

'So this is an unofficial test?'

'Yeah.' Jon smiled. 'If it links him to what I'm hoping, we'll pull him in on something else and then run a DNA mouth swab in line with the Police and Criminal Evidence Act.' Seeing Rick coming back in, he quickly hid the cup in his drawer. 'Right, I'll leave you to it.'

'Sure there's nothing else?' she said sarcastically.

'No, that'll do for the moment. Cheers.' He hung up as Rick sat down. 'I've just spoken to the CSM. The glove you found at the crime scene was made by a company called Mediquip.'

Rick raised a finger. 'Same as the ones Pete Gray was wheeling to the surgical ward.'

Jon winked. 'Have a check on the PNC, see if he's got any priors. I'll see what the internet has on Mediquip.'

Less than a minute later, Jon was reading out the company's home page in an American accent. 'Mediquip is one of the world's leading manu-facturers of latex and vinyl gloves for surgical and medical use. Our factory employs the very latest quality control standards in order to produce a range of gloves recognised across the globe for their reliability.' A row of thumbnail-sized photos popped up across the the screen. 'Powder-free vinyl. PE gloves for industrial use. Powder-free in natural colour. Latex surgical sterilised by EO gas. Copolymer sterile latex. Pre-powdered nitrile examination.' He scanned the column on the left of the screen. 'Here we go: suppliers.' He keyed

'United Kingdom' into the search field. Four names came up, one based in Manchester: Protex Ltd, Unit 15, Europa Business Park, Denton.

Rick's eyes were on his own screen. 'Pete Gray. Cautioned for sexual harassment back in eighty-nine. Was going to court, but charges were dropped by his then wife, Helen Gray. There's an addendum to contact the Domestic Violence Unit for more information.'

He called the unit and got them to pull their intelligence file on Pete Gray. There were two other incidents involving violence towards females, one in 1993 and another in 1999. Neither had resulted in a caution or conviction.

'So he's not had his DNA added to the national database,' Rick announced, hanging up the phone.

'Looks like he has an attitude problem with the ladies, though,' Jon replied, printing off the contact details for Protex. 'OK. I think it's time for a word with McCloughlin.'

As he got up, he saw the business card for Cheshire Consorts lying on his desk. Flipping it over, he looked at the mobile phone number scrawled there and groaned. He'd assured Fiona that he'd look into it, and now he'd have to waste valuable time keeping his promise.

'Two seconds, I just need to do a favour for a colleague of my girlfriend. She thinks she heard someone being strangled in the room next to her in a motel last night.'

Rick smirked at Jon's tone. 'Whereabouts?'

'Belle Vue,' Jon replied, picking up the phone.

'Really? Near where the body was this morning?'

Jon nodded. 'Yeah, but don't get excited. Whatever she thinks she heard, it was at three thirty in the morning. The third victim's time of death was hours before that.'

He called the communications liaison office. 'DI Spicer here. Could you run a check on a mobile phone number for me, please?'

Next he flipped the card over and rang Cheshire Consorts itself. 'Hello, this is DI Spicer from Greater Manchester Police. Who am I speaking to, please?'

'Joanne Perkins. Are you on duty, Detective Inspector, or is this call for leisure purposes?'

But for a calculating note, the voice was very seductive. Jon imagined long, shimmering blond hair, arched eyebrows and full red lips. 'I'm on duty, yes. Could I speak to the manager or owner, please?'

'You are. I'm manager and owner.'

'Ms Perkins—'

'Please, call me "Miss". You'll find we're feminine, not feminist, at Cheshire Consorts.'

Jon smiled; the lady was good. 'Miss Perkins. Do you have a girl on your books called Alexia?'

'Why?'

'A possible missing person. We have reason to believe she worked as an escort for your company.'

A cigarette lighter flicked and breath was exhaled against the mouthpiece. He could almost feel the smoke washing over his face. 'No surname?'

Jon shook his head. 'Afraid not.'

'No, I don't.' The answer was too abrupt.'

'Have any girls failed to check back with you since their last job?'

'DI Spicer, I'm not their nanny. The customer gives his credit card number to me, I send the girl to him. Apart from passing a percentage of his payment to the girl, I'm out of the equation.'

That was more like it, Jon thought. Cold and selfish. He guessed her experience of customers wasn't limited to just the management side of things. 'And you're sure no one of that name works for you? It sounds like an alias to me.'

'All my girls use aliases. Go to Cheshire Consorts dot com. They're all listed there. Now this is a business line. I really must go.'

Jon made sure he got the phone down first. Small recompense for being brushed off. A few seconds later he knocked on McCloughlin's door, opened it and let Rick step in first. McCloughlin's face lit up. 'DS Saville.' His eyes moved to Jon. 'And DI Spicer.' Less enthusiasm in his voice. 'Sit down.'

'Sir,' Jon began, 'we spoke to Pete Gray, the porter at Stepping Hill hospital.'

'And?'

'As soon as Carol Miller was mentioned, his mouth clammed shut. In fact, he got up and walked away, not prepared to talk any further.'

'Interesting.'

Rick spoke up. 'He was arrested for sexual harassment in 1989. His ex-wife.'

McCloughlin inclined his head. 'And I can tell you have more.'

Jon nodded. 'When we saw him at the hospital, Rick noticed he was wheeling a box of surgical gloves. They're manufactured by a US company called Mediquip, but distributed in this region by a British firm called Protex Ltd.'

McCloughlin's eyes lingered suspiciously on Jon before turning to Rick. 'Have you called Protex yet? We could do with knowing who the area rep is, at least.'

'Not yet,' said Rick. 'We – I've only just got the information.'

McCloughlin obviously sensed Rick wasn't being straight. He pushed his phone across the desk. 'Make the call.'

Rick looked down. The only thing on his lap was Pete Gray's record. Sheepishly he looked at Jon. 'I think you have the company's details?'

Jon whipped the sheet out from his notebook. From the corner of his eye he saw McCloughlin's lip beginning to curl.

Rick called the number, introduced himself and asked to speak to the sales rep for the north-west. He started jotting information down. 'Since when? . . . I see . . . And his name's Gordon Dean? . . . Where was he staying? . . . OK . . . No, if we hear anything we'll call back.' He hung up, looking baffled. 'It appears he's vanished. He was staying in Manchester, seeing clients around town yesterday. Since then they've been trying to

93

contact him. He missed a big sales meeting this morning.'

Without lifting his forearm from his desk, McCloughlin pointed a finger at the door. 'A blood-spattered glove is dropped at a murder scene and the area rep for that company goes missing the very next morning? I don't need to tell you which lead to pursue, gentlemen.'

As they made for the door, McCloughlin called Jon back. Without looking up, he said, 'Next time, don't use your partner to front up information that you've sourced. Understood?'

'Sir.' Jon closed the door quietly behind him.

CHAPTER 7

The body in the bed didn't move.

Sunlight slanted in through the open window, spilling across the crumpled white sheets and creating a lunar landscape of miniature ravines. Silence dominated the room, pierced at regular intervals by a thin whistle. It came from the bandages encasing the patient's face.

Eventually a hand slid upwards. A forefinger and thumb picked delicately at the nostril holes and shoulders flinched as pain lanced outwards. After a few moments the patient tried again, this time successfully getting the tip of a varnished nail into a nostril that still throbbed from where the blows had landed. A large flake of dried blood was prised away and a sob of self-pity was released.

The hand fell back on to the sheet as a soft whirring came from the window. A robin had alighted on the metal arm holding the window open. Head cocked to one side, it surveyed the room with a keen eye.

From the bed, a pair of swollen and bloodshot eyes looked back, hungry for company of any kind. The patient tried to encourage the bird forward with a kissing sound, tears spilling over the layers of gauze.

CHAPTER 8

Immaculate grass borders flanked the entrance to the Europa Business Park. The spotless white gates were open and, as soon as they turned in, the car tyres seemed to start gliding over the smooth tarmac. A large sign stood at a fork in the road. Rick's eyes moved over it. 'Units ten to twenty. Right turn.'

Jon spun the wheel and they followed the gently curving avenue. Side roads branched off to low buildings made from a type of corrugated material that appeared to come in only three colours: blue, green and white. Protex Ltd had chosen white.

They parked in one of the spaces reserved for visitors directly in front of reception. Grey glass doors slid silently open as they approached them and they stepped into a foyer which was tidy to the point of being unwelcoming. A photo of a proudly beaming man was on their right. Directly below it a brass plaque: *Keith Bradley founded this company in 1973.*

And doesn't his tie just show it, thought Jon, making an effort not to wince at the ugly splashes of colour jumping off the man's chest.

Photos of various gloves lined the wall, each one bathed in coloured lighting to add interest to a totally lifeless product.

A young woman with a headset cutting into her wavy brown hair nodded to them from behind the reception desk. 'Can I help you?'

They held up their warrant cards and her smile slipped.

'Could we speak to your head of human resources, please?' Jon asked.

'One moment.' She pressed a button on the switchboard. 'Martin, I have two policemen wishing to speak with you.' She listened for a second, then looked up. 'Could I ask what it's in relation to?'

Jon leaned closer and, for the benefit of the person on the other end of the line, said loudly, 'Gordon Dean.'

The receptionist listened again. 'He'll be right down. Please take a seat.'

Jon glanced at the chairs. Like everything else, they were stiff and unused. He remained standing. A minute later footsteps could be heard on the stairs. A middle-aged man in shirt and tie walked over to them. 'Martin Appleforth, head of HR.' He hesitated, not knowing who to shake hands with first.

Jon stepped forward. 'DI Spicer and DS Saville.'

Appleforth's office was slightly too warm. The blinds on the end window were lowered, but sunlight cut through the gaps, one sliver dissecting

97

the photo of a plain-looking woman trying to smile in some crowded beauty spot.

'I hope Gordon's all right? Has something happened?' He positioned his pen in the exact midpoint of a Protex notepad.

'We're not sure at present,' answered Jon, un-buttoning his jacket. 'What sort of employee is he?'

Appleforth turned one palm upwards, as if the necessary information would drop into it. 'Hard-working, reliable. He's been with us for around eight years.'

'And his sales patch is the whole of the north-west?'

'The Manchester area and south into Cheshire. Another rep takes care of the Liverpool area and up into the Lake District as far as the Scottish border.'

'So Mr Dean has a company car?' asked Rick.

'Yes, a silver Passat – same as me, in fact.'

'Do you have his registration?'

Appleforth swivelled in his seat, consulted a sheet of paper pinned to his noticeboard and read out the registration.

Jon noted it down. 'What sort of companies do you deal with?'

'Hospitals and GP practices mainly, as you can imagine, but any sort of business in the health sector. Private surgeries, NHS clinics, even a few tattoo parlours and beauty salons, though I class them in the cosmetics sector.'

'Tell me, do you have a contract with Stepping

Hill hospital in Stockport?' Jon asked, thinking of Pete Gray.

'I'd have to phone the sales department.'

'And it would be useful if we could have the list of clients Mr Dean saw in the last three days. Is that possible?'

'Again, I'd have to ask the sales department.'

'How old is Mr Dean?'

'Late thirties, I'd have thought.'

'Married?'

'Yes.' Appleforth looked down at his desk and rubbed a forefinger against his temple. 'Angela, if I remember.' Jon guessed he'd just been looking at Gordon Dean's file.

'Have you spoken to his wife today?' Rick asked.

'Yes.' Appleforth admitted. 'She rang earlier, very worried. When I said he hadn't shown up for the meeting here, she said she was going to report him as missing.' He looked at them as if they should already know this.

Rick nodded ambiguously. 'Which station did she go to?'

'Her local one in Stoke.'

'I see. Mr Appleforth, we could do with speaking to her ourselves. Could you give us her phone number?'

He reached for the mouse, but his hand stayed hovering above it. 'I'm not sure if I should give his personal details out . . .' His eyes were calculating. 'She said the police told her that, although he's missing, they couldn't treat it as anything but low priority for a few more days. How come you're here now?'

'Mr Appleforth.' Jon hunched forward in his seat, shoulders suddenly tight against his jacket. The desire to move the investigation forward was nagging away at him and there was no way an officious little prick like this was going to slow things down. 'We're investigating a serious crime here, one the press are also very interested in. There's reason to believe that Mr Dean, in his capacity as a sales rep for Protex, could help us. Now, I don't want this turning into a matter for your PR department.'

Appleforth hesitated a moment longer before clicking his mouse. Sure enough, Gordon Dean's details, including his address in Stoke, were already up on his desktop. 'We'd appreciate being kept up to date with Mr Dean's whereabouts.'

Jon sat back. 'Of course.'

They were heading back out of Appleforth's office when Jon paused in the doorway. 'Does Mr Dean have a workstation in the building?'

'Yes, office number five at the end of the corridor.'

'May we take a quick look inside?'

Appleforth hesitated but, unable to think of a decent reason why not, nodded and got up. He led Jon and Rick along the silent corridor, past smoked-glass windows and shiny wooden doors. They stood back at number five, allowing him to open the door for them.

To Jon's annoyance Appleforth used the opportunity to step in ahead of them and position himself in the corner by the window. 'What are you looking for?' he asked.

Jon shrugged. 'Nothing specifically.'

The room was small, too small for three men. Jon tried to look around, but his view was obscured by Rick and Appleforth. Picking up on his look of annoyance, Rick stepped back and watched from the doorway. Immediately in front of Jon was a small desk with a computer monitor and keyboard taking up one half. A phone with a notepad occupied the opposite corner and between them sat a desk tidy. Jon looked at the three cylindrical tubes, noting each one held a different colour of biro, blue, red and black. The shallower tray at the front was filled with paperclips. Jon looked again; they were actually stacked in neat little piles of decreasing size.

He examined the rest of the room. A filing cabinet was next to Appleforth, each drawer clearly marked: A – F, G – L, M – R, S – Z. Next to the cabinet was a bin. Jon craned forwards, it was spotlessly clean inside. His eyes wandered over the bare walls. No pictures, prints or photographs. He reached round the desk and tried the uppermost drawer. Locked. 'Does he ever actually work here?'

Appleforth looked confused. 'Yes. He's on the road most of the time, but here about three times a week I'd say.'

'And is he as neat in his personal appearance as his office suggests?'

Appleforth frowned briefly. 'I suppose so. And we'd expect him to be, too. Protex is a medical supplies company. We need to be neat, organised, efficient.'

'Clinical,' Rick added from the doorway.

'I'm sorry?' Appleforth asked.

'Nothing,' Jon replied, glaring at Rick.

At that time of day the drive down to Stoke took just over an hour. Rush hour, and you could double that, Jon thought. Gordon Dean's house was in a private development bordering agricultural land, cows dotting the fields alongside. The cluster of houses was large, all of them detached and with separate garages. They pulled to a halt outside Ravenscroft. Fake wooden timbers criss-crossed the front of the house, lattice windows adding another feeble period touch.

They'd phoned en route and Mrs Dean opened the door as they walked up the front path. She ushered them into a spacious living room dominated by pastel shades and the scent of polish. The pale pink carpet was covered in hoover marks and a yellow duster lay on the coffee table. 'I'm sorry,' she said, removing it. 'I need to be doing something.' Her eyes searched theirs, seeking information from their expressions.

'I'm afraid we haven't anything to tell you as to

your husband's whereabouts as yet,' Jon said, turning and gesturing to the large sofa and its plumped-up cushions.

'Oh, sorry, please.' She perched nervously on the edge of a matching armchair and her fingers started teasing the corners of the duster. As Jon sat down he realised the room had the same feeling of sterility as her husband's office at Protex.

Jon took out his notebook. 'When did you last speak to your husband, Mrs Dean?'

'Yesterday morning, when he set off for Manchester. But he should have rung this morning. He always rings me between eight and nine if he's staying in a hotel.'

'And how often is that?'

'Three or four times a month. Usually he stays in Manchester. Most of his big clients are around there, so he saves hours of driving by booking into a hotel.'

'Does he stay in a particular one?'

'Yes. They built a Novotel for the Commonwealth Games last summer. That's his usual one nowadays.'

'I see. Mrs Dean, this may sound silly, but have you looked in your husband's wardrobe?'

'Why?' Voice defensive.

'To see if any of his clothes are missing.'

'Yes, I have,' she replied with a stiff nod. 'The hangers aren't jangling.'

Jon wondered what she was holding back. 'And you've been trying his mobile?'

'Yes. It just rings through to answerphone.'

Thinking of the precise incisions that had been employed to remove the third victim's face, Jon leaned forwards. 'Mrs Dean, how did your husband come to work for a medical company? Does he have an interest in that area himself?'

'Sorry, I don't quite understand you.'

'Did he read medicine or have ambitions to practise it?'

'Oh no. He worked for a paper merchant's before this job, a manufacturer of franking machines before that. According to Gordon, it's all just sales at the end of the day.'

Jon glanced around. 'Does your husband have an office here?'

She pointed through the archway into the adjoining dining room. 'He plugs his laptop in there.'

Jon looked. On the table in the far corner of the room was a small printer. Two box files stood on a shelf unit beside it. 'May we?'

Mrs Dean nodded.

As Jon crossed into the other room, he was aware of her trailing along behind. He said, 'Could I be cheeky and ask for a cup of tea?'

'Of course. I do apologise, I should have offered.'

Once she was out of the room Jon and Rick each took a file. They put them on the dining table, sat down, opened the lids and started flicking through. Jon's contained plastic folders with information on Gordon Dean's clients. Rick's was used for receipts and literature about Protex products.

Both men were so absorbed in their task, they didn't hear Mrs Dean come back into the living room.

'Are you looking for anything in particular?' She was standing by the coffee table, carrying a tray with a teapot, milk jug and three cups.

Jon shook his head. 'Not really. We're just trying to get an idea of his typical movements.'

She put the tray down and approached them. Rick was flicking through the receipts for that month. Mrs Dean watched him, fingers of one hand massaging the thumb of the other. Jon waited for her to come out with whatever it was she wanted to say.

Eventually she spoke. 'I had a look through his suits earlier on. I found some statements there.'

Jon raised his chin. 'What sort of statements?'

'Credit card ones. The bills go direct to his office, but it's not a company credit card. They're old statements from the last two months.'

'Do you still have them?'

She dropped her hands to her sides. 'I'd never go through his pockets normally . . .'

Jon stood up. 'I understand, Mrs Dean, but these are special circumstances.'

She nodded in agreement. 'They're here.' She opened the drawer beneath the dining table but, rather than get them out, walked back into the living room. 'Do you take milk and sugar?'

'One, please.' Jon's eyes were on the sheets of paper as Rick shook his head politely at Mrs Dean.

Jon put the statements on the table and sat down. The card had taken quite a hammering. 'Piccolino's. That's the new Italian near the town hall,' he murmured.

'Twenty-six quid. Probably a meal for one,' Rick whispered back.

'Via Venice, Stock, Don Antonio's. He likes his Italian food.' Jon pointed at an item on the list. 'Is that a restaurant?'

'You've never heard of Crimson?' Rick's voice was barely audible.

Jon checked that Mrs Dean was still out of earshot and whispered, 'No. But he was there three times last month. What is it?'

'It's in the Gay Village, on a side road behind Canal Street. A wine-bar upstairs, cabaret and dance floor downstairs. Very trendy.'

'With who?'

'It started as a gay venue. There's a drag queen called Miss Tonguelash. All sorts go nowadays to hear her bitching.'

Jon glanced at Rick, ready to ask how he knew so much about a place in Manchester's Gay Village. But his partner's eyes were frozen on the statement, a red flush creeping up his neck. The words died in Jon's throat.

Mrs Dean walked back through the archway. As she held the china cups out, they began to rattle in their saucers. Tea started to spill. 'He's not coming back. The bastard.'

The word seemed so foreign coming from her

lips. She started to cry. Jon quickly stood up and took the drinks from her quivering hands. Rick pulled a chair out and she collapsed into it, raising a hand to her face.

Awkwardly, Jon stood to the side. Rick fetched her cup of tea and sat down next to her. Taking her hand in his, he said quietly, 'Why do you say that, Mrs Dean?'

She looked up, tears brimming. 'Those.' She pointed accusingly at the credit card statements. 'He's been hiding something for a long time now. There's always been something distant about him, but recently there's been a change. He's found someone else, I know it.'

'How has he changed recently?' Rick asked.

She extracted her hand from his and pulled a hanky out of her cardigan cuff. 'His behaviour. Like he's having a midlife crisis. He was talking about getting a motorbike, for God's sake. And he got a tattoo. Of all things.'

Jon sat down. 'What sort of tattoo?'

'A ladybird, on his shoulder. What came over him? He's thirty-nine.'

Jon looked at the framed photo on the wall: Mrs Dean standing stiffly next to a thin man with a sweeping side parting and feeble moustache, the Eiffel Tower rising into the sky behind them. They were in the city of romance but a good ten inches separated them.

Jon searched the walls for photos of children. There were none. 'Mrs Dean, is there anyone

Gordon may have gone to? A close friend, a son, a daughter?'

'We don't have children,' she replied, the corner of her left eye beginning to tick. 'I've already called all the people I could think of. No one's heard from him.'

Jon's eyes went back to the snap of them in Paris. 'Mrs Dean, it would be a great help if we could have a recent photo of your husband.'

They drove back up the M6 in the last light of day. Jon's mind switching between Gordon Dean's disappearance and Rick's intimate knowledge of a bar in the Gay Village. Was the bloke a homosexual? Something odd was definitely going on.

As they approached the Knutsford services the sky darkened and, minutes later, drops of rain started hitting their windscreen.

'Welcome to Manchester,' Jon commented with ironic cheer.

The manager at the Novotel was a woman of around forty, with wiry ginger hair fighting to break free from a cluster of hairclips. 'How may I help you?' An Eastern European accent added a brusqueness to her greeting.

Jon checked her name tag. 'Hello, Kristina. I'm DI Spicer, this is DS Saville.' The enthusiastic way she responded to the sight of their warrant cards surprised him. Perhaps it was something to do with attitudes to authority in her native country. She listened to their request, then looked at the computer before confirming that Gordon Dean had booked in the day before. 'The room is now occupied by another guest.'

'So Mr Dean checked out. Can you tell me at what time?' asked Jon.

'It is not possible to say. Many guests leave the key in the door, others drop it in the box at the end of the counter. The room is paid for at check-in and should be vacated by eleven the next morning.'

'Can you tell us if anything was left in his room? Bags, a laptop, that sort of thing?' Rick asked.

'I will check Lost Property.' She disappeared into the back room, returning a minute later. 'No, nothing from his room.'

Jon pondered the information. Gordon must have returned at some stage, packed his things and moved on. He pointed to the CCTV camera above the entrance. 'Do you keep the tapes from previous days?'

She nodded. 'For the last two weeks only. But I would need permission from head office before you can take one. They are shut now, I'm sorry.'

Jon tapped a finger on the counter. More and more, he suspected that Gordon Dean had simply eloped. However, he knew McCloughlin would be tracking him closely on this one. 'Actually, Kristina, we could seize the tape as evidence here and now. But don't worry, I'm happy if you could just put in a request for us to borrow yesterday's.'

CHAPTER 9

Jon clicked his biro shut and dropped it on the pile of paper and messages on his desk. Among them was a note saying the check he'd requested on the mobile phone number Fiona Wilson had given him had shown it to be a pay-as-you-go: untraceable. It was almost ten o'clock at night and the incident room was nearly empty.

'I'm calling it a day,' he announced.

Rick stretched his arms above his head. 'Yeah, good idea.' He pushed a batch of forms aside. 'This can wait until tomorrow. I'd never have believed getting someone's credit-card records would take so long.'

'That's data protection,' Jon replied. 'Lots more paperwork for us.' As he got up he saw the card from Cheshire Consorts on his desk. Shit, he'd promised Fiona he'd have a word at the motel. 'One more job to do,' he said, sitting down again.

Rick was hesitating, jacket draped over an arm.

'That favour for my other half's friend? I said I'd check the motel she stayed in. You get on.' Jon nodded towards the door.

'Oh. OK, see you tomorrow.'

Jon tried to look up the number for the motel but couldn't find it in the Yellow Pages. However, a quick visit wouldn't take him too far out of his way.

In the deserted car park he was surprised to see Rick standing by his vehicle. Jon was parked almost next to it. 'Car not starting?'

Rick flicked a distracted glance at his Golf. 'No, it's fine. I just wanted to get something sorted out.'

This'll be interesting, thought Jon, crossing his arms.

Rick's chest filled out slightly as he nervously breathed in. 'Back at Gordon Dean's house, you looked at me when I was describing that place called Crimson.'

Jon nodded, surprised that this wasn't about McCloughlin.

Rick swallowed. 'I hope the fact that I'm gay won't affect how we work together.'

Jon was suddenly relieved that it was dark: Rick couldn't see his blush. 'No. Of course not.'

Rick continued facing him a moment longer. 'Good. It's best that we dealt with it straight away.'

'Absolutely. And it's really not an issue for me,' Jon replied, hearing his language slipping into the politically correct. 'I'll see you tomorrow.'

'See you tomorrow.'

Simultaneously they unlocked their cars, opened the doors and got in. As Jon turned the ignition key, he heard Rick's engine start, too.

Both sets of lights came on together. Jon leaned forward and gestured to Rick. The other car drove quickly away. Jon sat back in his seat. Jesus, his partner had just admitted he was gay. He wondered if it was common knowledge around the incident room.

Despite all the anti-discrimination regulations, homosexuality was still something plenty of his colleagues regarded as a laughable affliction. They were usually the same officers who believed most blacks were thieving, lazy niggers.

He hadn't received any piss-take comments about working with a poof, so he concluded that no one could know. Then he remembered McCloughlin's wink on telling Jon that he was getting a partner. Could it have been a hint?

Five minutes later he pulled into the Platinum Inn's car park and looked across to the greyhound stadium behind. The floodlights were on and a crackly voice was announcing the runners for the final race.

Jon glanced around the car park. Two other cars, a Ford Mondeo and a Citroën Xara. Salesman choices. He pushed open the doors to reception. The place had obviously seen better days. The glut of cheap chain hotels in the town centre was slowly strangling it to death. Another few months and it would be boarded up, and shortly after that probably burned down by local kids.

Behind the counter was an alarmingly thin woman. You've had a tough paper round, thought

Jon. He held up his warrant card. 'DI Jon Spicer. And you are?'

'Dawn Poole, night manager.'

'Just the person I need to speak to. Were you on duty last night?'

'I'm on duty every night.'

Jon looked around, not envying her lonely job in an area where women's corpses were turning up, stripped of their skin. 'Seems quiet. How's business?'

She shrugged. 'It's been busier.'

'Who do you get staying here? Company reps, mainly?'

'Mainly. Some younger sorts having a night out in Manchester. Three to a room can work out cheaper for them than a taxi home, specially if they manage to sneak in an extra mate.'

'Who else?'

'That's about it.'

'So if I take a seat here, there's no chance of any couples coming in to book rooms by the hour?'

Her mouth tensed up and she pointed to the tariff sheet on the wall. 'The rates are for the night only.'

'Come on, Dawn.' Jon leaned on the counter, sensing it wouldn't take much to make her crumble. It never did with the mouse-like types. Usually they'd do whatever it took to keep attention off them. 'This place is used as a knocking shop. I don't work Vice. Help me out here and I won't need to get them involved.'

She crossed her arms, the bones in her elbows jutting out painfully. 'What do you want to know?'

That's more like it, he thought. 'The girls you get coming in here, do you know their names?'

'Some of them.'

'Ever heard of an Alexia?'

The skin below her eyes flinched. 'I don't think so.'

Jon didn't break his stare. 'You don't think so? How about a yes or a no?'

She dropped her head. 'No, I haven't.'

He took a breath in. 'Last night, someone heard something. It could have been the sound of an assault. Did you have any trouble? A girl coming out of her room looking injured?'

'No.' She was still looking down.

'Look at me, please. It was around three thirty in the morning.'

'No. That Fiona what's-her-name made a report, right? Listen, she staggered in pouring with blood. I helped patch her up, gave her some booze.'

'How much?'

'A lot. There wasn't much left in the bottle by the time she went to bed. Probably shouldn't have given her any, the state she was in. Totally stressed out, she was. Then she thinks she heard something in the middle of the night.' Bony fingers fiddled with her necklace. She sighed. 'Look, it can get pretty busy here, but I'd have noticed. Honestly.'

'What about side doors? Emergency exits? Is there one at the other end of this corridor?' He

114

pointed through the double doors at the corridor beyond.

'Yes.'

'If someone left by that route would it set off an alarm?'

'No, it doesn't work on that door. But why would they? It leads straight out to the bin area. They'd have to walk right round the building to get back to the car park.'

'My informant believes the commotion was coming from room nine. How about I take a look in it?'

Dawn handed him a key. 'Be my guest.'

Jon could tell searching the room was going to be a waste of time. His eyes shifted to the clock in the back office. Quarter past ten and he was dog tired. He knew she was holding something back. Probably just afraid of him finding out that she was putting the night's takings straight into her pocket.

He weighed up the two women's stories. Given the third victim's time of death, Fiona's emotional state and the hefty amount of booze it appeared she'd got through, he decided her claim was a waste of time. He gave the key back. 'OK, Dawn, take care.'

Her mouth opened with surprise. 'That's it?'

Out in the car park he glanced towards the rear of the building. It was plunged in shadow and he'd have to get a torch if he was to look around properly. Bollocks to that, he thought.

In his car, he called Fiona's mobile. 'It's Jon Spicer.'

'Have you been to the motel?'

'I'm in the car park right now. I've spoken to the night manager, Dawn Poole.'

'That's her. What did you say?' The words were slurred and Jon wondered how much she'd been drinking.

'She didn't notice anything suspicious last night.'

'Well, did you check the room?'

'It was spotless, like you said. And there was nothing round the back of the building, either.'

'What about Cheshire Consorts? Did you call them?'

'Yes. The owner told me there's no Alexia on her books.'

'She could be lying.'

'There's a web site. Have a look yourself. All the girls are listed there.'

'So what now? I really think I heard someone being killed.' Her voice was rising.

'Fiona, there's nothing more I can do. I'll keep an eye on the police computer. If an unidentified female body shows up, I'll look into it.'

'That's it? You're not doing anything else?'

A wave of irritation washed across him and he ran a hand through his cropped brown hair. 'What do you suggest I do?'

'I don't know. You're the policeman. If this was an angelic little girl or a copper's wife, things would be different, wouldn't they?'

Jon felt his jaw clench. 'You think you heard something. You were traumatised and pissed.' He paused to let the comment sink in. 'You could contact the Missing Persons Bureau, I suppose, but without a surname I doubt they can help. I can't think of anything else.'

'So you're washing your hands of it?'

'For fuck's sake, Fiona, I'm working on a big murder case. You can probably guess which one. I don't have time for this.'

Her voice was twisted with sarcasm. 'No, I suppose not. After all, it's only another whore who's disappeared.'

Jon hung up.

Ten minutes later he pushed his front door open. Claws scrabbled in the kitchen and Punch peered eagerly through the doorway. The dog gave a delighted *hrrmph!* through its squashed nose and bounded down the hall.

Jon scooped the animal up and began rocking it in his arms like a baby. Punch craned forwards, trying to lick Jon's face. 'Who's my stupid boy?' Jon said, lifting his chin and allowing a wet tongue to lap at his throat.

'I don't know how you can stand that.' Alice had come out of the TV room. She was wearing a dressing gown and clutching a mug in both hands.

Jon put Punch down. 'What a day. How are you, babe?'

'Good,' she smiled. 'Have you eaten?'

'Only some crap pizza, unfortunately.' He hung his jacket on the banister post and walked over to her. Careful not to put any pressure on her swollen stomach, he hugged her lightly. 'How's the bump?'

'Fine. I could feel some kicking earlier. Here.' She took his hand and placed it on her stomach, inside her dressing gown. 'On the right there, that's where the legs are.'

They stood motionless, Punch staring up at them with a bemused look on his face. Jon was careful to maintain an inquisitive smile, although privately he felt freaked out every time something began moving independently inside Alice's body. He kept his hand there for a few seconds longer. 'No. The little thing must be asleep.' With a twinge of guilty relief, he slid his hand out of her dressing gown, went into the kitchen and cracked open a beer.

As soon as he took a seat, Punch lay down on the lino floor and rested his head on Jon's foot.

'Did you ring Fiona?'

Jon sighed. 'Rang her, met her and went to that motel. She's got quite a temper, hasn't she?'

Alice grinned. 'Fiona? Yes, she's got a strong sense of right and wrong.'

'So why has she stuck by a husband who knocks her around for so long?'

Alice gave a sad frown. 'We've tried to work that out in the salon many times. You should hear her with customers who don't keep their appointments. She's straight on the phone asking where they are, demanding to know why they haven't shown up. But then she goes home and seems to adopt this submissive personality with her husband.'

'What the hell does she see in him?'

Alice ran her hands through her long hair. 'I don't think it was that bad to begin with. She's always reluctant to talk about it – pride I suppose – but I think they were happy for a while. God knows, something happened to turn it sour.'

He ran a finger down his beer can. 'Has she got a problem with the booze?'

'Why do you say that?'

'The night manager at the motel she stayed in said she'd downed a load of brandy, and she was slurring her words on the phone tonight as well.'

Alice nodded. 'She turns up for work late some-times. There's always a legitimate excuse, but you can smell it on her some mornings. If it was a big chain salon she'd have probably lost her job by now. Lucky for her Melvyn's happy to turn a blind eye.'

'Well, she certainly believes she heard something the other night. And she certainly wasn't happy when I said I couldn't do much.'

'Can't you?'

He took a long gulp, almost shuddering as the ice-cold beer went down his throat and hit his stomach. 'I'm not convinced she heard anything more than a bit of energetic shagging.'

'Why not?'

He hooked a nail under the tab of the can, lifted it up and then let it snap back with a ping. 'She only heard something. There's no evidence of anything else. The night manager says she didn't see anything, and I believe her. Didn't believe everything she told me, but I believed her on that count. All Fiona has is this.' He flicked the card from Cheshire Consorts on to the table. 'It could have been lying in the room for weeks, if not months, judging by the state of the place. A name that's probably made up, and a disconnected mobile phone number that isn't registered to anyone.'

Alice bit her lip. 'Oh, well. She's got her own life to sort out. She'll let it drop soon, I expect.'

Jon took another gulp of beer. 'The other big news is that I can't decide whether my new partner's reporting everything I do straight back to McCloughlin.'

Alice rolled her eyes. 'You mean he's still sulking about . . .' She stopped, unwilling to refer directly to the case that had almost cost them so much last summer.

'Just a hunch, but yeah.'

Alice blew a strand of blond hair out of her eyes. 'The arsehole.'

He gave a rueful smile. 'Oh, and another thing about my new partner. He's gay.'

'So?'

Jon examined his knuckles.

'Oh, please. Don't tell me you're scared he'll

threaten your masculinity by trying it on with you?'

Jon picked at the can's tab again. 'Well, I don't know. It makes things awkward, you have to admit.'

'Why? It only makes things awkward in your head. Don't flatter yourself. A big grunt like you with scars all over your face? He might prefer smooth-skinned, gentle types.'

'Let's hope so.'

Alice sighed. 'Surely you've worked with other gay officers?'

Jon shook his head. 'It's not like your job, Ali. We don't have people flouncing around like Melvyn.'

'Not every gay man's as camp as Melvyn. Besides, he puts a lot of that on for the blue-rinse brigade.' She smiled. 'The old dears reckon it's like getting their hair done by Graham Norton.'

'Yeah, well, this is the police.'

Alice put a hand on her hip and extended one foot slightly in front of the other. Jon called it her barrister stance, because it was a posture she adopted whenever they got into one of their verbal tussles.

They'd started seeing each other almost twelve years ago after a chance meeting in a city centre pub. Jon and several team mates were sitting at the centre table to watch the final of the 1991 Rugby World Cup on the pub's giant screen. As the match ground its way to England's eventual defeat at the hands of Australia, a few of his friends had got increasingly annoyed at the referee's decisions.

When the drinks on Alice's table were all knocked over she had no hesitation in standing up to have a go at their entire group. Before offering to replace them, Jon had watched her feistiness with admiration. It was the first thing he'd noticed about her and whenever it reappeared he was reminded why he'd fallen in love with her.

'What about all the equal opportunities stuff we're always hearing about?' she demanded. 'Those posters around town . . . What was the headline? Something about "All walks of life walk the beat"?'

Jon rolled his eyes, relishing every second of the exchange. The recruitment campaign posters, with their Home Office allocation of ethnic minorities in the photo, had generated plenty of jokes around the station, but not many non-white job applicants. Besides, bobbies walking the beat? They were too busy stuck at their desks completing paperwork for that.

'There's a culture in the police, Alice. You know it, I know it. It doesn't matter how much lip-service they pay to the drive for ethnic minority officers and all that.'

'And all that,' Alice tutted. 'Watch out, Jon, you might find yourself left behind in the last millennium.'

'I don't agree with it, Ali, but it's life. Besides, you say society's changing, but what you actually mean is that your experience of society's changing. I'd say that, on the whole, the age-old prejudices are just as alive and healthy as ever.' He thought about the poster's headline. 'It's just that your walk of life doesn't take you into contact with them.' He gave her a glib smile and waited for her response.

She scowled. 'You're bound to get racists and anti-gays in the deprived areas you get called out to. You always will until people are educated differently.'

Jon laughed. 'I'm not talking about housing estates. I'm talking about country estates. Those living at the top of the pile, not the bottom: the aristocracy, the establishment, the elite, whatever you want to call it.' He pictured the huddles of senior officers, the judges, the politicians. Old, white, married and male. 'I'm talking about people who've had the best educations money can buy. It's that lot who are most against change. The system suits them just fine. After all, it was created by them, their fathers and their fathers' fathers.'

Alice was silent for a moment. 'That's depressing.'

Jon realised he'd come out of this one on top, but the victory gave him precious little satisfaction. 'That's life,' he shrugged. 'Anyway, don't worry. I'm not going to creep around the canteen whispering to everyone that Rick's gay.'

'I know that.' She tipped her head back to yawn and saw the clock on the wall. 'You coming to bed?'

Jon finished his beer and nodded.

CHAPTER 10

Dawn Poole could almost see the waves of pain radiating out from the back of the patient's throat with every swallow. Breathing was obviously still difficult because, after a few more sips, the straw was released.

'Enough?' Dawn asked, her concern showing in her face.

The patient leaned back against the pillows and gave a single slow nod.

Dawn put the carton down. 'You're being so brave.' She ran her fingers gently through the short spikes of hair on the patient's head. The haircut reminded her of a singer's, someone who sang of bruised feelings and life's injustices. Annie Lennox? Sinead O'Connor? She couldn't remember.

Bloodshot eyes turned towards the window. A finger was held up, red nail varnish contrasting with the white sheets. 'Can you crumble a biscuit on the window sill?'

The words were little more than a rasping whisper. Unsure if she'd heard correctly, Dawn stood. 'Crumble biscuit on the window sill?'

The patient nodded. 'For a robin. It lands there.'

She smiled uncertainly. 'Of course, my darling.' She took a digestive biscuit from the untouched packet and broke off a small piece. 'Outside? Here?' she asked.

'And on the inside, too.'

Dawn began crumbling the biscuit between her forefinger and thumb.

CHAPTER 11

*T*ake a few moments to browse through our
selection of handpicked ladies. Prices start at
£150 per hour.

Fiona stared at the computer screen. Jon was
right: all the girls were listed there. She read a few
of their details.

*Becky, age 19. Holly, age 20. NEW! Kim, age 20.
Mel, age 22.* The list went right down to women
in their forties. By each name was a tab saying,
More info.

Fiona clicked on Mel's.

A new screen popped up giving the girl's height,
bust, dress size, hair, ethnic origin and occupation
(5′6″, 34C, 10, brunette, shoulder-length straight,
white British, customer service adviser).

At the base of the screen was a subheading,
Reviews. Fiona clicked on it and was taken to a
different page called 'Punter Opinion'. The report
was enthusiastic but matter-of-fact, like a review
of a well-designed electrical item. The punter
would definitely be seeing Mel again, it concluded.

Appalled at the commercial sophistication of the
process, Fiona went back to the main listings page.

She scanned down the column of names; the word '*NEW!*' was by about a quarter of them. The girls obviously came and went fairly frequently. Alexia could easily be an ex-employee.

Trepidation made her hesitate as she reached for her mobile. But all-too-familiar feelings of guilt flared up in response, and with them a determination to find out if Alexia was OK. Knowing she couldn't live with herself if she did nothing, she slowly dialled the number at the top of the screen. A woman answered almost immediately, her voice warm and attractive.

Fiona wasn't sure what to say. Suddenly, the words were coming out of her mouth. 'Hello. I'd like to speak to someone about working for Cheshire Consorts.'

'What's your background, love?' The voice had lost some of its pleasantness and become more matter-of-fact.

'Well, my name's Fiona. I work as a beauty therapist, specialising in manicures. I've also done a course in Swedish massage, but that was some time ago. What else? Um, I enjoy going out to the theatre when I—'

The woman cut her off. 'You're new to this, aren't you?'

'Yes.'

'How old are you, Fiona?'

'Late thirties. Thirty-eight.'

'That's OK. Some of my busiest escorts are your age.' A small crumb of encouragement;

Fiona's spirits lifted. 'Why don't you come and see me?'

'I'd like that.'

The address was a house in Mellor. Fiona had heard of the area. Big houses at top prices. More expensive than where she used to live. She closed Hazel's computer down, then went to the kitchen. 'Cathy,' she said, nerves making her stomach feel light and empty. 'Could I borrow some make-up, please?'

A short while later she was driving along the M60 ring road. She turned off on to the A626, following it all the way to Marple Bridge and the turning for Mellor. The road was narrow, leading through a pretty little village, antiques shops dotting the high street.

The road went up a hill and Fiona spotted a pub called the Royal Oak. She parked outside it as instructed and looked across the road to number 133. It was a large semi-detached house with a wooden front door. Nothing remotely seedy or dangerous about it. Crossing the road, she knocked a couple of times and waited on the steep stone steps. The door opened to reveal a woman about her age with an immaculately cut brown bob. She wore hardly any make-up and the skin was stretched tight over her cheekbones. Slightly sunken eyes looked down and her thin lips parted. 'Fiona?'

Conscious of the generous layer of concealer masking the worst of her injury, Fiona smiled. 'Yes.'

'Come in. First room on the right.'

She stepped past the woman, sensing that she was being assessed. She sat down in a pleasantly decorated front room. Although it was homely, something was missing. Fiona looked around. No family photos.

The woman sat down in a leather chair by a corner table which held a computer, printer, boxes of disks and other business gear. She surveyed her visitor. 'My name's Joanne Perkins. What happened to your face?'

Fiona lifted her fingers to her eyebrow. 'Some trouble with my ex.'

'Fiona, I don't send girls out with damaged faces. The men pay a lot of money, so they expect some class.' Her eyes shifted to Fiona's borrowed shirt and too-large skirt.

Fiona coughed self-consciously. 'To be honest, I've just left my husband. I didn't have time to pack much. These aren't my clothes.'

The phone rang. Joanne held up a finger at Fiona, then picked it up. 'Cheshire Consorts . . . Yes, that's right, sir . . . Whereabouts are you? . . . The one at the airport? . . . What sort of time? . . . And who did you have in mind? . . . Victoria? Oh, she's lovely, she really is.' She turned to the computer, clicked the mouse a couple of times and consulted the screen. 'I think she's available. If I can I take your telephone number, I'll get Victoria to give you a call.' She jotted a number down. 'And your name is? . . . OK, Gerald, you two have a chat, and if

129

you like the sound of each other I'll call you back to confirm the booking. Is that all right? . . . Lovely. Do you have a credit card? . . . No, don't give me the details now. Wait till I call you back, OK? Victoria will ring you shortly.'

She hung up, consulted the screen again and dialled a number. 'Victoria? It's Jo. Can you do a booking at the Radisson, Manchester Airport, for ten o'clock tonight? . . . He sounds fine – salesman I imagine . . . OK, he's called Gerald. Here's his number.' She read it out and hung up. Turning back to Fiona, she said, 'Now, you've just moved out?'

'Yes.' Fiona blinked, shocked at how prosaic Jo made selling sex seem.

'Your life's just been turned upside down. You need cash.'

'No,' Fiona protested. 'Well, yes. Things are all different. But—'

'I don't take on people who are going through stuff like that.'

'I'm sorting myself out.'

'Could you stand up?'

Slowly, Fiona did so. Her hands fluttered nervously and she had to make a conscious effort not to fold her arms. They hung at her sides, feeling awkward. She looked at a point on the wall well above Joanne's head.

'You aren't at all comfortable about this, are you? Somehow I don't think you really want to work in this business.'

130

Fiona's shoulders relaxed. 'No.' Gratefully, she sat down again. 'I'm looking for a girl. She's gone missing.'

'You're not the only one.' Joanne's lips tightened to a thinner line, and she lit a cigarette.

Fiona nodded awkwardly. 'I'm sorry. It was me who asked the police to ring you.'

Joanne took a sharp drag on her cigarette, shadows deepening beneath her cheekbones. 'Is this girl your daughter?'

The question caught Fiona off guard and a sudden image of Emily caused her eyes to sting. 'No. She was in the next room of a motel I was staying at. I heard something terrible happening to her. Like she was being strangled. I checked her room the next morning, but all I found was one of your cards with her name and a mobile phone number written on the back.' Joanne's face darkened at the news. 'I really want to know what happened to her,' Fiona concluded.

The phone went, and Joanne picked up. 'Cheshire Consorts . . . Hi, Victoria. You're happy with it, then? . . . Yeah, I thought he sounded quite nice, too, and he offered his credit-card number straight off . . . OK, I'll ring him to confirm it.' She called the man back. 'Gerald? Hello, it's Cheshire Consorts. Victoria would be delighted to meet you at ten o'clock. If I could take your credit card details, we can confirm the booking. I gather that you agreed an hour with Victoria, so the charge is £150. OK, the name on the credit card

131

is?' She took the rest of the details down. 'Thank you for using Cheshire Consorts, Mr Richmond, and I hope you enjoy your night.'

She replaced the phone, looked at Fiona and took another drag. 'No one of her name has ever worked for Cheshire Consorts. I checked after that pushy detective called. I turn away a lot of girls who'd like to work for me. Usually ones with drug habits – they're unreliable and they'll try and give their own phone numbers to clients to cut me out of future deals. I've been in the business long enough to spot them and I've worked harder than you can imagine to be where I am today.' She waved a hand towards the window and the pleasant surroundings beyond. 'I've got here because I only employ real ladies. Now, I don't know how one of my cards came to be in that motel room, God knows, there are enough men around town who use my escort agency. But I did have someone in here calling herself Alicia a while back.'

Fiona frowned. 'Sorry, you mean Alexia?'

Now Joanne looked confused. 'No, she said she was called Alicia, and that copper said Alicia, too, unless I misheard him.'

'You must have done. It was definitely Alexia written on the back of the card,' Fiona replied, wishing she hadn't given it to Jon.

Joanne sighed. 'I don't know. Maybe it was Alexia, then. No one of that name has worked for me, either.'

'How can you be sure without checking?'

Joanne said impatiently, 'Because I help them choose their working names.' She pointed to a Perspex container of business cards. 'After the interview I noticed half my cards had gone.'

'Why would she take your cards?'

'Trying to gain a bit of credibility, I'd imagine – at the expense of my business's reputation. The best place you can start searching for that little bitch is back where she crawled from.'

Fiona raised her eyebrows questioningly.

Joanne stood up. 'She claimed she was working the massage parlours. I'm fairly sure she said the Hurlington Health Club. You know where that is?'

Fiona shook her head.

'Just past the Apollo on the A57. You can't miss it. All the windows are blacked out, for a start.'

Fiona ignored Joanne's movement towards the door. 'What did she look like?'

Joanne sighed. 'Skinny little thing – a good sign she was using. About your height, late teens, early twenties. Hair darkish brown. Down to about here.' She held a hand to her collarbone. 'She was still pretty, not for much longer. The bruises round her eye certainly didn't help.'

'Bruises? Someone had been hitting her?' Fiona asked with dismay, imagining the wretched life the poor girl must lead.

An indifferent shrug. 'Goes with the territory, that end of the market.'

Fiona almost felt sick, acutely aware that Emily would have been roughly that age now. She held the image of the girl in her mind's eye as she finally stood. 'Thank you. And sorry to have wasted your time.'

Joanne looked her up and down. 'Listen, when your face has cleared up and you've got your own clothes back, call me.'

Fiona stared at her, unsure of what she meant. Realisation struck and she quickly made for the door.

By the time she got back to the outskirts of town, it had gone ten o'clock. The information Joanne had given her burned in her head. The Hurlington Health Club. A skinny girl with dark brown hair, around twenty years old.

The desire to find her dragged Fiona towards the city centre and she found herself driving along the A57 towards the Apollo. A few minutes later purple neon lettering caught her eye. The Hurlington Health Club. It was halfway down a short row of shops, sandwiched between a place selling antique fireplaces and another selling second-hand furniture. The doors and windows of both shops were concealed behind grey metal pull-down shutters.

She eased into a lay-by and looked across the road. The front of the Hurlington Health Club had been returned to something resembling a residential, not business, property. A terracotta pot holding a miniature conifer stood on either side of the front door, and in the front garden a tiny fountain sprinkled water, lit mauve by an under-water light, into a small, square pond.

She peered more closely at the windows. The curtains, of red material which had the heaviness of velvet, were open, but even so it was impossible to see inside. Joanne was right: there was an inner layer of glass and it had been blacked out.

Nervously, she checked in her rear-view mirror. There was no traffic coming. She climbed out and crossed the road. The front gate was open; water tinkled into the square pond. A small sign on the door read: *Open 11 am until late. All major credit cards accepted.*

Fiona took a deep breath and walked quickly towards the door. It opened and a man stepped out, buttoning up his coat. Their eyes met and his immediately moved down to her chest. He stared with no attempt at subtlety.

Fiona shrank back, bumping into the gatepost. He realised she wasn't coming in. The look that came into his eyes reminded Fiona of her husband before he punched her. He moved towards her and she turned and scuttled back across the road to her car.

Once inside she locked the door. He sauntered off towards the small car park by the Apollo. Her eyes turned to the front door again. She couldn't go in now, not at night. Any visit would have to be during the day when, she hoped, the place would be quieter.

CHAPTER 12

Jon checked his watch. Eight thirty-five, not too early to ring. 'Morning. Martin Appleforth, please. It's Detective Inspector Spicer.'

A few seconds of Handel's *Water Music* before Martin spoke. 'Morning, DI Spicer. I was just going through my emails. The sales department have sent over Gordon's client list as requested. Is there any news of him?'

'I'm afraid not. We're trying to locate his Passat, but nothing yet. And it hasn't shown up on the national database as abandoned or burned-out. Anyway, thanks for getting the information on Mr Dean. Did you find out if your firm has a contract with Stepping Hill hospital?'

'I did and we haven't. Have you an email address I can forward Gordon's client list to?'

Jon gave it to him and the message appeared a few seconds later. There were two attachments, a complete list of Gordon Dean's clients and a shorter one of the people he was due to visit in the last days before he vanished.

Jon dragged his eyes from the screen to see Rick hanging up his jacket. 'All right?'

'Morning.' Rick's voice was reserved, the comment made over his shoulder.

Jon watched him sit down. Rick glanced across, then broke eye contact and reached for the paperwork on his desk.

'I've got the last clients Gordon Dean was due to see,' Jon said.

Rick looked up, the tension around his eyes easing. 'Yeah?'

'On the day before he disappeared he had one client to see in the morning, then another three in the afternoon, two in central Manchester and one in Worsley.'

'Shall we start with his last ones first?'

'I reckon so.' Jon printed the list out. 'Might as well go over to the NHS clinic in Worsley.' He looked at his watch. 'No point in setting off now – the M60 will be a nightmare.'

They spent the next forty or so minutes filling out report sheets until the receiver called across the room to them, 'The preliminary analysis has come in for the footprint recovered at the latest crime scene.'

Heads across the room turned.

'It's a shoe, not a trainer. Size eleven, left foot. Owner likely to weigh in excess of twelve stone. The grip on the sole is quite distinctive and it's completely worn away on the inside edge, suggesting that the wearer pronates quite heavily. As a result, he's highly likely to have an unusual gait.'

The scene in the hospital corridor flashed into

Jon's mind. He had thought Pete Gray swaggered as a result of his beer belly. Now he wondered if the swivel in his hips could have been the result of one foot turning inwards with each step.

The clinic in Worsley was tucked away behind the pleasant green. It was part of a cluster of council buildings including a small swimming pool, exercise hall, doctor's surgery and the clinic itself.

The reception area was plastered with a haphazard collection of posters. Professionally produced NHS ones on giving up smoking sat alongside home-printed ones on dieting groups, childcare support and mothers' meetings. Jon looked with interest at a cluster of smaller, hand-written cards advertising everything from breast pumps and second-hand prams to babysitters and exercise bikes.

He heard someone cooing. A young woman in the seating area was bouncing a baby on her knee. The infant's head rocked gently back and forth but its eyes were locked on its mother's, the rest of the world completely irrelevant to them both. She held it up and the sight touched something in Jon. Just as he was about to smile, the baby vomited down its mother's shirt.

'Good morning.' The rosy-cheeked receptionist was studying them through the glass screen.

'Hello, there,' Jon replied as they produced their warrant cards. 'Who could we speak to about the medical supplies the clinic orders?'

'For my sins, that's me,' she replied, sliding a plate with a half-eaten muffin to the side.

'Does that include such things as medical gloves?' asked Rick.

'Yes,' she beamed. 'In fact, I took a new order the other day.'

'From Protex?'

'That's right.' Her voice slowed down. 'From Protex.'

Rick took out Gordon Dean's photo. 'You dealt with this man?'

'Gordon,' she started to smile again, then stopped. 'What is the . . .' Her voice faded away.

'How did he seem to you?' Jon asked.

Her eyes swung between them, settling back on Rick. 'Friendly as ever. He doesn't come in that often. It's a rolling order – once every few months.'

'Do you remember what time he left?'

'I don't know.' She flicked back through her appointments book. 'He came in after the nurse's post-natal clinic started at four. He probably left at about quarter past. Is he in some kind of trouble?'

Rick shook his head. 'No. We just need to trace him. Did he mention anything not related to work?'

'No. I didn't have time to chat that day – the post-natal clinic's always very busy.'

'But you do chat sometimes?' Jon asked.

'Yes, sometimes.'

'What does Gordon like to talk about?'

She thought for a few seconds, then smiled

sheepishly. 'Actually, come to think of it, he usually asks about my family and then lets me rabbit on about what my kids have been up to recently.'

'Nothing about himself?'

'Not really. Just how the job's going, if he's busy. You know, small talk, I suppose.'

They drove back to the city centre, heading for the next client. The business was in a smart modern building just off the prime shopping area of King Street. Eventually they found an empty loading bay on the edge of St Anne's Square. Leaving a police sign on the dashboard, they walked back round and examined the list of companies listed at the entrance. Firms of solicitors seemed to be the dominant force. A uniformed security officer in the lobby directed them towards the lifts. 'Sixth floor. They've got it all to themselves.'

As the lift rose silently, Rick said, 'I've heard of the Paragon Group. Big ads at the back of women's magazines. Must cost a fortune.'

The doors opened on a plush foyer, the green of tropical palms complemented by walls washed with a subtle turquoise paint. The carpet was pale blue, the lighting recessed. The result was very soothing. Trust us, you're in good hands, Jon thought.

The receptionist wore a starched white tunic and her hair was pulled back so tightly it looked like the follicles might bleed. As they approached her desk, she reached for a couple of forms.

Rick stepped up, his warrant card out. 'DS Saville

and DI Spicer. May we speak to whoever orders your medical supplies, please.'

She looked confused. 'Oh, I'm sorry. I thought you'd just popped in to enquire about, er . . . We don't have much here.'

'If whoever orders your medical examination gloves could spare us a minute.'

'Oh, that's our head nurse. She's with someone at the moment. Please help yourself to coffee.' She gestured towards an open door. A pot of coffee was in the corner of the room and satellite television played softly on a plasma screen mounted on the wall. A middle-aged woman squirmed with embarrassment as they stepped in. She pulled her magazine tight into her lap, and kept her head bowed over it.

Jesus, you'd have thought it was a sexual diseases clinic, Jon thought as they sat down. He picked up a brochure. It was printed on expensive stock, plenty of white space between the words. Printing costs had obviously not been a problem.

'Here you go,' Rick said, holding a woman's magazine out. The Paragon Group's ad dominated the page. A nude woman was sitting on a polished wooden floor. Her legs and arms were artfully crossed, screening a figure that was faultless. Below it the locations of the group's centres were listed. Every major city seemed to have one.

'Big business,' Rick stated.

Jon turned to the brochure's contents page. Surgery for the face and body, liposuction, hair

141

transplants, tummy tucks, reshaping and enhancing of genitalia. Curious to see how revealing the images might be, he flicked to an inner page. The photo was harmless: a woman gazed off to the side, a benign smile playing at the edge of her mouth. Ear reshaping, lip reduction and enlargement, chin implants.

'Gentlemen, please come through.'

A statuesque woman in what might have been her mid-thirties stood in the doorway. The same crisp outfit as the receptionist. She led them into an examination room.

'You have a question about our examination gloves?' She picked up a box from the corner of her desk. The label said: *Powder-free surgical gloves. Non-sterile latex.*

'Actually, it's about the person who supplies them,' Rick said.

Her immaculately painted lips contracted to form the word 'Oh?'

'Gordon Dean, he works for Protex,' Rick continued.

'Mr Dean, yes. He was here two days ago.'

'At what time?'

'About quarter past three, I'd guess.'

'And did he stay for long?'

'About three minutes.'

'Did you chat to him? How did he seem?'

'Chat with him?' The suggestion seemed to bemuse her. 'No. I signed for the delivery and he left.'

Jon saw this was going nowhere. He looked around. 'What goes on here, then?'

Her eyes turned to him. 'In terms of what?'

'Treatments. Have you got surgical theatres and doctors hidden away here? It seems very quiet.'

She shook her head. 'The only things performed here are non-surgical procedures requiring, at most, local anaesthetic. Botox injections and laser treatments, for instance. The primary function of this office is for consultations. An initial one with myself or another nurse, then one with a surgeon. Once the paperwork is complete, the patient will see their surgeon for a further pre-operative medical examination and briefing prior to the procedure at a local private hospital nearby. We rent the theatres from them.'

'Who are your surgeons, then?' Jon asked.

'Is this part of the original reason for your visit today or merely curiosity on your part, Detective Inspector?' There was a challenging, almost provocative, look in her eyes.

Jon stared back at her for a moment. 'A bit of both, I suppose.'

'Our surgeons are employed from a variety of backgrounds. But if you're concerned as to their credentials, as some prospective patients are, I can assure you they possess all the necessary qualifications.'

'Fascinating,' Jon replied, irritated by her brittle manner.

The woman seemed to sense this. She leaned

forwards to assess him, then turned to Rick. 'You have very good skin. Do you use a moisturising regime?'

'I do.' Rick smiled uncertainly.

She nodded, then turned back to Jon. 'And you, DI Spicer? I suspect that you don't.' She raised a forefinger and touched the skin at the outer edge of her eye sockets. 'Your starbursts show when you speak.'

Wrong-footed by the sudden turn in conversation, Jon was about to ask if that was the new name for laughter lines, but she carried on. 'The scar above your left eyebrow and the bump in your nose – where it has been broken, I presume – are both easily remedied nowadays. We could take years off your face with some very simple procedures.'

Her eyes continued to probe him, and Jon realised she was searching for flaws, imperfections, anything which might trigger an insecurity she could play on. He was thankful that his hair hadn't started to thin.

'Just imagine how delighted your wife would be.'

'I'm not married,' Jon said.

'Many of the men we treat find improvements to their face do their career prospects no harm, either.'

Jon shook his head. 'Are you a nurse or a saleswoman?'

'Just something for you to think about.' She smiled and handed him a business card.

Jon glanced at it, then dropped it back on her

desk. 'No, you're all right, thanks,' he said, walking out.

As they headed back towards St Anne's Square an indecipherable phrase was shouted out in front of them. Jon spotted the *Manchester Evening News* seller and the headline on his stand: BUTCHER STILL STALKS BELLE VUE.

The town hall bells started to slowly toll. The chorus came to an end and a single, funereal strike let them know it was one o'clock. Jon's eyes flickered from the gargoyles on its gothic spires to the people around him. Not for the first time, he wondered how close the killer might be at that very moment.

Rick said, 'Shall we get some lunch? I'm starving.'

'Good idea,' Jon agreed.

'The sandwiches are excellent in there,' Rick said, pointing at the Pret a Manger further down the street.

Jon groaned inwardly, thinking of the variety of breads and choices of fancy fillings. He nodded towards a Gregg's bakers on their side of the road. 'They do a decent bacon barm in there.'

Now distaste showed in Rick's face. 'Aren't those places a bit . . . you know . . . ?'

Jon looked at him. 'If you mean they do no-nonsense stuff without ripping you off, yes.'

Rick glanced in and spotted a couple of construction workers still wearing their hard hats in the queue. 'Shall we just meet back at the car?'

'Your money,' Jon replied. Rick crossed the road, and Jon went into Gregg's.

He ordered two bacon barms with brown sauce and a cup of coffee, then wandered into the square. Rick was already sitting on a bench in front of the ancient church overlooking the square, enjoying the intermittent bursts of sun breaking through the broken cloud above.

Deciding there was no immediate danger of being doused in a sudden spring shower, Jon sat next to him. As he did so he glanced across towards the glass-panelled corner of the Marks & Spencer's built on the site where the IRA bomb had gone off in 1996.

His mind went back to the event and the years leading up to it. He didn't suppose there ever was an ideal time for becoming a copper. He'd joined in 1991 at the age of twenty-one, suddenly finding himself patrolling the streets in a policeman's uniform. He'd kept on expecting members of the public to laughingly point at him in disbelief.

The city's nightclubbing scene was then in its prime and the place was known throughout the world as Madchester. But, as the nineties wore on, venues like the Hacienda were increasingly being taken over by gangs from Cheetham Hill and Salford. Every night was turning into a scrabble for the police station's bullet-proof vests as they were repeatedly called out to shootings. The gangs didn't care who died in their battle to control the lucrative drugs trade, and the press had started to call the city Gunchester.

Many of his colleagues had spent their weekends working undercover in nightclubs and bars, shitting themselves as they tried to gather evidence of drug dealing so the places could be shut down. Even now the thought made Jon almost laugh with relief – thanks to his conspicuous size, and the fact he was playing for the Greater Manchester Police rugby team each Saturday afternoon, it was a role he was spared.

As the Madchester period began to stutter and fizzle the city had seemed to be searching for a new identity. He remembered mentions of somewhere called Canal Street, rumours of it being a safe drinking haven for gays. Sankey's Soap opened in Ancoats. Alice started raving about a local band called Oasis and suddenly Manchester appeared to have rediscovered its spirit.

Then came the coded phone call on the fifteenth of June. A bomb was set to go off in one of the city's busiest shopping areas, just as the Saturday crowds were pouring in.

He remembered running down Market Street in his bobby's uniform, one hand holding his helmet on his head, the other furiously waving members of the public away from the Arndale. Intelligence was shaky and he had no idea when the bomb might go off. The only times he'd sweated so much was on the rugby pitch.

Within an hour they'd cleared an area in the

immediate vicinity of a large white van. He was keeping the crowds back from the cordon tape at the far end of Market Street when the thing went off. It was the loudest noise he'd ever heard, a roar that jarred the air so violently it made him stagger. Then came the cascade of glass. Even a good four hundred metres away, shards rained down all around them. Miraculously, no one was killed, but the centre of the city had been devastated.

He looked towards the gleaming building. Another example of how the city had evolved and adapted from its origins as the world's first industrial city.

As he bit into his large flat roll, he spotted Rick sipping from an absurdly small bottle. 'What's in there?'

'Banana and mango smoothie.'

Jon shook his head, thinking of Alice's love of reducing perfectly good fruit and vegetables to mush. 'You should meet my missus.'

It was just a short drive to the next address on the list. The building was on the Rochdale Road, imposing and dark. They parked in the rear yard, next to a brand-new Range Rover. 'Jesus, there's some money to be made in this game,' observed Jon.

They walked back on to the main road, clangs from a construction site clearly audible over the sound of traffic rushing past. Rick gestured to several cranes that towered like sentinels over the nearby roofs. 'Something major's going on over there.'

'That's Ancoats,' Jon replied. 'It's received huge amounts of regeneration money from the EU. The place is finally getting a facelift.'

Rick checked the printout and then the brass plaque by the door. 'This is it. 'The Beauty Centre, Dr O'Connor.'

Jon looked dubiously at the stone surrounding the door. It was stained almost black by exhaust fumes.

Rick had to buzz twice before a voice sounded on the intercom.

'Who is it?' A faint Irish accent, the voice casual and friendly.

Jon was surprised; compared to the glossy organisation they'd just come from, it was hardly a businesslike greeting.

'DS Saville and DI Spicer, Greater Manchester Police.'

Plastic clattered as the handset was dropped. 'Sod it! Sorry, come right up.'

They exchanged a look as the door clicked open, allowing them to enter a softly lit lobby. The air was slightly musty and Jon looked down at the deep-red carpet at his feet. The ground-floor doors were all plastered over and Jon guessed the rooms on the other sides were offices of companies in the adjoining buildings. The only way to go was up the stairs, and the heavy carpeting completely muffled their footsteps as they climbed. At regular intervals were facial portraits of models, a small notice below each photograph. Collagen. Restylane. Hylaform.

Laser skin resurfacing. Temporary wrinkle filler. Cool touch laser.

Jon nodded knowingly at Rick, 'Non-surgical procedures only.'

At the top of the stairs was a short corridor with two doors leading off. The one marked 'Treatment Room' was closed, the other open.

'Please come in,' the same voice called from inside.

They entered an office that looked like it should have belonged to a lawyer. A huge wooden desk dominated the end of the room, rows of books weighing down the shelves behind it. The daylight that made it through the windows seemed to be instantly soaked up by the red carpet and wooden wall panels.

A distinguished-looking man was seated behind the desk, wiping the handset of the intercom phone with a cloth for cleaning glasses. 'Slippery bugger. Hope it didn't sound too loud your end. Take a seat, why don't you.'

Jon drank in the Irish lilt. As they walked across the room, he took in the doctor's full head of white hair, guessing he was in his late fifties. Closer, he reassessed the doctor's age. If he was approaching sixty, he wore his years incredibly well. His jawline was firm, the skin around his eyes smooth.

When he smiled, his teeth were perfect. 'How can I be of help?'

Rick took out his sheet of paper. 'Do you run this place all on your own, Dr O'Connor?'

'I have a nurse on the days we carry out procedures.

150

But there's no point in paying her to be here when it's just paperwork that I'm tidying up.'

'Perhaps we should be talking to her. It's about whoever orders your medical supplies.'

'I do a lot of that myself.'

'Including medical gloves?'

'Indeed.'

'We're trying to ascertain the recent movements of a sales rep from Protex.'

'Young Gordon Dean? He was in here only two days ago.' He plucked a tangerine from the pile of fruit in a polished wooden bowl on his desk, then nodded towards it. 'Gentlemen?'

Jon and Rick shook their heads and the doctor held up a finger. 'Five pieces a day.' He leaned forwards conspiratorially. 'If more people kept to that little maxim there'd be a lot less work for me.' He dropped the peel into a bin and popped a segment of tangerine into his mouth.

'How did Gordon Dean seem to you?' Jon asked.

'His usual cheerful self.'

'He normally strikes you as happy?'

'He does. Seems to enjoy his work visits to Manchester, at least.'

'How about non-work issues? His personal life, for instance?'

The doctor paused. 'He's married, I gather. No children, though I don't know why. I'm not sure what answers you're looking for.'

Jon smiled. 'Neither are we. We're just trying to get an idea of him.'

'He's in trouble, I take it?'

'No. We just need to trace him. He seems to have disappeared. The last time you saw him, was there anything out of the ordinary? Was he agitated or preoccupied, perhaps?'

O'Connor shook his head.

'Was he here for long?'

'No longer than usual. He left at about three o'clock.'

'Did you chat at all?'

'We talked about the current best dining options in Manchester.'

'Those being?'

'Gordon loves his Italian food. He mentioned he was staying over in Manchester, so I recommended a place I visited the other day. Piccolino's. Have you tried it?'

Rick and Jon shook their heads.

'Ah, Gordon had. I think he was eating at one of his regular places. A person's name. Now let me think.' He closed his eyes.

'Don Antonio's?' Jon asked.

The doctor clicked his fingers, opening his eyes and bowing his head fractionally at Jon. 'Don Antonio's. I've not been there myself. Have you?'

'No, but I think we will be.' Jon started to get up, but paused. 'We've just come from the offices of the Paragon Group. What do you think of them?'

The silence was a second too long before he answered. 'A very efficient organisation.'

Jon sank back in his seat. 'And your personal, not professional, opinion?'

Dr O'Connor looked into Jon's eyes. 'My confidential personal opinion?'

'Won't go further than us three,' Jon replied.

'A bunch of mercenary money-grabbers.'

'Go on,' said Jon.

'They'll employ anyone as long as they have one ethic.'

Jon raised his eyebrows in encouragement.

'That they're prepared to treat anyone, regardless of need or suitability.'

'You mean surgery?' asked Rick.

O'Connor nodded. 'Their staff all have medical qualifications and a basic knowledge of cosmetic surgery. But they don't need any sort of track history – actually, they don't need any history or experience at all. Add to that the fact that this is an industry woefully lacking in regulations. New procedures and techniques are appearing all the time, and all too often they're driven by profit rather than patient well-being. Not, in my opinion, a healthy state of affairs.'

'So you've never applied to work for them?'

O'Connor snorted. 'Absolutely not. The reverse, as a matter of fact. They've tried to buy me out once or twice, but I'm not interested. I've also had doctors approach me looking for work. I've turned them away due to their lack of experience, only to hear they're employed by Paragon weeks later.'

'Performing full surgical procedures?' Jon asked.

'Full surgical procedures.'

'As opposed to what you perform here?'

'Correct. I specialise in aesthetic medicine – laser treatments, botox and filler injections, on the whole. Nothing more than skin deep. But the industry's expanding at an incredible rate. Everyone wants a slice of the action, to employ the prevalent terminology. Dentists now offer Botox treatments on the side. Got a medical qualification and a syringe? Then join the party. There are rich pickings for all.'

Jon contemplated the doctor's words. 'Going back to the surgical side of things, how many people would you say are employed in the industry?'

'Nationwide or just Manchester?'

Jon toyed with the idea of letting the doctor know which investigation they were on, suspecting that he'd soon guess. 'Manchester for starters.'

O'Connor frowned. 'Well, Paragon and their three main competitors have a total of around twelve doctors on their books, I'd say. Some of those work as surgeons in local NHS hospitals and do the private stuff on the side to boost their incomes. Of course, if you were going under the knife, that's the type of surgeon you want. In addition, they employ several who do private cosmetic work full time. Those guys may do a couple of days a week in Manchester, one in Leeds and one in Liverpool. They go where the business is. I'd hesitate to say how many of them are in Manchester altogether. Fifty, maybe?'

'Thanks for your time, Doctor,' Jon said, getting to his feet.

Out on the street Jon wrinkled his nose as a noisy lorry roared past, leaving a light haze of exhaust fumes in its wake. 'We'd better recommend to McCloughlin that all surgeons employed by the likes of the Paragon Group are traced and interviewed.'

'Should be easy to check the alibis of the travelling ones,' Rick said.

'True,' Jon agreed. 'Let's see Gordon Dean's appointments list again.'

Rick got the sheet of paper out, holding it taut against the buffets of air created by passing traffic.

Jon pointed to the final appointment of the morning. 'Jake's, in Affleck's Palace. That's a tattoo artist.' He looked towards Great Ancoats Street. 'It's only over there. Shall we get it done?'

'Why not?' Rick folded the sheet up.

Jon led the way across the main road and into the jumble of narrow streets and derelict cloth shops that made up the Northern Quarter. Soon they rounded the corner of a multi-storey car park, the smell of curry filling the air.

Rick looked at the little café with its never-ending menu painted on the windows. 'That must be the sixth one of those places we've passed.'

Jon nodded. 'This is where Manchester's first curry houses sprang up, serving lunch to all the Indian workers from the mills and warehouses that used to thrive around here. It was only after they'd

155

made enough money from these places that the owners opened up other premises out in Rusholme.'

'You mean the curry mile?' Rick said, referring to the stretch of road just outside the city centre crammed with dozens of glitzy Indian restaurants.

'That's the one,' said Jon. He pointed across another car park to a hulking old warehouse with strange flower-like lamps attached to its walls. 'And that's Affleck's Palace.'

They walked past a row of market stalls selling fruit and vegetables, and stopped by a side entrance to the Palace. Rick looked at a montage of broken tiles mounted on the wall. Blue fragments spelled out, *And on the 6th day, God created MANchester*. He smiled. 'What is this place?'

'Affleck's Palace? Come and take a look.'

They pushed through the doors and found themselves in a room crammed with racks of old denims, corduroy jackets and military-style clothing. Joe Strummer bellowed that they should know their rights, the music unbalanced by the heavier beats of an Eminem track coming from the next room. They went through a doorway into a narrow space lined with T-shirts. Rick pointed out the lettering on one: *Fat people are hard to kidnap*. 'Strange, but true I suppose,' he said.

'Just about sums this place up,' Jon answered. He was about to point out another that read, *Roll me in chocolate and throw me to the lesbians*, but changed his mind.

They crossed into another room, this one piled

high with memorabilia. A seventies-style telephone with a blue neon dial glowed from its position on an impossibly chunky Betamax video recorder which sat next to a ZX Spectrum. Finding a flight of stairs, Jon scanned the list of stalls. 'Jake's, third floor.'

When they reached a relatively quieter landing, Rick took the opportunity to speak. 'What a bizarre place.'

'Yeah, it hasn't changed in years. In fact, most of the stuff for sale looks like it hasn't changed in years, either.'

They emerged on to the third floor, the sound of the Fun Lovin' Criminals booming out from a stall selling semi-precious stones and wind chimes. Jon pointed down the narrow aisle. 'It's in the corner I think.'

They passed through four more zones of music before reaching a stall which differed from the rest in that it had a glass front. *Jake's Body Works. 2 for 1 on all piercings*. Close-up photos of tattoos filled the windows, most so fresh they were fringed by angry red skin.

Jon leaned closer, trying to work out the part of the body each image had been drawn on. Nipples, pubic regions and stomach buttons emerged from the patterns. They went inside. There was barely enough room for both of them to stand, but at least the cacophony of music outside dropped a fraction.

A man sat in the corner, shaved head bowed over a manga comic. He looked up, face glinting with clusters of studs. They protruded from his ears, lips, cheeks, nostrils and eyebrows. One ran through the upper part of his nose and Jon wondered how it didn't make him go cross-eyed.

He folded his comic shut. 'A Prince Albert, gentlemen?'

Jon was unsure what he meant, but knew from the man's expression they'd been sussed immediately for police.

He took out his ID card anyway. 'DI Spicer and DS Saville.'

'You don't say,' he interrupted, eyes moving to Rick for a second. 'I'm Jake.' He waved a hand so covered in tattoos, it was almost blue. 'You'll be wanting a seat before we get started.'

The comment was phrased so Jon wasn't sure if the man was referring to them asking questions or getting a Prince Albert, whatever that was. A mischievous light danced in Jake's eyes and Jon wondered just how much pressure would be required to rip the bolt out of the bridge of his nose.

Rick sat down on one of the stools and said, 'We're trying to trace the movements of Gordon Dean. You purchase your medical examination gloves from him.'

Jake's eyes were still on Jon, who remained standing by the door. 'Ease up, man. I'm only fooling around.'

Jon raised and then dropped the corners of his mouth, the smile over in a blink.

Jake turned his attention to Rick. 'Gordon?

He was in here two days ago.' He shook his head and laughed.

'Why's that funny?' Rick said, half smiling, too.

Jake clicked a tongue stud against his teeth. 'He was just passing through. He was on a voyage.'

If the man's eyes hadn't been so alert, Jon would have guessed he was on something.

'What sort of voyage?' Rick asked.

Jake leaned back. 'Self-discovery.'

'Meaning?'

'You tell me. After all, you're looking for him. I just spied him off my port bow, heading God knows where. Perhaps you know more about the course he was plotting.'

Jon shook his head. 'Jake, you're making me feel seasick. Just let us know why you thought he was on a voyage.'

Jake burst out laughing. 'OK, man, I like your style. For a start, he came back after his other appointments for another tattoo.' He twisted round, took a large book off the shelf by his head and opened it up. 'This little baby. Right on his left arse cheek.' He tapped a design of a pudgy red imp with red skin, horns and a trident.

'You did his first tattoo?' asked Jon. 'The ladybird?'

'That's right.' Jake looked up and his smile faltered. 'You've seen it? Don't tell me he's in the morgue?'

'Why? Is that where you'd expect him to turn up?' Jon held his eyes.

Jake's shoulders shifted. 'No. The guy was excited, a bit hyper even. But it was more . . .' He grasped at the air. 'Positive, you know? He was bursting with energy. He's not dead, is he?'

'As I said, we're trying to trace his movements. We don't know where he is.'

Rick said, 'So he was bursting with energy.'

'Yeah, like he'd just had some good news. Grinning all the time.'

'Didn't say why, though?'

'No. But he was on a mission. Said he was getting a haircut, too. That horrific side parting of his was going.'

'Did he say where was he getting it cut?' Rick said, pen and notebook out.

'Zaney's, downstairs.'

They clattered down the wooden steps, the incessant music and claustrophobic atmosphere beginning to get to Jon.

'Yeah,' said the hairdresser, sweeping a mane of crimson hair off her shoulder, 'he was my last customer. Left just before six. Don't get to lop fringes like his off very often.'

'What sort of cut did you give him?'

'The chopped look. Grade two back and sides, a bit longer on top. All messed up and spiky. He took a pot of extra-strong styling gel to make sure it stayed that way. Oh, and he let me get rid of that moustache, too.'

'Did he say what he was doing, why the sudden drastic change in hairstyle?' Rick asked.

160

'Nah. Just gave me a good tip and skipped on out the door.'

Rick rubbed his hands as they walked back to their car. 'A voyage of self-discovery. You reckon he was manic? About to go off the rails?'

Jon's hands were in his pockets, eyes on the pavement in front. 'I don't think so. He was still seeing clients, chasing sales targets. Did you notice his house? There was something dead about it. I think the wife's right – Gordon was on the verge of getting out.'

'Yeah, but to do what? I think he was building up to something. Maybe it was his next murder.'

Jon looked away. 'Just a gut reaction, but I can't see it.'

Rick remained silent.

'You don't agree?' Jon asked after a few seconds.

'He was hiding a completely different side of himself from his wife. Maybe he was hiding a lot of rage, too. That tattooist said he was bubbling with excitement. Could have been with the prospect of skinning another woman.'

Jon jangled the change in his pocket, still not convinced. 'By the way, what's a Prince Albert?'

Rick snorted, but kept looking ahead. 'It's a ring. One that goes down your Jap's eye and out under the rim of your fireman's helmet.'

'Oh, sweet Jesus,' Jon groaned.

CHAPTER 13

Cathy whispered, 'It's ringing.'

Fiona stood on the other side of the desk. She took the tip of a finger out of her mouth and, anxiously chewing a fragment of nail, hissed, 'Don't forget to say it's a personal call if she asks.'

'I know,' Cathy mouthed. 'Hello, could I have the fax number for Jeff Wilson, please?' She jotted a number down. 'And is he in the office at the moment? . . . OK, thanks.' She leaned towards the phone in readiness to replace the handset. 'Sorry? . . . No, it's a personal call . . . No, that's OK, there's no message . . . No, really, it's not important.'

She hung up and said, 'Jesus, she was desperate to get my name.'

'It's him,' Fiona said knowingly. 'He goes mad if you fail to take a name and number when someone calls. It was the same for me at home – even though he refused to take messages for me. My friends gave up trying eventually.'

The comment made Cathy look exhausted. 'Fucking men. Anyway, he's in a meeting until lunch.'

162

Fiona nodded, but didn't move.

'Well, go, then!' Cathy shoved her towards the door.

'Yes, sorry.' She whipped the car keys from her pocket and rushed outside. In her car she immediately began to fret again. What if the meeting was cancelled and his PA said someone had rung asking where he was? Would he guess it was her and rush home?

The mid-morning traffic was light, allowing Fiona to reach the house with reassuring speed. The driveway was empty, but she parked slightly further down the road, ready for a quick getaway if needed. At the mouth of the driveway she paused. If he did reappear and find her, she didn't know what he'd do. But he won't be drunk, she assured herself, using the knowledge to summon up enough resolve to approach the front door.

It opened to reveal that morning's post on the doormat. He's at work, she told herself, stepping inside and bolting the door behind her. She hurried through to the kitchen and unlocked the back door. Her escape route prepared, she went upstairs.

She pulled the big suitcase out from under the bed, opened the wardrobe and hastily started to fold clothes. Then she dragged it across to the dressing table and used her forearm to sweep all her bottles and pots into it. They cascaded onto her clothes, perfume bottles clinking. The noise was brief, but lasted long enough for her to imagine it could have masked the sound of his car pulling up. She looked from the window and saw an empty street. Breathing a sigh of relief, she rushed into the bathroom for all her toiletries.

The suitcase bumped down the stairs and she hauled it into the kitchen. He kept control of all their finances, including her wages from the beauty salon. But she knew some emergency cash was hidden in the biscuit tin. She flipped off the lid only to see a handwritten note: *Rot in hell, you whore.*

She flung the lid against the cooker, a cry of frustration escaping her. Looking around the kitchen, she yanked open the cupboard under the sink. The bottle of gin went into her suitcase, then she grabbed the bleach and squirted it all over the contents of the fridge. After flinging the empty bottle in the sink, she lifted up her suitcase and staggered round the side of the house.

She could hear a vehicle slowly approaching. She crouched down behind the wheelie bin. A driving instructor's car, teenager at the wheel. Breathing out, she dragged the suitcase across the lawn and along the pavement to her car. Only when she was actually pulling away did she dare to believe she'd got away with it.

Her next stop was Melvyn's beauty salon. She parked round the back, then rummaged in the suitcase for her concealing cream. After touching it over her bruises, she walked round to the front of the salon and went in.

Melvyn glanced in the mirror, a segment of wet

hair between two fingers. He met her eyes, and his scissors paused for a moment. 'Where've you been, you bitch?'

Behind him, Janice also paused, halfway through plucking a woman's eyebrow.

Oh Jesus, he's genuinely annoyed. Fiona's knees felt like they were about to buckle as Melvyn looked back down at his customer's head. But then he turned to face her again, a big grin on his face. 'Come here, you gorgeous woman!'

The scissors were discarded and he crossed the floor with small steps, jeans hanging off his hips. Hugging her with unusual force, he whispered in her ear, 'Did that bastard do that to your face?'

He pulled back to get eye contact and Fiona nodded, hand going to her eyebrow as tears welled up.

'Right!' He gestured to a girl sweeping up strands of hair. 'Zoe, get that kettle on and bring out the posh biscuits. You' – he took Fiona's shoulders and directed her towards a chair – 'put your feet up and relax. It's time you had some pampering.'

Fiona fell into the chair, laughter bubbling in her voice. 'Melvyn, really. You don't need—'

'Don't tell me what to do in my bloody salon.' Fingers adjusting his straggles of highlighted hair. 'By the way, Zoe, Fiona. Fiona, Zoe. She's with us on a work placement for a fortnight.'

He went back to his customer, and Zoe smiled uncertainly from under a low-hanging fringe. 'Would you like tea or coffee?'

165

Alice came out of her side room. Her smile didn't falter when she saw how Fiona looked. 'Hiya, babe, good to have you back.' Slowly, she crossed the room and carefully lowered herself into a seat beside Fiona. 'You OK?'

Fiona nodded too vigorously. 'I've left him. For good, this time.'

'You go, girl,' Melvyn called – his customer looked totally bemused at the goings-on.

'How are you?' Fiona said, looking at Alice's huge stomach.

Alice's face was glowing. 'Great, thanks. Where are you staying?'

'It's not that far away. Some really decent people live there.' She swallowed back her shame. 'It's a refuge, you know.'

Alice nodded. 'Listen, we've got a spare room. It's going to be the nursery, so if you can put up with a few cans of paint while Jon finishes decorating it . . .'

Fiona laid a hand on Alice's forearm. 'That's so kind, but I really want to make a go of it on my own.'

'I understand. But if you feel different, the offer's open.' She looked back towards her room. 'Customer's waiting. See you in a bit?' She pushed herself to her feet.

Ten minutes later Melvyn finished with his customer. He slumped down beside Fiona and picked up the carton of biscuits. 'Is that all that's left? Zoe, grab a tenner from the till and get us some nice ones from Marks and Sparks.' He turned to Fiona. 'So you've really moved out?'

'Yeah, I'm getting my own place. I can't stay where I am much longer. Actually . . .' She paused awkwardly. 'You know it's pay day next week?'

Melvyn held up a finger. 'Of course, love. You can have your money, and some extra, too. You'll need it for the deposit on your flat.'

He stood up and began to gently knead the back of Fiona's neck. 'Listen, love. About work. We can cover for you. Once you're feeling better and you've settled into your new place, give me a call. We could always come round for a little house-warming do.'

Fiona leaned back and closed her eyes. 'I don't know what to say, Melvyn, except I'll make it up to you.' Suddenly she tensed and her eyes snapped open. 'If he comes looking for me, you mustn't say a thing.'

'Bloody hell, Fiona.' Melvyn lowered his hands. 'I thought I'd trapped a nerve. Don't worry. If that fat bastard comes in, I'll tell him you don't work here any more.'

Fiona smiled.

After they'd finished their cups of tea, Alice caught Fiona on the street outside. 'Jon said you spoke to him,' she said, slightly out of breath with the effort of taking just a few quick steps.

Fiona's face tightened. 'Yes. I'm sorry that I lost my temper.'

'That's all right. He's used to it in his job.'

'Yeah, well, I had good reason. If you'd heard what

I heard, Alice . . . It's right here.' She tapped behind her ear. 'I can't get the noise out of my head. And no one cares. I know your Jon's busy, but no one cares what happened. Well, I do. I'm going to find out what happened to her. The poor thing is little more than a child.' She looked off into the distance.

'Who?' Alice said.

Fiona blinked. 'Oh. I talked to the woman at the escort agency. She does remember someone, though whether she was called Alexia or Alicia I'm not really sure. Whoever she was, the woman wouldn't take her on. Suspected a drug habit and sent her back to the streets, even though she was barely twenty.'

'What are you going to do?'

'I don't know. Try and find out what happened to her.'

'But you don't know if you're even looking for the right girl.'

Fiona shrugged. 'I just need to find out if she's OK.'

Alice was frowning with confusion. 'How?'

'Well, if she was sent back to the streets, I could start asking the girls who work there.'

'Prostitutes?'

Fiona nodded. 'Someone must know her.'

'Fiona, be careful. Until they catch this man . . .'

'I've shared a house with a monster for long enough. I can watch out for myself, don't you worry,' she replied, not feeling the bravado she was trying to show.

CHAPTER 14

Tentatively, she inched the door open and looked inside. The curtains had been opened and morning sunlight was streaming in. The air in the room reflected the temperature outside, and she realised the window was open as far as it would go.

The patient was half sitting up in bed, bandaged face directed to the world beyond the window, tips of spiky hair catching the sun's rays.

Seeing him staring off to the side like that reminded Dawn Poole of how they'd first met. It was in the hair care aisle of Boots just over four years ago. She had seen him scrutinising the bottles, a slimly built man not much bigger than her. He looked strangely helpless. He'd sensed her watching and turned awkwardly to face her.

His clumsy request for advice about hair dye had almost made her laugh. She'd assumed he was buying it for his elderly mother or some other female relative. As she explained the different choices that were available, the mixture of vulnerability and embarrassment in his face started to interest her. She wasn't used to a man relying on her for help and then attentively listening to everything she had to say. Normally in her relationships it was the other way round.

She gave him a couple of tips on how best to apply the colouring, and enjoyed the feeling of being needed as he eagerly absorbed her advice. Then he had surprised her by tentatively asking about how to apply false eyelashes.

Realising he was asking for the benefit of himself and not someone else, she had offered to let him know about applying false nails, too. He'd accepted with a smile.

An hour later they were sitting in a coffee shop, him with a large bag of make-up on the seat next to him.

'He came right into the room just now.'

The words were whispered with hardly any movement of the lips and Dawn was reminded of a novice trying to master the art of ventriloquism.

'Who?' she replied, walking into the room and sitting on the end of the bed.

'The robin. I put some crumbs on the bed. He hopped right in and ate them. So beautiful, so delicate.'

She could tell the bandages hid the beginnings of a smile. The feeling of foreboding that had been building since the policeman questioned her dissipated slightly and was replaced by a warm glow of admiration.

She couldn't imagine the pain he was going through. Knowing that she wouldn't have been able to endure it, she took one hand in hers and stroked the smooth skin. 'It's good to see you looking happier.'

The patient was still looking out of the window. 'Speaking, eating, sleeping. Everything still hurts. But now I feel it's worth it again. Worth it for who I'm going to be.'

Dawn nodded. 'That's the attitude. You know, I'm happy just to be out of that miserable motel. The place is falling apart. If it gets inspected, they'll close it straight off.' She hooked a strand of hair over her ear. 'Your dressings are due to be changed later on. I'm sure he'll bring some more painkillers, too.' The room was silent as she judged how to articulate the next sentence. She opted for a casual tone. 'A policeman called at the motel a few nights ago.'

Eyes swivelled towards her, blood still caught in the lower half of their orbits.

'He was asking questions. Someone thought they heard choking coming from one of the rooms. Choking like the person was in serious trouble.'

She waited for a response, but nothing came.

'I told him no one came to me needing help.' She glanced up seeking affirmation, but the patient had turned back to the window.

She reached into the bag and got out some women's magazines and a copy of the local paper. The outside column of the front page was devoted to conjecture about the Butcher's latest victim, who still remained unidentified. 'I brought you some things to read.'

CHAPTER 15

At 11:17 the next day Jon's computer pinged. Someone had entered the registration of Gordon Dean's car in the Police National Computer's database of stolen or abandoned vehicles. The system had then matched it to the flag he'd left earlier and relayed the alert to his computer.

He raised a hand and clicked his fingers at Rick. 'Bingo! There's a silver Passat at Piccadilly train station that has outstayed its welcome in the short-term car park. Registration matches our man's.'

The car-park attendant looked at their identities with surprise. 'I was just going to get it towed.'

'No need for now,' Jon replied. 'Where is it?'

He led them up to the third floor, Jon's head barely clearing the low concrete ceiling.

'Over in the corner. See it?'

'Cheers.'

They walked over and peered in through the windows. Rick leaned across the bonnet to see on to the dashboard. 'Ticket purchased at five past seven in the morning five days ago. Fits with him checking out of the Novotel and coming straight here.'

Jon checked the back seat. 'Empty. What do you reckon, then?'

'Seems a bit early to be catching a train,' Rick replied.

'Unless you're catching a train to catch a plane. They're practically round the clock to the airport.'

'Why not just drive there?'

'True.' Jon put his hand in his jacket pocket and hooked his fingers under the driver's door handle. To his surprise, it opened. 'That's a result.' He leaned inside; the interior was filled with the chemical smell of a cheap air freshener.

Rick used the same trick to open the passenger door without leaving any prints. He crouched down and popped open the glove compartment with the end of a pen. A tin of mints, a pile of compliments slips and an *A to Z* of Manchester.

Jon pointed at the music system. A tape was poking out of the cassette deck. 'That's a blank tape. Something could have been recorded on it.' He took an evidence bag out of his pocket, pulled it over his hand, removed the tape and placed it in his pocket. Then he pulled up the lever for the boot. Inside were a few crushed boxes of latex gloves, a picnic blanket and a golfing umbrella, the Protex logo just visible among its folds.

'Something heavy squashed those boxes,' Rick observed.

'Yeah,' Jon nodded. 'And my money's on it being some well-packed suitcases.'

Rick put his hands on his knees to push himself upright, then stopped. His head angled to one side and he got down on one knee to lean forwards into the boot. 'Hello, this doesn't look like Mrs Dean's taste in cosmetics.'

'What?' Jon asked, trying to look in.

Rick took out a set of keys and used the tip of one to hook the tiny object up. It stuck to the jagged edge like an exotic insect clinging on for dear life.

'What is that?' Jon frowned.

Rick studied it, rapt as an entomologist discovering a new species. 'A false eyelash. And look at the size of it. That's a real beauty.'

'Yeah,' Jon agreed, now able to see it. 'Normal habitat, streetus prostitutus.' He produced another evidence bag from his pocket.

As Rick dropped it in he said, 'The thought of this is making me feel ill, but I wonder if its mate is in the pile of skin that used to be victim number three's face?'

Jon nodded grimly. 'We'd better go over the autopsy report.'

'Maybe he's washing their faces, stripping off all their make-up before stripping off their skin.'

Jon weighed up the comment. Try as he might, the impression he was forming of Gordon Dean didn't fit with that of a killer. Unlike the thought of Pete Gray. Now there was a man he'd like to take somewhere private, a place where he could exert some real pressure. He stopped the thought right there, worried at how easily his mind could switch to the contemplation of violence. 'Let's see what's on this tape.'

Back in their own car, he turned the ignition key until the dashboard lights came on. Then, using an evidence bag as a glove, he carefully slid the cassette into the machine.

It was a recording taken from the radio, the DJ speaking loud and fast, Manchester accent easily apparent. 'OK, people, as I promised before the break, here's the tune that's setting the airwaves on fire at the moment. I heard a whisper from their record company that it's not being released until well into next year, so until then you'll just have to keep tuned to Galaxy FM, because we can't get enough of playing it here.'

A faint chorus of trumpets rapidly grew in strength. Nodding in time as the drumbeat started up, Rick said, 'It's called "Lola's Theme" – can't remember who it's by.'

By now the music was in full flow, female vocals blending with the uplifting tune. The trumpets built higher, reaching a crescendo as the triumphant chorus kicked in.

> *I'm a different person, yeah,*
> *Turned my world around,*
> *I'm a different person, yeah,*
> *Turned my world around.*

When they walked into the incident room, the receiver waved a sheet of paper at them. 'Gordon Dean's most recent credit-card transactions.'

'Cheers, Graham.' Jon made his way to his desk and laid the paper on it. He and Rick both went straight to the transactions on the night when Dean disappeared.

'Jesus Christ!' whistled Rick.

Jon made a quick mental calculation. 'That's over a grand and a half in one night.'

Rick sat down to study the transactions more carefully. 'Don Antonio's, like Doctor O'Connor said. And Crimson – surprise, surprise. Between those, a few drinks in Taurus and a stop in Natterjacks. He was certainly hitting the pubs and clubs around Canal Street.'

'Are these all places you know?' Jon realised he'd lowered his voice slightly.

Rick nodded. 'Gay ones, on the whole – Natterjacks gets quite a mixed crowd. But look at those last three transactions. £150 from a cashpoint, £9.99 from what looks to be a garage and then another £1,100 from another cashpoint.'

Jon pointed at the date. 'The final one is from the next morning at six forty-three. That one must have maxed his card out, then, twenty minutes later, he's buying a ticket for the car park at Piccadilly station.'

'So he deliberately cleared his bank account,' Rick murmured.

Jon dropped a ten-pound note on the table.

'That says he's holed up in a cottage somewhere, probably in the sack right now.'

Rick matched his money. 'You're on.'

'OK, I'll ring Visa for the exact locations of those two last cashpoints. Shall we drop by Don Antonio's?'

In the dull light of day the Hurlington Health Club looked almost innocent, only the blacked out windows jarring as odd.

Relieved that the place was so much less imposing than the first time she'd tried to visit, Fiona went up the pathway. The door opened into a room dimly lit by a variety of flame-effect lamps. An aquarium bubbled in the left-hand corner, the water glowing with crystalline light that spilled out across darkly coloured sofas.

A young woman wearing a towelling dressing gown was sprinkling fish food in. She turned round, a look of surprise across her face.

'Cindy, someone's here!' Heavy accent, Russian perhaps.

Fiona looked at the counter to her right, empty except for a swipe machine and a pot crammed with cheap biros, cellophane from the stationery shop still clinging to its lower half. A vacuum cleaner came on and an overweight woman with hair coiled on top of her head straightened up behind the counter. The girl by the aquarium slumped on a sofa and perched her bare feet against the rim of the glass coffee table.

'Hello, I'm hoping you can help me.' Fiona stepped off the doormat, almost shouting to make herself heard above the vacuum's aggravating whine.

'You what?' The fat woman's lips remained slightly apart as if the weight of her chins was pulling her lower jaw down.

'I'm trying to find a young woman,' Fiona replied self-consciously as the woman registered the cut to her eyebrow.

She carried on hoovering and Fiona wanted to rip the machine's plug from the wall. 'I think she works here. Or did recently.'

Still the woman said nothing and Fiona felt her words were being absorbed without impression by her bulk. 'Her name is Alexia.'

'She's not working here any more,' the woman snapped without looking up.

'Why? What happened?'

'Who are you?'

'Me? Just someone who knew her once.' The woman's eyes narrowed suspiciously. Clearly, the answer wasn't good enough. Fiona resorted to a lie. 'I'm a friend of her mother's. We're very worried about her.'

'A friend? Who do you work for, social services?'

'No, I'm a beauty therapist.'

Fiona saw the woman look at her hands. She'd given herself a manicure the day before. Since her face was a mess, something needed to look good.

'She did herself no favours by tapping up regulars

with her phone number.' She stopped pushing the vacuum in order to jut a thumb towards the door. 'I told her to sling her hook.'

'Where might she have gone?'

The woman swivelled a paw of a hand so her thumb pointed to the floor. 'Only one place she was heading for. Back to the streets.' She shuffled towards Fiona, thrusting the machine back and forth before her.

Fiona retreated a step. 'Which ones?'

'Which ones?' The woman repeated. 'What do you mean?'

'Which streets?' Fiona asked.

'I don't know. Try Minshull, for starters.'

'Minshull Street. Thanks.'

Fiona opened the door and was bathed in dull grey daylight. 'What did this girl look like?'

'I thought you knew her,' the fat woman said.

Fiona retreated on to the front step. 'Shoulder-length hair? Chestnut brown? My height? Thin?'

The woman was looking at the doormat, running the vacuum over it. 'That's her,' she said dismissively, moving the machine back on to the carpet and letting the door swing shut.

Copies of the autopsy report on the Butcher's third victim were doing the rounds of the incident room, several detectives chewing sandwiches as they digested its details.

'Same as the other two,' Jon commented. 'Evidence of being strangled. Blood in the surrounding tissues and fascia suggests he began to remove her skin within minutes of her death.'

Rick was hunched over his photocopied sheets. 'Well, at least she wasn't alive for it. Substantially more flesh taken off, too. And her missing teeth had been removed shortly after her death. Not wrenched out, removed professionally.'

'So along with surgical skills he's got some knowledge of dentistry. Fuck, what are we dealing with here?' Jon asked, an ominous shadow passing over him.

Rick looked up, face slightly pale. 'Why would he take out a selection of her teeth?'

'I reckon he's covering his tracks,' Jon said. 'He's making it as hard as possible to identify her. No face, only a few teeth to compare against dental records – he doesn't want to get caught.'

Rick looked down again. 'Because he wants to carry on. Jesus.' He turned to the photos of the skin itself. The first image was of it piled up next to the corpse on the waste ground. Jon glanced across the table then turned away as memories of having to eat tripe at his grandma's flashed up in his mind. 'No mention of false eyelashes.'

Rick flipped the photo over. The next one was the same pile of skin in the morgue. The pathologist had then taken the pieces of flesh and fitted them together like a grotesque jigsaw.

He turned to the section titled, 'Distinguishing Features'. 'Row of four piercing holes in the upper right ear. Tattoo on the lower left abdomen.'

180

Jon looked up. 'What of?'

'Betty Boop. Three inches high.'

'Betty Boop? That cartoon character? Oversized head, little kiss-curl, miniskirt and heels?'

'Yeah, I think that's her.'

'Is the cartoon on TV at the moment or something? I've seen that character recently. God, where was it?'

Rick was frowning. 'If he's covering his tracks, why leave her tattoo? Especially when virtually all the skin from the rest of her torso had been removed.'

'He leaves their knickers on. I don't think he saw it. We didn't at the crime scene, remember?'

'You're right,' Rick answered. 'It was under her knickers. He fucked up.'

Jon clicked his fingers. 'It was in the book in Jake's tattoo parlour. That Betty Boop character.'

Rick's eyebrows were raised. 'Gordon Dean and victim three could have got their tattoos done in the same place?'

Jon shrugged. 'Might be worth checking how often that Jake character is asked to do Betty Boop.'

'Back again, gents? I can see you're tempted. You know it's two for one on all body piercings? You could go halves, one nipple each.'

Jon leaned over the desk, his frame filling Jake's vision. He knew his size was intimidating. But when the person was as annoying as this little twat, who gave a shit? Remaining silent, he stared until the provocative smirk began to wilt. Then he raised a hand and swept it towards Jake's head. Jake's shoulders came up, his eyes screwing shut in readiness for the cuff. But Jon's hand carried on over his head and came to rest on the book of tattoos on the shelf by his side. 'Ease up man, I'm only fooling around,' Jon mocked, taking a seat.

Jake's eyes opened again. 'Oh, you're after a tattoo?' But the riposte was delivered weakly.

Jon ignored the comment and flicked through the plastic sheets until he found the right page. 'Betty Boop. How often have you done tattoos of her?'

Jake curled the corners of his mouth downwards. 'Dunno. Not that often. Why?'

'Do you keep a record of tattoos as you do them?'

'Yeah.'

'What about paperwork? Receipts, sales dockets, that kind of stuff?'

He nodded. 'Of course. I keep accounts and pay my tax. Anything to help cover the wages of servants of the state such as yourselves.'

'Good man,' Jon smiled. 'Here's what we need to know. Not counting his latest delivery, when was the last time you bought gloves from Gordon Dean?'

Jake slid a file off the shelf and started working backwards. 'Here, fifteenth of January.'

'Great. Was that also the date you gave him his ladybird tattoo?'

Jake thought. 'Could have been. Yeah, in fact I think it was.'

'Can you tell us which other tattoos you did that day?'

He took a ledger down. Each page covered a month, with names of tattoos and their prices listed. His finger stopped halfway down the entries for January. 'Yeah, there's the ladybird. Twenty-five quid.'

Jon looked at the page. Immediately below it was an entry for Betty Boop, with sixty pounds written in the next column. 'I know it was a few weeks ago, but do you remember who had the Betty Boop tattoo?'

Jake closed his eyes and raised a hand to his face. His forefinger and thumb twiddled the silver bar in the top of his nose as if it was a dial that turned on memories. 'A young girl. I asked her for ID to check she was eighteen.'

Jon raised his eyebrows. 'And?'

'Yeah, she was. Well, she had one of those proof-of-age cards for pubs.'

'Can you remember the name on the card?'

Jake frowned, silent for a couple of seconds. 'No, sorry.'

'On which part of her body did you do the tattoo?'

He tapped the left-hand pocket of his trousers. 'Here, just below her knicker line.'

'What did she look like?'

'I don't know. About five and a half feet tall. Slim, pretty. Little button nose, brown eyes and short brown hair.'

'How short?'

Jake held a hand to just below his ears.

'Any distinguishing features? Scars, birthmarks, piercings, that sort of thing?'

'Could have had a few piercings at the top of her right ear.'

Jon and Rick exchanged a glance.

'Do you take customers' addresses? Perhaps for a mailing list?' Rick asked.

Jake snorted. 'I'm not that hi-tech. Keeping this thing up to date is about my limit,' he said, hand on the ledger.

Jon glanced at the payment column. 'How did she pay?'

'Cash. That's all I accept.'

'Do you remember if Gordon Dean was in here at the same time as the girl?'

'Yeah, he was. It was busy.' He gestured to the curtain at the back of the tiny room. 'I was doing another one.' He looked at the book. 'There you go, a Maori arm ring, seventy-five quid. They waited out here together while I was doing it.'

'Were they chatting?' Rick asked, leaning forward eagerly.

'I don't know. When the machine's buzzing I can't hear much out here.'

'But they were here for a while, sitting next to each other?'

He nodded. 'Easily for half an hour.'

Jon stood. 'Thanks a lot. You've been a massive help.'

As they trooped back down the stairs, Rick started humming 'I'm in the Money'.

'Don't get cocky,' Jon said, wagging a cautionary finger. 'There's nothing to link him with Angela Rowlands or Carol Miller.'

'True. But Angela Rowlands was in the dating game and Carol Miller disappeared while on some mysterious errand. The sooner more information's entered into HOLMES, the sooner a link to Gordon Dean will emerge. You wait.'

'I am, and I'm not holding my breath.'

Except for a few waiters laying tables, Don Antonio's was deserted. The manager sat down at a table by the door and tilted Gordon Dean's photo to the window. His accent had the necessary elongated vowels for Italian authenticity. 'Ah yes, Mr Dean, he dines here regularly. But this photo is from before his new haircut.'

'And he was most recently in when?' Rick asked.

The manager waved a hand. 'Four or five nights ago?'

'Five,' answered Rick.

The manager looked surprised. 'You know already.'

Rick nodded. 'Where did he sit?'

A finger was pointed across the room. 'The corner table, for two people. But he was alone.'

'And he left at what time?'

'Early – he always eats early. We cleared his table well before eight, I'm sure.'

'Do you remember what he was wearing?'

'Chinos, maybe, a black shirt. Smart casual, as they say.'

'And how did he seem to you? You mentioned he had a new haircut.'

'Yes. Very short and sticking up. His moustache had gone also. He looked like a new man, much younger.'

'Did he seem happy?'

'Of course.' The manager spread his hands. 'Always happy. But yes, he ordered a glass of champagne, even though he had no one to toast it with.'

Back at the station they started typing. A couple of hours later their reports were ready for handing to the receiver, who would read them for any vital information before passing them on to the indexer for entering into HOLMES.

Leaning back in his seat, Rick stretched his arms above his head. 'So, next stop, Gordon's choice of late-night venues?'

Gay Village here I come, Jon thought uneasily. 'Yeah, I suppose so.'

Rick glanced outside at the darkening sky. 'There's no point in going now – far too early. A swift one instead?'

Jon rubbed the back of his hand across his lips, thinking of Pete Gray's duty roster. His shift at Stepping Hill finished at eight o'clock. Under an hour's time. He wondered whether to suggest they follow him, see what he got up to after work.

But then he imagined Rick's response: their orders were to investigate Gordon Dean's disappearance, and that's what they should stick to until instructed otherwise.

Jon clicked his tongue. 'Actually, I'd better show my face at home. My other half will be forgetting who I am.'

'No problem, I've got some stuff to sort out.' Rick's smile was overdone and Jon suddenly wondered if he had someone waiting for him wherever he lived. Rick looked at his watch. 'Shall we meet at around nine?'

Jon was putting his jacket on. 'Sounds fine. Whereabouts?'

'Will you get the train in?'

Jon nodded.

'The Yates's in Piccadilly station, then?'

'OK. See you there.'

CHAPTER 16

Jon followed the A6 all the way to Stepping Hill hospital. The car park was three-quarters empty and he reversed into a shadowy corner space from where he could watch the porter's lodge unobserved.

I should be at home, he thought guiltily, picturing Alice sitting on her own yet again. Outside, splinters of rain started lacing the air. They hit the windscreen, fragmenting into diagonal lines of minuscule droplets. A swirl of wind pushed a flurry of little needles against the glass from another direction, cutting the lines and creating a crosshatch effect. Seconds later the shower picked up in strength and the delicate effect was lost forever.

Bang on eight o'clock Pete Gray emerged through the doors, a US-style leather flying jacket over his uniform. He made straight for a Staff Only bay and got into a pale blue mini van. Its lights came on and he pulled out, heading for the main road. Keeping his distance, Jon shadowed him back on to the A6, then to a terraced house near Davenport train station.

Jon parked on the opposite side of the road and turned his lights off. The droplets clinging to his windows twinkled under the streetlights as he watched Pete Gray unlock his front door and go into the dark house. The hall lit up, quickly followed by the front room. Gray walked across to the corner, stooped to turn the telly on, then plucked the remote control from a shelf crowded with large books. Standing there, he flicked through a few channels, his other hand wandering round to his buttocks, where it began a lazy scratching.

The flickering light abruptly died and he put the remote back on the shelf, walked over to the front windows and drew the curtains.

Jon's eyes shifted to the blue van parked on the drive. The rear windows were facing him and he could see a Confederate flag in the corner of one of them. There were another two stickers in the other window, but the writing was too small to be legible.

Jon waited until an upstairs light went on, then climbed out and crossed the road. From the end of the driveway the writing on the stickers was plain to see: *Shaggin' Wagon* and *If it's a-rockin' don't come a-knockin'*. He tried to see into the back, but the windows were heavily tinted. Perfect for ferrying around cargos you didn't want anyone else to see, Jon thought. Back in his car, he jotted down the house number and the van's registration.

★   ★   ★

'Hi, babe, it's me.'

'In here.' Alice's voice floated back to him from the kitchen.

He shut the front door behind him, eyes fixed on the corridor. Punch's head appeared in the doorway to the living room a second later. Jon dropped to one knee and slapped his thigh. 'Come here, you stupid boy!'

Once their customary wrestling match was over, Jon planted a big kiss on Punch's muzzle, then stood up and walked into the kitchen. Alice's back was to him as she passed the iron over one of his shirts.

'You're late,' she said, looking at him over her shoulder.

'Yeah, I know. Sorry. It's this case.' He stood behind her and slid his hands across her stomach. 'How's you and the bump?'

'We're fine.' Alice smiled, hooking a hand round to stroke his cheek. 'Been snogging your dog again?'

'No,' said Jon guiltily. OK, then, he thought, I'm a liar.

'Well, someone's given you dog-breath.'

Jon glanced down at Punch. 'Haven't you brushed your teeth?'

The dog looked upwards, the skin above its eyes wrinkled into a frown.

Alice resumed her ironing. 'Seriously, Jon, you'll have to be careful about playing around with Punch once the baby arrives. I was reading about

190

these parasites dogs can carry. They can make a baby go blind.'

Jon knew the parasites were only found in dog faeces, but he didn't want to reply in case doing so opened up a wider discussion that led to whether they should keep Punch at all.

'Did you hear me?' Alice said.

'People have kept dogs in family homes for centuries. I've never heard of babies going blind.'

'It's true. I read about it in *Joys of Motherhood*.'

Fucking stupid magazines, Jon thought. Filling their pages with any old shit, nothing more than a vehicle to carry advertisements for extortionate baby equipment. He unwrapped his arms and addressed the back of her head. 'I'll wash my hands each time I've touched Punch.'

'And no kissing him, either. It can't be healthy.'

Still behind her, Jon made a face, then looked down at his dog and gave him a big wink.

'Have you eaten?' Alice asked, folding up the shirt.

'No, but don't worry. I'll just grab a sandwich – I've got to go back out.'

'Again?' Alice's voice had gone up a notch.

Jon sighed and moved into her line of vision. 'We need to trawl some of the bars a suspect was last seen drinking in. See if anyone knows where he is.'

'Which bars?'

'Just some around Canal Street.'

A smirk appeared on Alice's face. 'With your new partner?'

'Yeah, why?' Jon replied, not liking where this was going.

'People will think you're a couple.'

Jon rolled his eyes. 'I hadn't thought about that.'

Alice grinned. 'You'll look lovely together.'

'Yeah, yeah. Actually, what should I wear? I forgot to ask him.'

Alice wasn't able to drop her smile completely. 'For Canal Street? That white ribbed T-shirt I got you from Gap. The fitted one – it shows off your muscles. And your old 501s – they hug your arse beautifully.'

Jon shook his head. 'You're bloody loving this aren't you?'

'Yes,' she giggled. 'It's hilarious watching you squirm. What if any of your rugby mates see you?'

'Well, they're not going to, are they? The last place any of them would drink in is the Gay Village.'

Alice cocked her head to one side. 'You might be surprised.'

'I'm not listening,' Jon said, walking towards the door with a hand held up. If men wanted to shag each other, fine. Just as long as they did it behind closed doors. Problem was, now he was heading behind closed doors himself.

After a quick shower he came back downstairs with his jeans and T-shirt on. Bracing himself, he went into the kitchen.

Alice looked him up and down, eyes lingering at his crutch. 'They'll be like flies around shit,' she lisped in a camp voice.

Jon gripped his temples. 'Just stop it, will you? This is really doing my head in.'

She laughed again. 'Seriously, though, nice touch. Black leather belt and black leather boots.'

Jon studied her face for signs of a piss-take. 'They're my old shoes from when I was in uniform. Doc Martens,' he said uncertainly.

Alice kissed him on the mouth. 'You look fine, honey. And stop worrying, will you? Anyone would think you're about to climb into a cage full of pit-bulls.'

As Jon slapped squares of ham between two slices of granary bread, she started folding the ironing board up.

'Here, I'll do it,' Jon said. Licking margarine from his fingers, he took it from her.

'Cheers,' she answered, one hand on the small of her back. 'Oh, I saw Fiona today. She called into the salon.'

'How was she?' Jon asked, sliding the ironing board into the cupboard under the stairs.

'Can you get the hoover out while you're in there?'

'Alice, forget vacuuming. You should put your feet up.'

'And who'll clean this place?'

'I'll do it. Tomorrow before work, OK?'

Alice shrugged. 'I'll have to get pregnant more often.'

Christ! The prospect of one baby was frightening enough. He looked round, hoping to see an expression on Alice's face that would tell him she was joking. But her back was to him as she sorted through the pile of ironing.

'So how was Fiona?'

Alice's hands paused. 'She worried me, actually. I mean, she's sorting herself out, looking to rent somewhere, so she's finally free of that arsehole she married. But she was going on about what she thinks she heard in that motel room.'

Jon stood in the doorway, arms crossed.

'She's determined to find out what happened to that girl Alexia, or whatever her name was. She went to some escort agency, the one whose business card she found.'

He nodded.

'The owner had interviewed someone, but didn't take her on. So Fiona said she's going to start asking street hookers if they know her.'

Jon pictured what went on in Manchester's red-light areas after dark. It was a sad fact, but even many of his colleagues considered the working girls fair game for a bit of fun. Stories occasionally circulated of prostitutes being invited into the back of police vans, of freebies demanded in return for increased patrols whenever a violent punter was on the prowl. It was a brutal place for Fiona to be wandering around asking questions. 'She needs to be very careful.'

'I know. But she's determined to find out if she's alive. It's like some sort of fixation.'

'Listen, if she tells you anything more about what

she's up to, let me know. I don't want her getting into trouble. There's some very nasty operators making their living from those women.'

As Fiona drove through Belle Vue her eyes were drawn to the Platinum Inn. Lights shone behind the curtains in a few of the ground-floor rooms. Several couples were walking along the pavement, and she wondered which were genuine and which were not.

Five minutes later she was driving round the back of Piccadilly station. Spotlights ran along the top of a huge billboard poster. Stretched out in their glare was a bikini-clad woman, leaning towards the camera, lips slightly apart. Fiona just had time to see the ad was for a forthcoming plastic surgery programme on TV before the road turned left, leading her down a dark street bordered by several locked Manchester University buildings. It was a part of town she was unfamiliar with, and she slowed to a crawl. At once she became aware of women she'd been oblivious of a moment before. Now that she was looking properly, she could see more of them, some hanging back in the cobbled side streets that branched off from the road. A sign caught her eye. Minshull Street. One woman stepped to the edge of the kerb and started to beckon. The car passed under a streetlight and, seeing that it was a woman at the wheel, the prostitute's hand fell.

Fiona speeded up a little, shocked by the existence

of a world which, until a few seconds ago, she had only been vaguely aware of. She carried on, the bright lights of Canal Street just visible away to her left. The girls here were dressed more gaudily, and had exaggerated perms and overdone lipstick. She glimpsed silver platform shoes and microskirts and couldn't decide if they were just drinkers heading into the Gay Village.

Soon she was approaching the brightly lit area of Whitworth Street. As pubs and restaurants began springing up the girls evaporated away. She did a U-turn and drove back, scanning the dark doorways and shadowy areas under trees. How had they ended up here? she wondered. How many were escaping violent fathers, husbands or partners? She stared at them, feeling sick with the realisation that, in many ways, the only thing separating her from them was the thickness of her car window.

Jon looked around the Yates's pub. A few commuters with coats and briefcases were sipping pints before their trains home. No sign of Rick. He leaned on the bar and decided on a pint of Stella to help settle his nerves.

The change in his hand didn't cover the cost of the drink and, sheepishly, he had dig out another fifty pence while making the decision to never drink there again.

He chose a table in full view of the entrance, put his drink down and started to shrug his leather jacket off. Then he remembered his figure-hugging T-shirt and changed his mind.

The top half of his drink disappeared in two gulps and he began fiddling with a beer mat, pondering the possibility that his new partner was reporting back to McCloughlin. Although he had initially suspected he was, now he wasn't quite so sure. The limited exchange between them at the third victim's crime scene indicated that Rick and McCloughlin had met, but it was a big jump from that to concluding they were in a hidden agreement.

Jon stared at his drink, considering his options like a chess player. Booze. That would be his next move. Get him drinking, then drop in an awkward question or two.

A couple of minutes later Rick walked in, still wearing his suit. Wilting with the realisation he had misjudged his dress, Jon gave a weak wave.

Rick spotted him and crossed the room, taking in Jon's clothes as he did. 'Shit, I didn't think we were going casual.' His eyes caught momentarily on the rip in the knee of Jon's faded jeans.

Jon moved his leg under the table. 'I thought we were trying to mingle a bit.'

There was an awkward pause, broken by Rick's half-chuckle. 'Well, you'll certainly manage that. Drink?'

Jon tipped his glass to the side. 'Go on then. Another Stella please.'

Rick returned with two drinks, Jon eyeing the other glass suspiciously. 'Is that a Coke?'

Rick took a long swallow. 'With a double gin.'

Resisting the temptation to pick up the drink and sniff it, Jon gulped down some more beer.

Rick took out the credit-card company's breakdown of Gordon Dean's last transactions. 'So, his card was swiped in Don Antonio's at seven forty-nine. Next is a bill for thirty-six quid in Taurus. Transaction went through at eight forty-one.'

'What's Taurus?'

'It's a sort of restaurant bar at the very top of Canal Street. Nice cocktails, decent menu. Might as well start there.'

Jon tried to form an impression of Taurus as they walked through the doors – muted lights and clusters of candles were fighting a losing battle with the shadows encroaching from all sides. He almost stumbled on the sloping floor that led up to the tables, half of which were taken by people dining.

The shelves behind the bar at the top of the room glowed with an impressive assortment of spirits. A glass-fronted fridge was stacked full with bottles of champagne.

Jon tried to look relaxed as he perched on a corner stool. A large glass bowl was at his elbow and he casually picked up one of the things in it. Holding it close to his face, he squinted at the writing. *Free safer sex pack for men – two extra-strength condoms and two sachets of water-based lube.*

He dropped it like a hot coal and glanced at Rick, just able to see the smile at the corner of his mouth as he addressed the barman. 'Hi, there. A double gin and coke and . . .' He looked at Jon. 'Pint of lager?'

'I'll get these,' Jon said, standing up and taking a ten-pound note from his pocket. They watched in silence as the barman poured their drinks. As he placed them on the counter, Rick laid down the photo of Gordon Dean, his warrant card beside it. 'We're trying to trace the movements of this man. He was in here last Thursday night.'

The barman looked barely past the legal age for drinking. He ran a hairless hand across the black top that clung to his perfectly flat stomach. Rings glinted on three of his fingers.

'Black shirt, hair was cut much shorter, and the moustache had gone,' Jon prompted.

The barman snapped his fingers and said to Jon, 'Yeah, he sat where you are now. I remember because he put his credit card behind the bar, even though he was on his own. He was drinking champagne by the glass.'

'Did he remain on his own?' Rick asked, elbows now on the counter.

'Yeah, I think so. He chatted to people a bit as they were waiting for drinks, but no one actually joined him.'

The barman moved off to serve another customer. Jon risked a look at the two women eating at the nearest table. They were engrossed in conversation, a bottle of Pino Grigio between them. He found himself studying them, wondering why they looked slightly odd. Then it clicked: their hair wasn't natural. The styling was overdone and he realised they were wearing wigs. Masculine fingers picked up a wine glass, and Jon looked away.

The barman returned a moment later. 'Why, what's he done?'

Rick put the photo back in his pocket. 'We just need to ask him a few questions. So, do you think he was cruising?'

The barman pouted. 'Not really. He was just getting merrily pissed. He left after a bit – gave me a good tip, as well.'

Rick straightened up. 'Thanks for your help.' Once the barman had moved out of earshot he said to Jon, 'Not much happened for him in here, then.'

Jon had to make an effort not to let his eyes stray back to the couple. 'No, but I guess it was early in the evening. What about all this champagne? He was celebrating something.'

Rick finished his drink. 'Maybe it was a case of him celebrating the anticipation of something. Like his next murder, for instance.'

He's not the killer, Jon thought, knocking back the rest of his pint. 'When did he get to the next place?'

'Natterjacks?' Rick studied the record. 'He paid the entrance fee at eight fifty-six, so he must have gone straight there.'

Music was thumping through the plate-glass

windows making up the front of Natterjacks. Two bouncers stood at the entrance, barely acknowledging the flow of customers heading through the doors.

In the small lobby area people were flicking ten-pound notes under the window of the till counter, then heading into the bar. When it was Jon and Rick's turn to pay they flashed their warrant cards at the cashier. 'Mind if we have a quick look around?' asked Rick.

She looked towards the customers behind them and called, 'Next!'

Inside, it was getting towards uncomfortably busy. Throngs of people filled the area in front of the main bar. Jon looked around, relieved that there were at least a few groups of women in the mostly male crowd.

Rick pointed to a flight of stairs. As they headed down them Jon took in the ornately carved wooden balconies. Male faces peered down from all around. He followed Rick into a quieter side bar where the music was lower but the temperature far higher.

'This place is busier than I expected,' Rick said, taking his jacket off and loosening his tie. 'Aren't you hot in that?' he asked, nodding at Jon's battered leather jacket.

'No, I'm all right,' Jon replied, aware of the sheen of sweat on his forehead.

Once again Rick took the initiative with the bar staff. The girl serving them shook her head.

'Wasn't on that night. Hang on, I'll get Steve.' She moved to the till.

A thin man appeared, the low ceiling behind the bar causing him to stoop slightly. After looking at the photo he scratched his head. 'I'm fucked if I know, mate. The capacity of this place is over seven hundred. There are bars and dance floors on three storeys.'

Rick took the photo back and looked at Jon. 'Drink?'

'I'll need a piss first. Where's the men's in this place?'

Rick pointed to the side. 'Nearest ones are down those steps and on the right.'

At the bottom of the steps was a small dance floor. A line of men stood with their backs against the wall, each holding a drink in his hand. As Jon came down the steps he could feel their eyes crawling over him. Suddenly he realised what it must feel like to be a woman. Self-consciously, he wove between the few people dancing, noticing that the song playing was the one on the tape in Gordon Dean's car. Relieved to find that the toilets were empty, he took a corner urinal, hoping no one would come and stand next to him.

Back in the bar upstairs he walked straight over to Rick, 'Listen, there's no point in staying here, is there?'

Rick glanced at him. 'No, you're right. Let's move on.'

Jon made straight for the stairs.

Outside, Rick said, 'That place not really your style?'

'What do you mean?' Jon answered, surprised at how uncomfortable the crude assessment he'd experienced on the stairs had made him.

'Loud music, cramped bars. All that stuff.'

Jon looked up at the sky, relishing the cool air on his face. 'I felt like a right twat. Do you drink in those places out of choice?'

Rick smiled. 'If I'm out to party.'

Jon sighed, not knowing if that was a euphemism for picking up. The basement dance floor hadn't looked like it was being used for much else. 'Nah. Give me a proper boozer any time. Somewhere you can be comfortable and have a conversation.'

As they were talking, Rick had led the way to a darker side street. Halfway up it a red sign seemed to float in the air. Crimson. 'Here we go,' said Rick, examining the printout. He paid to get in here at ten twenty-one, then forked out another thirty-eight quid at two thirty in the morning. Closing time.'

Jon took a deep breath in. 'Is this going to be like the last place?'

Rick couldn't help laughing. 'This isn't like any other place.'

'Oh, Jesus, I don't like the sound of that.'

Dodging the debris scattered across the cobbles, Rick went up to the door. 'Usually there's a queue.' There was a notice stuck to the door. 'Ah. Miss Tonguelash is away. The place is shut for the night.'

Jon looked at him questioningly.

'He owns the place as well as being the resident DJ, cabaret artist and stand-up comedian. Look.' He read out the notice, 'The bitch is back tomorrow.'

'So is it a nightclub or what?'

Rick stared at the doors. 'I'd call it a meeting of many minds. But yeah, basically it's a nightclub.'

'A gay nightclub?'

'Not exclusively, no. We're right on the border here between the Gay Village and the rest of the city. All sorts turn up, gay, straight, lots of cross-dressers. You even get working girls popping in off Minshull Street to grab the free packs of condoms. You know, like the one you were looking at in Taurus.'

Jon felt his face flush. 'But it's ten pounds to get in. That's more than any pack of condoms.'

'No, the entry fee is for the downstairs area where the cabaret and other stuff goes on. It's free to drink upstairs.'

'I can't work out what Gordon Dean was up to, trawling these places. Is he gay? Is he lonely? What?'

'You don't have to be gay to be drinking in the Gay Village. A lot of people come here because you don't get fights breaking out. A lot of women come here because they know they won't get hit on the whole time.'

Hands in his pockets, Jon looked down at his feet. 'Do you remember ever seeing Gordon Dean? It seems he was a bit of a regular around here.'

Rick shot him a glance. 'No. That occurred to me, too, but I don't think I ever did. Besides, if I had I wouldn't have kept it to myself.'

Jon looked at him quickly. 'I wouldn't blame you if you had. Admitting something like that would certainly get the tongues wagging round the incident room.'

Rick said nothing.

Jon stared off down the street. 'OK. Assuming for a moment Dean killed the Betty Boop girl, do you really think this is where he also picked up Angela Rowlands and Carol Miller? Can you see those two visiting an area like this?'

Rick sniffed. 'Doesn't seem likely.'

'So what's he doing drinking around here on his own?'

'I don't know. But we need to come back when this place is open, that's for sure.'

'Because?'

'I've just realised: the entry fee Dean paid? It was for two people, not one.'

'So maybe he did get lucky that night.'

'Maybe,' Rick replied, looking at his watch. 'Quarter to ten. Time for another drink?'

'On one condition,' Jon replied.

Rick raised an eyebrow.

'I choose the bloody venue.'

Jon marched to the top of the road. They emerged on to the slightly better lit Minshull Street, girls hovering in the shadows beneath the trees bordering an empty parking lot.

'Where are we going?' asked Rick, trying to keep up.

Jon crossed over, heading back towards Piccadilly station. 'A proper pub.'

Standing in the hushed and cosy confines of the Bull's Head a few minutes later, Jon turned an ear towards the low music coming from the speakers and nodded in appreciation. 'Police and Thieves', from the original version of *Black Market Clash*. 'What'll it be?' he asked.

Rick was studying the fireplace and leather-upholstered seats. 'Same again. Cheers.'

They sat at a corner table. Jon leaned back, closed his eyes and stretched his legs out. 'That's a relief.'

Rick looked amused as he took his jacket off and hung it on the back of his chair. 'Do they keep your pipe and slippers behind the bar?'

One of Jon's eyes opened. 'I wish they did.'

Rick chuckled. 'Is that leather jacket welded to your back or what?'

Jon's other eye opened. 'I owe my girlfriend for why I've kept this on all night.'

'How come?'

'When I told her we were going round Canal Street, she recommended I wear this.' He held the jacket open.

Rick couldn't see a single wrinkle in the T-shirt. He laughed and said, 'Is it sleeveless, too?'

'Almost.' He gestured to his upper arm. 'They come to about—' He stopped, realising Rick was taking the piss. 'Yeah, yeah, nice one. You should meet Alice. You'd get along.'

Rick glanced around the pub again. 'It's bizarre to think this place is just a minute away from Canal Street. I didn't know it existed and I must have walked past it dozens of times. I only live round the corner.'

Jon sat forwards and took a long pull on his pint. 'Whereabouts?'

'Off Whitworth Street. In the new development of flats on Venice Street.'

Jon looked blank.

'You know the Japanese restaurant on Whitworth Street?'

'Yeah, Samsi something.'

'The Samsi Yakitori. I live above that.'

Jon was thinking how much a flat in a spot like that would cost. 'That must practically overlook Canal Street.'

Rick nodded.

'What about the noise?'

'Doesn't bother me. Besides, it's what living in the centre of a city's all about. Part of the vibe.'

Jon looked down at the table and noticed Rick's manicured nails. He thought of the hair-removal treatment Alice said Melvyn offered male customers at the salon. 'Back crack and sack', he called it. He wondered if Rick went in for that sort of thing. Still looking down, he said quietly, 'How far back do you and McCloughlin go?'

He raised his eyes and studied Rick's reaction.

His partner didn't blink. 'How do you mean?'

Jon took another sip of beer. 'Have you not worked on an investigation with him before?'

Rick looked bemused. 'Never even met him.'

Jon kept his eyes on Rick, watchful for any body language that suggested otherwise. He spotted nothing. 'I assumed he'd drafted you in because you'd crossed paths somewhere in the past.'

Rick's eyes narrowed for a moment and a smile of realisation flickered across his lips. 'And you thought I might be a plant, sent to keep tabs on the detective who stole his glory over the Chewing Gum Killer?'

Jon held his glass up and tilted it in silent acknowledgement of Rick's powers of deduction.

Rick gave a short, sour laugh. 'Cheers.' His face turned more serious. 'The order appeared in my pigeonhole the day before I met you. Until then I thought I was staying in Chester House for another desk rotation. I've never said a word to McCloughlin before joining this investigation. I think he's a great SIO but I'm not his fucking lackey.'

'I'm sorry. It just seemed a bit dodgy to me, especially given the wink . . .' He realised he'd slipped up in his eagerness to appease his partner.

'Wink? What wink?' Rick leaned forwards.

Jon looked away, cursing himself. 'Just something McCloughlin did.'

'I don't follow you. Just something McCloughlin did when?'

Jon sighed, realising he was cornered. 'When

McCloughlin told me I was being paired with you, he gave me this wink.'

Rick frowned and Jon knew he was turning over the implications of what such a signal could have meant. 'As in suggesting something about me?'

Jon sat back, wondering how often Rick had suffered with this kind of thing in the past. 'I suppose so.'

Anger shone in Rick's eyes. 'Word soon gets round, doesn't it? Apart from you, I've told two people in the force that I'm gay. I thought I could trust them both.'

Jon drank from his pint, considering whether to offer some insincere assurance that, career-wise, it didn't make much difference. He decided to stay silent.

After a few seconds Rick took a massive swig of his drink and breathed out. 'Fuck him.'

'Who? McCloughlin?'

Rick nodded.

Jon clinked his glass against Rick's. 'I'll drink to that.'

Both men sat with their own thoughts, but this time the silence between them was relaxed. Jon traced his mind over their encounters with McCloughlin during the investigation so far. In retrospect it seemed obvious there was no agreement between Rick and their SIO. He realised McCloughlin's bitter attitude toward him was, in turn, souring his own perception. He'd have to make an effort not to let it affect him.

Still thinking about his partner, he said, 'So when did you know you were gay?'

'That old chestnut.'

Jon wondered if the question had caused offence. But Rick didn't seem bothered. 'I've always known. It wasn't like a bolt from the blue at eighteen.'

Jon thought about this. 'How do you mean always? You fancied men even as a little kid?'

Rick toyed with his drink. 'Did you fancy women even as a little kid?'

'I don't know. I remember watching *Top of the Pops* and getting pretty excited by Pan's People's dance routines.'

Rick laughed. 'Well, Brian Jackson doing press-ups on *Superstars* made more of an impression on me. But I didn't consciously fancy him – it was just that he was more interesting, somehow.'

'But how did you find it at school? Playgrounds can be pretty brutal places.'

'Never a problem,' Rick stated. 'I'm not a screaming queen. In fact, if it wasn't for this one girl, most people would never have guessed.'

'A girl you turned down?'

'Basically, yes. I confided in her, thinking we were mates. She went off and told her friends, so pretty soon I was rumbled.'

'And?'

'One particular bloke tried to turn things on me. I walked straight up to him and burst his nose. It's the only punch I've ever had to throw. Luckily it was a beauty.'

Jon smiled. 'Sounds it. So no problems after that?'

'None.' Rick finished off his drink 'Again?'

Jon found himself reassessing another pre-conception about gay men. 'When you started on the gin and Cokes I thought, here we go.'

'Here we go?'

'You know,' Jon faltered. 'Well, I thought, that's a bit of a ladies' drink. Then I thought, two of those and he'll be all over the place. But fair play, you look more sober than me.'

Rick grinned. 'Think about it. Which thing more than any other drains people's money, time and energy, ensuring they have to get up early every single day of the week?'

Jon frowned. 'I don't know. Kids?'

Rick clinked his glass against Jon's. 'Precisely. And what would a segment of the population do if they had no parental responsibility, plenty of cash and lie-ins every weekend? They'd go out and have a good time. Restaurants, bars, clubs, nice holidays. Here's to the power of the pink pound.'

Jon was left to stare into the dregs of his pint, mind wandering to the early-morning feeds now only weeks away.

CHAPTER 17

The manager of the women's refuge wrapped her arms round Fiona, engulfing her in a fiercely protective hug. 'You take care of yourself,' she whispered, tilting her head back to look Fiona in the eyes. 'And let me know how you're doing.'

Fiona smiled, thinking about the six precious nights she'd spent in the refuge. 'Thank you so much, Hazel. You've been a life-saver. You are a life-saver.' Waving once more to the women on the doorstep, Fiona turned to her car. Her bags were packed safely in the boot and she climbed in.

The drive to her bedsit took less than a quarter of an hour. She had chosen a place with good transport connections to Melvyn's salon. After all, in the absence of anything else, it was now the main part of her life.

She could accept how the majority of her friends had been slowly driven away by her husband's cold and suspicious welcomes every time they tried to visit. Her resolute denials that anything was wrong had hardly helped.

But the rift she'd opened up with her parents

was a deep and aching wound. She'd enjoyed a happy childhood, supported and encouraged by a mum and dad she rarely heard argue. That made it all the more painful when she began to realise her marriage to Jeff wasn't destined for the same level of success.

She'd married him in her late teens. At first everything seemed great as he got a graduate job at a firm of surveyors and she completed her final health and beauty qualifications. Then she got pregnant and gave up work. With the birth of their daughter Jeff became more preoccupied with work. He'd been given new responsibilities and they made more demands on his time. Time he seemed only too happy to give.

He started coming home later and later, often smelling of whisky. It was a way of relaxing, he assured her. The management encouraged a bit of bonding outside work hours.

But his promotion never came and he became more irritable, forever screening the household bills. She was no longer earning and he made her feel guilty about spending money he said wasn't her own. The balance of their relationship had shifted and her role edged more and more to the subservient. It resembled, she realised one day with a mixture of surprise and disappointment, that of her own parents. Dad the breadwinner, mum the housewife. Only her mum had never seemed unhappy with her role. Perhaps she was being selfish in wanting more. So she kept quiet about her doubts, playing the part of happy mum, hoping things would improve.

Then one day he punched her. A simple movement of his arm, but an action that set in motion a chain of events that led to the death of their daughter. After that he retreated into himself, drinking more and more, questioning every penny she spent. Getting his permission to start working again was a huge struggle. He feared the loss of control it would entail and paranoid fear began to consume him: 'You're going to leave me . . . You'll meet someone else . . . Isn't what I earn good enough?'

He didn't lay another finger on her for many years. But gradually the bullying moved from mental to physical. Pushes and slaps at first, then heavier cuffs. Finally, punches.

She thought about her parents. She'd shut them out after their granddaughter's funeral, too ashamed to admit how the accident had happened. But they'd known something was wrong. She couldn't stand her mother's entreaties, her father's furious stares. Both of them powerless to help her while she refused to admit there was a problem. Now she wanted to make amends but pride prevented her from calling them. Not until she was properly back on her feet.

The bedsit occupied the corner of the ground floor in a large Victorian house in Fallowfield. It was a student area, the bus shelters permanently full of people in faded jeans, baggy tops and battered trainers. How they chose to carry their books vaguely amused her. Some went for simple sports bags, others opted for ethnic-looking canvas pouches. All avoided briefcases, but that was just a matter of time. She smiled wistfully, wondering what Emily would have chosen if she was still alive.

After reversing into the yard at the back of the building so her car was facing towards the road, she removed the spare car key from her purse. Once out of the vehicle, she checked that no one was watching, then slipped it into a crack between two bricks at the base of the wall. That was a quick means of escape, if it was ever needed. After all, if he did somehow track her down and turn up with a few drinks inside him, she knew what he was capable of.

The hallway of the house was littered with unwanted junk mail and a couple of old copies of the Yellow Pages, still wrapped in plastic. A door opened and a man appeared, a box of old cooking utensils in his arms. He looked to be in his late twenties, but he still wore student clothes.

'Morning. You just moving in?' he asked cheerfully.

'Yes,' Fiona nodded, holding her handbag tight against her stomach.

'Me too.'

She smiled, glancing at the box.

'Cooking things. If you ever need any, just help yourself. People have dumped loads of stuff down in the cellar.'

Fiona looked at the door he'd just emerged from. 'Thanks.'

'Are you a mature student?'

Fiona felt herself flush slightly. 'No. I'm, I'm . . . just in between places at the moment.'

His smile faded as he assessed her answer, eyes shifting to her damaged eyebrow. 'Sorry, I didn't mean to pry.'

'No, that's fine. So, are you? A student, I mean?'

'Yeah, I'm doing an MA.'

'Which subject?'

Now he looked embarrassed. 'Classical studies. Latin, Greek. Don't ask why. I think it was my mum's idea, really. She wants me to be a journalist.'

Fiona smiled. 'Well, I'd best get sorted out . . . ?' She raised her eyebrows enquiringly.

'Oh, it's Raymond. Raymond Waite.'

'Nice to meet you, Raymond. I'm Fiona.' As he carried on up the stairs, she looked with amusement at his cumbersome trainers, complete with little Perspex windows in the thick soles.

Then she opened the door to her room and looked around, refusing to be dismayed by its dour interior. It was hers, that was the important thing. Another small step towards freedom.

She paused to sniff the air. The fusty smell she'd noticed on her first look-around still remained, despite the window being open. She brought her suitcase in, eyes lingering on it, attracted by the bottle of gin inside. Fighting back the temptation to have just one drink, she picked up her handbag instead. Air freshener, bleach and scouring cream were what she needed. The bare mattress on the single bed was patchy with stains. With some difficulty she lifted it up and saw the underside was only worse. As she headed out of the door, she added a duvet, sheets, towels and a new mattress to her list, aware that the cash Melvyn had given her was rapidly running out.

She returned a while later, ferried the smaller things through to her room, then returned to the car and began trying to pull the new mattress out from where it lay across the boot and folded-down back seats.

A first-floor window opened and she heard hip-hop music before a voice said, 'You need a hand, Fiona?'

She looked up to see Raymond leaning out of the window. 'Would you mind?'

'No problem.'

He shuffled round the corner a few seconds later, crouching to tie the laces of his absurd trainers. The oversized tongues lolling from the tops reminded her of a pair of thirsty spaniels.

They carried the mattress through to her room, and placed it by the side of the bed.

'I don't know what to do with the old one – it's disgusting,' Fiona said.

'Yeah, I see what you mean,' Raymond replied. 'Why not dump it in the cellar? That's what everyone else seems to do with unwanted stuff.'

'Do you think it would be all right?'

'Yeah. Come on, I'll give you a hand.'

They hauled it off the bed and carried it out into the hall. Raymond kicked the cellar door open, then pushed the mattress down the short flight of stairs. It came to a lopsided halt at the bottom. He flicked the lights on and carried on down, Fiona following uncertainly behind.

'There are all sorts down here,' he said, pointing to the haphazard stacks of boxes. 'Old clothes, crappy portable televisions, records, textbooks, files of work. Do you need any saucepans? There's a whole crate of them in that corner.'

Fiona looked around, shoulders hunching up at the sight of the huge cobwebs nestled in the exposed rafters above her head. Raymond tipped the mattress on its side and slid it across the dusty floor into a side room. In the centre of the room was a table with what looked like a stone top.

'What on earth is that?' Fiona asked.

Raymond leaned the mattress against it. 'This house would have been built for a wealthy merchant. This room was the pantry. In the days before fridges, the servants would have stored meat on it.' He slapped the bare stone with his palm. 'It's always cool down here. See the gutter running round it? They'd cover the meat with muslin and ladle water over it occasionally. It would have kept for days.'

Fiona shivered. 'Well, I never knew that.'

Two hours later, she peeled off her Marigolds and looked around her room. That was more like it. A bunch of flowers on the windowsill; the bed covered by a plump duvet, the creases still showing on its cover.

Once again, she found herself looking at the suitcase. *No*, she thought. A good vacuuming, that's what this place needs. She smiled. It was the perfect excuse to call in at the salon. Melvyn wouldn't mind her borrowing the Dyson.

'Hi there,' she chirped, stepping through the door. She caught a tense look in Melvyn's eyes before his face broke into a smile.

'Fiona!' he said, taking in her designer jeans and crisp white shirt. 'You're looking more shaggable every day. If I didn't swing the other way . . .'

'Oh, stop it, Melvyn,' she laughed.

'Cuppa?'

'Thanks, yes.'

Melvyn turned to Zoe, who was replacing curlers on a rack. 'Zoe, will you be Mum?'

Fiona waved a hand. 'Don't you worry. I'll do it.' Without waiting for a reply, she walked across to the kitchen area and started setting out the cups.

'So how are you, darling?' Melvyn asked over his shoulder while wrapping a strand of his customer's hair in tin foil.

'Great, thanks. I'm feeling so much more positive.'

'Brilliant – you look like you do.'

'I've just moved into my own little place. It's not much, but it's a start.'

219

'Where is it?'

'Ridley Close in Fallowfield.'

'Near City's old ground?'

'That's it.'

Melvyn adjusted the towel round his customer's neck. 'OK, that's you for a half-hour. Are you fine with those magazines? The latest *Heat*'s around here somewhere. It's got a great article about the contestants for that plastic surgery show they're doing on telly soon.'

'I've read it, thanks.' She sat back in her seat and began reading one of the magazines on her lap.

Melvyn scooted over to the kitchen area. 'I bet you've got it all spic and span.'

Fiona nodded. 'Just about. Though I was hoping to borrow the Dyson. Once the place is properly clean, you'll all have to come round for a drink.'

'Just say when.' Melvyn picked up the biscuit tin and gave it a rattle. 'Empty again? God, do we get through them in here. Zoe, be a love and nip down the street for some more biccies.'

As the door shut behind her, Alice appeared from her side room. 'Fiona. I thought I heard you.'

Fiona looked at Alice and her eyes widened. 'You sure your due date is still a few weeks away?'

Alice's shoulders sagged. 'Oh, don't. I feel like a beached whale.'

Laughing, Fiona pointed to the kettle. 'Tea?'

'Thanks.' Alice perched on the edge of a stool and made a cradle for her stomach with her hands.

'Fiona was just saying she's moved into her own place,' Melvyn announced.

'Where is it?' Alice asked.

Fiona grabbed a pen and paper from her handbag. 'Flat 2, 15 Ridley Close. Over in Fallowfield.' She handed the scrap of paper to Alice. 'You're all welcome to come round, but obviously the address has to stay secret. He has no idea where I am.'

Fiona caught that tense look on Melvyn's face again. 'What is it?' she asked.

'Nothing,' he said with a little shrug.

Fiona turned to Alice, but she was watching Melvyn. Fiona looked back at him. 'He's been here hasn't he?'

He didn't answer.

'The bastard,' Fiona hissed, fear and anger flaring up. 'What did he say? What did he do? Did he threaten you? He did, didn't he?'

Melvyn gave her a brief smile. 'Nothing more than a raging poofter like me's used to. Don't worry, he soon ran out of steam. Especially when I blew him a kiss.'

Fiona gasped, one hand over her mouth. 'You didn't!'

'That was a bit much,' Alice added with a grin. 'I thought the veins in his neck were about to burst.'

Fiona felt sick. 'Oh, I'm so sorry.' Her eyes cut to the front of the shop: could she be seen from the street? 'What if he comes back?' Now she felt genuinely scared.

'That's probably why it's best you stay away for a bit,' said Melvyn. 'I told him you don't work here any more. He'll soon give up.'

Alice went over to the reception desk and tucked Fiona's address into the back of the appointments book.

'Thanks, Melvyn, I really appreciate this,' Fiona said more quietly.

Melvyn fidgeted on his stool. 'Only thing is, Fiona, I can pay you your holiday money. But, you know how it works in here. Without you doing any treatments . . .'

'You want me to leave? Find a job somewhere else?' Her nausea increased.

'No!' Melvyn protested with a dramatic wave of his hands. 'You're one of the team. I didn't mean that. But what will you do for money? I mean, I could lend you some . . .'

Fiona shook her head defiantly. There was no way she was becoming a charity case for her friends. 'I'm fine for now. Listen, I'm just glad you're prepared to give me unpaid leave.'

They all heard the front door open and Fiona shrank backwards. 'Is it him?' she whispered, knowing her face was draining of colour.

Alice looked round the corner. 'Hi, Zoe. Chocolate Hobnobs? Good choice.'

When Fiona eventually set off for her bedsit, the salon's Dyson in the boot of her car, guilt hung heavy over her. She'd caused so much trouble to so many people. Dawn Poole appeared in her head. Another one she owed an apology to. Especially after sending Alice's other half round to question her.

At the end of the street she turned towards the A57, deciding to put things right at the Platinum Inn straight away. When she pulled into the car park a short while later she couldn't decide which slot to take, it was so empty. Inching slowly forwards, she decided on the far side, away from the day manager's silver Volvo and near the gap in the hedge she'd squeezed through several days before.

How hopeless her life had seemed that evening. Not that it was a whole lot better now. She thought about the cramped little bedsit that was her new home. Her money had almost run out and she had no idea how she was going to meet next month's demand for rent.

Her mind turned to her husband and she pictured him during his more pleasant moments. Laughing at something on the radio, delightedly rubbing his hands when his football team scored. She wondered what he was doing, how he was coping without her. He spent so much time at work, he'd never find the opportunity to clean the house. She imagined the state of the kitchen. Maybe she should call and see how he was. If he showed remorse for his violence and agreed to seek counselling, perhaps they could discuss the possibility . . .

She shook her head, realising where her train of

thought had so insidiously led her. 'What are you doing even considering it?' she asked her reflection in the rear-view mirror, focusing on the first glimmers of a life free of fear. 'You're not going back.'

She turned the radio on. The seven o'clock news on Smooth FM mentioned the Butcher of Belle Vue case. The police still hadn't been able to identify the third victim – once again, anyone who knew of a missing female in her late teens to early twenties with shoulder-length brown hair and a distinctive tattoo on her lower body was asked to call the incident room. A tattoo? she thought. That was a detail they hadn't included before.

A thin figure came hurrying up the path and went into the motel. Dawn. Fiona waited for the day manager to drive off before climbing out.

Dawn's face remained blank as Fiona walked through the doors.

'Hi there,' Fiona announced uncertainly.

'What do you want?' Dawn replied, busying herself with some paperwork.

'I've come to say sorry. I didn't mean to cause you any bother.'

'Didn't you? Well, you fucked up there, then. What did you expect would happen if you went to a copper and told him you heard someone being killed in the next room?'

Fiona sighed. 'What I heard really shook me up. Then, when I read the report in the paper later that morning . . . Do you realise her body was found only just down the road?'

'Of course I know that. Jesus, I've got to walk from the bus stop to here every single bloody day.'

'Oh, Dawn,' Fiona frowned in sympathy.

They regarded each other for an instant.

Dawn brushed a stray hair from the counter. 'It's all right, as it happens. He buggered off after a few minutes.'

Fiona kept her voice casual. 'So he didn't go poking around?'

'No, thank God.' Dawn reached for a cigarette, offered one to Fiona. 'I thought he was going to look around the room at least, but he just asked me if I'd ever heard of a girl called Alexia.'

Fiona was seething at Jon's claim to have searched the place. 'And have you?' she asked. 'The woman who owns that escort agency, Cheshire Consorts, reckons someone using that name tried to get a job with her. I think the same girl worked in a massage parlour just down the road near the Apollo. A place called the Hurlington Club.'

Dawn lifted the counter flap. 'You've been busy. Come on, let's have a coffee.'

They went into the back office and sat down on the comfy seats.

'Go on,' Dawn prompted.

'Well, I think it was the same girl. It could have been an Alicia, though – there was a bit of confusion with names.'

Dawn was searching for her cigarettes. 'And what did this girl look like?'

Fiona frowned. 'I don't know. Around my height with shoulder-length brown hair. Pretty, apparently, but quite thin in the face. She may be using drugs.'

Dawn looked up, a pinched expression on her face. 'How old?'

'Young. About twenty at the most.'

Looking relieved for some reason, Dawn opened a desk drawer and drew out a fresh bottle of brandy. 'Doesn't sound like anyone who comes in here. Fancy a splash?'

The glowing liquid shifted in the bottle. Fiona felt the muscles in her throat tighten with the anticipation of its warmth. She knew that having just one drink would be impossible and the thought of ending up in one of the motel's grim rooms again was just enough incentive to turn it down. Swallowing back a rush of saliva, she said, 'No, I'd better not. You know, driving and all that.'

She looked away and listened as Dawn poured a dash into her own cup. There was a clink as the bottle was replaced in the drawer.

'Why are you so determined to find this Alexia? If she even exists.'

Fiona looked fixedly at the tip of her thumb as it probed at the tops of her fingers, like a creature checking its brood. 'I just hate the idea of this poor girl being out there so alone in the world.'

'So do I. But there's only so far you can go. I think you should try and forget it. This search of yours is dangerous, Fiona.'

Fiona's eyes were still locked on her hand and when she finally spoke her voice seemed to have retreated deep inside her chest. 'I had a daughter once. Emily. But she died.' Her thumb foraged about, touching the tip of each finger. Counting them in. 'I lost her because I wasn't there for her.'

'What happened?' Dawn whispered.

'Jeff – my husband – had really gone for me. It was the first time he ever did. He stormed back from work early one afternoon. He'd been drinking and I did something – I don't know what – to aggravate him. He turned round and punched me in the stomach. No warning, nothing. He hit me so hard I knocked the kitchen table over as I fell. Emily saw everything. He'd left the front door open and she ran out into the road shouting for a nee-nar. She was four years old and that was her word for an ambulance.'

Tears broke from Fiona's eyes.

'He'd knocked the wind out of me and I couldn't get up. I could only lie there, gasping like a fish. It was a car. I heard its tyres screeching. I still hear its tyres screeching.' She swallowed a moan, unable to mention the thud of metal on flesh that followed.

Dawn put her drink down and grasped Fiona's hand. 'You can't blame yourself for that, surely?'

'I try not to, but it doesn't help much. After that

things were never the same. One moment's loss of control and our lives were ruined. I could see the knowledge of what he'd done eating away inside him. At first I was glad, but I forgave him eventually, trying to salvage something between us. He's never been able to talk about it. I tried so hard to make things work. He was my husband and, despite everything, I still loved him. But the more I reached out to him, the more distant he became. Then, maybe five years ago, he attacked me again. And you know what?' She smiled sorrowfully, shaking her head. 'Afterwards was the only time he'd shown me any affection in years.'

Dawn squeezed her hand. 'Don't waste your time. It's not you who's provoking him. He's the one to blame, not you.'

Fiona nodded. 'I know. But now I've got my head full of the noise of that poor girl choking. Apart from the man who attacked her, I may be the last person to hear her voice.' She looked up at Dawn. 'That room was used, wasn't it? You did let a couple in there.'

Dawn raised her cup to take a sip, using it as a way of breaking eye contact. 'Yes, I think so. It was a pretty busy night, though. People were coming and going and I was a bit worse for wear after all that brandy we drank.'

'But surely you remember handing the key over? Surely you'd remember a couple checking out again?'

'No. The key's missing and the lock doesn't work

228

properly, anyway. And if they went out by the fire escape, I wouldn't have seen a thing. What makes me wonder if it was used at all is the fact it was so immaculate. I certainly didn't clean it.'

'He did. That's what I heard him doing after it all went quiet.'

Dawn shrugged. 'Who knows what happened?' She raised her cup and took a generous sip.

Watching her, Fiona thought, God, I need a drink. She put her coffee cup down. 'I'd better go. Listen, I want you to know how much I appreciate your help that night. Are we still friends?'

Dawn smiled. 'Still friends. I just wish I'd put you in an upstairs room. It's all but untouched up there.'

As Fiona stood she said, 'Oh, I've got a place of my own. It's not much, but I'd love it if you could pop round.'

Dawn looked genuinely pleased. 'I'd love to. So you moved out of Hazel's place. What about your husband?'

Fiona flexed a wrist backwards. 'History. He'll never find me. I've been back and taken all the stuff I need.'

'Good for you. I'm so pleased.' Dawn reached for her handbag and produced an address book.

'I feel so excited.' Fiona said, then dictated her new address and mobile number. 'You'll call me soon?'

Dawn closed the book. 'Will do.'

★　　★　　★

Fiona ran the Dyson backwards and forwards over the same small, tired square of carpet. After a while she turned it off and looked around the bedsit. There was nothing left to clean. Deep inside her something began to stir. It felt like despair. I need something to do, she thought as the hazy image of Alexia appeared in her head. She looked at the clock. Quarter to nine. Would many girls be out on Minshull Street yet? Probably not. Her eyes snagged on the suitcase. The bottle of gin was like a beacon inside, emitting a signal she could no longer resist.

'Just a couple – God knows I'll need it where I'm going,' she said quietly to herself, grateful now the decision had been made.

The bottle chinked against the rim of the glass and gin glugged inside. She allowed the level to rise the width of another finger before righting the bottle. The tiny fridge was full, the bottle of tonic nicely chilled. She filled the glass to the top, then took a series of small sips, soon swallowing as much as if she'd given in and gulped it straight down.

Almost immediately the alcohol caused a lifting sensation in her head and without realising it, she let out a satisfied sigh. Now, what to wear? Nothing remotely dressy, that was for sure. She laid out a baggy top and plain trousers then, after sipping the glass dry, set off for the shower room on the first floor.

★　★　★

The train pulled in to Piccadilly and she walked slowly through the station, mentally running through what she'd say. Out on the concourse she looked down the slope towards the road that led into the city centre. The Malmaison Hotel dominated her view, yet now she knew that just a few streets behind a different world existed in the shadows. She broke off from the flow of people marching up to the bright lights of Piccadilly Gardens, headed down a dark side street and emerged into a nearly empty parking lot.

She heard the hoot of a tram as it emerged from the tunnels beneath Piccadilly station. The noise had a desolate note that echoed clearly through the night air. Seconds later the tram nosed into view, trundling round the bend in the hard metal tracks, wheels whining and squeaking in protest. Emotionless faces looked at her from within the bright carriages and then it was gone.

Making her way across the parking lot, she scanned the dark areas behind the trees lining Minshull Street on the other side, and soon caught sight of a lone female figure.

Unsure suddenly of what to say, she walked straight past the woman and found herself being dragged towards Portland Street. She emerged on to the busy road and looked around. A garish bar was on her immediate right and she went in.

The double gin disappeared in no time. She looked in her purse. She didn't have the cash to afford city centre prices, not after spending so much on things for her room. As she swung her knees round to climb off the bar stool, she nearly bumped a man who had appeared at her side, a fifty-pound note in his hand. He was late forties, thinning hair, but nice eyes.

'Sorry,' she said.

'Time for another?' he asked, nodding at her empty glass.

Fiona's mouth opened and shut. She hadn't been bought a drink by anyone other than her husband in years.

'Don't look so surprised.' He tapped the menu card on the counter – until then she hadn't been aware of it. *Thursday night – Singles night! Bottles of bubbly half price!*

His smile revealed a row of white teeth, one canine slightly chipped.

'Sorry.' Fiona shook her head. 'You caught me by surprise.' She felt her hand going up to her face. The cut over her eyebrow was becoming less and less apparent, but it still made her feel uncomfortable.

'Are you waiting for someone else? I mean, I hope I'm not . . .'

'No.' she shook her head again. 'I just popped in. I'm on my way somewhere else.'

'Anywhere interesting? I'm only here on business and I haven't a clue where to go.' He lifted a hand to his chin, allowing it to linger, the lack of wedding ring obvious.

'Er, actually, I'm just delivering a message. I shouldn't be long.'

He blinked, trying to work out what she meant.

'If the person's not there, I should be back in five minutes,' Fiona explained, trying not to look at the money in his hand. Thinking of how many drinks it would buy.

'So, maybe see you here in a short while?'

'Yes, hopefully.'

'I'm Martin, by the way. Martin Mercer.' He extended a hand.

'Fiona,' she answered, shaking it and climbing down simultaneously.

Minshull Street stretched off to her side like a dimly lit tunnel. In its murky depths she could see silhouettes of girls caught in the headlights of a slowly approaching car. Before apprehension could take hold, she strode purposefully forwards.

The first girl she got to was dressed in a surprisingly conservative way. Her skirt was a little too short, but the shoes weren't ludicrously high heeled and the jacket looked practical. She had heard Fiona's approaching footsteps and was keeping one eye on her and one eye on the road in front.

As Fiona slowed to a halt, the girl turned to look at her properly. Fiona guessed she was in her late twenties. 'Hello.'

She nodded back.

'I wonder if you could help me. I'm looking for a girl. I've heard she's often around here.'

The woman raised her eyebrows, so Fiona pressed on. 'She uses the name Alexia, but I'm not sure if it's her real one.'

'How come you're looking for someone and you don't even know their name?'

Her voice had a pleasant Scottish brogue and visions of unspoilt glens sprang up in Fiona's mind. How had she gone from there to here? 'Well . . .' Fiona dried up. The question cut straight through her story of Alexia being a friend's daughter. 'It's a strange story.'

'I bet,' the girl replied looking away. 'Never heard of her.'

Another car was slowly approaching and she stepped nearer the kerb, one hand on her hip. Fiona moved back against the tree trunk until the car had passed. When it had, the girl didn't turn back and Fiona guessed the opportunity for questions was over.

The next girl was older and slightly overweight. She also wore a sensible jacket but it was almost fully unzipped. A white lycra top bulged with flesh underneath. This time Fiona chose a more direct approach. 'Hello, I'm looking for Alexia. Have you seen her around?'

She turned, jaw moving and lips apart as she worked on a piece of chewing gum. Her open-mouthed expression lent her a vacant air. 'You what?'

'I'm looking for a girl called Alexia. Have you seen her?'

The girl scratched at her neck. 'Reddish-brown hair? This tall?' She held a hand up to the level of her ears.

Fiona nodded.

'Not for a bit. Who are you?'

'A friend. Her mum and me are best mates.'

The girl's voice hardened. 'Maybe she doesn't want to see her mum. Not after she sided with the dad over what he did to her.'

Despite the implications of the comment, Fiona felt a surge of excitement. This girl was more than just a casual acquaintance. 'She's sorry. And he's gone now. Her mum just wants her back. Listen, can we go for a coffee and talk?'

Another car was coming. The girl looked at it, then back at Fiona. 'If you're paying. It'll be thirty quid.'

Fiona's hopeful smile gave out. 'I'm sorry. I haven't got that kind—'

The girl cut her off. 'Prime time, love. I can't afford to be sitting in cafés right now.' She stepped towards the kerb and the car slowed to a stop.

Fiona turned away, feeling as awkward as if she was watching another person going to the toilet. She started towards the other side of the road.

The girl opened the passenger door. 'Try Crimson,' she called. 'She might be hanging around there, pocketing the free rubbers.' She got in and the car pulled away.

Crimson? What was that? Fiona started back towards the first girl, but she'd obviously heard the exchange. 'Second on your right, back that way.' She pointed behind Fiona towards the area of Canal Street.

'Thanks,' Fiona replied, turning round.

The side street was like a narrow alleyway, barely wide enough for a car and she hesitated before setting off down it. Black forms crouched menacingly in the doorways and Fiona couldn't be sure they weren't all full bin liners. With her first step, her heels caught uncomfortably on the cobbles. Up ahead people mingled in a pool of soft red light. They were going in and coming out of a doorway. She looked back towards the normality of Portland Street, bathed in brilliant light and she thought about the man in the bar and his bulging wallet.

CHAPTER 18

Jon was hunched over his pint, enjoying Beth Orton's tremulous vocals when he heard Rick's voice behind him. He looked round, relieved to see that he was dressed casually in a striped shirt that hung outside his trousers.

'Yeah, I'm all right, mate,' Jon replied. 'What are you having?'

'Gin and Coke. Cheers.'

As Rick took the bar stool next to him, a wave of aftershave washed over Jon. 'So, you all set?'

'Ready as I'll ever be.' Jon picked up his pint and took a sip.

They went over the day's progress, or lack of it. Still no one had come forward to report a missing female who matched the third victim's description. Missing reports from all over the country had been checked for matches on fingerprints, DNA and dental records, but with no joy.

All the information about Gordon Dean and the tattoo artist from Affleck's Palace had been entered into HOLMES and a new index on 'Body Art/Piercings' opened. Despite Rick's optimism, it failed to make any cross-connections with Angela Rowlands or Carol Miller.

They saw off their drinks, then headed for Crimson. Down the narrow side street they saw a number of people disappearing into the red glow. Jon thought of moths being drawn into a flame.

A group of three lads – late teens or early twenties – were gathered at the doors. They were wearing jeans, trainers and baseball caps.

'No chance,' Rick said quietly as they got closer.

Sure enough, the bouncers were letting other people in, but not those three.

'Fucking full of poofters, anyway!' one snarled, realising the type of venue they'd stumbled across. They backed out of the bouncers' punching range and began hurling abuse.

Jon automatically increased his pace, keen to get there before things escalated.

Rick put a hand on his arm. 'Let the bouncers sort it.'

One stepped out into the side street and the group shied backwards. They were all mouth. After spitting towards the door and making a last few gestures, the group of three walked straight towards Jon and Rick.

The first held up a hand, face red with excitement. 'I wouldn't bother. It's full of shirt-lifters.'

One of his mates cut in. 'Sharpy, leave it. They're probably a pair of bum bandits, too.'

The lad looked at Rick, his expression rapidly turning ugly. 'You fucking are, aren't you?'

In the periphery of his vision, Jon saw the lad's hand curl into a fist and shoot towards Rick's face in a vicious uppercut.

Jon swung his forearm out in a short chopping movement, knocking the punch away before it even got to chest height. The movement left his hand close to the lad's throat. Before either of his mates could react, Jon grabbed his windpipe, digging his fingers into the ridged cartilage. Then, locking his elbow, he propelled the lad across the alley, putting distance between him and his mates before slamming him into the wall. A jerk of his arm sent him stumbling away, coughing and gasping simultaneously.

He spun round and faced the other two. Air was pumping in and out of his lungs, the oxygen making him feel light-headed. He stepped forwards, waves of energy radiating through him, every muscle in his body singing. And in that instant he wanted – more than anything in the world – one of them to go for him. Knees slightly flexed, he stared at them, picturing the havoc he could wreak on their faces. 'Who's next, then?'

They looked at him uncertainly, neither prepared to make a move. Things hung in the balance as, off to the side, their friend started vomiting down the wall.

'Listen, mate, no bother, hey?' one said quietly.

Jon said nothing.

The other took a step back. 'Let's go.'

His fists still clenched at his sides, Jon watched

as they cautiously helped their friend upright and guided him away. With their retreat the adrenalin drained away and he suddenly felt dizzy. He leaned a hand against the wall.

'Why did you do that?' Rick was staring at him, shocked.

'He was swinging for you. Didn't you see?'

'The one you grabbed by the throat?'

Jon held up a thumb and finger slightly apart. 'You were this close to getting chinned. That would have been you flat on your back – the last place you want to be in a fight.'

Rick shook his head. 'Shit. I didn't see a thing.'

Jon dropped his hand and sucked in a deep breath.

'You all right?' Rick asked hesitantly.

He held his hand up again. 'Yeah, just give me a second.' He concentrated on taking regular, slow breaths and after a few seconds his heart rate levelled out.

By now the trio had reached the end of the alleyway. The two who could speak turned and shouted a quick chorus of 'Does he take it up the arse?' before running away.

Shaking his head, Jon pushed himself upright. 'Let's get a beer.'

When they reached the door, the bouncers waved them straight in with a smile, and one of them said, 'Good to see a bit of bashing back, mate.'

Fucking great, thought Jon. They think I'm gay, too.

The upstairs area was dominated by the bar spanning the back wall. The lighting was subdued, small spotlights directed on the swathes of red velvet that hung down the bare brick walls. The same material was draped round marble pedestals on which stood full-length nude male statues. Apart from the figleaves over their groins, they were styled like Michelangelo's *David*. Cascaded over the material at the base of each pedestal were piles of fresh oranges, lemons, apples, tomatoes, melons, grapes and peppers.

'Is that all real?' Jon said, trying to make it out in the half-light as he headed for the bar.

'Absolutely,' Rick replied. 'It's based on this amazing bar in Majorca apparently. The display gets changed every night. I think it helps that Miss Tonguelash's brother runs one of the biggest grocers at Smithfield market.'

As Jon watched, a barman plucked a few lemons from the top of a pile and threw them to a colleague preparing cocktails behind the bar. The place was about half full, with many people heading down a staircase to the floor below.

'What are you drinking?' Rick asked.

'Pint of strong lager,' Jon replied.

They found a space at the end of the bar next to more glass bowls of the same safe sex packs he'd picked up in Taurus. Jon leaned against the counter and looked around. Immediately he spotted a group of transvestites at a nearby table. Seeing their big shoulders, square faces and bad wigs, he remembered an end-of-season party at his previous rugby club where drag was the obligatory costume. The rest of the clientele looked fairly ordinary, though dominated by men. Rick was talking to the barman and Jon had to concentrate to make out their words over the music floating up from downstairs.

'That's great. Thanks for your help.' Rick slid a pint across to Jon.

'What did he say?' Jon asked, ducking his head and taking a massive gulp.

'He remembers Dean. A bit of a regular. Says he often saw him in here chatting to various people.'

Jon knew more was to come. 'What about the night in question?'

'Usual thing, floating around up here, went downstairs for a bit.' Rick smiled. 'But thinks he saw him leaving at the end of the night with a working girl who sometimes pops in to grab free condoms off the bar.'

'Any description?'

'Shoulder-length reddish hair, five feet eight, slim build.' Rick held up his drink and they clinked glasses. 'I reckon if we ask about in here, we could find out more.'

Jon looked around. 'I'll let you do the honours.'

Rick gave a little snort. 'Coward.' He walked over to the nearest table, the photo in his hand. From the corner of his eye, Jon saw heads shaking.

Five minutes later Rick returned. 'Nothing. You know what this means?'

Jon finished his drink. 'Time to go downstairs.'

There was a small counter at the bottom of the steps. After flashing their warrant cards to the woman behind it, they showed her the photo of Gordon Dean, but she couldn't remember seeing him.

Rick peered through the windows in the double doors before them. 'Not too busy yet.'

Inside was a lot darker. A glitter ball hung over the dance floor and several couples were milling around to 'Dancing Queen'. In the DJ box was a tall figure with a hairdo like Marge Simpson's. She was wearing a satin dress covered in what looked to Jon like a collection of luminous ping-pong balls. As he and Rick made their way round the edge of the dance floor the song came to an end. But rather than another starting up, a beam of light swung across the room and settled on Jon.

Shielding his eyes, he squinted at the DJ box, the figure now barely visible behind the spotlight's glare. 'Fuck me, this one's new in town.' The voice was high, the words drawled. 'Look at the size of him, girls. He can slip up here and butcher my snatch any time.'

As laughs of disbelief at the joke's poor taste erupted all around, the spotlight was cut and the next song kicked in. Despite his embarrassment, Jon recognised the trumpets building in strength before the drumroll started. 'Lola's Theme'. Whoops of delight came from the dancefloor and a group of transvestites started sashaying around singing, 'I'm a different person!'

When he reached the bar, Rick grinned at him and said, 'That was Miss Tonguelash.'

Jon could feel his face was still burning. 'I see how she gets her name.' He looked around uneasily and saw Fiona Wilson staring at him. A slimy-looking creep was standing next to her. She lurched over, her large gin glowing faintly under the ultraviolet light mounted behind the bar.

'Fiona.' Jon nodded. 'Enjoying yourself?'

She raised a forefinger and tapped him on the chest. 'You never checked that room. I spoke to the receptionist. She told me.'

Jon noticed that Rick was looking totally bemused. 'Rick, this is Fiona. She works with my girlfriend. Fiona, Rick, my partner.'

Her eyes slid unsteadily towards Rick. 'You're his what?'

'We're partners,' Rick replied with a grin.

She looked lost.

'In the police,' Jon added.

She started giggling. 'For a moment there I thought you meant—'

'Yeah, I know,' Jon interrupted.

The slimy creep appeared behind her. Jon instantly saw that he was trying to appear friendly and inquisitive but couldn't hide the look of concern that his shag was escaping him.

'Martin Mercer,' he said, extending a hand towards Jon.

'Jon Spicer.' Briefly, they shook.

'Fiona's certainly got an interesting taste in night venues. One minute we're in a place on the main road, next she's dragged me in here!'

Jon looked away from his shining teeth. 'So, Fiona, what are you up to?'

'Trying to find out what happened to that girl. You know, the one you couldn't give a shit about.' She was tilting towards aggression again.

Taking her elbow, he guided her towards the corner of the room, out of earshot of the creep. 'Fiona, Alice mentioned you've been making enquiries. You need to be careful.'

Fiona curled her lips in distaste. 'Someone's got to try and find out if she's OK. No one else is.' She took a large gulp of her drink.

'What did the woman at Cheshire Consorts say?'

'She had an Alexia come and try to get a job with her. But she thought she was on drugs. Sent her packing.'

'And now you're trawling round the red-light district, searching for her? Fuck, Fiona, it's not safe. Specially at the moment.'

Fiona leaned against the wall and rolled the back of her head against it. 'Not just trawling. I was told she comes in here sometimes. But no one's seen her since the night I heard someone being killed.' Abruptly, she tipped the last of her drink into her mouth, spilling an ice cube down her front. 'Bollocks,' she said, leaning forwards and shaking her top so it fell to the floor.

Jon glanced at the creep. He hadn't moved an

inch, unwilling to walk away from his claim. 'Who's the bloke?'

Fiona's head lolled in his direction. 'An old acquaintance.'

'Is that right?' Jon didn't believe her.

'See you around, Mr Spicer.' She tottered away.

The salesman whispered something to her, and they moved off towards the stairs. As they went past, Jon pointed at his own eyes then at the man's face. I've clocked you, the gesture said. Next instant, they were gone.

'She's heading for the mother of all hangovers,' said Rick.

'I hope that's all she's heading for.'

'So what was she on about?'

'She's the one who thought she heard a prostitute being strangled in the next room at that motel. She thinks the girl worked for an escort agency and now she's trying to track her down.'

'Sounds dodgy.'

'Exactly,' Jon replied. He looked around. 'I need a piss.'

The red bulbs lighting the toilets made the narrow room disorientating. Jon peered around in the half-light for any urinals, but saw only safe-sex posters lining the walls. He realised there were only cubicles. He took an end one and started emptying his bladder. Halfway through he noticed a waist-high hole in the partition wall between his cubicle and the next. At first he thought it was where the toilet roll holder had been ripped off.

But the hole was properly drilled and, besides, the toilet-roll dispenser was mounted on the back wall.

He re-zipped his fly and bent down for a closer look. He could see straight through into the next cubicle, where an identical hole had been cut in the next partition wall. He realised he was looking through a series of holes that ran the entire length of the toilets. The music got louder suddenly as someone entered the toilets. Jon quickly straightened up.

Back in the main bar he was shocked to see Rick sitting at the bar talking to Miss Tonguelash herself. Resisting the urge to flee up the stairs, he walked over and picked up his pint.

'Jon, this is Miss Tonguelash.'

She swivelled round, one leg crossed over the other, a slit running up to mid-thigh. 'Call me Andrea.' Absurdly long eyelashes fluttered and the back of a hand was proffered, fingers pointing down.

Not prepared to kiss it, Jon grasped it lightly. 'Hello.'

Looking mildly disappointed, she said, 'You've just been holding your penis. I do hope you used the sink afterwards.'

Jon hadn't. 'Of course.' He put his hand in his pocket.

Rick looked amused. 'I was asking Andrea about the night we're interested in.'

'Mmmmm,' she said, sipping her cocktail through a long straw, talon-like nails giving her fingers a more feminine taper. 'He was larking around down here with some little hussy on his arm.'

'A slim girl with brown hair?' Jon asked.

Miss Tonguelash nodded at the people on the dance floor. 'What colour hair do you think they all have?'

Jon looked. Banks of lights flickered on and off, bathing the dancers in a succession of colours. 'OK, I take your point. But you'd say this girl had darkish hair?'

'Girl? I used the word "hussy".'

'OK, hussy, then. But why call her that?'

'I imagine she'd only come in her to help herself to free condoms before her next trick. Looks like this Mr Dean was it.'

'You mean she was a prostitute?'

'Absolutely, darling.'

'And you don't mind prostitutes roaming around in your club?'

'Not if they're in here to pick up condoms. I'm all for safe sex, whatever form it may take. Aren't you, Mr Spicer? In favour of safe sex?' She brushed her lips over the end of her straw and fluttered her eyelashes at him.

Jon gave a businesslike smile. 'Of course. And did they leave together?'

'I can't say for sure, but it seemed pretty likely.'

He looked at Rick. 'Is that all we need?'

Rick nodded. 'Thanks for your help, Andrea.'

'Not at all,' she answered, eyes still on Jon as they turned to the door. 'Oh, one more thing.'

They stopped and turned back.

'You two make a lovely couple.'

Out on the street Jon breathed a sigh of relief. 'Christ, that was embarrassing.'

Rick chuckled. 'I thought you handled her very well.'

'Her or him?'

'Her when she's working.'

'But him at other times?'

'I don't know. Probably.'

Jon shook his head. 'And another thing. The partition walls in the toilets all had these holes cut in them.'

'Glory holes. Surely you've heard of them?'

Jon rolled his eyes. 'Yeah, it's just I've never imagined them to be fitted as standard. What a place.'

'But worth going. Now we know he didn't leave alone.'

'Yup.' Jon took the credit-card company's report out of his pocket. 'From here, he headed to the twenty-four-hour garage up near the Apollo. Two transactions. Cashpoint for £150 and the petrol station itself for £9.99.'

'OK, let's head there.'

They walked up to Minshull Street, Rick looking with surprise at the number of women hanging around. 'Jesus, do Vice realise it's got this busy along here again?'

'I'm sure. But until enough people start complaining, what's the point?'

'Bring on licensed brothels,' Rick said, dismissing a hopeful girl with a wave of his hand. 'Save everyone a load of hassle.'

They hailed a cab on Whitworth Street and pulled up on the petrol station forecourt a few minutes later. Jon tried the door, but it was locked. 'Intercom service after ten,' he said, reading the notice. 'I hate this.'

They held their identity cards up at the cabin window. The bald man inside reached to his left and a small speaker crackled. 'Can I help you gents?'

'Could you let us in? We'll talk inside,' Jon answered.

The man stepped round the counter, crossed the deserted shop and opened the door.

'Cheers,' Jon said, locking it behind him. 'Were you on duty last Thursday night?'

'Yup, I'm on duty every night but Sundays and Mondays. Those nights are my weekend.'

Rick showed him the photo of Gordon Dean while Jon got out the credit-card record. 'We believe this man called in here at 3:08 a.m. and purchased something to the value of £9.99,' Rick said.

The man smiled. 'Yeah, I sold out of three-packs that night.'

'Three-packs?'

'Condoms. Didn't you see the report in the *Manchester Evening News*?' He said proudly, 'Per head of the population, Manchester has more massage parlours than any other city in Britain.

And we sell more condoms than any other petrol station in the country. What with the Hurlington over there and all the saunas and working girls around Piccadilly station . . .'

'So what costs £9.99?' Jon asked.

The man pointed behind him to a twelve-pack on the shelf. 'There you go. I'd sold out of them by the end of that night, too.'

'Do you remember this man? He'd had his hair cut short and his moustache shaved off.'

He leaned over the photo. 'No, 'fraid not.'

Jon looked at the security monitor. 'Is that CCTV on all the time?'

'Yes. You want the tape from that night?'

'If you don't mind,' Jon replied, impressed by the man's willingness to help.

'There's a VCR in the back office. Can you watch it in there?'

'Sure,' said Jon. He paused at the coffee machine. 'Can I get you a drink?'

'I bring my own flask in, cheers.'

'Don't blame you,' replied Jon, getting a couple for him and Rick.

The tape was dated and timed, allowing them to picture-search through until 3:05 a.m. 'Here we go,' said Jon, sitting back and stirring his coffee.

The camera was set up high, looking down on to the forecourt below. Within seconds the grainy black-and-white footage revealed a Passat pulling up next to the cashpoint built into the wall by the cabin window. Gordon Dean, hair cut short and spiky and wearing a black shirt, got out first.

Then the door on the far side of the car opened. Jon and Rick leaned forward. A woman with dark shoulder-length hair got out. From the way she walked, Jon could tell she was wearing high heels before she came round the back of the car. Now she was fully in the camera's gaze, Jon took in her body. Quite tall, slim hips and a hard, tight arse. His eyes rose to her breasts as she turned. They were high and jutting, the type only possible with the help of surgery or a push-up bra. To his dismay, Jon felt sexual interest stirring in him. The thought of fast and dirty sex in an anonymous hotel. He suppressed the thought by saying, 'Gordon Dean's happily driving round town with a load of champagne in him.'

Rick nodded, eyes on the screen as the woman caught Dean up at the cashpoint machine. She reached out a hand and cupped his buttocks. The entire time he was withdrawing money her face was out of sight, nuzzling at his neck.

Next, she said something into his ear and disappeared back inside the car. He went to the cabin window, handed over his card and seconds later it was returned with a box of condoms.

The tape ran on and they watched as the car moved off, started to indicate right then disappeared out of the picture.

'Is it the girl in the morgue? I reckon it could be.' Rick commented.

'Time of death's totally wrong,' Jon answered. 'Victim number three died early to late evening, according to the pathologist.'

'There's always a margin for error. Especially when the body's been exposed to the coolness of the night air.'

Jon rubbed the back of his neck. 'OK, it's a possibility.'

Rick looked at the screen. 'I get it. The £150 from the cash-point is her charge for sex. Then she taps him for the condoms, too.'

'But I thought she snaffled all the condoms she needed from Crimson?'

Rick shrugged in reply.

As they got up, Jon snapped his fingers. 'Shit! We forgot the tape from the Novotel. That woman on reception was keeping it for us.'

'I'll bob in first thing tomorrow morning. Shall we call it a day?'

Jon looked at his watch and saw how late it was. 'Good idea.'

Rick wrote a receipt for the garage's tape and they let themselves out. The door clicked shut behind them and Rick buttoned his jacket up. 'I'll walk from here, I'm only five minutes away. The cab rank by Piccadilly station is probably your nearest.'

Jon glanced at the traffic. 'No, you're all right. There should be plenty of cabs passing this way. Nice work tonight, mate. I'll see you tomorrow.'

As they shook hands Rick said, 'Cheers for that outside Crimson by the way.'

Jon met his eyes. 'My pleasure.'

Rick let go of his hand and laughed. 'Yeah, I got the impression it was.'

As he wandered off Jon looked down, embarrassed that Rick had witnessed him in the alley spoiling for a fight. He found it hard enough to accept that, rather than fear or anxiety, the prospect of violence gave him a jolt of excitement. But he couldn't deny it was there, ready to erupt whenever anger flooded his veins.

He looked up the road, forcing his thoughts back to the investigation. Gordon Dean had signalled to turn right when he left the forecourt. The centre of town and the Novotel were to his left. He stared in the other direction, towards the roundabout and the start of the A57, leading towards the Platinum Inn and Belle Vue.

Even if Gordon Dean had driven the hooker from the CCTV footage straight to the motel and Fiona Wilson heard her being murdered, time of death was all wrong for her to have been the third victim. But as he shifted from foot to foot, uneasiness was gathering at the back of his mind like the beginnings of a headache.

CHAPTER 19

It was the angry throb bouncing back and forth between her temples that dragged Fiona from the depths of unconsciousness. She kept her eyes shut, trying to gauge if more sleep might be enough to make it go away. But then other parts of her mind started to function. She heard the sound of traffic passing in a continual stream. The smell of stale sweat and alcohol filled the air. Her eyes were still shut but she could tell it wasn't dark. She tried to turn over onto her back, but her arms were restrained.

Her eyes snapped open, trying to focus. She couldn't see. Something was covering her face and she started to panic. As she tilted her head back the material slipped from her face. A bedside table, the surface bare except for a lamp and a small foil square, almost ripped in half.

She began to wriggle and realised her arms were only caught up in the sheet that had been covering her face. Behind her someone grunted in their sleep. Her eyes went back to the square of ripped foil. It was a condom wrapper. As she sat up and straightened her legs she could tell that she'd

255

recently had sex. She was naked and a wave of nausea welled up. Looking over her shoulder she saw the salesman, his face pressed against the pillow and saliva glistening at the corner of his mouth. Meredith? Mercier? He was asleep next to her, a half-drunk bottle of champagne on his bedside table. Slowly she looked around. She was in a hotel room, her clothes lying in a pile on the floor next to the bed. Carefully she climbed out, scooped them up, let herself into the bathroom and locked the door.

She just got to the sink before violently retching. Two mouthfuls of acrid brown liquid came out and a sour, fruity smell filled her nostrils. She turned on the taps and as water started to wash the liquid away, strings of mucus-like saliva were revealed in it. She retched again.

Her brain felt like it was clenching in on itself, sending waves of pain right down into her molars. She grabbed a glass, filled it with water and started to sip. Her stomach heaved, but it stayed down. The self-loathing that trailed her heaviest drinking sessions, like a rusting old tanker being pulled by a tug-boat, loomed over her. But this time it was compounded by shame. She wanted to curl up and cry, but not here. Anywhere but here.

She climbed into her clothes, careful to keep her head up to minimise the pounding in her temples. A wash bag was on the shelf above the sink. Guiltily, she lifted out his toothpaste and squirted some onto her finger. She smeared it over her teeth and worked it around her mouth. Her tongue soon felt like it was burning and she thought that the pain served her right.

Looking at herself in the mirror, she adjusted her hair and used a tissue to wipe off the smears of mascara. The bathroom door clicked loudly as she opened it. Round the corner, in the main part of the room, she heard movement and held her breath.

'Jesus, what a night,' he groaned.

Fiona moved quickly to the door and let herself out. She eventually found a lift, walked through reception and out on to the street. Wincing in the bright light of day, she looked to her left and right. She was on Portland Street, Piccadilly Gardens and the bus terminal almost opposite. A digital clock read 8:43 a.m., cars filled the road and people hurried by, freshly showered and ready for work. Fiona folded her arms across her stomach and set off towards the bus station, eyes fixed on the pavement in front.

After thirty metres she realised the bar where she first met him was on her right. The doors were shut and a couple of cleaners were clearing the tables of glasses, many half finished. Her stomach flipped over.

The station was filled by a disorderly procession of buses, some trying to pull in and drop off passengers while empty ones queued to pull out. Engines revved, horns blared and exhaust fumes filled the air. Fiona felt like she could die at any moment. Miserably she approached a notice-board, trying to work out how to get back to her bedsit.

The bus dropped her off at the top of her road half an hour later. Breathing a sigh of relief, she slid the key into the front door and almost walked straight past the small pile of post with her name on.

Dreading they were bills, she opened her room, threw the envelopes on the bed and headed straight upstairs for a shower. Quarter of an hour later she sat down, a dressing gown on and a towel wrapped round her head. She selected the hand-written envelope first. A card from everyone at the salon, wishing her the best in her new home. Looking at their signatures, a tear sprang up in her eye and she forgot her headache for a moment. But the next letters brought it back with a vengeance. Payment forms for electricity, gas and water. Recommendation to pay by Direct Debit, £5 off if she did. Fiona looked at her purse – she'd barely had enough money for the bus fare home.

Woodenly she got to her feet and opened the cupboard above the sink. There was a couple of inches left inside the bottle of gin. She tipped it into a glass and sat down, tears springing to her eyes as she thought about the last few years of her marriage.

As Jeff's intimidation worsened, she'd started taking the odd nip of gin in the evenings when he was at the pub. Had fear or loneliness prompted it? Take your pick, she thought, raising a silent toast.

The nips became larger and more frequent. Finding the money for new bottles became ever more difficult. She'd got Melvyn to pay her partly in cash, hiding her supplies under the sink or inside the big casserole dish. Places he'd never look.

She hadn't dared consider how much she was growing to need it. Empties were spirited out of the house in her handbag, dropped in shop bins or even the hedge if the street was quiet.

Fiona looked at her glass and a wave of self-pity washed over her. God knows, if anyone deserves a drink it's me. It doesn't mean I have a problem, she thought, gulping the gin down.

CHAPTER 20

Once again Rick was in before him and Jon felt a slight pang of irritation. 'Up with the chirp of the sparrow again.'

'Where's that expression from?'

Jon thought for a moment. 'My grandpa used to come out with it. Must be an Irish one.'

'Yeah, you mentioned your family was originally from Galway.'

'A little fishing village called Roundstone. Ever visited the west coast of Ireland?'

Rick shook his head.

'You should do. Catch it right and it's the most beautiful place on earth.'

'So have your family always been in the job?'

Jon laughed. 'No, I'm the first. My great-great-granddad moved over here with his two brothers. They all worked as navvies on the Manchester Ship Canal. My great-granddad did, too, only he supplemented his income in another way.'

'Oh, yeah? Doing what?'

Jon couldn't keep the pride from his voice. 'He was a champion bare-knuckle fighter. Made enough from it to get the family out of their slum in Little Ireland.'

Rick grinned. 'Well, that explains a few things.'

Jon felt his face flush as he realised Rick was referring to the confrontation in the alley the previous night. 'Bare-knuckle fighting was a big thing back then. He was a real celebrity. Anyway, never mind that. What have you got there?'

'The tape from the Novotel. The receptionist had it ready in an envelope, bless her.'

'Have you been through it yet?'

'I wasn't in that bloody early.' He stood up. 'Shall we?'

They went through to the side room that housed the VCR unit. Jon immediately opened a window, then picked up an ashtray full of cigarette butts and placed them outside on the windowsill. Rick slid the tape in, turned the telly on and picked up the remote. The tape was time-lapse, comprising of a series of images taken at two-second intervals. The result was infuriatingly disjointed footage of the hotel foyer.

'God, shall I get the paracetamol now?' Jon sighed.

'From the hotel's records, he checked in at two seventeen p.m.,' said Rick, turning the tape on to picture search, making the images seem even more random. After ten minutes of the machine whirring, he hit Play again. 'There he is, still with his moustache.'

They watched Gordon Dean check in, then vanish into a lift carrying one large bag and a protective cover for suits.

Jon went to his notebook. 'Right, he was the last customer at that hairdresser's in Affleck's Palace at about six p.m., and he was eating in Don Antonio's by around seven.'

Rick hit the picture search again, stopping it at 6:15. A few minutes later Gordon Dean appeared at the top of the picture, crossing the corner of the foyer on his way to the lift. His hair was short, his moustache shaved off.

'I'm a different person now,' Rick sang under his breath.

Thirty-five minutes later he reappeared, now in his black shirt.

'OK, so far so good,' said Jon, consulting his notes. 'Now, he's out around town for the next few hours. We know he used his card at the petrol station at Ardwick Green at three oh eight a.m. Next activity is the cashpoint on Miller Street where he maxed out his card at six forty-three. After that he paid for the car park at Piccadilly station at seven oh five. That's another thing that strikes me as odd.'

'What?' Rick pressed Pause.

'That cashpoint is way out of the route you'd take driving from the Novotel to Piccadilly station. What's wrong with the Barclays just up on Portland Street or the ones in the station itself?'

Rick was looking blank.

'Come on, I'll show you.'

They walked into the main room and crossed to the street map of Manchester pinned to the wall. 'Here. Miller Street. Why drive all the way to there?'

'I see what you mean.'

Jon held up a finger. 'Unless you're avoiding city-centre cashpoints because you don't want to be seen.' He waved his finger in a circle over his head. 'Manchester has the most comprehensive network of cameras in any British city. Almost every cashpoint is covered by CCTV. But I'm almost certain that one out on Miller Street isn't.'

'Why the sudden subterfuge?'

'I don't know.'

Rick turned the remote over in his hand. 'How about this? He whisks her off to a rented property somewhere, snuffs her out and removes her skin. Then he dumps her on the grass in Belle Vue. But something goes wrong, making him panic. So he empties his bank account and flees town.'

'Or how about this? He picks up the condoms at the petrol station, and they head back to the Novotel and get down to business. An hour later, she's given him such an incredible time, he thinks, Fuck it all, let's get out a wedge of cash, jump on the train and go off somewhere to enjoy ourselves for a few days. Somewhere remote, no cashpoints anywhere near.'

Rick rocked his head from side to side, weighing

the argument up. 'Doesn't explain his shady behaviour. I'd say seven to one my theory's correct.'

'Bollocks,' Jon replied. 'That tenner's mine.'

Rick laughed. 'OK, we need to scan the Novotel tape for when he got in. Some time between leaving that petrol station and visiting the Miller Street cashpoint.'

'That's almost four hours,' Jon said, walking away. 'I'll get the coffees and paracetamol now.'

They'd got to 6:04 a.m. on the videotape when it clicked to a halt. They stared at the blank screen for an instant before looking at each other.

'Shit,' they announced simultaneously.

Rick ejected the tape and looked at the label. 'It runs from six in the morning to the same time next day.'

'So we need the next one. That's bloody typical.'

Rick pointed to the telephone number on the label. 'No worries, I'll phone her.' He got out his mobile and keyed in the number. 'Hello. Can I speak to Kristina, please?' He waited for a moment. 'Hi, Kristina, it's DI Rick Saville. I picked up the security tape this morning . . . Great . . . Listen, we need the one from the next day, too. You've got it there still? . . . Lovely. We'll be there shortly.'.

It was strange to walk into a scene they'd been observing as a recording for the past four hours. Kristina was there, the usual smile on her face.

'Hi, there,' said Rick. 'Thanks so much.'

264

'That is OK,' she answered, blushing slightly. 'Are you, how did you say, seizing it?'

Jon and Rick glanced at each other.

'Tell you what,' said Jon. 'Why don't we just whiz through it in your back office first? We're only interested in the first hour.'

'Oh, yes, of course. Please.' She lifted the counter flap and showed them through. After loading the cassette, she pressed Play and stood aside. Static swarmed the screen, before stuttering frames began cutting in. Then the picture took hold properly. The foyer was busy. Too busy for six in the morning.

Jon pointed to the time frame. 'Six fifty-eight a.m. Where's the first hour?'

Kristina looked crestfallen. 'The night porter must have forgotten to change the tapes over. I'm very sorry.'

Outside the hotel he kicked the base of the wall. 'Fucking typical.'

'So that's it, then. Until something else happens, the trail goes cold.' Rick said angrily.

'There's always the CCTV footage from Piccadilly station,' Jon said reluctantly. 'If we pick them up there we may even be able to work out which train they caught.'

'Of course!' Rick replied.

'Don't look so pleased. My other half got her bag snatched in the station last summer. I've seen the number of monitors in the CCTV control room. Since they redid the station for the Commonwealth

265

Games, you can't pick your nose in that place without it being on film.'

'Surely that's good?'

'Not when you're the mug who's going to be trawling through all the tapes. There must be twenty cameras in the main part of the station. More on each platform.'

Rick sighed. 'When are we interested in? The car was parked at seven oh five a.m., so let's say for the next hour.'

'Call it thirty-five monitors.'

'Thirty-five hours of footage. Surely it would be best to divide that out across anyone who's not on Outside Enquiries?'

'A job that dreary? I'll go another ten quid McCloughlin will give the lot to me – and that means you, too.'

Rick grimaced. 'No, I think I'll pass on that one. If we watch seven hours a day, that's five days in the video room.'

Jon groaned, thinking about the spartan furnishings and smell of old ashtrays. 'Have you got a video in your flat?'

'No, just DVD.'

'We've got one at home. We'll go through it all there.'

Rick nodded, 'So what now?'

Jon looked at his watch. 'We'd better check back in with McCloughlin. But I intend to make the most of the quiet spell.'

CHAPTER 21

Jon shouldered open the door of Cheadle Ironside's clubhouse and plonked his kitbag down in the bar. A scattering of other players were there, some gathered round a table as one flicked through a copy of the *Sport*, semi-naked girls pouting on every page.

'Hey, Jon! So you are playing – I thought you'd gibbed out.' This from a gnarled old man with bushy eyebrows.

'All right, Heardy. I got a break from work so I thought, Fuck it, it's Saturday, I'll go and sweat blood and tears with the boys.'

'You mean Alice has let you out for a few hours,' a young man with a shaved head called over, fingers curled round a bottle of Lucozade Sport. A chorus of knowing laughter broke out.

'Just wait till your missus gets up the duff, Westy,' Jon replied with a grin.

'I'll have to nip round and service her before that ever happens,' Heardy cut in, and the laughter turned on Westy.

The door to the changing rooms burst open and the captain, already in first-team strip, came in.

'Come on, you bunch of tossers. Kick-off's in forty minutes. Get changed.'

The changing rooms stank of Deep Heat. Jon shrugged his jumper off, loosened his club tie enough to slip it over his head with the knot still intact, then hooked it over a peg. He sat down, opened his kitbag and took his boots out.

The captain crouched in the middle of the room, a pile of rugby shirts at his feet. As he called out a number he threw the shirt at the appropriate player with an accompanying comment.

'Number three, Chico. We want those scrums solid as a rock today.

'Number six, Bamby. I want you leaping like a salmon in the line-outs.

'Number fourteen, Cookie. Have a run at your opposite man – he shat it last time.

'Number seven, Slicer.' A shirt hit Jon in the chest. 'The usual, please. Make them regret ever turning up here.'

Jon nodded, faintly amused that his nickname from when he played for Stockport had finally caught him up. The two players on the bench next to him were sniggering over a camera phone.

'Here, Jon, check this out. Ash's bird's had a tit job. Look at the pair on that.'

The mobile was thrust into his hand, the screen filled with a full-colour image of a young woman. She was smiling proudly at the camera, a mammoth pair of breasts straining beneath her crop-top.

Jon held the phone closer to his face, then looked over at Ash. 'She's really your girlfriend?'

He nodded, beaming, then cupped his hands in the air and wriggled them from side to side. 'B cup to a double D, just like that. The wonders of modern medicine.'

Jon took another look at the phone. 'What do they feel like?'

'Rock-hard mate. Don't even move when she's lying on her back as I'm giving her one. Marvellous, they are.'

A shirt hit him full in the face. 'Ash! Mind on the match, not your bird's plastic tits!'

Jon handed the phone back with a bemused shake of his head. Alice's breasts had ballooned during her pregnancy and, although he found the novelty of it amusing, he couldn't imagine her heaving them around on a permanent basis. To his relief, she had said exactly the same thing.

Half an hour later they trooped back in from the training pitch for the pre-match talk. Studs clattered on the concrete floor as they milled around, sheens of sweat covering their faces. Jon sat quietly in the corner. Breathing deeply with his eyes fixed on the floor, he enacted the first seconds of the match in his head. The need to immediately stamp his authority on his opposite man in order to shake his confidence and upset his desire to even play.

'Right,' the captain announced. 'Get your last-minute pisses out of the way, I want you back here in one minute.'

Jon rested his hands on his thighs and jiggled his knees up and down, thinking forward to the moment the referee's whistle would start the game.

'I want your minds on the match. First ten minutes, boys, we hit them like a fucking steam train. Are we letting this bunch of whining scouse bastards come to our back yard and turn us over?'

A few players growled, 'No.'

'I said: are we letting this bunch of whining Scouse bastards come to our back yard and turn us over?' the captain roared.

'No!' the team shouted back.

By now the captain was prowling up and down the middle of the narrow room, smearing Vaseline over his eyebrows. 'Get up! In a circle!'

Everyone stood, arms going around teammates' shoulders. The captain stood in the middle, rotating slowly. 'Look me in the eye, every one of you. Good, I can feel it, I can see it. You want this. First tackles: make them count. I want them knocked on their arses before they even think about getting a drive on. Right boys, let's get out there!'

As they marched towards the doors in single file, the coach, an ex-Royal Marine with no neck, stepped forward and yanked Jon to one side. Quietly, he said, 'Slicer, you missed the match at theirs, but the open-side flanker did all the damage. He's a dirty bastard, creeping offside, handling the ball in rucks, killing it every time he could. If he even shows a finger on our side of the ball, I want him taken care of. Understood?'

'OK, Senior,' Jon nodded.

The bar after the match was packed with people from both clubs, but the eyes of the Ironsides players were brighter. Standing around in small clusters, they went over the highlights of the match – the try-scoring moments, the big hits, the slick passing.

Jon stood at the end of the bar, a tubi-grip packed with ice covering his right hand. He took another gulp from his pint of orange juice and lemonade, his body still crying out for fluids after the demands of the match.

The captain stepped over to him and nodded. 'Great game today, Jon.'

'Cheers,' he replied, eyes shifting to the other side of the bar where a group from the opposition team were sitting.

The captain saw the direction of his gaze. 'I just had a word. He's a bit groggy, but otherwise fine. That was some punch you gave him.'

Jon shrugged. 'He was asking for it all afternoon.' Despite the casualness of his answer, he felt relieved. He always did what he needed to win a match, but after the final whistle he knew the opposition were ordinary people like him. They also had jobs and families to feed. And they couldn't do that if they were off work with concussion.

'How's the hand?' his captain asked.

'It'll be OK.'

'You ready for a beer?'

Jon glanced down at his near-empty glass. 'No, mate, I need to be going.'

The captain nodded in unspoken understanding. 'See you at training?'

'I'll try and make it. This case I'm on is a bastard, though.' He finished off his drink and slipped out of the side door.

Punch scrabbled to his feet as Jon stepped into the kitchen. Alice and his younger sister, Ellie, were sitting with heads bowed over a magazine. He swung his kitbag so it slid across the linoleum towards the washing machine, then reached out to his dog. Punch immediately sniffed his injured hand.

Jon was marvelling at the dog's ability to sense injuries when Alice said, 'Jesus Christ!'

'What?'

'Your hand. It's like a bloody balloon. What happened?'

Jon held it up, as if noticing it for the first time. 'Oh, someone stamped on it, I think.'

'Oh, yeah, I've heard that one before,' Ellie said with an impish grin. 'Sure someone's face didn't run into your fist?'

Jon shot her a look.

'Why you play that stupid game, I don't know,' Alice sighed. 'There's ice in the freezer compartment.'

Jon opened the fridge. 'Want a beer, little sis?'

'Oh, go on, then.'

'Alice? Anything to drink?'

'No, I'm fine, thanks.'

He took two cans off the top shelf, sprang the tabs a little awkwardly with his left hand and put one on the kitchen table. 'What rubbish are you two reading?' he asked, peering down at the glossy magazine spread out between them.

'It's an article called "Botox Babes",' Ellie replied without looking up.

The text was interspersed with photos of famous females snapped outside the premises of well-known cosmetic surgeons.

'Ha!' said Alice triumphantly. 'I knew she was looking too damn good.'

'You're right,' Ellie answered. 'What was that premiere she appeared at looking dog rough?'

Jon realised he was well and truly excluded from the conversation. He emptied the ice tray into the sink, scooped up a handful of cubes and placed them in a tea towel. Twisting it into a knot, he swung it hard on to the floor. There was a sharp crack and the ice shattered. Punch immediately started to sniff tentatively at the point of impact.

Jon sat down, then reached his left hand across to Alice's swollen stomach. 'How's the wee one?'

'Sleeping at the moment. But he was kicking like a bugger earlier on.'

Jon smiled and sat back.

A page was turned and, pointing at the magazine,

273

Ellie said, 'Oh, I was thinking about going on this diet. It's worked for loads of celebrities.'

Jon cocked his head to look at her. 'You don't need to lose any weight.'

Ellie smiled. 'Aah, thanks.' Her attention went straight back to the page. 'It looks really simple. And you can still have the occasional treat.'

'Alice,' said Jon, 'tell her. She doesn't need to lose weight.'

But Alice was studying the page. 'Yeah, it does look good. Maybe we could go on it together, once the baby's here. I'll definitely need to lose a bit then.'

Jon looked despairingly at Punch. 'Fancy watching *The Simpsons*?'

He'd just settled into his armchair when Alice leaned through the doorway. 'Don't get too comfortable. We're going out, remember?'

Jon made a show of slowly stretching out his legs, racking his brain for what had been arranged.

'You've forgotten, haven't you? Christ, Jon, you can be crap.'

He massaged a non-existent pain in his knee, mind furiously working. 'No, I hadn't.'

'So where are we off to, then?'

Just as the silence reached breaking point, he remembered. 'The parenting class at the health centre. Is it time to go already?'

Alice kept looking at him, suspicion showing in her eyes. 'Yeah, six thirty, just like the last three weeks. You're driving.'

She manoeuvred her stomach back out of the doorway into the hall. Wistfully, Jon put his can of beer on the table. The atmosphere in the meetings made him cringe, something about the happy looks on the organisers' faces as they cheerfully outlined all the trauma ahead. Or it could be the fixed smiles of the parents-to-be, happily grinning but all betrayed by the trepidation shining in their eyes.

'See you later, Punch,' he said, switching off the telly and walking resignedly to the door. Out in the corridor he could hear Ellie clattering about in the kitchen. 'You cooking, little sis?'

'Yeah. Only spaghetti, though. See you in a bit.'

'Good evening. Tea or coffee?' The elderly woman beamed at them as he held the health centre's swing doors open for Alice. After picking up their drinks, they proceeded across the tiles of felt carpet and into the meeting room. The hard plastic chairs were half taken by other couples and a pair of slightly embarrassed-looking women sitting on their own.

Jon glanced around, wondering how many of the other men resented the fact the classes had been arranged on Saturday nights. Quite a few, he guessed, judging from the looks on most of their faces.

He and Alice sat down, nodding hello to the couple beside them. Jon noted the prison tattoos on the man's fingers and wondering how many times he'd been inside.

'Oooof, that's a relief,' said Alice, stretching her

275

feet out in exact imitation of the woman next to her.

'Innit?' she agreed. 'My ankles are so swollen it feels like I'm on a plane the whole time.'

Alice smiled, 'Have you tried any of those soothing creams they do for feet? They're lovely.'

'No, but that sounds a great idea.'

The two women slipped easily into conversation about their shared experiences of pregnancy. Jon and the other man sat back, Jon relieved that the presence of their partners between them prevented conversation.

'Lovely to see so many of you here,' said the health visitor a few minutes later. She started drawing plain blue curtains across the windows. 'This evening we're watching the birth video I mentioned last week. It's not something you get to see on an average night's television, but it's well worth witnessing in advance of your own births I can assure you.'

Jon sipped his tea, realising to his annoyance there was no sugar in it.

'OK,' the health visitor continued. 'Are we all sitting comfortably?' She turned the telly on, then stood to one side with the remote for the video in her hand. Holding it within an inch of the machine, she pressed a button. The screen remained blank. 'Oh, bother,' she said, instantly flustered. 'This was all meant to have been set up. Mary, can you work this thing? The little screen on the video recorder says it's playing.'

Jon groaned inwardly as the woman who had

made their tea got up uncertainly. Hooking strands of grey hair behind her ears, she leaned towards the handset, unwilling to actually take it off her colleague. 'I don't know, Marjorie. Did Trevor plug the scat lead thingy in?'

'He said it was all ready. I don't know.' Marjorie thrust the remote at the video recorder again. 'Nothing.'

'Is it on AV?' Jon asked, sitting forward.

'Sorry?' she replied, sounding relieved and instantly offering the handset to him.

Jon stood up and, after checking the leads were properly in at the back, pressed the TV/AV button. Immediately the screen was filled by a close-up of the view between a woman's legs and a fast panting filled the room. 'Unless this is one of Trevor's private collection, I think we're in luck.'

'Quite, thank you,' Marjorie replied, a tight smile on her face as a couple of the men suppressed snorts of laughter.

Jon sat down, only to receive a sharp jab in the ribs from Alice.

Screaming started and a bulbous blue lump started trying to push its way out of the woman. Blood and slime were smeared across her inner thighs.

'We've missed the first bit, but never mind,' announced Marjorie. 'As you can see, the baby's head is just showing. The mother has been in labour for five hours and is fully dilated. Everything's in the right place.'

Her screams faded into sobs and a voice off-camera said, 'That's brilliant. You're doing brilliantly, Karen. Tell me when you feel the next contractions coming. Have some gas and air if you like.'

The camera panned upwards, revealing the distended belly, then the head and shoulders of a wild-haired woman. Jon was shocked to see she was totally naked, enormous and swollen nipples pointing off to the sides.

An ashen-faced man was sitting by the head of the bed, holding a plastic mask over her face. When he saw the camera was on them he tried to arrange the sheet across her breasts. As soon as they were covered she yanked it off again, eagerly gasping away behind the mask. He tried to take it off her face after a few more seconds and her hand clamped instantly over his, fingernails biting deep into his flesh.

'Karen here opted for a natural birth. At first. By the time she changed her mind, it was too late for an epidural,' Marjorie intoned.

Alice angled her head towards Jon. 'I want every drug they've got. Understand?'

'You've got it.'

'Oh God, oh God, oh God,' the woman on the screen started repeating.

Jon saw the muscles in her thighs snap tight. 'Oh Jesus, this is worse than that scene in *Alien*,' he whispered, making Alice choke on her sip of tea.

On the screen a pair of hands reached out and grasped the top of the baby's skull. 'OK, push Karen. This is it. Push!'

There was no way the head could fit through, Jon thought. A nerve-shredding shriek erupted and suddenly the head popped out. A glistening blue body laced with a waxy substance quickly followed, releasing a gush of bloody fluid behind. Unable to watch any more, Jon shut his eyes and heard the health visitor say, 'Now, as you can see, Karen is bleeding quite heavily from a tear here, but the hospital staff are waiting for the afterbirth to emerge before giving her some internal stitches.'

Jon thought of the cold can of beer on his living-room table. The film ended a few minutes later and he was able to open his eyes again.

'So,' said Marjorie, pulling back the curtains, 'you've now seen one of the most incredible things Mother Nature has to offer. And soon you'll be witnessing it for yourselves.'

She smiled at a room full of grey faces.

Jon took Alice's hand and gave it a reassuring squeeze. 'I'll be there for you, Ali,' he whispered.

She looked up at him and murmured, 'You might want to wear gardening gloves to the delivery.'

'What do you mean?'

She sank her nails into the soft skin on the back of his injured hand. 'If my birthing's any where near as horrendous as that, I fully intend you to share in the pain.'

Jon tried to extricate his hand, but she dug a little deeper, the sweetest of smiles on her face.

CHAPTER 22

Jon was buttoning up his shirt in front of the bathroom mirror when the doorbell rang.

'Ali! That'll be Rick. Can you let him in?' he called down.

He heard the front door open and a man with a foreign accent started speaking.

'Cheap videos! Latest Hollywood blockbusters! Three quid each.'

He peered down the stairs to see Rick standing on the front door step, a stack of cassettes in his arms.

'You must be Rick.' With a smile, Alice stepped back to let him in.

'Hi, there,' he said in a normal voice, adjusting the videos so he could shake her hand. 'And you're Alice?' His eyes dropped momentarily to her stomach. 'How long before the baby's due?'

Self-consciously, Alice placed a hand over her bump. 'Around six weeks.'

'Well, you look great. You've got that lovely glow no amount of make-up and sunbeds can achieve.'

Alice's smile widened and she glanced up at Jon. 'Thanks. Could you give my partner a few tips about paying compliments?'

'Yeah, mate, very smooth,' said Jon, sounding like a stampeding elephant as he came down the stairs.

Alice rolled her eyes. 'Right, I've got a train to catch. Enjoy the blockbusters,' she said to Rick, before turning to Jon and giving him a kiss. 'See you later.'

The door shut and Jon showed Rick towards the front room. Punch stood in the doorway, an inquisitive look on his face. Rick hesitated.

'That's Punch, my stupid mutt. Don't worry, he's soft as shite.'

Rick stepped forward and Jon watched as he gave the dog a cursory stroke with just the tips of his fingers. He moved into the front room.

'Want a brew before we get started?' asked Jon.

'Yes, thanks,' Rick said, looking at the photos of Jon, Alice and Punch in various outdoor settings. 'Who's she?' Rick asked, pointing to a younger girl who shared Jon's bright blue eyes.

'My little sister, Ellie,' Jon answered, watching him from the doorway.

Rick stepped across to the CD collection. The mix was fairly eclectic, including Miles Davis, Paul Weller, Radiohead and the Smiths. He searched in vain for anything more lively. 'Don't you have anything you can dance to?'

'Like what?'

Rick ran a finger along the collection. 'I don't know. Diana Ross, Kylie, Madonna?'

'Oh, you mean gay stuff?' Jon replied with an

innocent smile. 'I think Alice has got a copy of *Saturday Night Fever* somewhere.'

Grinning, Rick held up two fingers as he placed the videos by the machine.

When Alice got in at six they were still sitting there, dirty cups, plates and the remains of a packet of digestives on the table. Punch was stretched out next to an untidy scattering of videos on the floor.

'Mind if I let some air in, you stinky boys?' Alice asked, her nose wrinkling.

Rick looked mortified.

Jon hit the Stop button and stretched his legs out. 'What a nightmare.'

Alice undid the window latch and Punch's head was suddenly jerked up by the shift in scents as outside air blew in. 'Any luck?' she asked.

'Not a glimpse,' Jon yawned. He looked at the heap of videos beside the machine. 'We've been over seven platforms. Only another six to go. If we find nothing there, we start on the recordings taken from inside the main part of the station.'

'How about some tea? Rick, would you like to stay for some food?'

Rick glanced uncertainly at Jon, who was still staring mournfully at the pile of untouched videos. 'Er, thanks, but I've got something else already arranged.'

'No problem. How about tomorrow if you're carrying on with this?'

'Yeah, thanks, that would be great.'

'Good,' said Alice, heading off to the kitchen.

Rick turned to Jon. 'We're narrowing it down at least. Only platforms eight to thirteen to go.'

Jon nodded. 'Trains for Manchester Airport leave from platform eight upwards.'

'Yeah, but there's no record of him on any flights from that day.'

'And the trains out to Liverpool and up to the Lake District usually go from platform thirteen.'

'Which would fit with your theory of him being holed up in some remote beauty spot.'

'True,' Jon replied. 'But something doesn't feel quite right.' An image of Pete Gray popped up in his head. He'd still be on the daytime shift, due to finish at eight in the evening.

He was wondering whether to mention his visit to Stepping Hill hospital when Rick began clearing up the mess on the table.

'Don't worry,' said Jon, only just noticing it. 'I'll take care of it.'

Rick straightened up. 'Same time tomorrow, then?'

'Same time tomorrow,' Jon replied grimly.

Once Rick had left, Jon called down the corridor. 'Alice, have I got time for a quick you-know-what?' he said, knowing that if he uttered the word 'run', Punch would start leaping all over the place.

'Whatever,' Alice called back.

Her offhand tone of voice set off a small alarm at the back of his head as he poked his head into the front room. 'Punch, fancy going for a run?'

The dog arched its back and seemed to bounce on to its feet in a single movement. Jon climbed the stairs, the mess on the table forgotten behind him.

They ate in silence, Jon faintly aware of the pile of plates and cups Alice had carried through from the front room and left by the sink.

He wolfed his food down, then mopped up the remains of sauce with a hunk of white bread. 'So what did you think of Rick?'

'Nice,' Alice replied, sounding distracted.

Jon stopped chewing for a moment to study her. 'Just nice? Doesn't sound like you, Ali.'

She sighed and turned slightly in her seat. 'How old is he?'

'Almost thirty, I think.'

'He's doing well, then.'

'Accelerated promotion scheme. Graduate and all that. This is just a stint with us at FMIT. He'll be moved to another rotation in a few months, in between taking tests.'

He cleared their plates and carried them over to the others at the sink, noticing the time as he did so. 'Oh shit, babe, there's something I need to check out quickly.'

'You what?'

But he was already heading down the corridor to the front door. 'Shouldn't be long.'

He only just made it to the car park at Stepping Hill before Pete Gray emerged through the doors.

Again he went straight home and Jon watched his hazy form as it moved around behind the frosted glass of the bathroom window. He was shaving, getting ready to go out. Thirty minutes later he emerged through the front door, wearing brothel creepers, black jeans, a white shirt with metal collar tips and with his hair arranged in a glistening Elvis quiff.

Jon eased his car out behind the minivan as it set off towards the centre of town. They parked on a side road near Piccadilly station, and Gray hurried across the road and into a pub with faded curtains hanging behind its dirty windows.

Jon waited a couple of minutes, then jogged over the road. The poster behind one of the grimy panes of glass announced, *Karaoke Night. Singles Welcome.* Dotted round the poster were little stars with names written inside: the Beatles, Frank Sinatra, the Stones, Fleetwood Mac, Elvis.

Obviously aiming for an older crowd, thought Jon, slipping through a side door and making straight for the end of the bar. He kept his head down, aware of several glances in his direction. Safely in the shadows he looked around, assessing the atmosphere. A veneer of jolliness just succeeded in holding a feeling of nervous desperation at bay. More alcohol was required for things to improve. Luckily, doubles with mixers were half-price all night.

Pete Gray was sitting on his own at a table near the karaoke machine. A middle-aged woman was up on stage, ruining something by Alicia Keys. She reached the last line, flabby skin swaying slightly as she flourished her arm. A wave of applause washed weakly across the bar and her semi-embarrassed bow revealed a deep and doughy cleavage. As she stepped off stage Pete stood up. His body language was enthusiastic, short hand movements indicating how impressed he was. The gesture merged into a wave towards the bar, and the woman accepted with a smile that etched the crow's feet deeper into the skin round her eyes.

Jon hunched lower on his stool, eyes on the cocktail menu in front. Two drinks were ordered and Pete led her back to his table. After twenty minutes he returned for two more, but Jon noticed the barman only put vodka in hers.

The compère announced an Elvis song and Pete duly took the stage. It was a rendition of 'Love Me Tender', complete with wavering end notes achieved with a slight curl of his upper lip. Most of the song was directed at the woman. He even braced his legs and gave it a couple of pitiful hip shimmies. Jon wanted to gag but, from the size of her smile, the woman seemed mightily impressed.

Warding off the applause, Pete sat down again and quickly made his move. He put a business card on the table, then his hand slid across to hers and their fingers entwined. He leaned his head closer and said something to make the woman instantly stiffen. She leaned back, putting distance between them, and her eyes started cutting around the room. Somehow Pete had blown it. A minute later she got up and made her way to the ladies'. Clearly irritated, Pete picked up a straw and stabbed at the ice cubes in his drink. When it became obvious she wasn't coming back, he pushed both glasses away, retrieved his card and left. With Jon trailing along behind, he drove straight home. Seconds after going inside, the glow of a TV showed from behind the bedroom curtains.

Checking his watch, Jon saw it was just after ten at night. It was past the reasonable time for a phone call, but he couldn't resist. He opened his notebook and looked at the phone numbers at the front. Deciding that it wasn't fair to rouse Mrs Miller, the elderly mother of the second victim, he called the mobile of the first victim's daughter instead.

It was answered after a few rings, the sounds of a bar loud in the background.

'Lucy here. Who's this?'

'Lucy, it's Detective Inspector Spicer. I'm working on the investigation into—'

'I remember you.'

'Good. Sorry to call this late, but I needed to ask you something. Do you have a minute?'

'OK.' The two syllables were heavy with caution.

'You mentioned that you took your mother to a few singles' nights in town.'

'That's right.'

'Did you ever take her to a place near Piccadilly station called the Coach and Horses?'

'Yes – it was pretty much a disaster.'

'Pretty much? Did anyone make a pass at her?'

'No. Well, no one nice. There was this one guy who gave her his card. But he was such a creep I made her promise to never ring him.'

'What makes you say he was a creep?'

'Just his general attitude. I didn't want my mum being added to his list of cheap one-night stands.'

'What did he look like?'

'I called him the Fat Elvis.'

Jon looked across at Pete Gray's bedroom curtains and the blue light that flickered there.

It was almost eleven by the time he let himself back in through the front door. To his surprise Alice was still up, sitting reading a magazine in the front room, with the telly on low.

'Hiya, babe. Just getting a glass of water.'

Ruffling Punch's ears, he walked down the short corridor into the kitchen, noticing that the vacuum was back in the cupboard under the stairs. The carpet was spotless. In the kitchen he grabbed a glass from the cupboard and had half filled it before realising all the plates and cups had been washed up and put away.

He went into the front room and sat down in his armchair. 'You've done all the clearing up. I was going to do that.'

Alice sighed. 'When?' Her voice was flat and she didn't look at him.

'Tonight. Now.'

'I got tired of waiting.' She looked up and he saw her lips were pale and thin. The alarm bell that had started ringing earlier on returned, much louder now. 'You'd have started vacuuming at this time of night? I'm usually in bed by now.'

'Maybe tomorrow morning, then.'

'Or maybe fucking never!' She slammed the magazine on to the table.

'Where's that come from?' Jon said, surprised by her anger. From the corner of his eye he saw Punch slinking out of the room and he wished he could do the same.

She struggled to get off the sofa. 'Where's that come from? God, you're a prat at times, Jon Spicer.'

He stared at her thinking about how the investigation was floundering. McCloughlin was getting more wound up by the day, and his prowling round the incident room was making everyone tense. 'Ali, I'm not a bloody mind reader. I didn't do the washing up. Is that what this is about?'

She glared at him for a moment longer. When it became obvious that was the best he could come up with a cry of frustration escaped her. She swung her stomach round and waddled out into the corridor.

Jon remained seated for a few seconds, irritation

washing over him. 'We're trying to catch someone before he strips the skin off another victim, Ali,' he said, getting up and crossing the room to the door. 'You know the score with my job. Murderers don't tend to work office hours.'

She'd managed to get halfway up the stairs, one hand clutching the banister. He watched her shoulders rise and fall as she tried to get her breath.

'You're also about to become a dad. I'm struggling here. Struggling with this pregnancy, struggling with my job, struglling to keep this place clean for when the baby arrives.' She turned around and pointed down at him. 'I won't have you messing it up. And another thing. That bloody nursery isn't finished yet, Jon, and you promised – you bloody promised!'

A tear broke and she wiped it away furiously. Jon suddenly saw how vulnerable she was, saw how hard she was fighting to keep it together. The knowledge that he was responsible for her distress tore a hole in him.

'And don't ever bring details of your work into this house. That's a rule you made with me, remember? So don't fucking break it to try and justify your shit behaviour.'

Jon opened his mouth but couldn't think of anything to say. She turned and laboriously climbed the rest of the stairs. The bathroom taps came on.

He walked slowly into the kitchen, mind going

back over the last few days. He tried to remember when he'd last cooked, cleaned, tidied or thanked Alice for covering for him. He looked down at Punch, who stared up at him with sad eyes. 'I've fucked up big time, haven't I, Punch?'

The dog looked back at him in silence.

He climbed the stairs two at a time, knocked on the half-open bathroom door and looked in. She was brushing her teeth hard enough to remove their outer layer.

'Sorry, Ali.'

Still scrubbing, she looked in the mirror and he saw her eyes were wet. Guilt mushroomed in his chest. He stepped across to the sink, curled a forearm around her stomach and gently gripped her wrist in his other hand, stopping the toothbrush moving.

Leaning his forehead on her shoulder, he whispered, 'I've been a complete prick. I'm sorry. I didn't realise.'

The hand gripping her toothbrush lowered. 'I want this pregnancy to be a good experience.I don't want to be stressed and crying with our baby inside me.'

'I know,' he murmured, eyes shut. 'I'm going to make sure it is.' Gently, he began to kiss her neck, feeling her posture slowly soften.

After a few more moments she whispered his name.

'Yeah?' he said, head still bowed.

'I think I've got rabies.'

'What?' His eyes snapped open and he saw the white foam at the corners of her mouth.

'Grrrrr,' she smiled and, seeing her playful look, he felt his heart actually leap in his chest.

He turned her round. 'I promise, Ali, I'm going to—'

She cut him off by pressing her lips against his. He kissed her back, using his tongue to lick the minty mess away.

He felt one of her hands settle on his thigh and he leaned forwards, tracing his fingers hopefully towards her swollen breasts. His hand was lightly gripped and he opened his eyes to see her looking at him with her eyebrows raised. 'Right now, I'd rather scrub the toilet than do what's on your mind.'

Jon sighed. 'Not even a—'

'No way,' she replied with a grin, extricating herself from his arms and leaving the room.

Jon leaned his hands on the sink and stared at himself in the mirror, trying to remember the last time they'd had sex.

CHAPTER 23

Dawn Poole leaned forward and gently applied a finishing touch of mascara to the patient's eyelashes. 'There, you look wonderful.'

'Really? How bloodshot are my eyes?'

The bedside mirror had been moved, so Dawn didn't lie. 'They're not clear yet, but compared to a few days ago, they're so much better.'

The patient's head fell to the side, face bandages rasping lightly against the pillow. The front doorbell went.

'That'll be him!' Dawn jumped to her feet and hurried from the room.

As soon as the bedroom door shut a whir of wings came from the window. The robin sat there, head cocked, expectantly looking in.

The patient reached slowly for the biscuit on the bedside table, broke off a piece and crumbled it on the bedcover. With a hop and a flutter, the bird alighted centimetres from the red fingernails. It pecked a fragment, looked up and around, then pecked another.

Apart from the occasional blink, the patient could have been a statue. Or a corpse.

Footsteps were coming up the stairs and the bird stopped feeding to listen. As soon as the door began to open, it darted back out of the window.

Dawn stood aside, allowing Dr Eamon O'Connor to step into the room. The patient tried to smile.

Dr O'Connor walked slowly round the bed, brushed the crumbs off the cover and sat down. 'OK. Let's get these bandages off and see how your face is mending.'

'Will it hurt?' the patient said, fingers fluttering at the collar of the nightie.

'Not at all,' O'Connor said, opening his brief-case. After methodically cleaning his hands with an antiseptic wipe, he took out a pair of stainless-steel scissors. 'Now, hold that pretty head still and I'll just snip your bandages.'

The blades of the scissors came together and the outer layer of gauze fell away.

'Good,' O'Connor said, laying the scissors down. He took a loose end and slowly unwound the layers obscuring the patient's lower face.

As he reached the final lengths watery brown liquid had stained the material. 'You still have some discharge from the wound, but that's to be expected. Keep taking the antibiotics I prescribed.'

Carefully he eased away the final strip, revealing an oval face marred by a thin lacer-ation running along the entire length of the jaw. More bandages held a couple of splints in place down each side of the patient's nose. The wounds on the jaw were held together by a thicket of incredibly fine stitches.

Dawn stared with affection at his face. The masculine edges had been almost totally smoothed away. She thought the feminine look suited him far better.

O'Connor leaned forwards to survey his handiwork. 'Excellent, if I say so myself.'

The patient's eyes were wide. 'Will there be any scarring?'

O'Connor shook his head. 'With sutures applied this well? Keep out of direct sunlight and use the cream I give you, and no one will be able to see a thing. Now, my dear, let's take a look at your nose.'

He took a pair of tweezers from his briefcase and used them to prise away the gauze. Then he slid the lower blade of the scissors beneath and carefully snipped upwards. The patient sat rigid in the bed, eyes tightly shut.

Gently, the doctor pulled the covering away, easing out the little splints and eventually revealing a swollen nose, the skin stretched so tight it shone. Ugly bruising spread away from it, staining the skin beneath the patient's eyes a purplish yellow.

'Hold still. We're nearly done.' O'Connor took a pencil torch from the briefcase, bent forward and shone it up the patient's nostrils. 'Can you breathe through your nose?'

'Just. But the left nostril feels blocked.'

O'Connor nodded. 'It looks like dried blood to me, not how the cartilage has settled. Dawn, can you fetch some warm water and a towel?'

She jumped to her feet and went into the bathroom.

'So I'll be OK, Doctor?'

He smiled at the frightened-looking figure in the bed. 'Of course. We talked about how the process of becoming who you want to be will have its ups and downs, didn't we? You're doing well and I'm certainly happy with how things are going.'

Dawn came back into the room. 'Here you are, Doctor.'

'Thank you.' He arranged the towel like a bib over the patient's chest, tested the water with a forefinger, then removed a cotton bud from a small pot and dipped it in the bowl. He inserted the end into his patient's left nostril and rotated it very slowly. It came out stained dark brown with dried blood. 'Any pain?'

'No,' the patient whispered.

He turned the cotton bud over and repeated the action, slowly dissolving away more blood.

'Very gently now, try breathing in through your nose.'

The patient did so, eyes opening wide. 'I can.'

'Well, thanks for sounding so surprised,' O'Connor said, standing up.

'I'm sorry.' The patient tried to smile.

The doctor clicked his briefcase closed. 'I'll be back to remove the sutures in a few days. In the meantime, keep taking the antibiotics and don't, whatever you do, start to pick.'

The patient nodded meekly. 'Doctor, what about my other pills?'

'Absolutely not, I'm afraid. Not until you've completed the course of antibiotics. Don't worry, no appreciable differences will manifest themselves before then. You can go back on them soon enough.'

CHAPTER 24

The call to the incident room came in at just before six in the evening.

Barely controlled hysteria created cracks in every word the woman uttered. 'We've just seen the local paper. My daughter isn't here. She's not here. There's post in our hallway.'

'Please slow down, madam. What's in your hallway?'

'Post. We've been away in Lanzarote and she's not here.'

'Can you give me your name and address?'

'Debbie Young. Her name is Tyler. She has shoulder-length brown hair.' She dissolved into sobs and a man came on the phone, voice as flat as the fens.

'We live at 61 Rowfield Road, Stretford.'

'Thank you, sir. Was that your wife just speaking?'

'Yes.'

'And you say you've just got back from holiday?'

'We've been in Lanzarote for the past ten days. Tyler was meant to come with us, but there was an argument and she stayed at home. She's eighteen. About five and a half feet tall.'

'Does she have any distinguishing features you can tell me about?'

'Piercings in her ear, her right ear. And a tattoo.'

'What sort of tattoo, sir?'

He paused, having to force the next words out. 'It's of Betty Boop. Just near her hip.'

'Confit duck leg with grilled spiced fig?' the waiter asked, tendrils of steam rising from the plate in each hand.

'That's for my wife.' The man gestured across the immaculate white linen.

'And slow-braised lamb with sweet pepper mash for you,' the waiter replied, setting the other plate down with a smile. 'Enjoy your meal.'

He backed away, leaving the couple to examine their food, anticipation making their eyes shine.

'This smells lovely,' the woman said, picking up her fork and spearing a fig. She popped it into her mouth and bit down, eyelashes lowering in appreciation of the flavour.

'Good?' he asked, teasing a strip of meat from the cut on his plate.

She nodded, leaning back and staring across the choppy waters of the Manchester Ship Canal to the dramatic silver angles forming the Imperial War Museum North. 'You know, from here,' she commented, dabbing the corner of her mouth with a napkin, 'you can really see the meaning of Daniel Liebeskind's design. The Earth shard, the Air shard and the Water shard, all interlocking.

The three different arenas of twentieth-century conflict.'

Her husband sipped from his glass of Cabernet Sauvignon and nodded. 'He doesn't win the world's most prestigious building projects for nothing I suppose.'

Her eyes trailed back across the water, savouring the setting and atmosphere. Then they stopped, attention drawn to a large, pale object in the water directly below. A seagull was perched on top of it as it drifted slowly past, sharp beak tearing at the eye sockets of the corpse's hideously puffed-out face.

Jon stood motionless, staring at the body of Tyler Young. She'd left school at sixteen, flitting between several McJobs, bored, restless, convinced the world had to be a more exciting place. When she was younger, she'd won a beauty competition and she'd aspired ever since to be a catwalk model.

But her height had never progressed beyond five feet seven, a world away from the Naomis, Giseles and Carmens. More recently she'd been to Tempters, hoping to get work as a topless barmaid, hungry for paid recognition of her beauty. But the management had turned her away, with the advice that she needed to go up a bra size or two if she wanted a job.

That's what had caused the row. Tyler said she'd prefer to spend the money her ticket to Lanzarote had cost on plastic surgery instead. They'd refused to entertain the idea and she'd stormed out of the house.

Jon looked at her chest now, the skin of her breasts removed, pectoral muscles showing through the waxy layer of fascia. Could Pete Gray have done this? Tyler Young wasn't the same as the first two victims. For a start, she was over twenty years younger. The only way someone like Pete Gray could get access to a girl like Tyler was if he paid for it. Had she gone on the game to fund her operation?

He tapped a finger against his chin, arms pressed close to his chest in the cool air of the mortuary.

Or was she the prostitute from the CCTV footage of Gordon Dean?

He shut his eyes, trying to sift through his thoughts.

A door opened somewhere and he heard metal clang as a trolley was wheeled down a corridor. Soon the plastic curtains parted and the gurney entered the room, two technicians behind it. Jon glanced at the fibreglass shell coffin as they came to a halt by a stainless-steel autopsy table.

'If you're staying in here, you might want to hold your breath.' This from the pathologist, who entered the room in full protective clothing.

'What is it? Jon asked.

'He bobbed up in the Manchester Ship Canal, right outside the Lowry theatre's terrace restaurant. Ruined a lot of pre-performance dinners he did.'

301

'A floater?' Jon said. 'I think I'll head for the goldfish bowl.'

'Good move. He's been in a good week or so, I'd say.' The pathologist nodded towards Tyler's corpse. 'Can we put her away?'

'Yes. Thank you.' He stepped out of the theatre area and into the viewing room, wondering how to tell Rick that he'd been following Pete Gray.

In the theatre, the technicians opened up the shell coffin and hefted a large plastic sheet containing the body on to the autopsy table.

The pathologist prepared his implements on a side counter while one of his assistants cut through the adhesive tape sealing the sheet. Then she peeled away the folds to reveal a monstrously bloated corpse, the yellow skin marbled with a network of bluish lines. He was in a foetal position, ankles and wrists bound together.

Oh Jesus, Jon thought, never failing to be shocked at how death could turn the human body into a gruesome parody of its former self. He watched with a grimace as she carefully removed the plastic evidence bag the pathologist had placed over the victim's head. The neck was twisted round, the eyeless face a blob of marshmallow, short brown hair on top of his head looking like a skullcap.

That was enough. Jon started to walk out, but paused, eyes drawn to a red mark on the corpse's buttock. He pressed the intercom button and his voice came through the speaker in the theatre.

'Excuse me. Could someone take a closer look at the mark on his arse?'

One of the technicians stepped round and leaned over the body. 'It's a tattoo of a red devil, I think. A small figure holding a trident.'

A jolt shot down the length of Jon's spine. 'I can't see from this angle, but is there another one on his shoulderblade?'

She moved to the head of the table and peered down. 'Yes. The skin's distorting it pretty badly, but it looks like a ladybird.'

'Thanks.' Jon got his mobile out and called Rick. 'You can let McCloughlin know that Gordon Dean's just surfaced.'

'So the pathologist reckons he'd been in the water for about ten days?' said Rick, sipping his gin and Coke.

Jon put his pint down on the table. 'Yup.'

Rick's lips moved slightly as he counted out a sequence. 'That still puts him in the time frame for Tyler Young's murder. Maybe he killed her then, for some reason decided to top himself.'

Jon shook his head. 'You're not having that tenner. With his wrists and ankles bound as they were, it couldn't have been suicide.'

Rick rubbed his temples. 'But if he didn't kill Young we're no closer to catching the Butcher.'

'Actually, that might not be the case.'

'Why not? What do you mean?'

Jon flipped a beer mat over, but failed to catch

it. He looked Rick in the face. 'We've still got the Pete Gray lead. I've been following it up.'

Rick crossed his arms and sat back. 'When have you found the time for that?'

Jon shrugged. 'Evenings. I've only caught him coming off his shift a couple of times. Followed him to a bar the other night.'

'When were you planning on letting me know?'

'I was about to when Gordon Dean's body was wheeled in.'

'Really?' Rick asked sarcastically.

Jon met his eyes. 'I was. He went to a singles' karaoke night dressed like Elvis. Got chatting to a woman there, looked like he was about to pull. Gave her his card, then said something to scare her off.'

Rick was looking more and more pissed off. 'You did all this behind my back?'

'I didn't think you'd be interested in shadowing Pete Gray after the amount of hours we've been putting in during the day.'

'Don't give me that shit. You didn't even ask. We're meant to be working this together.' He drained his drink and stood up to go.

'We are. Just hear me out, will you?'

Rick remained standing.

'I rang Lucy Rowlands, the first victim's daughter. She said a guy gave her mum his card at a singles' night one time. It was in the same bar I followed him to the other night. Lucy said the guy was a total creep, called him The Fat Elvis.'

'Did you speak to the woman he scared off?'

'No, because by the time I got back to the bar after following him home, she'd gone. But it means he could have had contact with Angela Rowlands and Carol Miller.'

'Good work. I'll let you fill in McCloughlin.' Rick walked out without another word.

Jon sighed, then took a mouthful of beer. It didn't make him feel any better.

His mobile started buzzing in his pocket. Nikki Kingston, the crime-scene manager's name showed on his screen.

'Hi, Nikki. How are you?'

'Good, thanks. Why're you sounding depressed?'

'Long story.'

'Good. You can tell me over those drinks you owe me. Where are you?'

He'd finished his pint by the time Nikki walked in to the Bull's Head, a small briefcase under one arm.

Jon waved her over. 'So what news have you got?'

'Uh-huh.' She held up a finger. 'Drinks first.'

Jon smiled and got to his feet. 'What'll it be?'

'Gin and dry martini, thanks.'

Jon returned with their drinks and sat down.

Nikki was checking the ashtray for recently stubbed-out butts. 'Still not smoking?'

'Yes,' Jon protested.

She looked provocatively at him out of the corner of her eye.

'What?' he laughed, holding out his hands. 'What do I have to do to convince you?'

Looking at the ashtray, she said, 'There's only way I could really tell none of these were smoked by you. But the night's a bit young for that.' She moved the ashtray to another table. 'So what's the long story?'

Jon's smile disappeared. 'That guy I'm working with, Rick Saville?'

'Oh yes?' Nikki took a sip, looking over the rim of her glass.

Jon remembered the glance that had passed between them at Tyler Young's crime scene. The pang of jealousy returned and he found himself saying, 'Liked him, did you?'

She smiled. 'He's not bad. Doubt I'm his cup of tea, though.'

Her answer confused him.

Nikki gave his hand a sympathetic squeeze. 'I think he's gay.'

Jon's mouth dropped open. 'He is.'

'No shit, Sherlock? How long did it take you to figure that out?'

'A bit. How did you know?'

'Call it feminine intuition.' She paused, then looked at him. 'Was that a glimpse of the little green monster I just saw?'

'No.' He felt a blush creeping up his neck. Shit!

'It was,' she smiled, a note of triumph in her voice. 'You were feeling jealous! Even if he wasn't gay, he's not my type.' Her eyes went to Jon's scarred hands, travelled up to his lips, then his eyes. 'I like my men a bit rougher at the edges.'

Jon looked away. 'I've been following up a bit of a lead, but in my own time.'

'So?'

'I didn't let him know. Or rather, I just did let him know and he spat his dummy out.'

'Well, there you go. Gay men can get a bit emotional.'

Jon sprang to his defence. 'No, it was fair enough. I wasn't being straight with him.' A look bounced between them. 'If you know what I mean.'

'I think so,' she smirked.

Jon took a gulp of his drink. 'Actually, the lead has to do with the tests I asked you to run. So come on, what's this hot news you have for me?'

She reached for her briefcase. 'You asked me to run an ACE-V on the fingerprints and a DNA analysis on a plastic cup.'

'That's right.'

'I didn't come back with anything conclusive on the fingerprints.'

'You said you'd recovered a partial from the inside of that glove we found by the third victim's body.'

'Yes, but it was only a partial. Comparing it to the couple on the cup you gave me resulted in, as I said, nothing conclusive. A couple of points matched, but that's nowhere near enough, as you know. However, I ran the print through NAFIS. You do know the owner has a record?'

'Yes, don't worry.'

'OK. Are you ready for the good news?'

'Go on.'

'The DNA test from the plastic cup was successful, although not with anything from the scene of the third victim.'

'But?'

'You still owe me another drink, yeah?'

'Yes! Come on, what is it?'

'I ran it against the DNA samples recovered from Carol Miller and Angela Rowlands.'

'And?' Jon crossed his fingers.

'It matches the DNA found on the vaginal swab from Angela Rowlands.'

Jon clenched his fists tight as he leaned forwards. 'Yes! This means a guy I've got my eye on has been in contact with two of the Butcher's victims. Nikki, I could kiss you.'

Before he could move, she brought her lips up against his. A hand slid along his jaw, round the back of his neck, and he felt the softness of her tongue probing his lips. For a second he remained still, his nerves zinging. Then he pulled back.

Her eyes slowly opened. 'You really haven't been smoking.'

'I'd better get those drinks,' he whispered hoarsely.

Nikki smiled.

He stood at the bar, mind racing. A raw desire for sex was threatening to overwhelm him and he knew that staying for another drink would lead to the point of no return.

The barman came over. 'Same again?'

Jon hesitated, hand on the fiver in his pocket. 'Yes, please.'

As the drinks were poured, Jon tried to focus on Nikki's revelation. It had to make Pete Gray the prime suspect. They had enough to haul him in there and then. He paid for the drinks and carried them over to the table. But the look of hurt on Rick's face refused to fade in his mind. After putting the drinks down, he said, 'Nikki, I'm really sorry to do this, but I've got to catch Rick up and let him know the news.'

She looked at him, a half-smile on her face. But when she saw he was serious, her expression turned sour. 'Go on, then, off you run,' she said, waving a hand dismissively towards the door.

CHAPTER 25

In the glow of the streetlights the drizzle swirled in the air like pollen. It drifted helplessly, pushed and pulled by erratic currents of air, finding its way beneath the umbrellas of the few people walking the pavements, coating their clothes in a damp layer.

Fiona paused long enough outside the bar to scan its windows for drink offers. Then she rounded the corner into Minshull Street. A couple of girls were out and she walked towards the first, who was sheltering under the overhang of a seventies office building, the doorway of which stank of piss.

After listening to Fiona's question, she sucked deeply on her cigarette and shook her head. Fiona thanked her and set off towards the other girl. She was huddling in a doorway on the other side of the street.

Fiona was halfway across the road when she noticed a car rapidly approaching. She had to jump over a large puddle to make it on to the pavement in time. A split second later it drove into the water, sending a cold sheet splashing against the backs of her legs.

'Whore!' a male voice yelled through the vehicle's open window as it sped away.

'Fucking wanker!' the girl screeched back, jabbing her middle finger up.

Fiona tried to brush the worst off, but her trousers were soaked.

'You all right?' asked the girl.

'I'll survive,' replied Fiona a little shakily. 'I was coming over to have a word. I'm looking for Alexia.'

'You just missed her. She's had enough for the night, said she was off to the bus station to get some chewing gum, then going home.'

'Really? A girl around my height, about twenty, reddish-brown hair?' Fiona asked, already setting off towards Chorlton Street.

'Brown, red, bleached – she changes it all the time.'

Fiona half jogged along the side street. Soon the bright lights of the recently revamped bus station came into view. A couple of National Express coaches idled in their bays behind the barriers, a miserable clutch of passengers waiting to be let on.

She approached the doors, eyes scanning the main hall. The newsagent's was long shut and Fiona was afraid she'd missed her quarry. But then she saw the vending machines in the corner. A young girl was standing at them, counting out change in the palm of her hand.

She was taller than Fiona, but wearing heels and

a miniskirt. Her thin legs were mottled with bluish marks, the same way Emily's had been whenever she got cold. Fiona could see she was shivering, her hair soaking wet with rain.

'The ten twenty-eight National Express service to Glasgow Buchanan bus station is now ready to board. Please proceed to bay number four.'

Fiona was right behind the girl as she pushed coins into the slot and pressed the buttons. A coil of wire rotated forward, releasing a packet of gum into the abyss. It clattered into the tray at the bottom of the machine and the girl leaned forward to pluck it out, one knee bending more than the other. As she turned around their eyes met and the girl began to move past.

'Alexia?' Fiona said in a whisper, having to hold back the torrent of apologies trying to escape her.

The girl paused. 'Huh?'

'I was in the next room at the Platinum Inn. I heard you being attacked. Oh God, I'm so sorry I did nothing to help.' Tears made her vision swim. 'Are you OK? I was so afraid, so afraid for you . . .'

The girl was frowning. 'What the fuck are you on about?'

'Room nine of the Platinum Inn. I was there, Alexia.'

'Alicia, not Alexia. And it's not even my real name, anyway.'

Fiona stiffened, remembering the mix-up of names with the owner of Cheshire Consorts. 'You worked . . . Did you work at the Hurlington Health Club?'

Her face was becoming suspicious. 'What if I did?'

'I'm trying to find a girl called Alexia. I think something terrible might have happened to her.'

She was moving away now. 'Yeah? Tell me something new.' The bitter laugh should never have come from someone her age.

Fiona crumpled into one of the plastic seats. Her surge of optimism had been sucked away, leaving her with a dry despair. Looking at the time, she got to her feet. The twenty-four-hour Spar was only five minutes away – she was sure they sold alcohol right up until eleven.

Twenty minutes later Fiona pulled up outside the Platinum Inn. The car park had three other vehicles in it. She walked towards the doors, her handbag heavy in her hand. Dawn's smile faltered when she saw Fiona's expression. She looked like she couldn't decide whether to scream or cry. 'Are you OK?'

Fiona lifted the neck of the bottle of gin clear of her handbag. 'Fancy a nightcap? I really need one.'

They sat side by side, each holding a full glass in one hand and a lit cigarette in the other. Dawn watched the twin streams of smoke twisting up from their fingers. 'So it was all a mix-up of names?'

Fiona sighed, took a long sip and sighed again.

'I don't know. But yes, it seems that I've been chasing a girl called Alicia, not Alexia. The owner of Cheshire Consorts was a bit confused about what the girl she interviewed was called.'

'But didn't the card you found here have "Alexia" written on the back?'

'Yes.'

'So surely an Alexia visited her?'

'Not necessarily,' Fiona replied, dragging on her cigarette. 'The owner said there's loads of her cards floating around town. The one I found could easily have belonged to a punter.'

'What about the Hurlington Health Club? The woman there gave you the same description.'

'The woman there didn't listen to a word I said. She wouldn't even turn the bloody vacuum cleaner off to talk to me properly. There is an Alexia out there somewhere, but who knows what she looks like? What a mess.' She took another drag and breathed out in exasperation, a veil of smoke spreading before her.

Dawn clinked her glass. 'You did your best. Can't ask for more than that.' She regarded Fiona, waiting for a reaction.

Fiona stared miserably at the other wall, her bottom lip slightly red from where she'd been worrying it with her teeth.

Dawn's eyes travelled to the cut that emerged from Fiona's eyebrow. Despite the expert application of make-up, she could see it would leave an ugly scar. 'How's your eyebrow? Still sore?'

Fiona continued staring straight ahead.

'Fiona, hello! Anyone in?' She waved a hand in front of Fiona's face.

'Sorry. What?' Fiona blinked.

'Your eyebrow. Will you get a professional to look at it?'

Fiona smiled bleakly. 'A private hospital? I could never afford that.'

Dawn stubbed her cigarette out. 'There are other options.'

'Like what?'

Dawn shrugged. 'You know I mentioned the person I'm with?'

'Your companion?'

'Yes,' Dawn smiled. 'My companion. Our relationship, it's quite complicated. He's having surgery to change his . . . appearance. He's never been comfortable with how he is. I'm sure you'll meet him one day.'

She cleared her throat and waved a hand weakly, not prepared to elaborate. At least, not yet. 'Anyway, what I'm trying to say is, the doctor treating him does it all for cash. And cheaply, too. I think he enjoys the challenge.'

She registered Fiona's sceptical look. 'He's no quack. He has his own clinic and really knows his stuff.' She winked at Fiona. 'Pretty dishy, too, in an older-man sort of way.'

'How old?' asked Fiona, looking more interested.

'Late fifties, I suppose. Why don't you ring him, explain your circumstances? I honestly believe

315

he'd treat you. Probably even let you pay him when you can. It's worth a try, don't you reckon?'

Fiona traced a finger over the raised line of damaged tissue. 'He can get rid of something like this?'

'God, yes,' Dawn said eagerly. 'I've seen what he can do. It's amazing.' She got up, stumbling as the alcohol pulsed in her head. 'He's called Dr O'Connor. I'll write his address down.'

Fiona drained her drink. 'OK. No harm in just popping in, is there?'

The next morning Fiona turned over in bed and looked around. To her relief she found herself in the tiny room that was home. The bottle of gin on the table acted like a magnet on her eyes. Immediately she started to fret about the fact that she didn't have enough money to buy another. Kicking the duvet off, she pulled her dressing gown on and shuffled over to the door. Peeping out into the hallway she saw some post on the shelf. Two letters for her, both looking ominously official.

Back in her bedsit, she made herself a coffee and sat at the table. The letters lay at her elbow, but she didn't dare open them in case they were demands for money. Chin resting on the heel of one hand, she watched the curls of steam rising from the coffee. There was no milk in the fridge, her bread had run out the day before, and her packet of cigarettes was empty.

Her mind went back to waking up in the

salesman's hotel room. She finally admitted that she'd only slept with him because he was a way of procuring more drink.

Was it so bad? She'd had a great time, forgotten all her worries for a while.

Far better, in fact, than any time she'd spent with her husband in years. Bitterly, she thought about their marriage. How many times had she endured sex with him through no will or desire of her own? And for what? A stifled existence behind the façade of a respectable house, her money rationed and her movements controlled.

Christ, the night with the salesman was a pleasure in comparison. At least he'd treated her with respect.

She stared at the empty gin bottle then picked up her purse. There at the back was the number for Cheshire Consorts. She remembered Joanne's phone conversation with the escort girl. A hundred and fifty quid an hour. It seemed so respectable, so above-board. They met in hotels and the men paid by credit card, for God's sake. There was a world of difference between that and the poor wretches she'd seen working Minshull Street in all weathers.

She tried to turn her mobile on but remembered the battery had died days ago. Searching in her purse, she found just enough money for the payphone in the hall.

'Hello. Joanne? It's Fiona Wilson here. I came to see you just over a week ago . . .'

317

'Yes, I remember. What can I do for you, Fiona?'

She took a deep breath to quell the tremors in her throat. 'Well, when I saw you, you mentioned that when I'd sorted myself out . . .'

'I did. And have you? Is the bruising on your face gone?'

'Yes,' Fiona whispered, fingers touching the cut on her forehead.

'How about your wardrobe?'

'I've been home and collected all my clothes.'

'So you're in your own place now?'

'Yes.'

Silence for a second. 'Then I'd like you to come and see me.'

Fiona said nothing.

'Fiona? Are you still there?'

'Yes.'

She heard Joanne light a cigarette. 'Fiona, the girls who work for me have made a rational choice to do so. They're paying their way through nursing college, saving the fees for law school, getting together a deposit for a house. It's not a permanent job, it's a stepping stone to something better. They are in control at all times and they most certainly are not whores.'

She arrived just before lunch, having made herself up and put on a simple black dress that suited casual or more formal occasions.

Joanne opened the door and smiled. 'Well, that's some change from the lady I saw two weeks ago.'

Fiona smiled back, trying to look confident and relaxed.

'Don't worry,' Joanne said, showing her inside. 'A lot of men find a touch of nerves very attractive.'

CHAPTER 26

The enquiry room was hot with bodies. Much longer like this and the condensation will start dripping from the ceiling, Jon thought as he opened a window.

The hum of voices started to die down as McCloughlin's door opened. He stepped out, followed by a thin man with long strands of greying hair swept across his head. Perched on his nose was a pair of rimless glasses that gave a clear view of his feminine eyelashes. Dr Neville Heath. Jon thought back to last summer and concluded that he should have stuck with the black frames he'd had then. After the two men had passed his desk he whispered to Rick, 'Thought it wouldn't be long before this guy got involved.'

Rick swivelled in his seat to regard McCloughlin and his companion, who took up position side by side at the top of the room. McCloughlin glared at the last two officers still speaking. Their conversation withered under his gaze.

'Right, people, as you all know, Gordon Dean's body was discovered yesterday. However, there is nothing to prove he killed any of our three victims, so this investigation is very much ongoing.' He waved the murmurs down. 'In fact, I want you to assume Gordon Dean wasn't the killer. Which means we have to redouble our efforts until we find out who is. To this end, I'd like to introduce Dr Neville Heath. He's a criminal psychologist and has been lecturing at Manchester University since some of you were in primary school. Dr Heath has been over all the information we've gathered so far. He isn't aware of any suspects we're pursuing – alive or dead – so whatever profiles he produces are not biased by our own suspicions. I think you'll agree he has some interesting thoughts to share.'

Jon's eyes turned to the doctor. If you've been lecturing for so long, he wondered, how can talking to us lot make you look so uncomfortable? This isn't the sort of case for someone with a nervous disposition.

'Hello,' the doctor said, looking down at his notes, failing to make eye contact.

The room remained silent.

Dr Heath glanced anxiously at McCloughlin. 'Actually, I haven't produced any profiles quite yet. More a number of observations that could be helpful.'

McCloughlin nodded politely, his expression saying: get on with it.

Registering the look, Dr Heath turned to the room. 'OK,' he said. 'The first thing I'd normally do in a case where more than one crime is being carried out by a person is map the locations where the attacks have occurred and draw a circle round them. It's been frequently found that the criminal lives within that circle, often towards its centre. That's because criminals – especially burglars, rapists and murderers – usually start offending in their own neighbourhood, where they're familiar with their surroundings, before moving further afield as their confidence grows.'

Jon could see people beginning to lean forwards and the doctor's confidence appeared to increase as a result.

'The problem with this case is that we don't know where the mutilations and killings were actually carried out. However, we can say where the victims came from. Number one, Angela Rowlands, lived in Droylesden. Victim two, Carol Miller, in Bredbury. From this we can extrapolate a midpoint around Denton, where the Hyde Road intersects the M60.'

'Hyde Road's the A57,' Jon muttered to Rick.

'Now, I realise this is close to where the bodies are being dumped, but I don't think it's where our killer lives. And here's why. When we add in the address of Tyler Young, which is in Stretford to the west of the city, our circle expands to cover the whole of central Manchester with a midpoint around Didsbury and Fallowfield. This is a far more likely area of residence, for reasons I'll come to in a minute.'

He flipped his top sheet of notes over and took

a shallow breath. 'Now, studying our killer's temporal patterns reveals a bit more about him. Our victims were all discovered on different day – a Tuesday, a Thursday and a Saturday morning. Times of death suggest they were all killed at some point during the evening before, so he's killed on a Monday, a Wednesday and a Friday. Angela Rowlands was last seen when she left her office in central Manchester at lunchtime. Carol Miller dropped her infant son at her mother's house in the late afternoon, and Tyler Young we're unsure about. Taking Angela Rowlands, there was a gap of about six hours between her last sighting and her time of death. This suggests to me she had initial contact with the killer during the office hours of a weekday.'

He took his glasses off and rubbed tiredly at the red marks on each side of his nose. Come on, Jon thought. The whole bloody room is hanging on your next comment.

With his eyes shut, the doctor continued, 'We can therefore suppose our killer isn't constrained by normal working hours.' Glasses back on, he opened his eyes and had to blink a couple of times to regain his focus. 'He has freedom of movement during the day to control his own movements. Keep that thought.

'Next is what he's doing to his victims. These aren't, to use the term our colleagues in America prefer, disorganised killings. They haven't been carried out in a fit of uncontrolled rage. They're

323

careful, meticulous and unhurried. He needs a private place to carry out his work, somewhere he has no chance of being disturbed. Therefore he's probably a property owner or has access to commercial premises.

'He's orgainsed and, judging from the mutilations themselves, skilled. I would also guess these characteristics apply to him in general. He's in a professional occupation, probably supervising his own movements during the day. Possibly self-employed in some capacity.'

Rick paused in his note-taking and held his hand up. Christ, thought Jon, does he think this is a classroom? The doctor nodded at Rick.

'Why do you assume he's got a job?'

The doctor lowered his notepad. 'Well, the bodies are turning up on waste ground in Belle Vue, having been moved there from somewhere else. That suggests he owns a car or has access to a commercial vehicle. It needs to be big enough for him to stash a corpse in it quite comfortably. It takes money to run any vehicle – hundreds a month if you build in the purchase price or cost of loan repayments. He needs a regular wage for that.'

'Like a salesman of latex gloves,' Rick whispered.

Jon shrugged, thinking of Pete Gray's van.

'I would also expect our killer to be very organised in his personal life. His place of work will be neat and orderly, as will his appearance – fastidious, even. Given his professional role, I would say suits for work, smart dress outside it. Shirts, leather shoes, trousers, not jeans. We're not looking for a dishevelled, wild-eyed maniac. Unfortunately, we rarely are. We're looking for a quiet, unassuming, individual. One with an understated type of charm. Think Jeffrey Dahmer. Unobtrusive, able to merge in without making much of an impression. Probably regarded as "nice" by his neighbours.'

While Rick eagerly noted down the doctor's words, Jon sat back and mulled the information over. Pete Gray drove a van with blacked-out windows. And God knew why, but it seemed some women believed he had a certain charm.

'How is he selecting his victims?' the doctor continued. 'They're from three different parts of the city. The first two mentioned they were going somewhere specific before disappearing. A liaison with our killer, but for what? A date? An appointment? They've made the decision to meet him. Has there been prior contact? If you haven't done so, check all three victims' neighbours for any recent visits. I don't mean by trades people such as window cleaners – too menial. Someone flogging conservatories, satellite TV, free holidays. Professional salespeople basically. As I said, he can turn on the charm when required.'

Jon glanced over and saw Rick shooting him a look of triumph.

'What is he trying to achieve through his murders? I'm not sure, but he's certainly settling into it. More flesh is being removed and, in the third instance, the face and teeth as well. I'm assuming the surgical avenue is being treated as a priority?'

McCloughlin gave a tight nod.

'It wouldn't surprise me if the next victim were to be completely stripped of her flesh.' The atmosphere in the room tightened perceptibly and the doctor flushed red on realising his gaffe. 'If he isn't caught before, of course. But he's getting more careful. Removing the third victim's face and teeth is a way of preventing identification. He's covering his tracks in order to carry on. This also links into the general lack of evidence recovered so far. He's wearing gloves, probably a facemask and gown. Of course, that suggests medical knowledge, but it also suggests forensic awareness. So he may well have a record for similar, more minor crimes. Mutilating pets, for instance.'

'What about sex crimes?' a female officer asked from the back.

The doctor shook his head. 'I don't think so. All three victims were discovered with their underwear on. There's no sign of sexual activity, forced or otherwise. Of course, they might have believed they were meeting him for that. But it's not his motivation. Mutilations of this nature are often ritualistic, and in ritualistic killings the genitals are frequently the focus of mutilation. But not here. He's seeking to achieve something else here.

'Another point to consider is this. Why is he

choosing Belle Vue as his dumping ground? It suggests to me that he has good familiarity with the area, but I don't think he lives there. More likely is that he regularly passes through, perhaps to and from a place of work. As I mentioned earlier, given his likely professional status and the level of house prices in Didsbury, I suspect that is his area of residence. Taking into account the need for privacy, we should be considering detached houses.'

Wrong! Jon had to make an effort to stop his head from shaking. Pete Gray worked at Stepping Hill hospital and lived in a terraced house near Davenport train station. Neither was particularly close to Belle Vue. He'd chosen the area for another reason.

'Also, he has to get the bodies into his vehicle and then dump them in Belle Vue. Perhaps he has a drive-in garage or a garden with a screening hedge. My final comment is this. From the intervals between his first three killings, we can unfortunately expect him to strike again any day.' He lowered his notes, stepped back and looked at McCloughlin.

Taking the cue, McCloughlin nodded. 'Thank you for that, Doctor.' He turned to face the room. 'A summary of Doctor Heath's observations will be coming round. In the meantime, we focus on Tyler Young – victim number three and a whole new avenue to investigate. You all know her details; now we need to start delving into her life. Her parents told us she was angling to get a job in Tempters, that topless bar in the centre of town. I want the management and all the staff questioned – barmaids, cleaners, glass washers, the man who stocks their condom machines, the lot. Gavin, your team can handle that?'

'Certainly, sir,' the DI replied. Jon could almost see the team rubbing their hands with glee at the prospect of interviewing the barmaids.

'We need to map out her last twenty-four hours. Usual routine – friends and family first. Obviously Mum and Dad were abroad on holiday, but she has two aunts living nearby. The reason they didn't come forward was because they thought she was on holiday with the parents. Nevertheless, we still need to talk to them. She didn't have a boyfriend as far as her parents knew, but we need to verify that with her mates.

'Vanessa, that's your team's shout. I also want you to get over to the family home and have a good look through her stuff. The mum doesn't think she kept a diary, but you know how it is with teenage girls. Go through her bedroom, check the backs of her drawers, under the carpet – you probably know better than me where she might hide stuff. We'll need the family computer, too, to see what email she's been sending or receiving.'

As Jon watched the young DI brush her hair off her face, he wondered what McCloughlin had in mind for him and Rick.

'Andy, I want your team to continue with your

TIEs on the members of the dating agencies Angela Rowlands met up with. How many have you got left to trace?'

'She was sent the profiles of twenty-seven men. It seems she had contact with sixteen of them. So far we've traced, interviewed and eliminated twelve.'

He turned to another officer sitting at the front. 'Simon, how's your team going with the surgeons?'

'Not bad, boss. We've just got to check the alibis for three who have contracts with the Paragon Group.'

'Good. Keep going.' He held up a sheaf of photocopies. 'The most recent photo of Tyler Young her parents could find. Help yourself.' He dropped them on the table and was turning back to his office when he said, almost as an aside, 'Oh yes, Jon and Rick, keep trawling through those videos from Piccadilly station. We need more footage before we can categorically say the woman with Gordon Dean wasn't Tyler Young.'

Jon uncrossed his arms, trying to keep the irritation out of his voice. 'Sir, doesn't it now appear that Gordon Dean's murder is unconnected to the Butcher investigation? I was hoping to invest our time in following up the Pete Gray lead Rick and I unearthed.'

'Rick and you unearthed?' McCloughlin replied sarcastically. 'Pete Gray is not a priority at this time. The whereabouts of that prostitute is. I want her tracked down.'

He ushered the doctor back to his office.

Shit, Jon thought, how do I let him know Gray's DNA showed up on Angela Rowlands's body? McCloughlin has enough doubts about my working methods without me announcing that I've run an illegal and unauthorised DNA test on a suspect. He pursued them into his boss's office. 'With respect sir, Pete Gray is definitely hiding something. He has free access to the type of latex glove found at the crime scene of Tyler Young, he works odd shift patterns, he drives a van with blacked-out windows, he's a regular at singles' nights around town. Surely that's grounds to at least ask the man for a voluntary DNA swab?'

He glanced at Dr Heath, who was peering at McCloughlin over his glasses, one eyebrow raised.

But McCloughlin's face had drained of colour. 'DI Spicer, there are many more avenues to this case than the ones you see fit to create. As SIO, it's my job to prioritise them. You'll go through that footage if you want to stay on this investigation.'

'And once we've been through it all?'

'If there's no sign of her, you can question Pete Gray. Now get out.'

Jon stepped out of McCloughlin's office and into a mass of excited conversations. He went back to his desk and slumped down in his seat, wondering how to get out of the mess he was in.

Rick looked across at him. 'Did you tell him about your dodgy DNA test?'

'Christ, no! I'd be off the investigation by now if I had.'

Rick whistled. 'You're sailing very close to the wind. Though personally, my money's still on Gordon Dean.' He put a few finishing touches to his notes, swivelled the pad around and pushed it across the desk.

Reluctantly, Jon started reading. *Works to his own schedule. Skilled or professional role, probably 'high end' of sales. Has his own vehicle. Fastidious in terms of organisation and personal appearance. Familiar with Belle Vue.* Rick had a satisfied look on his face. 'Gordon Dean fits all those criteria – every time he had to get to Protex he'd have driven through Belle Vue.'

Irritation itched Jon's scalp. 'It wasn't him.'

'On what basis exactly?'

'This,' said Jon, pressing his fist into his sternum. 'I can feel it in here. He's not our man.'

'Great! Discard all the techniques of twenty-first-century policing and go on good old gut instinct.'

Jon hooked a forefinger under Rick's pad and flipped it over. 'There's more to this job than treating it like some frigging university course.'

Rick retrieved the pad and stood up. 'I'm getting a coffee.'

Jon watched him go, waiting until he was out of earshot before saying, 'Fucking little smart-arse.'

331

CHAPTER 27

The lines of halogen spotlights came on and he crossed the concrete floor, the low cellar ceiling muting the sound of his footsteps.

On the other side of the small room he stood before a counter lined with his collection of surgical instruments. He surveyed the rack of scalpels before picking one out and examining its blade, eyes narrowing under the bright light glaring down from above.

With a deft movement he released the blade from the metal handle and disposed of it in a flip-lid bin that was spattered with specks of red. Then he lifted a small foil wrapper from a box labelled: *Carbon steel. Sterility guaranteed if packet unbroken.*

He tore the foil open, lifted out the new blade, fitted it to the handle and replaced the scalpel on the rack.

Shutting his eyes, he breathed in. Unable to escape the airless room, the coppery tang of blood hung heavy around him.

So many to choose from, he thought, opening his eyes and looking at the sheets of paper beside him. Women's names, addresses, hopes and desires were all listed there. He lifted the top sheet and ran his eyes over the form.

Should he select one of these? After a few moments' contemplation, he decided against it. None of them felt quite right. He wanted his next job to be really special. Something that would leave the crowds of imbeciles gaping with shock.

Another woman would come along soon. They always did.

As he put the forms back his eyes shifted to the collection of human teeth in the test tube. The corners of his mouth twitched with anticipation.

CHAPTER 28

Jon and Rick sat in the front room. Still treating each other a little warily after their argument the day before, they had now waded through the footage from every platform without success. Rick loaded the first tape from the main terminal building and sat back on the sofa with a sigh.

Jon couldn't concentrate on the screen. 'He's fucking sidelined us. This is a wild-goose chase and he knows it.'

Rick half turned his head, one eye still on the screen. 'Jon, we can do this in less than three days if we keep going.'

'Three days! We could crack this case in hours if we go after Pete Gray.' He began picking at the frayed armrest. 'Look, this is a waste of time, right? Gordon Dean pops up in the Manchester Ship Canal. So why are we looking for him catching a train out of Manchester? Someone else dumped the car at Piccadilly station to make it appear like Gordon Dean had eloped. Probably the prostitute's pimp.'

Rick was trying to watch the footage.

Jon sat forward to get in his line of vision.

'Whatever that prostitute's involvement in Gordon Dean's murder, it's a separate case from the Butcher. Tyler Young was killed and her flesh stripped off early in the evening. Dean and that prostitute are together on the CCTV film from the petrol station hours later that night. Tyler Young and that prostitute are different people.'

'That's not to say Dean isn't the Butcher. He skins Young, then goes out celebrating with the mystery girl from the CCTV. Later, he ends up in the Manchester Ship Canal. We still need to track her down and find out what happened.'

'OK, I agree the prostitute holds the key to Dean's death. But I bet she'll still be in Manchester, back on her old patch in all likelihood. What I'm saying is Dean isn't the Butcher. When could he have skinned Young? We have his movements mapped out from early afternoon until three in the morning.'

Rick stopped the tape and gripped his head in his hands, growling in frustration. 'So what do you suggest?'

Jon waited for him to look up. 'We fuck those tapes off. Let's tell McCloughlin we split them in two. We phone him later to say we did half each and there's nothing on any of them.'

Rick fiddled nervously with the remote control. 'And what do we do in the meantime?'

'Check out Pete Gray. Ask him for a voluntary DNA swab, maybe put some questions to his colleagues at Stepping Hill hospital.'

Rick remained silent and Jon could tell he was wrestling with the decision to actively deceive his SIO. Finally he said, 'I'll agree to take a break from these bloody tapes, but on one condition.'

'Go on.'

'We go back and talk to that tattooist in Affleck's Palace first. We take the photo of Tyler Young and see if it's the girl Gordon Dean spent time waiting with. I still reckon he's the Butcher.'

Jeff Wilson walked past Melvyn's salon, glancing quickly in. Where the fuck was his wife? He knew she wouldn't have been able to cut off all contact with her friends there. They must know where she was. The vacant-looking girl who seemed to have only just started was sitting at the reception desk, chewing a pencil. It seemed like no one else was there.

Looking at his watch, he realised he could only stay for another fifteen minutes. A business meeting beckoned. Suddenly he saw a way of finding out where Fiona was hiding. With a bit of luck, it might just work. And then he could teach the bitch a lesson for trying to leave him.

He crossed the road to a florist's and ordered a big bouquet of flowers. Once the girl had curled a sheet of cellophane round them, she asked if he'd like a message added.

'Actually, the lady doesn't even know me. But we got talking once in the queue for the sandwich shop and, well, it sounds silly I know, but I think

I've found my soulmate.' He feigned embarrassment and was pleased to see the girl's face soften. Would the stupid cows ever give up on their absurd faith in fairytale romance? 'I was wondering, could you carry them to that beauty salon across the road for me? I'll pay your standard delivery costs.'

She looked over his shoulder, an intrigued expression on her face. 'To that one? Melvyn's Salon?'

'Yes, that's where she works. I've been plucking up the courage to do this for days.'

'OK,' she smiled. 'But you do know it'll be £12.50?'

'A small price to pay, believe me. The lady's name is Fiona. Fiona Wilson.'

After writing down his message, she carried the bouquet across the road and into the salon. When she walked in, Zoe's eyes widened in hope at the huge spray of flowers.

'Hi, there,' the florist announced cheerfully. 'A bouquet for Fiona Wilson.'

Zoe looked disappointed. 'She's taking some time off work.'

The florist's shoulders slumped. 'Oh. Well . . . that's a shame.' She turned towards the door.

'Hang on!' Zoe exclaimed. 'Her home address is here somewhere.' She opened the appointments book and turned to a load of loose bits of paper at the back. 'Yes, I thought it was. They can go to Flat 2, 15 Ridley Place, Fallowfield. Here, I'll write it out for you.'

'Thank you.' The florist took the piece of paper.

Back in her shop she felt a surge of sympathy over her customer's concerned expression. 'Don't worry. She's off work for a while, but I've got her home address.'

'Really?' Jeff Wilson replied. 'That's smashing.'

When they walked into the tiny tattoo parlour, Jake was sitting behind the desk, blowing smoke rings at the ceiling. Jon hooked a finger through one and then withdrew it, the gesture making the pale loop bend and waver.

'Gents, good to see you again.' Jake sat up, not bothering with any clever comments. Jon stood aside to allow Rick up to the desk.

'Jake, we won't take up any of your time. The girl who picked the Betty Boop tattoo on the same day as Gordon Dean was in here getting his ladybird. Is this her?'

He laid the photo on the desk.

Jake leaned forwards and studied it. With his head still bowed, he said, 'She's the Butcher's third victim, isn't she?'

Jon and Rick said nothing and he looked up. 'The papers said she had a distinctive tattoo on her lower abdomen. It's her, right?'

'We're not at liberty to say,' Rick replied, voice tight.

Jake's eyes narrowed and moved to Jon. 'It is. That's heavy shit.' He let out a whistle and picked the photo up. 'Yes. I'm pretty certain that's her. She's got the line of earrings and everything.'

'What happened that day?' asked Rick. 'Think back. You finished the Maori armband. You showed the customer out. Gordon Dean and this girl are sitting here.' He pointed to the two stools. 'Their thighs must have been practically touching. What did they say?'

Jake shut his eyes and started twiddling the rod in his nose. 'Nothing. I took the armband guy's cash and then said Gordon Dean was next. He stood up, squeezed round her knees. She smiled and wished him good luck.'

'And what did he say?'

'Just thanked her, I think.'

'And afterwards? You've completed Gordon's ladybird tattoo. You show him back through the curtains . . .'

'Yeah, she's still sat there.' Jake opened his eyes and looked at the empty stool. 'Dean pays me, says he'll call again soon. Then he wishes her luck, says she's made the right choice, and walks out.'

'The right choice?' said Jon, pushing himself clear of the doorframe.

'Yeah, the right choice.'

Despite the street being bathed in cold sunshine, a flurry of raindrops started to fall around them. Squinting, Jon looked up but could only spot a few tiny clouds in the sky. Then a breeze whipped up from nowhere and the air abruptly cleared. Jon looked back down, thinking that nothing felt quite right.

'There's something in this,' Rick said, holding up a hand and testing the texture of the air between a forefinger and thumb.

Jon kept silent, desperate to get over to Stepping Hill hospital.

'"The right choice". What did that mean? Tattoo? Job? Decision to see him again?' Rick frowned. 'I want a word with that Dr O'Connor. He seemed fairly friendly with Dean.' He set off towards the Rochdale Road.

Just give it up, will you? Jon thought, following along behind.

As they reached the Beauty Centre, the door opened and a woman who appeared to be in her late thirties stepped out. She looked like someone had just punched her mouth and, on seeing Jon's stare, she raised a self-conscious hand to her swollen lips. She hurried past and Rick caught the door before it could shut, while Jon buzzed the intercom. 'Dr O'Connor, it's DI Spicer and DS Saville. Could you spare us a couple of minutes?'

'Of course. Please come up.' The lock clicked uselessly. Halfway up the stairs, Rick tapped a photo on the wall. 'Her with the trout-pout we just passed? That's what she'd had.'

Jon looked at the image of a woman with puckered, glossy lips. The words below read, *Softform. For enhancing lips and eradicating deep wrinkles.*

Jon shuddered. Why did women feel the need to do this to themselves? If it was to attract men, it did nothing for him.

O'Connor rose to his feet and extended a hand across his desk as they entered his office. After they'd shaken, he gestured to the pair of chairs and sat down. 'Officers, how can I help?'

Rick reached into his pocket. 'Doctor, we're still following up leads regarding Gordon Dean's disappearance.'

The doctor crossed his legs. 'Any progress?'

'The investigation is ongoing,' Rick replied. 'However, we're still trying to fill in some of his movements after he last saw you.'

At that moment they heard the door across the corridor open, and a woman came into the room. Mid-forties, hair tied back. Poking out from beneath her coat was the hem of a starched white dress. 'Sorry to disturb you, Doctor. Everything's locked up.'

'Good, then I'll see you tomorrow,' he smiled.

'See you tomorrow.' She disappeared down the stairs.

'Jenny Palmer,' said O'Connor, 'my nursing assistant. Wonderful woman.'

Rick nodded. 'Did Mr Dean ever mention any lady friends in Manchester?'

The doctor frowned. 'No. But wasn't he married?'

'Yes,' Rick answered. 'But perhaps not as happily as he might have been . . .'

The buzzer sounded on the wall. Rick waited but the doctor waved it away. 'Kids, I imagine. I have no further appointments this morning.' The buzzer sounded again and he leaned forward. 'You were saying?'

Jon got up, went over to the window and looked down at the street below. The receptionist from the Platinum Inn was staring up. On seeing Jon, her eyes dropped and she scurried off down the street. He was about to ask O'Connor what was going on but changed his mind, sensing that, for the moment, it might prove more useful to keep what he'd seen to himself.

'You seemed quite friendly with Mr Dean. Did he ever mention a girl fitting this description?' asked Rick, putting the photo on the table.

O'Connor took it. 'No, I'm afraid not.' He glanced at the image again. 'Pretty young thing, though a bit too young for Mr Dean, don't you think?'

Rick took the piece of paper back, disappointment obvious on his face. 'Well, thanks, that's all.'

They stood and shook hands again.

'Please let me know if you hear anything about Gordon,' said the doctor.

'Will do,' Rick answered after a moment's hesitation.

Jon waited until they were outside before saying, 'The buzzer, it was the night receptionist from a motel in Belle Vue called the Platinum Inn.'

'How do you know that?' asked Rick.

'Because I spoke to her a few days ago. Favour to that friend of my girlfriend – the one who

342

thought she heard a prostitute being killed in the next room.'

'Oh, yeah, the one who gave you that business card? What was the name on it? Alexia?'

Jon nodded. 'What was she doing here, I wonder? She practically ran off when she saw my face in the window.'

'Don't know. But Tyler Young and Gordon Dean definitely had an association. I think we should get back to those tapes.'

Jon held up his hands. 'Hang on. We agreed to pop over to Stepping Hill and ask Pete Gray for a voluntary DNA swab.'

Rick looked away, tapping his foot against the pavement. Eventually he turned back. 'One hour, OK? No more.'

At Stepping Hill hospital a grey-haired porter looked at Jon's warrant card then tapped his tunic. 'Twenty years in the Transport Police, me.'

'Really?' said Jon. 'When did you retire?'

'Twelve years ago. Trouble with the ticker. Mind you, I'm glad I got out, reading about how things are going for you nowadays. Can't touch those little yobs for fear of legal action, isn't that right?'

'There's ways and means.' Jon gave the old boy a wink and got a knowing smile in return.

'What's that pepper spray like? Does it drop them like flies?'

'Never used it myself, but the uniforms certainly like it.'

'Wouldn't have minded a can of that in my day. So, who are you looking for?'

'Pete Gray. Is he around?'

'It's his day off.' The porter put a couple of boxes of medical supplies on a small trolley.

'Could we ask you a few questions instead?' Jon asked.

'Certainly, if you don't mind talking on the move. I've got to get this lot over to the surgical ward. A rare trip for me.'

'Is that so?' Jon set off alongside the man, Rick just behind.

'Pete usually delivers everything to the surgical wards. He's very possessive about it.'

'Latex gloves, for instance?'

'Everything. He wheels everything over there.'

'Why's that?'

'He loves the surgical ward. Says he'd have been a surgeon if he'd had the education.'

The back of Jon's neck started to tingle. 'Really? I thought he was more into learning the lyrics of Elvis songs.'

The man laughed. 'You mean his karaoke stuff? Yes, he's certainly a bit of a ladies' man. In fact, I reckon the real reason he always delivers to this ward is because he fancies the medical secretaries.'

Jon smiled. 'A bit of a skirt-chaser, then?'

The porter nodded. 'Oh aye. I don't believe in bragging about your love life. But then I've been married for forty years, so I don't have one.' He laughed at his own joke. 'Bachelors like him? I suppose it's different.'

Jon thought about Gray's record of violence against his first wife. 'So he's never given marriage a go?'

'Pete? No. Says he's not the marrying kind. Not his thing.'

Jon flicked a glance at Rick walking just a pace behind. 'Are there many ladies he talks about?'

'If you believe everything he says, he's had more than I've had hot dinners. It's those singles' nights he goes to around Manchester. Always a new story to share with us on a Monday morning.'

'He never mentions regular girlfriends?'

'Too busy having fun for that, according to him. Not that I believe he's truly happy. Still sowing your wild oats at forty odd? There's only one hole he's filling at weekends, and that's the great big one in his life.'

By now they'd reached the doors to the surgical ward. Jon held them open and the porter wheeled the delivery through.

'No Pete today?' asked the woman behind the reception desk.

'Day off.' He pointed at the boxes. 'They're only light things. Shall I leave them here?'

'That's fine,' she replied, coming round the counter.

Jon helped him lift them off the trolley. As the porter made for the doors Jon said, 'Thanks for your help.'

'You're finished with me, then? Rightio.' The door swung shut.

Jon produced his warrant card and showed it to the receptionist. 'DI Jon Spicer. Could I ask you a question or two?'

'Yes?'

'It's about Pete Gray who you just mentioned.'

'Pete?' She looked amused, but her voice held a note of caution. 'Has he done something wrong?'

'Nothing like that,' Jon assured her. 'The other porter mentioned he has quite an interest in the surgical ward.'

'Oh, does he! You need to speak to Mr Anderson. He's let Pete observe him in the theatre once or twice.' Suddenly she looked concerned. 'That's not illegal, is it?'

'Not as far as I'm concerned.'

She smiled with relief.

'Is Dr Anderson in today?' Jon asked.

'Mr Anderson,' she corrected him. 'You call consultant surgeons "Mister". Yes. He's performing a laparotomy. Very busy.'

'Could you find out if he'd object to me asking him one or two questions?'

'What, now?'

'It's extremely important.'

Ten minutes later, Jon was standing at the end of an operating table, wearing green overalls, a facemask and surgical goggles. While a young man held apart flaps of flesh with retractors, the surgeon was delving around in someone's

346

stomach. Blood was being sucked away down a tube with the same sound as a child finishing a drink through a straw.

The surgeon turned to the scrub nurse. 'Number fifteen scalpel, please, Ruth.'

She handed it to him and he leaned forward to slice something within the wound. The vicious-looking scalpel was dropped with a metallic clink into a stainless-steel kidney tray and he straightened up. 'Pete Gray? Harmless enough fellow. Approached me in the canteen one time. Bit of an odd request, but whoever's fault it was he left school so poorly qualified isn't my concern. I was just pleased to see the fellow taking an interest. Yes, he's sat in on quite a few operations, even borrowed a few of my anatomy books.' His eyes narrowed above his facemask. 'Still got my *Gray's Anatomy*. Must remember to ask him for that back.'

'And what sort of operations has he observed you performing?'

'Oh, removing bowel cancers, mainly. Clearing blockages in lower intestines. Couple of abscesses, too.' He picked the scalpel up and began cutting again.

'Does he ask questions?'

'How do you mean?'

'Regarding surgical techniques. How you make incisions, that sort of thing.'

'Yes. Lots. In fact, it was usually easier for me to give a running commentary.'

Jon had heard enough. 'Thanks very much for your help.'

As soon as he was out of the operating theatre, he yanked off the surgical clothing.

'Well?' said Rick expectantly, as Jon entered the reception area.

He kept his voice down and tried to keep the flow of words under control. 'He's been in there watching all sorts of stuff. Observing the surgeon as he opened people up, asking questions about how he does it, borrowing books on anatomy.'

'Jesus Christ.'

'Now do you believe me?'

Rick coloured slightly. 'Yeah, I think you could be right.'

'Come on, let's get round to his house.' Jon set off towards the double doors.

'What about the boss?' Rick called after him.

Jon fished out his mobile phone. 'DCI McCloughlin please. It's DI Spicer.'

A moment later McCloughlin came on the line. 'Got some interesting news for me, Spicer?'

'Yes, I have, sir. Very interesting. Pete Gray has been sitting in on operations at Stepping Hill hospital, watching the surgeon perform. Only observing, but he's also borrowed books on anatomy.'

'What the hell are you doing there? I instructed you to go through the CCTV footage from Piccadilly station.'

Jon shot a guilty glance at Rick. 'We've been

through them all sir. DS Saville and I split the tapes. Went at them most of the night and all this morning. Not a thing sir, no. I think it was a ruse. The car was parked there to make it appear Gordon Dean had fled.'

'So where is this prostitute? We need to trace her.'

'Rick and I believe the prostitute is still in the area. I'm sure, given time, we'll find her. But as regards Pete Gray, I think it's imperative we talk to him and request a DNA swab to eliminate him from the enquiry.'

'And don't tell me, you just happen to have a chance of speaking to him now?'

'As it happens, we have, yes. We're about ten minutes from his house.'

'A chat, Spicer. And a polite request for a swab. No more, do you understand?'

'Absolutely. Thank you, sir. We'll keep you informed.' He snapped the phone shut, looking relieved. 'We've got the go-ahead.'

As they walked up the short drive Jon pointed out the stickers on the rear window of Pete Gray's van, *Shaggin' Wagon* and *If it's a-rockin', don't come a-knockin'*.

Rick raised his eyebrows. 'Classy.'

Jon pressed the doorbell and stepped back. They heard the jangle of keys a few moments later and the door swung open.

Pete Gray looked out at them. His hair was messed up, great greasy strands of it hanging down over his face. Nervously, he swept it back over his head.

'Mr Gray, DI Spicer and DS Saville. We spoke to you—'

'Yeah, I remember. What do you want?'

'Could we come in for a quick word?' Jon took a step towards the open door.

Gray shifted back and glanced over his shoulder into the house. 'Er, can you call later?'

'It really won't take long.'

Gray rubbed his unshaven jaw with the knuckles of one hand. 'It's not a good time.'

'As I said, we'll be out of your hair in two ticks.' Jon placed a hand against the door frame.

He glanced at it. 'Are you arresting me?'

'Why would we do that?'

'I don't know.' His eyes shifted to Jon's hand for a second time. 'OK, come through to the kitchen.'

The kitchen was at the end of a short corridor directly ahead. Before that were two doors, one on each side. Jon knew the one on the right led into the TV room, its shelves stacked with books. Pete Gray pulled the one to his left shut as he walked down the corridor.

Jon pointed to the closed door. Then he stepped into the house and walked into the TV room on the right.

Gray whirled round. 'Hey! The kitchen's down here.'

Jon was in the centre of the room, looking at the bookshelves. 'Sorry?'

Gray walked angrily into the room. 'You heard me. The kitchen, it's down—'

He heard the door across the corridor being opened and realised he was caught in between the two men.

Jon read out some of book titles. '*The Anatomical Drawings of Leonardo da Vinci. Andreas Vesalius: The Work of a Master. Clinical Anatomy for Medical Students*, Richard S. Snell. *Gray's Anatomy*. What a strange collection. What would you want with books like these?' He took *Gray's Anatomy* off the shelf.

'What? Put that down.' He looked towards the other room. 'Get out of that fucking room. This is illegal!'

'I'm sorry, sir, but you invited us in.'

'Jon, in here.' Rick's voice was thick with suppressed emotion.

Jon kept his eyes on Pete Gray. The man was highly agitated, but there was still red in his cheeks. Jon knew if he was about to fight or run his face would be white, the blood rushing into his arms and legs. 'After you, sir.' Jon extended a hand towards the corridor.

They went into the other room. Rick had a folder open on the dining-room table and was spreading out colour photos. What struck Jon at first was the redness of the bodies; torsos completely stripped of their flesh, skull-like faces with eyeballs exposed, lips missing and teeth bared to the world.

351

CHAPTER 29

Dawn Poole paused before the bedroom door, took a slight breath in and pushed it open.

The patient was sitting up in bed staring across the room. Rows of stitches along the jaw were merging with a light covering of stubble. The nose was still swollen from where Dr O'Connor had broken it, shaved down the bone, then reset it. Bruising lay heavy beneath the eyes. 'Did you get them?'

Dawn shook her head. 'I couldn't. That policeman was there, the one who came asking questions at the Platinum Inn.' She realised that she was still in the doorway, nervousness rooting her to the spot. 'He saw me and I had to walk off. What's going on? Why was he there?'

But her questions hadn't been heard. The top of the sheet was being twisted in a knot, red fingernails digging deep into the folds of material. 'I need fucking Androtone. Look at me! The hair's coming back. I'm disgusting.'

Meekly, Dawn stepped forwards. 'You've been in bandages for days. When I had my leg in plaster for a while it was covered in hair when the cast came off.'

'Your leg, not your face! Jesus!' The patient looked wildly around, scratching at the spiky hair on his head. 'My bust's shrinking, too. He can't deny me my tablets. I must have Progesterone!'

'They're not shrinking darling,' said Dawn, looking at the swelling under his nightgown.

'You're lying! In there.' A hand flapped towards the chest of drawers. 'Second drawer down.'

'Alex, you're scaring me.'

His eyes met hers. 'Listen, it's not my fault. It's the testosterone. It's flooding me like poison.' Wretchedly, he clutched a hand between his legs. 'Oh God, the sooner we go to Holland and I get the full operation . . . Now, please, the drawer?'

Dawn took a few more tentative steps into the room, increasingly alarmed at the aggressive way he was ordering her around. It had never happened before. At the start of their relationship she'd found things awkward, not knowing if they were stumbling towards something that would involve sex. Then, one night, he had gently resisted her hesitant advance, telling her that, although he loved her, it was as a soulmate. More than friends, but not quite lovers.

She was just glad to know one way or another, and actually quite relieved they could continue together as companions without the confusion. As the trust between them grew, he'd begun to describe his dream of being more than a transvestite, of becoming an actual woman.

She'd been shocked and worried. Was the operation dangerous? Would he want to leave her once the transformation was complete? But she soon realised that, in many ways, he needed her more. As a physical carer after each painful stage of surgery and as an emotional carer as he struggled with feelings of self-doubt and despair.

Cost was the hardest part. He'd never had more than the most basic jobs, same for her. She'd reacted with horror to his suggestion that he go on the game. But he told her that he'd done it before. He'd worked as a rent boy for spells during his teens and early twenties. He knew there was a thriving market for transvestites and pre-op transsexuals. Knowing his happiness depended on changing sex, she eventually accepted the idea.

The first night he went out in full drag she'd been terrified for his safety. But he reappeared the next morning with hundreds of pounds. Within a few more nights he'd earned enough money to pay Dr O'Connor for his cheek implants. So the process began. Alex selling himself to pay for the next stage of surgery, lying in bed being cared for by her as his wounds healed, then going back on the game to finance his next visit to O'Connor.

Of course, there were times when he was angry, hurt by punters' scathing remarks or cheated out of payment after servicing their needs. Her mind jumped to the night Fiona had thought she heard someone being killed. 'Alex, the night before Dr O'Connor operated on your nose and jaw, you were working, remember? You brought a punter back to the motel in the early hours. Did you end up in room nine?'

'Second drawer down!' A sudden falsetto scream.

She flinched, then hurried across to the chest of drawers. On top of it was a mannequin's head, covered by a chestnut-brown wig shot through with strands of red. Dawn opened the drawer and gaped at the pile of cash inside. 'Where did all this come from?'

'Take two hundred. Get over to Annabella's. Tell her I need a fortnight's worth of Androtone, two hundred and fifty mg a day. And Progesterone, five-mg pills, all she's got. Now go!'

Dawn peeled off four fifty-pound notes and almost ran from the room.

The patient sat back, arms over the covers, palms upwards. After a few seconds the robin flew in. It perched on the end of the bed, peered at him, then flew halfway up and landed by his hand. He watched it impassively until it alighted on his palm. Then his fingers clamped inwards, crushing it to death.

CHAPTER 30

'You've done what!' McCloughlin exploded. Jon kept his voice calm. 'Sir, he tried to run. We had no choice.'

McCloughlin looked at Rick for confirmation.

'It's true, sir. He saw me with this lot and went for the door.'

'At which point DI Spicer body-checked him so hard, he's claiming that his shoulder's dislocated.' McCloughlin voice was brimming with contempt.

'It's not dislocated, sir. Believe me, he'd have been squealing a lot louder if it was,' Jon answered.

'Shit,' said McCloughlin. He looked down at the clear plastic bag and the collection of images inside. 'So what the bloody hell are these?'

Rick stepped forward. 'It's the work of a German anatomist called Gunther von Hagen, sir. He's pioneered a process called plastination. Basically, he takes the corpses of people who've left their bodies for medical research, strips them of their flesh, dissects them to expose the internal organs, preserves the whole thing and puts them on display.'

McCloughlin was shaking his head. 'Yes, I remember there was a documentary on TV. I switched over after a few minutes.' He stared at a photo of a corpse, its own skin draped over its outstretched arm. Another of a man holding a basketball in one claw, tensed and ready to leap, all his muscles exposed, mouth open in an eternal gasp for breath. 'Where are these monstrosities put on show?'

'He has an exhibition called *Body Worlds*. It travels all around the world. These images are from when it came to London earlier this year. Loads more are for sale on the web site, too.'

McCloughlin pushed the images away. 'So Pete Gray was there. OK, go and interview him. I'll be watching.'

Jon and Rick sat down opposite Gray. He stared back at them in silence as the Neal twin-deck tape recorder whirred away.

'Strange hobby you have there. Collecting pictures of dead people, poring over anatomy textbooks. Why don't you talk us through it?' asked Jon.

Gray shrugged. 'You think I'm a ghoul.'

Jon stared back at him, thinking, too bloody right you are.

'If I were a medical student studying to be a doctor, you wouldn't be looking at me like that. You'd be full of respect at my desire to learn how the human body functions.'

'But you're not.'

'Why should that matter? Why should knowing about the secrets of our insides be confined to the medical establishment? Why should the Royal College of Surgeons deny people like me access to autopsies through their secretive Fellowships? We are all human, we're all entitled to understand how our bodies work.'

'Why?'

'Because it's fascinating. At least, I happen to find it fascinating. But, because I'm not a doctor, you think I'm a ghoul. If it helps you to understand, I wanted to be a surgeon when I was younger.'

'You wanted to be a surgeon? Why? Did some relative of yours write that *Gray's Anatomy* textbook?'

'No.'

'Was your father a surgeon?'

'No. He was a printer.'

'Was an uncle? A relative? A friend? You don't just take a fancy to being a surgeon.'

'I did. Leonardo da Vinci did, and he's regarded as a genius.'

Delusions of grandeur, Jon thought. The trait of a psychopath. He placed the plastic bag of *Body Worlds* images on the table. 'These pictures you had in your house. Why are you collecting images of corpses stripped of their skin?'

'They show the true workings of the human body in all its glory.'

'Like the corpses of Angela Rowlands, Carol Miller and Tyler Young show the true workings of the human body in all its glory?'

Gray looked disgusted. 'I've got nothing to do with them. Whoever did that is sick.'

'Paying to see skinned people and collecting photos of them isn't sick?' Jon lifted the bag and let it fall with a slap on to the table.

'Maybe you should be interviewing the other people who attended that exhibition, then. There were over eight hundred thousand of us.'

He was too glib, too well rehearsed. Time to shake him up. 'So when did you meet Angela Rowlands?'

Gray flinched. 'How do you mean?'

'I mean, when did you meet Angela Rowlands? It's a simple question.'

'Did I?'

Jon leaned forwards, aware that his next comment was about to leave him wide open with McCloughlin. But he was so close to nailing the bastard sitting opposite him, he didn't give a shit. 'How else did your sperm get inside her?'

'How do you . . . ?' The sentence faded out.

'You've got a fucking record, man!' Jon shouted. He remembered McCloughlin was listening, and lowered his voice. 'Kicking the crap out of your wife and then two other girlfriends, remember?'

'But I never gave a DNA sample. I don't understand.'

Jon's eyes flicked briefly to the mirror window

at his side and he imagined McCloughlin's face. 'We know everything about you. Now, tell me what happened!'

Gray's shoulders collapsed. 'It was at a singles' night in town.'

'Which one?'

'The Coach and Horses, near Piccadilly station.'

'And?'

'We talked, I gave her my number. I didn't think she'd call, but she did. Obviously didn't take her young friend's advice.'

'That was her daughter.'

Again Gray's face showed complete surprise at Jon's knowledge. When he proceeded, it was a lot more cautiously. 'She rang me about a week later. We met, she came back to mine and we had sex.'

'Just the one night?'

'Yes.'

'Any talking involved? Chat to her about your interest in human anatomy?'

'No! Look, I know you think I killed her. And you think I saw Carol Miller, don't you? I didn't. We talked on the phone about that bloody rowing machine, but she didn't ever come round to see it.'

'On the night she disappeared she was off to see someone about something.'

Gray started biting a thumbnail. 'Listen. When you came asking about Carol Miller that time, I didn't lie. I've never met her. But I had seen

Angela Rowlands. I thought if I told you that, you'd haul me in. And sure enough, here I am.'

Jon found himself scowling. The interview wasn't going as he'd hoped. 'How long before we find the link between you and Tyler Young? There are officers searching her home now. Will they find one of those cards you like to hand out at karaoke nights?'

'You've been following me!'

Jon ignored the remark. 'When did you meet Tyler Young?'

'How would I ever come into contact with a girl her age? Look at me.' He glanced down at his paunch. 'I'm a fat forty-three-year-old who does Elvis impressions.' He looked up, and Jon was shocked to see a tear running down his cheek. 'I'm a fucking hospital porter, for God's sake. I'd have as much chance of pulling a girl like Tyler Young as I did with Angela Rowlands' daughter.'

'You tried it on with Lucy Rowlands?' Jon asked emotionlessly.

By now Gray was openly crying. 'Yes, when her mum had gone to the toilet. She told me to fuck off.'

Jon kept at him. 'You'd have plenty of chance with Tyler Young if you were paying for it.'

Gray hauled himself up in his seat. 'I've never paid for it. Ever.' Defiance rang in his voice.

The silence stretched out until Rick nudged Jon and made a T shape with his hands.

Reluctantly, Jon reached over to the tape

361

machine. 'OK, interview suspended at three fifty-two p.m.' The tape clicked off and he got up.

'Cup of tea?' Rick asked gently.

'Three sugars,' Pete Gray replied, wiping the tears from his cheeks.

Jon was halfway down the corridor when McCloughlin's voice rang out behind him, 'Have you been following that man?'

Jon stopped. 'I was in a pub one night, sir, and observed him making a pass at a woman.'

McCloughlin gave a snort of disbelief. 'What was that about finding his DNA in Angela Rowlands?'

Jon bowed his head. 'After speaking to him in the hospital canteen the first time, I had a test run on the cup he'd been drinking from. We got a match from that.'

Fury made McCloughlin's voice squeak. 'Who the bloody hell do you think you are? I didn't authorise it, you arrogant prick. You knew it went against regulations.'

Jon turned. 'No one ever need know, sir. Now he's under arrest, we're entitled to take an evidential mouth swab from him. We'll get our match from that.'

'He's not under arrest – you're to release him without charge immediately.'

'What?'

'You've badly jumped the gun on this one, Spicer. He hardly had the look of a guilty man to me.'

'He's had a sexual encounter with one victim, phone contact with another, and we haven't even started looking into who the third victim was involved with.'

'Pretty much the same could be said for over a dozen men Angela Rowlands met through her dating agency. We haven't arrested any of them.'

'I doubt they have photos of skinned corpses in their homes.'

'So your little vendetta – which is what it looks like to me – should suddenly take precedence in this investigation?'

'I'd say it's a very promising lead.'

'A very promising lead,' McCloughlin sneered. 'DI Spicer, with Tyler Young's identification the incident room has turned into a fucking spaghetti machine. There are very promising leads oozing out all over the place. I've got three extra indexers and they still can't enter the information into HOLMES fast enough.'

Jon fought to suppress his rage.

It must have shown on his face because McCloughlin paused to let out a dry laugh. 'I'll give you one thing, you're a tenacious bastard, aren't you? The only reason you found those photos is because you barged into his home without a search warrant. And the only reason you know he had sexual relations with Angela Rowlands is because you obtained a sample of his DNA in a manner that will be laughed out of court. Now, in keeping with PACE procedures, you can put his mouth swab in for DNA analysis. It can join the queue along with our many other suspects'.'

'It could be days before we get a result.'

'So be it. I've got plenty of other leads you can be following up in the meantime. Now, process him, let him go and then report upstairs. It's time you fitted in with this investigation just like everybody else.' He brushed past.

As soon as the door to the stairway shut behind him, Jon spun round and slammed the heel of his hand against the nearest door. 'Fuck!'

Rick kept his distance. 'Easy, Jon. He isn't getting away – he's just got a stay of execution before we haul him in again.'

'Yeah, by which time he'll have destroyed any evidence in his house, had the inside of his van steam-cleaned, and thoroughly prepared his story.' He took several deep breaths. 'McCloughlin's got it in for me and it's tainting his judgement.'

Rick leaned against the wall. 'Let's just play it cool. There's time yet.'

'I need some air.' Jon strode down the corridor and out through a side door into the car park.

The scent of cigarette smoke wafted over him and he looked around. A couple of uniforms were standing there, puffing away. Before his conscience could stop him, he stepped towards them. 'Could I ponce a smoke off you?'

'No problem. You look like you need one.'

He put the cigarette in his mouth, bent towards

the lighter's flame and drew the smoke deep into his lungs. Then he leaned back against the wall and shut his eyes. Six months without a cigarette. Bollocks to it all, he thought, breathing out and immediately taking another drag. His boss, the case, the prospect of fatherhood; everything was getting to him. He thought about having to let Pete Gray back out on to the street and exhaled smoke in disgust.

When Jon and Rick walked into the incident room an hour later the place was full of excited faces. Glancing at the windows of McCloughlin's little office, they saw it was jammed with senior officers. They headed over to the receiver's desk.

'Hear you dropped a bollock with a suspect,' he said.

'We'll see,' Jon replied, lips tight. 'Why all the commotion?'

'DI Gardener's team found Tyler Young's diary in her bedroom.'

'Really?' said Rick. 'And what was in it?'

'Quite a few names.'

'Was there a Pete Gray mentioned?' Jon demanded.

The receiver looked down at a sheet of paper. 'I'm putting together a list at the moment, but no, I can't see him.'

'How about Gordon Dean?' Rick's voice was full of hope.

'No, we've looked for him already. Have a word with Sergeant Evans – he's ready to give out the first actions now.'

Jon and Rick drifted across to the allocator's desk, where a few members from the team tracing Angela Rowlands' contacts from the dating agency were already waiting.

'Tracked them all down, then?' Rick asked one of them.

'No. McCloughlin's given the Tyler Young leads priority.'

Jon glared out of the window, noting that the day's brightness had died. While they'd been in the cells a layer of grey had silently closed in over the city. In the distance he could see dark ribbons of fine drizzle drifting down. The cooler air that crept through the window had a musty smell, like that of a dank cellar.

Behind him the allocator announced, 'OK, you lot, come and get an action.'

Rick joined Jon a few seconds later, a piece of paper in his hand. He read it through and then looked up, bewilderment on his face.

'What is it?' asked Jon, turning away as the first droplets began hitting the glass and burrowing their way downwards.

'We're being sent to the Beauty Centre. Tyler Young had made enquiries with Dr O'Connor about lip implants. Then he told her he could do breast implants, too. Quoted her an amazingly low price if she could pay cash.'

CHAPTER 31

'**I**'m sure I could help with that,' Dr O'Connor said. 'Why don't you come in and see me?' He paused, a pencil balanced in his fingers. 'Tomorrow afternoon is good for me, too. I have a slot at three thirty . . . OK, that's grand. And the name was? . . . Fiona. Fiona Wilson.' He wrote it in his appointments book. 'See you tomorrow, Fiona.'

After replacing the phone, he pressed a button at the top of the unit and looked at the woman on the opposite side of his desk. 'Sorry about that. I've turned the thing off. Now, where were we?'

She crossed her legs. 'I was saying that I haven't discussed this with anyone.'

'I usually advise all my patients to seek the opinions of family or friends before embarking on any procedure,' O'Connor replied.

She shook her head. 'I want it to be a surprise, that's the whole point. I'm telling everyone that I'm going on holiday, then I'll turn up as the new me.'

'You haven't even let your partner know of your plans?'

'I'm single,' she replied. Moisture glistened in her eyes, but she blinked back the tear and sat up straight in her seat.

Yes, O'Connor thought. You've been through a traumatic experience, in all likelihood created partly by a fundamental flaw in your character. Perhaps you were too jealous. Maybe insecure. Probably just plain dull. And now, rather than address the real reasons for why things went wrong, you're going to re-invent yourself by taking out a bank loan and paying for a few cosmetic procedures. Probably treat yourself to a new hair-style, too. And that's it, the new you will carry on exactly as before because you really haven't changed a thing.

He shifted slightly in his seat, the ache in his bad knee bothering him as usual. He looked down at the patient form on the desk, and moved straight to the last section. 'Could I ask how you heard about the Beauty Centre? Were you recommended by word of mouth or did you see an advertisement?'

'I saw your advertisement in the 'Health and Beauty' section of the local paper. When I realised you were near my office, I thought I'd pop in.'

O'Connor nodded.

'So does this mean you'll treat me?' she said, as he began filling in the form.

'Well, let's start by assessing you. Which parts of your face are you unhappy with?'

She raised her chin and looked at him. 'My eyes

are sagging, especially the skin below them. And I'm developing these lines above my upper lip. My throat bothers me, too. The skin there needs tightening.'

O'Connor gazed at the face of a perfectly normal forty-five-year-old. Apart from the slight bagging off the skin below her eyes, which could be easily rectified with a blepharoplasty, she didn't need any treatment. Apart from reasons of pure vanity, at least. 'Well, I can certainly perform a couple of procedures to address those issues—'

'And my skin in general,' she interrupted, warming to her theme. 'It just looks tired, no matter how much I exfoliate and moisturise. I noticed on the stairs that you offer those lasers. How do they work?'

Her bleating had started to aggravate him, and keeping the pleasant lilt in his voice was becoming more of an effort. 'Just out of interest, how much do you spend on moisturisers?'

'Well, I use a Clarins programme. Let's say it's not cheap.'

'Anti-wrinkling properties in the treatments?'

'Of course.'

He nodded. 'I can save you that money. After all, why use anti-wrinkle treatments when you have no wrinkles to treat?'

She gasped. 'I'd never thought of it like that!'

Smiling, O'Connor swivelled the lamp on his desk so it shone directly at her face. He scrutinised her for a few seconds then said, 'Well, we offer Cool Touch laser. It works by stimulating cells to produce natural collagen, the supporting framework beneath your skin. That would take about twenty minutes. The pinkness fades very quickly and you could be back at your desk within an hour. You really haven't mentioned your visit to any of your colleagues?'

Smiling, she shook her head. 'I can't wait to see them when I walk back in.'

'But in your case I think we should opt for what used to be crudely known as a skin-peel. It's actually called laser skin resurfacing and I would admit you as a day case in order to perform it. Your skin will feel tender for about a week, but the results last much longer. You could forget about your monthly expenditure on Clarins – I'd prescribe you a moisturiser that's far less expensive.'

'That sounds better to me. And will it sort out these marks?' She held a finger to her forehead.

He leaned forward. 'Are they old acne scars?'

'Yes. They've bugged me ever since I was a teenager.'

He sat back. 'Everything would be removed.'

Eagerly, she probed her upper lip. 'What about these awful grooves that are appearing?'

Would she ever shut up? 'Well, we could eliminate those with filler. I favour Dermaleve. It involves a few injections, and the whole procedure would take half an hour. There's really very little impact on your time. If you like, I'll show you the treatment room. Then I can conduct a proper assessment prior to arranging a convenient date for your treatment.'

'Yes, I'd like that.'

He got up, straightened his stiff knee and limped round the desk. 'OK, this is where it all happens.' He unlocked the door to the treatment room. On the far side was an adjustable bed, a large roll of blue paper mounted behind it. By its side was what appeared to be a small printer or photo-copier. Grey plastic and a few buttons on the top. Cupboards lined two of the walls, and a small sink was in one corner. Next to that were several cupboards with all their doors closed. O'Connor hobbled across the shiny floor to the grey plastic machine. 'Cool Touch laser.'

She had sidled across to a poster of a smiling woman with immaculate skin. 'Doctor, you mentioned that you could do my upper lip in twenty minutes and I could go straight back to work.'

Nurse Palmer wasn't due in until the next day. Their privacy was assured. No one knew she was here. O'Connor saw the opportunity presenting itself. 'Yes. There would be a bit of pinkness and a slight numbness from the anaesthetic. I suppose if we perform the procedure now, we could fill out the rest of the form while your skin settles down.'

'How much would it cost?'

He waved a hand. 'Seventy-five pounds. But I'd only charge you once all your procedures had been successfully completed.'

'Oh,' she smiled. 'In that case, could you do it for me now?'

God, will your incessant whining never stop? He imagined how her voice box would look when the skin covering it had been stripped away. He pulled the roll of blue paper until a length of it covered the treatment bed. 'Hop up.'

She removed her coat, climbed up and sat back. 'Will it hurt? Needles really bother me.'

O'Connor flicked on the examination light hanging down from the ceiling. Then he turned on a tape recorder. As the sound of soothing pan pipes filled the room, he unlocked a cupboard. It was filled with bottles and boxes. He took out a pre-prepared syringe, the needle only centimetres long. Inside was a clear, gel-like substance. 'Here it is, five millilitres of Dermaleve. And no, you won't feel a thing. I'll apply some anaesthetic cream first.'

'That's a relief.' She sat back.

He moved out of her line of vision then took an empty syringe from the cupboard. Next he removed a tiny vial of Propofol from the shelf, washed his hands in the sink and dried them. After smearing her upper lip with cream he said, 'OK, I'll get everything ready back here while that takes effect. You just relax.'

He pulled on a pair of size eight latex gloves, picked up the syringe and sucked the Propofol into it. He placed it in a stainless-steel kidney tray, put that on a small trolley and wheeled it over.

Sitting down on a stool by the top of the treatment bed, he leaned forward. 'How does that feel?'

'I don't think it's . . .' she mumbled. 'Oh, my mouth won't work properly.' She tried to smile, but her upper lip wouldn't respond.

'Perfect. Now close your eyes and lift your chin up slightly.' Visualising what was beneath her skin, he traced the facial vein as it crossed the submandibular salivary gland and branched off beneath the skin of her upper lip. He slid the needle in and injected half the Propofol directly into it. He knew the anaesthetic would render his patient immobile in seconds.

Calmly, he returned the syringe to the tray and walked back over to the cupboards. 'How does that feel?'

She didn't reply. He returned to the treatment table and looked at her. Her eyes were fixed open and he lifted a hand to shield them from the harsh light above. Gradually her pupils widened a fraction. 'Good, you can hear me but you can't move.' He sat back on the stool and, keeping the soothing, doctorly, tone in his voice, took her hand. 'I want you to know that I despise you.'

Flecks of panic flew from her irises, though her breathing stayed steady and slow.

Needing time to quell the bile in his throat, he listened to the music for a few seconds. 'Don't worry, my skills are far superior to injecting bloody filler.' Angrily, he looked around the treatment room, then began breathing deeply. When he spoke again, his voice had a melancholy note. 'Not here. We're going to a place where I won't have to hurry. Mine is a delicate art, one that we don't want to rush.'

He lifted the half-full syringe, turned her head slightly to the side and injected the remaining Propofol directly into her external jugular vein. Her eyelids slowly lowered and she slipped from consciousness.

CHAPTER 32

'I'm afraid she wasn't in, Alex,' Dawn said miserably, taking off her soaking wet coat and laying the cash on the end of the bed.

He dropped the mirror on the bedsheet and started to sob. 'Oh God, look at me. I'm vile, absolutely vile.'

'You're not,' Dawn insisted, trying to take his hand. 'You're beautiful.'

She peered at him, always slightly amazed at how different the person she had fallen in love with now looked. When they'd met in Boots his blond hair had been long and swept back from a face which, although unmistakably masculine, had a curious delicacy. She sometimes thought that maybe there'd been a woman in there all along.

Gradually his appearance had then altered. Superficial changes like the removal of his hair were immediate. A simple laser treatment and female hormones saw to that. Then came the operations. His angular cheeks were smoothed over and filled out, his chin reduced and rounded off, his lips enlarged. Now his square jaw was gone and his nose had been turned into something dainty and petite.

When his breasts were inserted last year the switch in genders became startlingly real. But still he refused to let her call him 'she'. Only once they'd been to Amsterdam for his vaginoplasty. Then he'd be a real woman.

He picked the mirror up again and started to probe his Adam's apple. 'I need the tracheal reduction to get rid of this.'

'You can, Alex. You just have to be patient. You've come so far.' She reached out and embraced him, running her fingers through his short hair until he calmed down.

She'd never seen him like this before. However difficult things had got for them in the past, it had only made her more determined to stick with him. This rage was something new. The way he'd started shouting at her. It reminded her of previous relationships. Ones that had ended in her being beaten up and eventually having to flee.

Gently she said, 'That woman I told you about. Fiona. She called in at the motel again. She thinks the name of the girl she heard being attacked in the motel was Alexia. She's searching everywhere for her, trying to find out if she's OK. She won't give up. It's like an obsession.'

He raised his head to look at her. A muscle had gone into spasm at the corner of his mouth and he looked like he was repeatedly attempting a particularly miserable smile. 'What do you mean, searching everywhere for her?'

Dawn shivered. 'She lost a daughter years ago and now this Alexia is part of that guilt. It's like she believes that if she can find her and make sure she's safe, her own life can move on. So she's up and down Minshull Street talking to all the girls. Someone said she'd find her in Crimson, so she's been going there, too.'

'And she's been talking to a policeman about it?'

'Yes, the one I saw at Doctor O'Connor's surgery. Alex, do you know what this is about? That night in the motel—'

He slammed the mirror down on the bedside table, cracking the glass. 'Give me her address.'

'Why?'

He sat on the edge of the bed, knees sticking out from under the hem of his nightie. 'Gordon Dean was a pervert.'

Dawn stared at him in silence.

'He wanted to tie me to that bed, wanted to perform his sick fantasies on me.' He glanced at her. 'He wanted to humiliate me.'

Dawn's hand went up to her mouth. 'What are you saying?'

'God knows, he'd have tried to kill me if I'd let him bind my hands. But I asked to tie him up first. He liked that. He was the same as the others, not interested in me as a woman. Just interested in me as a freak.' His hand went to his groin and he grabbed his penis through his nightie. 'If this was gone, he wouldn't have been interested. Yes, I killed him and took his money.'

Dawn turned slowly to look at the fifty-pound notes on the bed. 'You killed him?'

'Dawn, we're so close to getting out.' He held his hand up. 'It's within reach. You and me, living together in Amsterdam. No fear of persecution. We'll be so happy together. But this Fiona's determined to ruin it for us. I need her address. What is it?'

'What will you do?'

'Just talk to her. Explain that I'm Alexia. Show her that I'm all right and ask her to leave us alone.'

He got up and pulled a purple tracksuit on over the nightie. 'Her address, Dawn. Give it to me please.'

Dawn was hunched over, gently rocking herself back and forth. 'You killed him?'

He regarded her for a second, then turned to the mirror and starting applying make-up, vainly trying to mask the bruising around his nose and below his eyes. After that he put the wig on, teasing strands of hair forwards so they hung over his eyes. Next he took a chiffon scarf and wrapped it round his neck, fluffing the folds of material up so his jaw was hidden. 'The address, Dawn.'

The room was silent.

He put on a pair of high heels, then turned round. Her handbag was on the bed. His footsteps were loud as he stepped across and picked it up. Her address book was in there and he began flicking through the pages. There weren't many entries.

Finally Dawn looked up. 'No, you mustn't! Give it to me.'

She made a feeble lunge for the book but he batted her hand away. 'Is this her? Fiona Wilson? It is, isn't it?'

'Leave her alone!' She tried to stand but he shoved her back on the bed. The first time he'd ever used force against her. She curled into a ball as he ripped the page out and strode from the room.

The buzzer made Fiona's hand jolt. She grabbed a tissue and wiped off the bit of misapplied lipstick. Then she looked towards the door. No one had arranged to come round. Besides, she had to be at the hotel airport in under an hour: her first client was expecting her.

The buzzer went again.

This time Fiona replaced the lipstick in her make-up bag and stood. She straightened her dress and walked over to the door. As she peered out into the hallway the buzzer went yet again.

She padded across to the outer door and looked through the peephole to the street. All she could see was rain drifting down and a huge bunch of flowers.

Joanne Perkins, she thought. It must be a good-luck gesture. Something she does for all her escorts before their first date. How sweet.

She opened the door and looked out. The flowers dropped to the doorstep and her husband's dripping face leered at her. 'Found you, you fucking bitch.'

The sour stink of whisky hit her in the face.

Fiona tried to slam the door, but he jammed his foot into the gap. Knowing she'd never get her bedsit door locked in time, she whirled round and darted for the stairs. As she raced up them his footsteps were heavy behind her. She ran into the bathroom and slid the heavy brass bolt shut. The window was half open when he started kicking the door. Climbing out on to the windowsill, she reached an arm round the wet drainpipe. Her car was parked directly below, spare key hidden in the gap between the bricks.

CHAPTER 33

'Can I remind you this is a murder investigation?' Rick shook his head disbelievingly at Jon. 'That's right, the investigation is ongoing . . . Yes, you go and check with someone more senior.'

He cupped a hand over the phone mouthpiece. 'Incredible. The General Medical Council. Protecting patients and guiding doctors, according to their web site. More interested in looking after their own, if you ask me.' Abruptly he took his hand off the mouthpiece. 'Yes, it's extremely urgent. Call it a matter of life and death if you like – the Hippocratic oath has something to say about that, doesn't it? . . . Thank you. Email is perfect.'

A message pinged on Rick's computer ten minutes later. He printed the documents out and sat down.

'Jesus Christ,' he whispered. 'He's a bit more than the plain old Dr O'Connor written on that brass plate outside the Beauty Centre.'

'Go on,' said Jon, leaning forward, elbows on the table.

'Try Dr Eamon O'Connor BDS, MB Bchir, FDSRC (Eng), FRCS (Eng), Phd. He's an oral and maxillofacial surgeon.'

Jon stared at him blankly. 'What's that?'

'Fucked if I know,' Rick replied, scanning down the top sheet. 'Born 5 August 1948, Dublin. Spent five years at dental school there, then two years training as a surgical dentist at Bart's in London. Then he took a postgraduate qualification at the Royal College. Passed it to become a Fellow in Dental Surgery.'

'So he's really a dentist?' Jon asked, thinking about Tyler Young's missing teeth.

'I haven't even started yet. Then he went back to medical school as an undergraduate. Four years at Cambridge, emerging as Dr O'Connor. One year as a junior houseman at Guy's, where he spent six months training in general surgery and six months training in general medicine.'

'General surgery?'

'Wait,' said Rick. 'There's plenty more. Next he spent two years doing a Basic Surgical Training Rotation. Six months at the Accident and Emergency at St Thomas's, six months in their cardio-thoracic unit, and finally one year learning plastic surgery at University College London hospital. Then he took another exam to become a Fellow of the Royal College of Surgeons. After that he spent five years as a registrar at Guy's. He got a consultant's post there, and he started specialising in cranio-facial surgery.'

382

Rick read the next paragraph in silence, shaking his head all the while.

'What?' Jon demanded.

'Get this. It says that while he was a consultant at Guy's he reconstructed a lot of faces that had undergone major traumas. Even worked on a couple of casualties from the Falklands conflict. But his particular area of expertise, and one that he pioneered new techniques in, was removing sections of patient's faces to allow neurosurgeons access to tumours located at the base of the brain.'

Jon got up. 'You're serious?'

Before he could walk round and look at the documents himself, Rick tossed the top one across the desk.

Jon sat back down and flicked through it, stopping at the last page. 'It says here that, in 1989, he attended a hearing of the Professional Conduct Committee. Something called an FTP.'

'Fit to Practise,' said Rick, consulting another sheet. 'The committee judged that his FTP was impaired due to mental ill health resulting from a drug dependency. He botched an operation and left a patient with brain damage.'

'What was he taking?'

'Diamorphine.' Rick whistled. 'He got addicted to smack. Mitigating circumstances according to this. He smashed his knee in a road traffic accident and that led to his dependency.'

Jon snapped his fingers. 'The strange footprint!

He's never emerged from behind that bloody great desk of his. We've never seen him walk.'

Rick traced a finger down his sheet. 'So they suspended him from the medical register. Then, three years later, they allowed him to practise again, but with conditions on his registration.'

'Don't tell me,' Jon said, dropping the print out on the desk. 'He's not allowed to perform surgery.'

'Exactly,' said Rick. 'He moved to Manchester and set up the Beauty Centre in 1994.'

They parked in the side street by the Beauty Centre.

Jon looked into the rear yard of the building. 'The Range Rover's there. He must be in.' Then he glanced up at the heavy sky. 'This is coming in off the Irish sea. It won't stop for a while yet.'

They hurried round to the front entrance of the blackened building and rang the buzzer. After waiting a couple of minutes, Jon stepped back out into the rain and looked up. Doctor O'Connor tried to shrink back from the window, but their eyes had met.

Jon held a finger to his chest, then pointed upwards. Seconds later, the lock on the door clicked open.

They moved quickly up the stairs, Jon anxious to close down his time to think. When they entered his room, O'Connor was sitting behind his desk removing the skin from another tangerine. 'Gentlemen? You caught me just as I was about to lock up.'

They shook hands again and sat down. Jon glanced at Rick, a cue for him to begin.

'We don't want to keep you,' said Rick.

'Go ahead.' The doctor smiled and sat back, the leather of his chair creaking slightly. 'News about Gordon Dean?'

'No.' Rick slid the photo of Tyler Young from his jacket and laid it on the desk between them.

Jon studied O'Connor's reaction. He looked down, put the half-peeled piece of fruit aside, then extended a forefinger and rotated the photo so it was in perfect alignment with the edge of his desk. As usual he kept a poker face, not a hint of emotion on it. He looked up and raised his eyebrows questioningly, the skin on his forehead barely wrinkling.

'Have you ever seen this woman?' Rick asked.

The doctor didn't look at the photo. 'No.'

'You've never spoken to her?'

'How could I say? I get a lot of telephone enquiries. I could have spoken to her, but I wouldn't know what on earth she looked like. To what is this in relation?'

'According to her diary, she was discussing lip implants with you. Then you mentioned breast implants, too. Your prices were extremely competitive.'

O'Connor interlinked his fingers over the photograph, concealing the smiling face below. 'That's impossible for two reasons. One, I only perform non-surgical procedures. Two, she's clearly under twenty-five and I've made it a condition of the Beauty Centre not to offer treatment to anyone below that age.' He slid a brochure across the desk. 'Here, you'll find it in my introduction on page two.'

Jon got up and walked over to the shelves of books behind the doctor. O'Connor clearly found his presence there unsettling and partly turned in his seat.

Rick ignored the glossy booklet and nodded at the photograph. 'The body of Tyler Young was recently found with her breasts, face and large amounts of her flesh removed. Have you ever spoken to Carol Miller or Angela Rowlands? Their bodies were also discovered not long ago with most of their skin missing.'

O'Connor turned his attention back to Rick. Still his expression was neutral. 'Of course I haven't.'

Jon spoke. 'Interesting collection of books you have here. Tell me, Doctor O'Connor, you only perform cosmetic procedures?'

'Aesthetic medicine, I prefer to call it.'

'So why have you got a copy of this?' He didn't identify *Gray's Anatomy* or take it off the shelf, trying to oblige the doctor to get out of his seat.

But O'Connor leaned forward and peered round Jon. Before answering, he looked at Rick, then back at Jon, his eyes calculating. 'Would you mind sitting down? I can't speak to you and your colleague if you're hovering behind me.'

386

Jon shrugged and took a seat, pleased to have rattled the doctor's apparent calm.

'I used to perform surgical procedures. Facial reconstructions for people who'd developed brain tumours or for the victims of car crashes and suchlike. Then, rather ironically, I was involved in a crash myself. My left knee was badly damaged and I developed an addiction to painkillers.'

'What sort of painkillers?' asked Rick.

O'Connor's eyes filled with shame. 'Diamorphine. I had free and easy access to it through my surgical work. Eventually it had a detrimental effect on my ability to perform. I was investigated by the General Medical Council and my licence was suspended. After attending a rehabilitation course, I was allowed to practice again – but with the condition I didn't perform surgery. That book is a leftover from my earlier career.'

The room was silent for a moment. Then Jon looked around and said, 'For a business, this place is always very quiet. When do you actually treat people?'

'Normally I use Thursdays and Fridays as my treatment days. It gives customers the weekend to recover. The rest of the week is given over to fielding enquiries, conducting consultations and, if I think it's appropriate, booking in customers for treatment.'

'So if those days are for, essentially, drumming up business, why did you ignore the door buzzer on our previous visit?' Jon stood up again and went to the window.

The doctor shifted in his seat. 'Probably because I was talking with you.'

'On our last visit I looked out of this window, like I'm doing now, and saw that your caller was a woman I recognised. She works in a motel on the A57. When she saw me looking down she couldn't walk away quickly enough. Why do you think that was?'

The doctor raised one shoulder a fraction. 'Perhaps she was coy about the fact she was considering aesthetic medicine. There's still a surprising amount of stigma attached, though it's lessening all the time, thanks to the exemplary lead provided by our celebrities.'

Jon thought he heard a cynical note in the doctor's voice. He walked over to the doorway and pointed across the corridor to the treatment room. 'Would you mind if I look around? Is this where you carry out your procedures?'

The doctor kept his seat but leaned forward, agitation finally showing. 'I'm afraid that room is locked.'

'Surely you have the key?'

'I've left it at home. My nurse has the other, but she's only here if we're treating customers.' He licked his lips.

Jon stared at him, sensing the man was telling lies. The blank expression was still clamped on the doctor's face, but a faint sheen of sweat glistened on his forehead. Jon's hand was outstretched to try the door handle. Instead, he crossed the room and, like a predator closing in for the kill, leaned in towards the doctor's face. Small beads of sweat oozed out of the shiny skin and began to run down his forehead.

'You're sweating, Doctor. Or can't you feel that? Perhaps you've been using Botox a bit too much. It wouldn't be the first time you've self-administered, after all.'

The doctor angrily wiped a hand across his forehead. 'I resent that insinuation and I don't like the direction this discussion is taking. I'm not prepared to say anything more without my solicitor present.'

'That's probably a good idea,' Jon replied.

O'Connor stood up and walked to the door: they saw that he had a pronounced limp. 'Good day, officers. You can show yourselves out.'

As they passed him, Jon smiled. 'I'm sure we'll be speaking to you again very soon, Doctor.'

When they emerged on to the street, the drizzle was still falling.

'Why didn't we just arrest him?' asked Rick.

Jon kept walking. 'After what happened with Pete Gray? The top of McCloughlin's head would blow clean off.'

'The man's bullshitting us! It's as clear as day.'

'I know.' Jon unlocked the car. 'Let's wait here and see what he does next. He's rattled. My bet is he'll be off like a shot.'

They moved further down the street and swung

the car round. While they waited Jon watched the giant cranes looming out of the haze shrouding Ancoats. One was silently turning, a load of girders suspended from its end. Jon was reminded of a gentle animal, quietly grazing. But it was a harsh clanging that carried from behind the buildings in front. The noise seemed more akin to destruction, as if that part of the city was being demolished, not rebuilt.

O'Connor's Range Rover appeared ten minutes later. He drove up to the junction with the main road and turned right. With their windscreen wipers on their fastest setting, Jon and Rick followed him as he headed along Great Ancoats Street, passing the black glass of the old *Daily Express* offices and assorted derelict industrial buildings. Soon he got to the junction with the A57, just up from the Hurlington Health Club. He turned left, away from the city centre and towards the Platinum Inn. The streetlights flickered to life as the sky darkened above them.

'We're right in the Butcher's dumping ground. It's him. It has to be him!' Rick whispered excitedly.

Jon kept a couple of cars behind. They passed the motel and the greyhound stadium, then crawled through Gorton, failed shops and the occasional massage parlour lining the road. When they reached the roundabout for the M60, the Range Rover took the final exit, heading south, keeping in the slow lane, speed never creeping above seventy miles per hour.

'The turn off for Didsbury is in two junctions' time,' Jon said, remembering Dr Heath's report.

But O'Connor took the next exit. They dropped back and shadowed him along the A560, passing a Safeway and then a boarded-up building with the name Quaffers just visible above the entrance.

Five minutes later they were driving through the centre of Romiley, one car behind him. The high street petered out, shops replaced by terraces of housing. Soon they changed to semi-detached, then finally detached as countryside opened up on the left of the road. Farm lights dotted the dark hills in the distance. After a couple of hundred metres the Range Rover's brake lights lit up and it swung into a driveway closed in by large fir trees.

Jon and Rick pulled up on the verge. A privet hedge shielded the house from the road and they squeezed through the soaking branches into O'Connor's garden.

Crouching behind a rhododendron bush, they saw him hobble up the steps to a large Victorian house with wooden gables and a band of decorative brickwork running above the ground-floor mullioned windows. The exterior light came on and he set his briefcase down at his feet in order to unlock the front door.

The hallway lights went on. He came back outside and walked over to the rear of the Range Rover. After glancing down the drive, he opened the boot. He leaned in and, with some effort, straightened up. In his arms was a large object wrapped in a sheet.

'Christ almighty!' Rick whispered as the material slipped and a pair of feet wearing women's shoes were revealed.

'Oh, my fucking God,' Jon said, straightening up.

He felt Rick pulling him down as the doctor plodded up the steps into his house and shut the door behind him. 'Wait, Jon. We've got to call for back-up.'

Jon shook his head. 'They'll take half an hour, easily. She could be dead by then.'

Squinting at the placard beside the front door, Rick scrabbled for his phone. 'DS Saville here. We need back-up. We have a potential hostage situation at The Briars, Compstall Lane . . . Yes, Armed Response Vehicle, everything. You'll see our car parked on the side of the road. It's a dark-blue Volvo, registration mike, alpha, zero, two, hotel, tango, foxtrot.'

He lowered the phone. 'They're on the way.'

A light showed in a tiny window at the base of the house, just above ground level.

'He's got a cellar,' Jon whispered. 'He's taken her down into the cellar. He's skinning them down there and then driving back into Belle Vue to dump their bodies.'

Keeping low, he splashed through the shallow puddles dotting the lawn, slowing when he reached the driveway. Carefully, he crossed the tarmac and crouched against the wall.

Rick emerged from the gloom and squatted down beside him.

Jon lay on his stomach and tried to look through the filthy pane of glass. A shadow moved across the room below and he was just able to hear a door open. 'He's down there. Taken her into a side room, I think.'

A car passed on the road. As the noise of its engine died away he heard a metallic clink. It was exactly the same sound as when the consultant at Stepping Hill hospital had dropped the long-bladed scalpel in the kidney tray. 'Oh, sweet Jesus. Rick, we can't wait. He's going to start skinning her.'

'You can't go in! We've got to wait.'

Jon got to his feet and went to the front door. It was made of solid-looking wood with two panels of stained glass running down it. He pressed the bell and heard it ring deep inside the house.

He counted to thirty, then pressed the bell again and kept his finger on it. Eventually he saw movement behind the glass. There was a rattling of a chain and the door opened a few inches. The instant O'Connor saw Jon outside he tried to slam the door shut.

Jon crashed his shoulder against it, just managing to prevent it clicking back on to the latch. The doctor pushed from the other side and for a few moments they were cheek to cheek, just the layer of wood separating them. Jon felt his strength begin to show and the door started inching inwards.

Abruptly the resistance disappeared and the doctor fled down the corridor, surgical gown flapping behind him.

Jon took a step back and kicked the door open, part of the security chain spinning across the hallway tiles.

He raced down the long corridor and into the kitchen. The doctor's briefcase lay partly open on the floor, files spilling out of it. Jon looked around. The door leading down to the cellar was in the opposite corner and it was slightly ajar.

He heard a voice behind him. 'Where is he?'

'Down there.' Jon pointed to the door and then whirled round. Against one wall stood a Welsh dresser and next to it was a wicker basket containing walking sticks and umbrellas. Jon grabbed a thick walking stick with a V-shaped split at the top and approached the cellar door.

He pushed it fully open with the end of the stick and looked down. A flight of bare wooden stairs led to a concrete floor. He started downwards, holding the stick before him. A shudder caught his shoulders and then snaked down his back as the air grew noticeably cooler. The cellar's central area was lit by a single bulb and three plywood doors led off from it, light shining from beneath two of them.

Jon stood listening.

To his side, an ancient-looking boiler came to life, a line of blue flames flaring behind a soot-speckled panel of glass. The row of pipes fastened to the bare brick wall above it started to creak and tick.

'Doctor O'Connor, there's no means of escape down here. Come out now.'

No reply.

Jon stepped up to the door for the unlit room and kicked it open. A dark and narrow space was beyond, the floor knee deep in coal.

He kicked open the next door. A larger room, lit by another single bulb which revealed stacks of medical journals, a pristine mountain bike, some folded-up deckchairs. At the back was a pile of clothes and women's shoes.

He turned to Rick and pointed at the last door.

Rick shook his head furiously and mouthed, 'Wait.'

The flames of the boiler went out and, as the cellar became silent again, they could hear a faint, wet hissing sound as if someone was blowing a thin stream of air through their teeth. They looked questioningly at each other, then Jon bowed his head and listened.

As he did so, a trickle of blood began to creep out from under the door. He jumped backwards, lowered his shoulder and charged. The door splintered off its hinges and he nearly fell into the room beyond. A cluster of halogen lights shone down, adding a glare to bright white walls that were spattered with dry blood. In the centre of the room was a concrete block, topped with a layer of what appeared to be marble. Stretched out on it was the woman, still partly wrapped in the sheet. Jon could see that she was still fully clothed.

The hissing was coming from the side of the room and Jon turned his head.

O'Connor was sitting with his back against the wall. His hands were slick and red and he was clumsily trying to pick up a scalpel caught in the blood-filled folds of his surgical gown. Blood spurted from his neck, each little jet hissing like a snake as it erupted into the air.

Rick came in. 'Oh my God, we need . . . we need cloth. Something to stem the bleeding.' He grabbed the corner of the sheet wrapping the woman and tried to tear it.

O'Connor at last got a grip on the scalpel with his right hand. He turned his left wrist upwards and moved the tip of the blade towards it. Jon lifted the walking stick and brought the V of it down on to the doctor's right hand, pinning it in the puddle spreading out beneath his legs.

He told Rick, 'Leave it. The woman's our priority. Has she got a pulse?'

With shaking hands, Rick felt her neck. 'She's alive.'

'Then get upstairs and find out where the paramedics are. Now!'

Rick's mouth opened and shut. He pulled his mobile phone out and hurried back up the stairs. Jon looked around. Next to the woman was a small trolley. In a stainless steel tray on top of it were two syringes and a pair of latex gloves. Medical instruments lined the back wall. More scalpels, blades becoming ever more thin and cruel. Next to them were saws, clamps, retractors, hammers, chisels. A drill with a shiny silver bit. His eyes were caught by a test tube filled with what appeared to be human teeth.

He felt the walking stick shift and he looked down. The doctor was feebly trying to lift his scalpel hand.

Jon leaned on the stick. 'You're not taking the easy way out. Not before you tell me why.'

The doctor slumped back against the wall and raised his eyes. Even under the harsh lights their shine was fading, and Jon knew he hadn't long left. The little jets coming from his throat were getting smaller, weaker.

'Why?' Jon repeated. 'Why did you do it?'

O'Connor's eyes swivelled to Jon's hands and his voice sounded like wind in a cave. 'Enjoyable, isn't it?'

'What?' Jon demanded.

'Playing God, controlling whether I live or die.'

Jon looked at his knuckles, saw they were white with the pressure he was exerting on the end of the stick. He took his weight off. 'I'm not like you, Doctor.'

O'Connor's lips stretched in a faint smile as his head sagged forward and his eyes slowly shut. The blood now just trickled from his throat.

Jon knocked the scalpel from O'Connor's hand and rammed the V of the stick against the man's forehead, cracking his head against the white plaster. 'Why? Tell me why!'

The tiniest slit opened between the doctor's eyelids and a faint whisper emerged from his bloodless lips. 'We're just the same underneath.'

Violently Jon shook his head. 'No. No, we're not. Tell me . . .'

His words faded to a whisper. The doctor had gone.

Jon stepped away from the pool of blood which was moving slowly across the floor like a living thing, easing itself into the gutter that ran around the table, dripping through the slats of the rusty drain.

He lifted the woman clear of the cold stone and carried her out of that terrible room with its cloying aroma of blood, both fresh and old.

Up in the kitchen he laid her on the table, lowering her head gently to the oak surface, tilting it back to make sure her airways were clear. He could hear Rick talking on the phone out on the front step. He sat down at the table, as if starting a vigil at the woman's side.

The doctor's briefcase and files still lay on the floor. Jon's eyes settled on the uppermost folder and the name written on its front: 'Alex/Alexia Donley'.

Alexia. The name of the prostitute Fiona Wilson was so desperate to find. He picked the file up and opened it.

A patient profile, Polaroid photo of a man in the

upper right-hand corner. He was staring at the camera, self-conscious in its uncompromising gaze.

Alex Donley
Age: *34*
Initial assessment: *3/3/01*
Patient background: *Alex came to me in a state of considerable agitation. In the last few years he has come to believe that he is a transsexual and has been seeking a gender reassignment through the NHS. His GP 'reluctantly' (to use Alex's word) referred him to the gender identity clinic at Charing Cross hospital. After fully assessing him, a consultant psychiatrist there judged that Alex wasn't a genuine transsexual. Alex scathingly told me that the consultant thought Alex is interested in becoming a woman because he believes it will resolve the violent outbursts to which he is susceptible. I questioned Alex more closely on this and he expressed his opinion that, once his testes have been removed and oestrogen prescribed, his masculine traits (which he sees purely in the form of aggression) will be replaced by feminine traits (which he sees purely in terms of compassion). Despite this obviously simplistic belief, Alex presents a rare and challenging case.*

Jon heard footsteps in the hallway. He looked up to see Rick and a couple of armed officers trooping towards him.

'Where is he?' the one in front asked.

Jon nodded towards the cellar door. 'Down there, but you needn't worry, he's dead. It's a crime scene now, so best keep out.' He turned back to the file on his lap, the voices around him fading away.

I explained to Alex that I do not have the expertise or facilities to perform a vaginoplasty – recommending that he pay privately for the operation in Holland. Despite this, he was keen for me to perform facial surgery in order to feminise his features. We agreed that he should start a course of hormone therapy in order to develop breasts, redistribute fat around his hips and thighs, soften his body and facial hair and lift the pitch of his voice.

In terms of facial reconstruction we agreed on the following areas:

Octoplasty (to reduce the protrusion of his ears)

Rhinoplasty (to create a thinner nose)

Thyroid chondroplasty (to reduce the prominence of his Adam's apple)

Mandibular osteotomy (to reduce the squareness of his jawbone)

Dermal implants to cheeks, chin and lips (to round out his face)

Laser hair removal (back of neck, chest, nipples, underarms, forearms and hands)

Breast augmentation (C cup)
*Alex appreciates that the treatment is on an
unofficial basis and that the prices I charge
reflect that. He has stated that he will pay
for the procedures on a stage-by-stage basis
as the necessary funds become available to
him.*

A hand shook Jon's shoulder and he looked up at
the officer who'd spoken earlier.

'I said, how is she? What's he done to her?'

'Sedated her somehow.' Jon held a finger to her
neck. 'Her pulse and breathing are regular. Where
are the bloody paramedics?'

'On their way.'

Cursing, Jon returned to the file and flipped the
page. A photo of Alex with bandaging around his
ears, cheeks swollen and red. *16.7.01 Octoplasty
and cheek implants. Paid cash.*

On the next page Alex was pouting at the
camera, make-up and mascara on. *23.3.02. Breast
augmentation, lip enlargement and laser hair removal.
Paid cash.*

On the next he was wearing a wavy red wig.
5.12.02 Chin implant. Jon realised he was looking
at the woman from the garage forecourt CCTV
footage.

His mind started ticking. The false eyelash in the
boot of Gordon Dean's car. The last withdrawal
on his credit card from a cashpoint that wasn't
overlooked by CCTV cameras. Gordon Dean's car

turning right as it left the garage forecourt, heading towards the Platinum Inn.

The pieces were coming together.

Alex Donley had killed Gordon Dean in that hotel room and put his body in the boot of the car. Then he'd driven to the Manchester Ship Canal and rolled the corpse in. After that, he'd cleaned out Dean's credit-card account and left the car at Piccadilly station to create a false trail.

Fiona Wilson had indeed heard a prostitute and a punter in the next room – but the person choked to death wasn't Alexia, it was Gordon Dean.

Jon turned the page and felt his scalp contract. There it was. *3.3.03* – the day after Gordon Dean had disappeared. *Rhinoplasty and mandibular osteotomy. Paid cash.* Alex Donley had funded the procedure with the money he'd taken from Gordon Dean's bank account the night before.

Rick sat down next to him. 'Just spoke to McCloughlin. He's on his way, though it nearly choked him to say it.'

Jon reached for his mobile, then realised he'd left it in the incident room. 'Give us your phone a second.'

Rick flinched at his abrupt tone but handed it over.

'Keep a check on her breathing,' Jon said, whipping out the notebook from his jacket. He flicked through to Fiona's mobile and rang it. Answerphone. He cut it off and thought for a second. It was evening opening at the salon. By the time Alice answered, he was standing on the front steps, noting with relief that the night was now clear. 'Ali, it's me. Your friend Fiona, where did you say she is?'

'She moved into a bedsit near Manchester City's old ground.'

'She still trying to find Alexia?'

Alice sighed. 'She thought she had the other day. But it was a mix-up of names. Yeah, she's out most nights I think.'

'I need her address, Ali. Have you got it there?'

'Jon, I'm with a customer. Can't it wait?'

'Alice, she's in real danger. I need it right now.'

Jon heard her making apologies to her client. Movement as she left the room.

An ambulance pulled into the driveway. The driver cut the engine and Jon heard the rear doors being opened. A moment later two paramedics appeared.

'Straight down the corridor into the kitchen,' Jon told them.

At the other end of the line he heard Alice call out, 'Has someone moved Fiona's address? It was in the back of the appointments book.'

A female voice just audible. 'Oh, sorry, it's by the till. I had to give it to someone trying to deliver her some flowers.'

Alice again. 'You what? Who did you give it to?'

'A woman. She had a bouquet for Fiona.'

'When was this?'

'Earlier today. Lunchtime.'

'Jesus Christ, Zoe, that address was a secret.

Jon?' Her voice was louder now. 'It's Flat 2, 15 Ridley Place, Fallowfield. Can you get over there now? I think her husband may have tracked her down.'

He turned and shouted down the corridor, 'Rick! I've got to go, that friend of Alice's is in serious trouble.'

Rick strode towards him, astonishment on his face. 'McCloughlin isn't here yet.'

'I know.' Jon handed back the phone. 'I'll let you fill him in.'

Rick's hand was still out, the phone resting on his upturned palm. 'You're not serious?'

But Jon was already jogging down the garden path, pulling the car keys from his pocket.

CHAPTER 34

Alex Donley paused at the front door of 15 Ridley Place. A huge bouquet of soaking flowers lay on the top step. The card read, *Together for ever.*

As he adjusted his wig and pulled the chiffon scarf up to hide the stitches running along his jaw, he noticed the door was slightly ajar.

With the tips of his varnished nails he pushed it open. The hallway was deserted. He could hear loud music upstairs. He looked at the doors in front of him and saw that number two was slightly open as well.

His heels clicked lightly as he stepped across the plastic tiles. Silence from Fiona's flat. Carefully, he pulled the kitchen knife from his handbag and eased the door open.

Thick fingers grabbed him by the wrist and he was yanked into the wrecked room beyond. A big man, growling with fury, swung him against the wall. The tip of the knife struck a radiator and was knocked from his grip. Another hand locked on to his jaw.

Alex smelled whisky as the man looked him up

and down before saying, 'What sort of a fucking freak are you?'

He tried to escape the man's disgusted stare by turning his head, but the man yanked his chin round. Sharp pain shot along his stitches.

'I said, what sort of a fucking freak are you?'

'Let me go.'

But the man's grip on his face was steadily increasing. He felt the stitches starting to tear. Rage erupted in him like a geyser going off. He brought his hand up between the man's legs, grabbed his scrotum and twisted as hard as he could. The hands clamped on his jaw and wrist instantly released. Alex's free hand came up under the man's chin, preventing him from doubling over. Their eyes met for an instant, then Alex crashed his forehead against the man's nose. He dropped to the carpet as if taken out by a sniper.

Alex felt his face. His fingers came away covered in blood. The pain, the days spent in that bed, all for nothing. 'You fuck!' He stamped on the man's face, high heel snapping off as it connected with his teeth. 'You fuck, you fuck, you fuck!' he screamed, bringing his foot down again and again and again.

As he turned away he spotted a hand mirror on the shelf. When he looked into it he saw that his wig was hanging off one side of his head, an eyelash was missing and a four-inch slit had opened up along his left jaw, blood streaming down into the folds of his scarf.

'You piece of shit,' he said to the prone form curled on the floor, aiming one last stamp at the man's blood-filled ear.

He took out his mobile phone, waited until his breathing slowed down. 'Dawn, she's not here. Where else might she be? Didn't you mention a sal—'

Dawn cut in. 'She's here.'

'What, now?'

'Yes. She's asleep in one of the upstairs rooms. She turned up around half an hour ago and drank half a bottle of brandy straight down.'

'What did you tell her? Did you tell her about me?'

'No, I hardly said a word. She was going on about her husband finding her. Alex, what are you going to do?'

'Don't let her out.' He kicked the bouquet into a bush and staggered down the steps.

Ten minutes later Jon slipped cautiously into Fiona Wilson's flat and looked down. A large man with tight grey curls lay on the floor, face bruised and swollen, blood oozing from his nose, mouth and ears. Jon couldn't tell if it was Jeff Wilson or not. Next to his head was the broken-off heel of a woman's shoe.

Jon crouched down and started to put him in the recovery position. An eye opened, slit-like in the puffy flesh.

Jon tensed, unsure of what the man might do. 'Can you hear me?'

'Bitch,' he mumbled through thick lips, blood bubbling out of his nostrils.

'I'm a police officer. Can you tell me your name?'

'Red-haired bitch.'

Jon opened his jacket, removed a mobile phone and wallet. He glanced at a bank card. Yes, it was the husband. 'Mr Wilson. Jeff. Can you hear me?'

The man coughed a few times and the eye swivelled round a bit.

'Where's your wife, Mr Wilson? Have you seen her?'

'She's gone.'

'Who did this to you?'

'Red-haired bitch.'

Jon's mind went to the person with Gordon Dean at the petrol station's cashpoint. 'A woman with red hair? About five feet eight or so?'

'Red-haired bitch.' His hand moved to his crotch and he winced with pain.

Jon got up. 'Don't try to move. I'm calling you an ambulance.' Fumbling through the unfamiliar menu on the phone, he called for help. Then he rang Alice. 'It's me. I'm at Fiona's place but she's not here. Where else might she be?'

'I don't know. Patrolling Minshull Street, maybe. That's where she's been looking for Alexia.'

Jon shut his eyes. 'Where would she go if she needed somewhere to stay?'

'Well, she just moved out of that refuge. Maybe back there?'

Jon ran upstairs and hammered on the door of

the flat playing loud music. It opened on a dingy interior, a student blinking stupidly out at him from a haze of cannabis smoke. His eyes nearly popped out of his head when Jon thrust his warrant card in his face and demanded, 'What's your name?'

'Er, er . . . it's Raymond. I can explain.' He waved at the thick fumes flooding out from his flat. 'I'm a student here at the university. But I also went to—'

'Raymond, shut up. I need you to look after a casualty until the ambulance arrives.'

Jon drove round to Stanhope Street, got his warrant card out and knocked on the door.

A very wary-looking woman answered. 'Hello?'

'I'm looking for Fiona Wilson. Has she turned up here this evening?'

'No. I'm Hazel, the manager. She moved over two weeks ago.'

'Do you know where to?'

'No, she didn't say.'

'OK, thanks.' He walked back to his car. Somewhere in the distance a burglar alarm let out an insistent wail into the night. He called Alice again. 'Think. Where else could she be?'

'What about the motel in Belle Vue? She mentioned the woman who runs it. I think they've become quite friendly.'

Dawn Poole stood behind the reception desk of the Platinum Inn, twirling a strand of hair round and round.

She'd run to the bathroom and vomited as soon as the front door had banged shut. Then she'd just sat on the bed for a while. None of this was happening. Her dreams of a life with him were falling apart.

Had he really killed that man? No. Coming off his hormones, and the business with Fiona, had upset him. Made him tell a load of lies.

So why are you packing your suitcase? she'd asked herself, pausing to look around their bedroom.

She stopped, a pair of jeans in her hand. Her usual response to violence was to curl up until it was over, then run away. But the thought of being alone again terrified her. She couldn't abandon everything with Alex so abruptly. Her mind swung back to how he'd pushed her. No. He wasn't really a violent man. She couldn't accept she'd got involved with one yet again.

Glancing at the half-packed suitcase, she'd had a desperate desire to talk to him. Unable to decide what to do, she'd caught the bus and gone to work as normal.

A gasp of shock escaped her as Alex tottered into the foyer. 'What have you done to your face?' she said, opening the counter flap and hurrying to him. 'You're bleeding!'

Alex slapped her hand away. 'Which room is she in?'

Dawn's voice faltered. 'Alex, you're making me so scared. What's happening?'

410

'Listen,' he hissed, bringing his face close to hers. 'Do you want her to ruin our future together?'

'No.' A tear started down Dawn's face and she bent her head.

'Good. We've got enough cash to get out of this country right now. Tonight. We'll make a new start together. You and me, Dawn. Just us. But this woman will wreck it all. She will. Now give me the fucking room number.'

Dawn's shoulders were drooping as she tried to control her sobs. 'What will you do to her?'

Alex slammed her up against the counter. 'Which fucking room!' he shrieked.

No. Oh God, no, it was happening again. She shut her eyes and heard a long moan coming from deep inside her. Be small. Don't do anything to make it worse. It will end soon.

His open hand crashed into her face, snapping her head back. 'The room!'

'Twenty-three – she's in room twenty-three. Please don't hurt me.' She fell to the floor as Alex kicked off his shoes and stormed towards the stairs.

Jon could see the motel foyer was empty as he raced towards the doors. He burst through and spotted a pair of woman's shoes on the floor. One was splattered with blood and missing a heel. Immediately he ran to the double doors on his right and scanned the corridor. Empty. The sound of sobbing was coming from the back

411

office. He vaulted over the counter and went in. Dawn Poole was huddled in the corner, arms wrapped tightly round herself. A nearly empty bottle of brandy was on the floor at her feet, sodden tissues strewn around.

'Dawn, it's DI Spicer,' he said, crouching in front of her and looking into her face. 'Are you all right?'

She couldn't control her crying, her whole body convulsing with sobs.

Jon took her gently by the arms. 'Easy, Dawn, easy. You're OK.'

Her eyes were tightly closed.

'Dawn, can you answer me? Is Fiona Wilson here?'

He felt her stiffen.

'She's here, isn't she? Her husband found her flat. She came here because she had nowhere else to go. I'm right, aren't I?'

Dawn took in a shuddering great breath.

'Dawn, is Alex Donley here? Alexia, the red-haired prostitute?'

She started to shiver. 'He said he'd never hurt me. Oh God, it's all gone . . . it's all gone wrong.'

Jon frowned. 'Who said that? Alex?'

She nodded.

'Alex is your partner?'

'He said he was different. Said he'd protect me.'

Jon gently squeezed her arms, aware how painfully thin they were. 'Dawn, none of this is your fault. Do you hear me? Dawn, open your eyes. Look at me.'

She took another breath and her eyes slowly opened.

Christ, he thought, seeing the look of utter defeat in them. 'I know people have made you a victim in your life. But you can put a stop to it now, do you hear me? You can put a stop to all of this by telling me where Fiona is. Please tell me before she gets hurt.'

She shut her eyes and Jon thought he was losing her. But she lifted her chin and said, 'Room twenty-three.'

He jumped to his feet.

She started to cry again. 'He's up there already. You must stop him – he's going to do something terrible.'

The door at the top of the stairs opened on to another empty corridor. Jon looked at the first door: fourteen. He crept forwards, passing fifteen on the other side. Seventeen, nineteen, twenty-one. Twenty-three. The door was shut. He listened, but no noise came from inside. Slowly he turned the handle and opened it a crack.

'You stupid cunt.' A man's voice, straining with effort. 'This is what happens to stupid cunts like you.'

Jon slipped inside, moved past the bathroom and looked into the room beyond. Alex Donley was straddling the chest of Fiona Wilson, pressing a pillow into her upturned face. Fiona's hands were scrabbling around, feebly trying to get a grip on the thing smothering her.

One step took Jon to the edge of the bed. 'Hey!' he barked, swinging with all his might.

Alex's head whirled round, streaks of long red hair flying out. Jon's fist caught him full in the mouth, lifting him clean off Fiona and sending him somersaulting backwards to the floor.

Jon plucked the pillow from Fiona's face, heard her gasping in air. He looked over the end of the bed.

Alex Donley lay crumpled and unconscious on the floor, both lips burst open, the upper one split right up to the base of his nose.

CHAPTER 35

Officers were clearing their drawers, packing files and personal effects into boxes. Rick held up a batch of reports and tapped their lower edges on the desk to square them off. 'How did you track them down?'

'I pulled all the reports for credit cards that had been lost or stolen in the city centre in the three days prior to Alex Donley paying for a new surgical procedure.'

'Quite a few, no doubt?'

'A few dozen. From those, I selected all reports made by men. Next I took the cases where money was withdrawn from a cashpoint after the card's disappearance had been reported. That narrowed it down massively, since you need the card's PIN to make a cash withdrawal. After that it was just a case of contacting the card owner, explaining it was a murder investigation and asking whether they'd lost their card in the vicinity of Canal Street.'

'I bet that got a few evasive answers.'

Jon smiled. 'It certainly did. But I explained that it was all confidential and they soon admitted involvement with a certain red-haired individual going by the name of Alexia.'

Rick shook his head. 'So who were these people?'

'All sorts. An immigration officer from Gatwick doing a placement at the airport, a builder working on the new apartments going up, and an out-of-towner who was in Manchester for the weekend.'

'What I don't understand is how he got access to all their bank accounts.'

'I've been thinking about that, too,' Jon replied. 'Remember the garage forecourt? He was snaking round Gordon Dean at that cashpoint. I reckon he skimmed the guy's PIN then.'

Rick rubbed his forehead. 'The sneaky bastard. So he'd rob someone, then go straight to Dr O'Connor and use the money for his next stage of surgery.'

'Exactly. There's a gap of several months between his visits to O'Connor. As soon as the wounds from one operation healed, he'd go back on the game and rob another punter. What I want to know is why he took the step of actually killing someone. What's the score with him? Has he spoken yet?'

Rick shook his head. 'Still scrawling on his little pad that he can't talk. They'll do a psychiatric assessment once his mouth's sorted out.' He glanced at Jon's bandaged right hand. 'That must have been some punch.'

Jon said nothing.

'In the meantime,' Rick quickly continued, 'Dawn Poole's proving extremely helpful.'

'She still under arrest?'

'No. We're putting her up in a hotel for the time being. Obviously she knew Alex was earning money by turning tricks on the ladyboy circuit, but McCloughlin's happy she had no idea he had murdered a punter.'

'Good,' Jon said. 'She didn't.'

'And Fiona Wilson?' Rick's question hung in the air.

'She's moved back in with her parents and is talking to the Domestic Violence Unit. I gather from Alice that she's pressing charges against her husband. The refuge has got photographic evidence. She's divorcing the prick, too. He's been on a decent salary for years, so she'll be fine from a financial point of view.'

Rick looked around. There were only a couple of other officers left. 'Good. Coming for a drink? McCloughlin's put a couple of hundred behind the bar, apparently.'

Jon thought of how McCloughlin had rubbed his nose in it about getting it so wrong with Pete Gray. He got up, a half-hearted smile on his face. 'I don't think so. Tell the lads I'm on painkillers. No alcohol allowed.'

'A Coke, then?'

Jon raised his eyebrows. 'Be serious. No, I'll pass.'

'Another time, then. The Bull's Head, perhaps?'

'Definitely. So where's your next stint?'

'I've got some time off to think about it. I'm not sure if the front-line stuff is really my thing. Maybe I'll head back to Chester House. There's something I could do on discipline and complaints.' He looked at Jon for his reaction.

'You've been excellent to work with, Rick. You're bloody sharp and you're meticulous with detail.'

'Thanks. But I froze at O'Connor's house. I didn't want to go in there. If you hadn't led the way . . .'

Jon shrugged. 'Another thing about that cellar. He had two syringes in the tray by the stone slab. Did you find out what they were?'

'Yup. Propofol, to keep her sedated. Diamorphine for him.'

'He'd started using again?'

'That psychologist, Dr Heath, reckons he was using it as a disinhibitor. To allow him to do what he did.'

Jon picked at the edge of the box of files.

'What's on your mind?' Rick asked.

'Any theories from Dr Heath on why he was doing it?'

'Only the usual ones – the thrill of playing God, that sort of thing.'

Dr O'Connor's final words echoed in Jon's head. Deep inside a little part of him agreed that there was a thrill in holding another man's life in his hands. The sensation, he realised, hadn't been a

418

lot different from swinging his fist into Alex Donley's face.

'Come on, mate, spit it out,' Rick said.

Taking a deep breath, Jon quietly spoke. 'Down in that cellar, after you'd gone upstairs to check on the ambulance, he said something to me.'

'Really? What?' Rick hunched forwards to hear better.

Jon caught Rick's eye for an instant. 'I let him die down there, Rick, and he smiled and said, "We're just the same underneath."'

His eyes dropped to his watch and he kept them there as the seconds ticked silently past.

Finally Rick said, 'Two things. You didn't let him die. He'd just about bled out by the time we got there. He'd gone through an artery. I doubt a team in an operating theatre could have saved him.'

Jon tried to smile. 'But I was happy to not even try. What's your second point?'

'"We're just the same underneath". Are those his exact words?'

Jon nodded.

'I don't think he meant we as in you and him. He meant we as in all of us. We're all the same underneath. Maybe that's what he was trying to show by skinning his victims. It was a demonstration, a display. Perhaps a protest against the way his art – one that took him years to acquire – is being debased and exploited to satisfy people's vanity.'

'You think so?'

'Yes.' Rick got up and came round their desks. They faced each other a little awkwardly. He held out a hand.

Jon glanced down at his bandaged fingers. Unable to shake, he raised his left hand instead and clapped it on Rick's shoulder. 'Good working with you, mate.'

'Likewise.'

They embraced, each slapping the other's back – a ploy, Jon knew, to keep up the required level of manliness.

As Rick set off for the pub, Jon called across the empty office. 'If you change your mind about the front-line stuff, I'd be happy to work with you again.'

EPILOGUE

Jon knelt on the nursery floor, spreading the same paint-spattered sheets of newspaper out. He put the tin of red paint on them, then tried to prise off the lid with his left hand. The fingers of his right were no longer bandaged, but gripping anything was still painful.

Reaching for the spoon, he lifted it with a quiet crack from the crusty blob of paint it lay in. The viscous puddle on the floor of Dr O'Connor's cellar appeared in his head. The file notes for Carol Miller, Angela Rowlands and Tyler Young had been found hidden in his surgery. All died trying to achieve some superficial ideal of beauty. Images flashed through his head. Melvyn's salon. Jakes' tattoo parlour. The Paragon Group. TV shows, magazine articles, newspaper reports. All about one thing: trying to look more attractive.

Jon put the paint-covered spoon aside and, still kneeling, rested his elbows on the windowsill. He stared through the glass, unable to stop dwelling on why Dr O'Connor had started to kill his customers. The explanation, if there ever could be one for things like that, had gone with him to the

421

grave. What a world this is, he thought, letting out a little snort of breath.

Alice's voice came from the doorway behind him. 'A penny for your thoughts.'

He looked round, and without getting up held his arms out. 'Come here.'

Slowly she crossed the room, her stomach looking like it was about to burst. She stepped carefully onto the sheets of paper, one foot covering the small ad for the Beauty Centre. It sat discreetly next to the columns of classified entries in the 'Health and Beauty' section. The opposite page was covered in boxed ads for Manchester's assortment of massage parlours and escort agencies, Cheshire Consorts' one of those at the top.

Still kneeling, Jon pressed his cheek against Alice's belly and reached his arms round her until he could grasp his own wrist. It was a gesture that sought to protect them from everything he knew existed outside the window and an attempt to bind all three of them closer together. But it didn't seem enough. A desire for something more tangible engulfed him and he found himself saying, 'Alice, do you fancy getting married?'

ACKNOWLEDGEMENTS

Once again a rough manuscript was transformed by the expert touch of Gregory and Company and Orion – special thanks to Emma Dunford and Jane Wood for all your time.

Keeping names anonymous for professional reputations, a big thank you to:

The Turnip – how you sat all those exams, I'll never know
Ian – for the medical advice and the tour of your cellar
Nessy – top marks on the police knowledge as usual
Jo – for showing me round your salon